The Secrets *of* Leaven

"A delicious mystery…exploring deep questions."

—*Deb Arca, Patheos.com*

i

TiLT
BOOKS

Reimagining the American way of life, starting
with our own.

The Secrets of Leaven is published by TiLT Books Taos, NM

Second Printing   TiLTBooks.com   leavenrising.com

Photography: Jonathan Kaufman / Todd Wynward

Cover design: Ken Gingerich @ TiLT Imagine

ISBN-13: 978-0615792958

For Margaret and Nico, who never give up on me

- - - - -

Art is not a mirror held up to reality but a
hammer with which to shape it.

--Bertolt Brecht

The Secrets
of Leaven

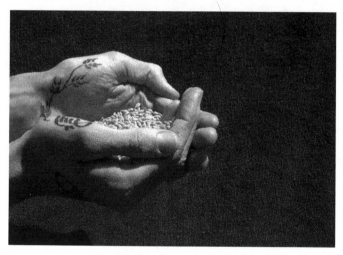

TODD WYNWARD

TiLT
BOOKS

1 AUTHENTICITY

Summer, Thomas Whidman rejoiced as he strode across the grassy quad of the Bay Area Theological Union. The late afternoon sun slanted through the maples, bringing out greens and golds. One more class, and he was free.

A bike approached from behind. He turned to see Talia Simmons cycling up to meet him. She hopped off her mountain bike, tousled his brown curly hair, and gave him a long kiss. "Happy last hour of the semester, lover."

"Feels good," replied Thomas. "Year two of seminary: done."

"What does that make you, two-thirds of a pastor? Should I call you a *past?*" They strolled toward class together, Talia walking her bike. "What do you think Paloma's got planned for our last session?" She turned. "He wouldn't throw a pop quiz, would he?"

"What? On how to meditate?" Thomas laughed. They entered the seminary's busy student union. "It's non-credit. He's more likely to throw a graduation party, Zen style. Maybe a tea ceremony."

"Well, we'll find out in a minute," Talia responded. They walked down the long hallway leading to Paloma's meditation dojo, a carpeted sanctuary of quiet in the heart of the bustling building. "I can't meditate in bike shorts," Talia said at the door. "See you inside."

- - - - -

A row of disembodied heads floated before Thomas' vision. If he squinted just right, the white robes of the meditation students seated across from him melted into the white wall behind. The visual was eerie: human heads, unnaturally calm, suspended in space.

1

Stop goofing, Thomas chided himself. *Center. Focus on the lungs. Peace comes with every breath,* Paloma says. *Thoughts will arise. Let them drift away like boats down a river.*

The echoes of the gong faded, and the *sangha* settled in for the last sit of the semester. Soon all Thomas could hear was deep breathing. Sixteen motionless students, barefoot in loose clothes, sat cross-legged in the thickly carpeted dojo. Thomas' mind continued to recite the basic precepts: *Back straight. Hands centered but not resting. Be still.*

In the center of the circle in a scarlet kimono was Stephen Paloma, their teacher, legs in full lotus. He sat erect, his hawk-like features and shaved head disciplined even when relaxed. His fierce eyes stared straight ahead, unblinking; his goatee, almost menacing. The small gong rested upon his lap.

Thomas breathed. *Yeah, baby,* he thought. One more year and it's *Reverend* Thomas Whidman. *Same title as Uncle Ben,* he realized, *but far from the same man.* Two Reverend Whidmans traveling very different paths.

Before he closed his eyes, Thomas glanced to his watch: 5:10 pm, June 1, 1992. Fifty minutes until summer break. Then nothing to do all June but hang out with Tal. A smile came to his lips. *God, her hair was nice this morning, right out of the shower.* His smile deepened. *Maybe June will be full of nice showers. Then two weeks with Ben and Mike in Guatemala...*

Fo-cus. Thomas groaned. He repositioned his lanky legs, but his mind still wandered. Mike had insisted that he join this Guatemala trip. *Just like old times, bra,* Mike kept saying. *Hope not,* Thomas thought. Church mission trips to Mexico had stopped being Thomas' thing in high school. But Mike was right about something: maybe going on this construction brigade trip *could* somehow make it better with Ben. If only he'd stop preaching and start listening.

C'mon, Whidman, focus. Thomas kicked himself inside. *One last class. Crap, my nose itches. Is Paloma looking?* Staying still, Thomas opened his eyes a crack. Through the slit he saw the outline of the room, the silhouettes of figures. And he saw his scarlet-robed teacher staring directly at him with a faint smile.

Busted. Thomas shut his eyes and focused on his breathing. Concentration still eluded him. He became convinced something was lurking on his nose. *Is he still staring at me?* After a moment, shame gave way to curiosity. Thomas risked another veiled glimpse. Paloma remained in the same position, eyes wide, the same inscrutable smile etched upon his face. This time, Thomas noticed the stare was aimed just above his head.

Had he been looking at me at all? Paloma's gaze seemed all-encompassing and vacuous at the same time. In one bizarre mental leap, Thomas realized his teacher's stare and smile shared the same disturbing qualities as the Mona Lisa. *What was Paloma smiling at? Nothing? Everything?*

Thomas opened his eyes fully and looked around the room. He spotted Talia across the circle, straight back, eyes closed, head tilted downward. Her wavy brown-blonde hair fell to her athletic shoulders. Her chest rose and fell evenly. *Sure do like that chest,* Thomas thought, admiring her poise. *Just a few months meditating, and she's already doing better than me.* He let his gaze linger. *Three months and I'm already in deep.*

Thomas caught himself. *Whidman, you're a lost cause,* he laughed. *Can you focus for one minute?* To leash his roving mind, Thomas engaged in his favorite mental discipline: reciting Koine Greek. Most seminarians considered studying Greek a necessary but onerous burden, but not Thomas. He reveled in it. Today he began near the top of the alphabet, choosing words that mirrored his mood. *Apoluo.* To set free, to detain no longer. He breathed deeply, finding solace in the familiar exercise. *Not meditation, but at least it's focused.* Another word arose: *Entheos,* to be possessed by the divine. *My favorite,* thought Thomas. One of the first words of Koine he'd ever learned. As an eight-year old, sitting on the knee of Uncle Ben, he'd been fascinated by the colossal tome that sat permanently on the reverend's immense wooden desk, the foreign Greek symbols shining out from gilt-edged pages as thin as butterfly wings. *Holy Scripture is the inerrant Word of God,* Uncle Benjamin would tell Thomas, *so we'd better understand it correctly.* Know your Bible, Reverend Ben would command his flock from the pulpit. Biblical literacy was the cornerstone of a sound faith--the only kind of faith worth having.

A faith worth having. That's why Ben allowed Thomas on his knee all those Monday evenings as a young boy, to inhale Koine Greek and keep the rest of the world at bay. Reverend Benjamin Whidman, the magnetic pastor who led *Church of the Harvest* in Orange County, treated himself to a two-hour rest late on Sunday afternoons. But every Monday found him busy at his desk again, already working the Greek and Hebrew translations for next week's sermon. Thomas remembered his uncle's knee, solid and strong beneath him. The knee, the desk, the great book: each warm and solid and strong. Always there. Once his mother died, Thomas came over to Ben's every Monday after school. Ben's house was across town, but at age eight Thomas already knew the way. The first time he didn't come home after school, Thomas was sure he'd get in trouble with Dad. To his surprise, his father barely noticed. He was readying for Monday Night Football.

Thomas came over that first Monday, and then the next, and soon it became

3

religion. The Greek flowed. "You have a gift," Ben told Thomas four years later, when he was twelve. His uncle was right: the logic of Biblical Greek merged in Thomas like liquid light. He didn't just translate the ancient tongue; he *consumed* it. Thomas tasted the words like honey, far sweeter than his native English. *Thalassa*, the broad ocean sparkling under the Mediterranean light. *Hagios*, a most holy thing, or a person set apart. *Hemiorion*, half of an hour of labor. *Metanoia*, the kind of radical transformation that led back to *entheos*, possession by the divine.

Ben's life, full of ancient wisdom and an ever-present God, was so much richer than his own that Thomas knew at age twelve he wanted to be a preacher just like his uncle. Thomas was baptized the following year, and Ben's church became his second home. Uncle Ben, with no children of his own, began to prepare his young nephew to be a pastor.

The sound of the gong brought Thomas back to the meditation room. He glanced at his watch. *Wow, class over*. His eyes found those of his teacher. Though silent, Paloma's presence commanded the room. When all the members of the *sangha* were attentive, their teacher spoke.

"Welcome to summer," Paloma declared, smiling. Small cheers popped up around the circle. "During this semester, you each followed busy schedules and important routines, including this class." He took a sip of water. "But summer is time to break from routine. Time to rejuvenate, to play, to try other things." *Anapausis*, Thomas translated: a season of rest.

Paloma continued. "As for me, I'm going on a trip to Israel. Ancient ruins, old friends, and timeless desert between my toes." His dark eyes twinkled. "Who else is doing something different this summer?"

"I'm training for a half-marathon with my grandson," said an old man near Thomas. When Thomas glanced down at the man's spindly legs, he chuckled. "Not as spry as I once was," he confessed. "But I'm going to try."

"Good for you, my friend," said Paloma. "If you feel you can do it, do it."

"I'm planning to paint all summer," volunteered a stringy-haired librarian from the seminary. "It might sound funny, but I've never taken a vacation in place," she confessed. "I want to see San Francisco with new eyes. I'll putter around the whole Bay Area, painting the things I love: the bridges, the streetcars, the hills, the coastal tide pools." The woman looked down, self-conscious. "I don't get a lot of time to do that during the regular year."

Paloma acknowledged her words with a smiling nod.

"I'm going backpacking in the Sierras," offered Talia from across the circle. "I lead trips for Outward Bound in the summers." Her gray eyes sparkled with excitement. "I get paid, but I'd do it for free. I love challenging people to be their best. It's a good balance for the social work I do in downtown Oakland. It does my soul good to get out into the wilds."

"I think it's how we were meant to live, Talia," Paloma commented. "You can discover much about yourself in wilderness. Enjoy." A brief silence ensued.

"I'm joining a construction brigade to Guatemala," said Thomas. "A Habitat for Humanity kind of thing."

"Oh?" Paloma turned. "Excellent. You've spent time in Latin America?"

"Just mission trips to Mexico, back when I was a teenager," Thomas confessed. "My best friend from high school, Mike, really wants to reconnect, so I said I'd go. It's with our old church, down in Orange County. My uncle's the pastor."

"But Guatemala?" Paloma raised an eyebrow. "Civil unrest has marked that country for decades."

"I know," Thomas replied. "That's why I'm going, actually. My uncle and Mike think this trip is about building a community center and saving souls. Me, I want to meet the *campesinos* and hear their stories." He paused. "It should be good."

"A little unsure about entering a conflict zone?"

"I probably should be." Thomas gave a half-smile. "Honestly, I'm more unsure about spending time with my uncle. We used to be close. But a lot's changed in ten years. Not sure how it will go."

"*Hacemos el camino al andar,*" Paloma said.

"Huh?"

"We make the road by walking," Paloma translated. "When I was a kid, my *tia* used to tell me that when I worried about the future." He shrugged. "You never know how something will turn out until you jump in." Their teacher gave a final smile to Thomas, then addressed the group. "I look forward to hearing about the roads each of you make this summer. Whatever you do—whether you train for a marathon, paint from your heart, backpack in the mountains, or plunge into another country—I challenge you to do it with authenticity. That's our goal: to become authentic human beings."

Summer was beckoning, but Thomas decided to take a risk. "Sometimes your words are a little cryptic," he said to his teacher. A few surprised chuckles erupted from other students. "What do you mean, authentic?"

Paloma turned, head cocked a little to one side. "Let me ask you this, Thomas. Do you think most of us act in a way that is in harmony with our deepest selves?"

Thomas paused to consider. "No. Most people seem to do things out of fear or habit. Or maybe to be protected, or accepted."

Paloma looked around at the class. "Fairly astute, wouldn't you say?" Several students nodded. "Thomas is correct. Modern humanity is in an identity crisis." Paloma paused a second to let that statement register. "How we act-- and how we truly want to be--are often two different things. Why? Because our inner and outer worlds are not one."

"You're getting cryptic again," Thomas said.

"We're often divorced from our true selves," Paloma explained. "Unconscious of our true motives and purpose. Until the inner is expressed in the outer, there is no authenticity. Be aware of the true self that is within you. Let it grow."

Okay, I asked, but now I've had enough, thought Thomas. *C'mon, do the clap.*

"Enough words," Paloma said good-naturedly, rising like a gymnast. He clapped, ending the session. His smooth scalp gleamed under the soft light. "May it be a good summer for all of us." With both hands lifted high, the kimono-wearing Zen instructor began his own benediction. "As of this moment, each of you has passed this course with distinction. By the utter lack of power vested in me by this institution, I hereby give you every bit of credit I can for this absolutely non-credit course." He smiled and turned full circle, his scarlet kimono trailing. "Be adventurous. See you in August."

2 THE EMPTYING

Stephen Paloma started out on foot into the Judean desert just before midnight. The meditation teacher's steps made dark hollows under the bright moon as he traveled across featureless dunes to reach the dry riverbed below. *Featureless*. Paloma smiled at the word. That's how he'd regarded this patch of desert the first time he came here, learning from Theologos how to be a Preparer. Over the years, however, he'd come to know the features of each sandstone mesa, each dusty river channel, each crumbling desert tower.

He traveled in the *wadis* when he wanted to make no mistakes—one dry stream bed interconnecting with another. But it was crossing the open spaces between the canyons that gave Paloma sheer joy, especially at night. Coming up out of Wadi Musa in the moonlight, he topped the mesa and laughed with delight. Arabs called an open plateau like this a *farsh*, a mattress, and the description particularly fit right now. The broad tabletop was pale and open, the expanse of the night world laid out like a blanket around him. Beyond the white mesa, the ringing mountains stood in deep blues and blacks: Jebel Suba, Jebel Umm-Shummar, Jebel Tarboosh.

As he strode across the stark moonscape, Stephen Paloma counted back. How many nights had he traveled through this land since he'd been named Preparer six summers ago? How many days had he spent preparing Leaven's initiates for their desert Trials and—hopefully--bringing them back? Over two hundred, he estimated. So far, all eighteen initiates he'd set out over the years had returned in one piece, but considering the risks of desert Trials, he didn't take chances. *Trust God in all things*, the old monk Theologos had joked during his training that first summer, *but make sure to tie your camel first*. That's why Paloma had begun his trek tonight after prayer with a pack that contained water, rehydrating salts, a med kit, refrigerated anti-venin, and an avalanche beacon. Emergencies still could happen, both of body and soul. A Preparer had to be ready.

Coming to the lip of the *farsh*, Paloma paused to view the vast desert below. The network of moonlit canyons spread away like veins in an oak leaf. Then, resuming his steady pace, he plunged down the sandy cliffside of Wadi Borma. At the dry river bottom, Paloma checked his watch, assessed his heartbeat and respiration rate, and grinned. All three good. With any luck, he'd locate his charges and bring them back before the moon had set.

- - - - -

He found Ryan Walker where he'd last seen him, next to an ingenious evaporative water trap the man had crafted in Wadi Borma's sandy bottom. Ryan was the easy kind: an initiate who claims a piece of desert and doesn't move for forty days. Angela Martinez had taken more time to locate; she'd migrated with her sparse rations since his last check fourteen days ago. The summer monsoons had been rare in recent weeks, so she'd left her dusty little *wadi* for better water. Paloma eventually picked up her trail a half-mile away. Following, he found her sleeping next to a murky pool on a mat she'd made of woven grass.

Now, six hours after starting out, he was back where he began, perched with his charges on a sandstone ledge. Sitting silently in their dust-colored cloaks, the trio drew as much attention as dead leaves strewn among rocks. Despite the delay finding Angela, Paloma was satisfied: both his initiates were alive and well, and they'd returned an hour before daybreak. Weak and filthy but glowing, Angela and Ryan sat calm and vigilant next to their Preparer as the sky brightened. They watched the activity below.

In the emerging light, pilgrims were arriving. The far-flung members of the Society of Leaven were joining together for their yearly gathering, coming to the desert place where Leaven had been born, thousands of years ago: the Cave of the Baptist.

Paloma heard footsteps, and peered down the sandy wash at two advancing figures. "That's Lauren Makwela, from South Africa," Paloma whispered to Ryan and Angela. "She writes for the biggest daily in Cape Town. She's brand new to us--just passed through her own Trial last year." The woman he indicated was lean and very dark in complexion, while the skin of the older man walking with her was the color of milk chocolate. "And that's Clarence Washington," Paloma murmured. "He's a retired professor from Portland, Oregon. One of Leaven's three elders." *And someone I trust with my life.*

Paloma wasn't surprised to see Clarence strolling up the desert *wadi* in a black t-shirt and blazer. That outfit, along with tortoise-shell spectacles and the tight gray curls at his temples, were the man's trademark. When Paloma came up to Portland from the Bay Area last year to spend time with Clarence, he couldn't help chortling when he looked in the man's closet. Clarence, however, felt no embarrassment. "Why are Americans so enamored with options?" Clarence questioned, thumbing through a stack of identical black t-shirts. "These do me just fine. I can look dignified no matter how bleak the circumstances." Paloma had to agree; after all, last April he'd picked the man up from Portland Correctional. It was Clarence's fourth conviction in as many years for unlawfully serving food to the homeless down on Burnside without a food handler's license, so it was significant jail time. Yet somehow even after serving three months in the lock-up, Clarence had looked sharp as he walked through the prison gates to Paloma's waiting car.

Three dozen pilgrims had traveled up the dry river bed in the last thirty minutes, Paloma guessed. Some came alone, others in groups, but Paloma knew them all. After each sojourner passed, he whispered the traveler's name and place of origin in the ears of his charges. The names were diverse, the locations even more so: Portland. Madras. San Salvador. Berkeley. Beijing. Loreto. Boston. Quito. Edinburgh. Brisbane. Santa Fe. Petrograd. Arequipa. Des Moines. Mount Athos.

Although Jerusalem International was only seventy kilometers away, the Cave of the Baptist was a world apart. In order to reach this desolate piece of Judean desert, the members of Leaven had to leave their motorized transport near the tiny ruined kibbutz of Suba, and then walk into the desert on foot. Using unnamed goat trails, the pilgrims followed a pebbly seasonal flood channel that eventually became Wadi Musa, the dry river canyon that funneled travelers to the base of the sacred Cave. No signposts beckoned them, but each knew the way to their spiritual home.

Paloma, sitting in lotus on the ledge, regulated his breathing. He felt a steady pulse in his wiry wrists. It was beating strong, very strong, and not because of his night's exertion. His whole body sang. As a Zen teacher for more than twenty years, he'd learned to become aware of shifts in his physiology, and the strength of the Spirit within him this morning was surprising. He felt it in his pulse, in the new initiates at his sides, in this gathering, and in the discovery that would be revealed in just a few hours. The Spirit of God was percolating through the world of men.

"Shouldn't be long now," Paloma murmured to Angela and Ryan, looking at the early morning sky. "Most everyone has arrived." He hadn't seen Collister and Adinah yet; he could only assume that the archaeologists' big announcement was keeping them away for the time being. Collister could get wound up like that, lose track of the present. He should get back to practicing Zen, Paloma thought.

9

Clarence Washington's big baritone laugh floated back down the canyon. About a hundred meters up the riverbed, Paloma could see Clarence greeting old friends. About forty members of Leaven had congregated in a natural rock amphitheater, encircled by a band of sandstone cliffs pock-marked by small caves. One dark cavern high up the cliff wall yawned wider than the others: the Cave of the Baptist.

From a distance, Paloma peered at the cave's mouth. Was the Shepherd within, preparing for the initiation? Or was she already at the clifftop, greeting the desert sun like she'd done every day for the last thirty years?

Approaching footfalls caused Paloma to look the other direction, away from the gathering. Somebody was coming up Wadi Musa. They were trying--but failing—to be stealthy.

"Stephen!" hissed an urgent voice out of sight down the dry streambed.

Surprised, Paloma and his two initiates perked up their ears.

"Paloma! Where the blazes are you?" the voice called again.

Paloma smiled. He could place his friend's accent anywhere. Dr. Simon Collister was finally coming, and the Brit sounded frantic.

The noise eventually came into view in the form of the final two members of Leaven. Dr. Simon Collister was in the lead, followed by his Israeli colleague Dr. Adinah Sharon. Sharon was attempting reason and advocating calm. Collister was listening to neither.

"Simon, this doesn't seem prudent," counseled Dr. Sharon, a tiny almond of a woman. Her black hair was captured in a bun, her hands thrust into her desert field jacket. Even from a distance, Paloma could hear the strain in her voice. "Simon, please. It's almost starting. Let's join the others and wait until it's our time."

"Blazes, Adinah, I tell you he's here!" After stumbling over a rock, the British archaeologist called out again. "Where are you, Stephen? Good God, man, show your face!" Collister kicked the pebbles in the bottom of the sandy wash in frustration. "He's here, Adinah, he has to be. Bollocks, that man's like a bloody ghost!"

Paloma rose on his hidden ledge and came to the rim to make himself visible below. "Looking for me, perhaps?"

"Paloma!" Collister blurted loudly, looking up. "I knew it!"

Paloma put a finger to his lips and pointed at the gathering a hundred meters away. Collister turned red. "So sorry," he said, whispering. "Just glad to see you. Very glad."

"What's the emergency, my friend?" Paloma asked. "Gained enough weight recently that you need another desert Trial?"

"Har har," the Brit responded. "No, my emaciated friend, one was more than enough for me. I'm just big boned, big boned." Collister patted his tummy, and squinted up at Paloma. "Stephen, I need an urgent favor."

"I gathered."

"We have to stop the ritual. Now."

"Patience, patience." From his ledge, Paloma leaped down to the *wadi* below. He put his hands on Collister's shoulders, and looked into the Brit's flushed face. "Simon, everyone knows your find is important. It's why we have such a crowd this year. But we'll get to it. First, let's deal with the initiation. Then, your discovery."

"*We don't have time!*" burst Collister. He brushed a shock of red hair back from his freckled brow. "Israeli officials might be here any bloody minute."

"Good one," Paloma chuckled. Collister wasn't laughing. "Wait a minute," Paloma said. He turned the other archaeologist. "Adinah, is he serious?"

"He's exaggerating," she said. "But yes, he's serious." Dr. Sharon pushed her sensible glasses back up the bridge of her nose, looking distinctly uncomfortable. "Someone at the Department of Antiquities caught wind of our discovery."

"What?" Paloma looked at the government archaeologist in disbelief. "Adinah, you promised our dig would appear insignificant. You said nobody cared about the upper Wadi Musa region." He looked around at the vast empty desert. "Historically uninhabited. No resources. Worthless."

"That was all true. Until yesterday." She looked down at her leather shoe. "Someone at the Department overheard me talking on the phone."

"Talking?"

"Simon called me at the office."

Paloma's head turned to Collister, astounded.

"I was excited!" The Brit threw up his arms. "I told you I'm bad at this undercover stuff!" Collister ran a meaty hand through his hair. "And now I've screwed it all up."

"It's not *that* bleak, Simon," Adinah said. "I keep telling you, it's Shabbat. No one from the Israeli Department of Antiquities will be coming out here *today*. Nobody investigates on the Sabbath. It's against Torah."

"Against Torah!" Simon retorted. "Are you living in some Zionist fantasy, Adinah? Sure, Israel's a Jewish state, but there are plenty of non-kosher government officials ready to make a good bust on a weekend." He turned to Paloma, chewing his fleshy lip. "We've got to stop the ritual, Stephen, and show everyone the Ossuary. Before it's too late." Collister scanned the desert horizon. "There could be Jeeps here any minute. And whatever the Department finds at an unauthorized dig, they take."

"Unauthorized?" Paloma arched an eyebrow at Dr. Sharon.

"More like undocumented," she explained. "We've got a permit on file, but I've been rather negligent in reporting what we've discovered. So a government official or two might be upset, and want to confiscate artifacts immediately. It's possible."

Government officials in Jeeps. Paloma reeled. *Tromping around our proving ground.* The Zen teacher performed a quick inner analysis. Elevated heart rate: Yes. Increased respiration rate: yes. Elevated level of anxiety: yes. *If I'm tense,* Paloma thought, *no wonder Simon's about to burst.* He glanced over to see Collister pacing in the sandy riverbed with red face and orange hair, a boiling carrot in a windbreaker.

Paloma slowed his own breathing, then tried to help Collister gain some perspective. "Simon, I've just brought Ryan and Angela back in after their Trials." He indicated his two charges squatting on the ledge. Collister squinted, seeing them for the first time, and waved.

"Remember the ritual after your own Trial?" Paloma hoped the Brit recalled what it felt like. "Descending into the Drowning Pool is what *makes* an initiate part of us, Simon. New members don't just join Leaven every day." The Preparer looked up at the faces of his initiates, then back to the archaeologist. "Angela and Ryan have just spent forty days alone in the desert, Simon. *Forty days.* Their lives are utterly changed. After undergoing that, you really think we should just say, 'jolly good show, thanks for joining our team. Now excuse us, we've got more important things to do?'"

"Blazes, man, that's *exactly* what I'm saying!" Collister blurted, then stopped. He looked to the pair on the ledge and held out his hands. "Forgive me," the Brit muttered. "Ryan, Angela, you're terribly important. This is just more so. No offense."

If either of the two initiates took offense, they certainly didn't show it. In fact, the calm light evident in their faces--even under weeks of dust and sweat—told Paloma that very little would perturb these two ever again. It was the quality he always wanted to see after a Trial: that hard-earned, unshakeable confidence in something bigger. He paused. *Did Simon still have it?*

"Look, something's happening," Angela said, smiling through dusty lips, bright eyes looking up the wash toward the sandstone amphitheater. "The Shepherd's starting."

Paloma turned. There, high atop the cliff face above the seated crowd, an aged woman wielded a long staff. She stood tall, silhouetted by the rising sun like a prophet of old. The ceremony was beginning.

"That's my cue," Paloma said. He looked at Simon and Adinah. "Yours, too."

"Weren't you listening?" Collister hissed, amazed. "We're out of time!"

"Easy, friend. We can't stop the ritual from here, can we?" Paloma placed a hand on Collister's shoulder and led him toward the gathering. Adinah followed. Paloma looked back over his shoulder at Ryan and Angela on the ledge. "Stay here, my friends, and wait for my call. Soon it will be your time to die."

3 SHOWDOWN

Peace Surplus. The huge sign came into view below them as Thomas and Talia crested the hill on Berkeley's Shattuck Avenue. Thomas knew of the store as a hippie-run bargain barn catering to army vets, boy scouts, wilderness trekkers and world travelers. Talia was a huge fan of the place, always coming here to restock before her Outward Bound treks, so Thomas figured it could meet his needs for his upcoming Guatemala trip: water purifying tablets, a thief-proof pouch for his passport, a small backpack, a few bandanas and a language phrasebook.

"School's out for summer!" Talia sang next to him on her mountain bike as they stopped to take in the view. "At least for you. Me, I'm a working girl. But you, you're done. For a while, anyway." She glanced over at him. "I forget, it's been so long. What does three months of vacation feel like?"

"Free." *Eleutheria,* his mind translated, the ancient Greek coming unbidden. From his bike Thomas looked sideways at Tal with a lopsided grin, his scruffy beard and curly brown hair framing his glasses and ruddy face. "Like Paloma said, time for rest and recreation."

"Time for slacking, you mean," Talia remarked. "Now that you've got a month with nothing to do, how about being my house boy 'til you go, cooking and washing all the dishes?" Talia proposed with a sly grin. "Attending to my every need when I come home from a hard day of work?"

"Sounds like my kind of prison," Thomas said, laughing in the evening light. He didn't want to admit how good that sounded. "You really want me to be there all the time?"

14

"That *could* get a little scary," Talia reconsidered. "My mom always warned me about boyfriends creeping into my life. First they take your toothbrush, she says, then they take over your car."

"Your mother needs some serious counseling," Thomas muttered darkly. "Thanksgiving with her in Portland's going to be a blast."

"Don't be like that. She's going to love you," Talia reassured him. "Of course, I think she'd love anyone I brought home wearing pants." Thomas chuckled. From what she'd told him about her teenage years, Talia had always found better things to do than spend time worrying about boys. Even through college, her coltish figure and her love for the outdoors kept her attention focused less on Oregon's men and more on its mountains.

"Glad wearing pants is a big plus for your mom," Thomas replied. "Since being a pastor certainly isn't." Talia was about to say something, but Thomas cut her off. "I'm one of those rabid Jesus followers she warned you about. You sure she'll take a liking to someone who might lure her daughter into a life of organized religion?"

"She'll probably be prickly at first," Talia conceded, "but she'll warm up. Honestly? She'll like you because *I* like you." Talia looked over at Thomas with her kind gray eyes, her face flushed with exercise. "Mom wants me to be happy. And I'm happy with you." With that, she pushed off and coasted down the hill to *Peace Surplus*.

As he followed her down the long hill, the low angling sun caught Berkeley's tree-lined boulevards below them in a blaze of light. Thomas thought he couldn't take in all the joy. Life was so good. He stood up on his pedals in his Chuck Taylor high-tops and howled, the breeze rushing through his Talking Heads t-shirt. He thought back to the first time they went out, just after Spring Break. He'd taken her to a hip mainstream coffee chain that seemed safe enough for a first date. He remembered being drawn by her unique look, attractive in an almost masculine way in her vest and jeans, trim and muscular, softened by a loosely-bound cascade of tousled blonde hair and striking gray eyes. Her nose was big, but she was asymmetrically beautiful, captivating and rough and utterly confident in herself. He found her fascinating.

He smiled to himself as he rode. He'd expected her to order a salad or something low-fat. Instead, she ate like a freaking horse. She took huge bites, laughing, talking with her mouth full, slathering butter on most everything. With her appetite and metabolism, she was a regular at both all-you-can eat buffets as well as Bay Area marathons. During the date, he discovered she was a social worker who specialized in troubled adolescents throughout the Bay Area. She was captain of a co-ed Ultimate Frisbee team that played down by the Presidio. She also led wilderness trips for Outward Bound, usually with teenagers but sometimes with older folks, and had just returned from a Spring Break backpack in the Sierras.

Why had he worried so much about finding a place that was safe? He should've known better. She'd been unusual from the first moment they'd met. When Talia walked in to Paloma's meditation class for the first time, the only open space left was next to Thomas. She took it. At the end of the hour of silent sitting, the master sounded the gong and clapped. One by one, each member of the *sangha* stood up and exited clockwise, formally, in silence. As her turn approached, Talia became aware that her entire left leg had fallen asleep while sitting in lotus, and her knee was locked. Frantically needing assistance, Talia reached up to tug at the nearest object. Instead of getting a lift up, she pulled Thomas' loose cotton pants down. A huge vertical gap of crack was exposed, enough to make a repairman blush. Thomas quickly recovered, first his drooping waistline and then his composure. After securing his pants, he reached down to help her. Within a second Talia was standing placidly in the line, as if nothing odd had transpired. Since that time, pulling one another's pants down to the knees in public places had become a regular part of their budding relationship, as had late-night talks, exploring the Bay Area for unknown hole-in-the-wall restaurants, and hikes in the nearby San Gorgonio range with Agnew, the Great Dane puppy they'd gotten together from the pound back in May. Thomas laughed to himself: the dog had been their first big commitment.

Talia, leading, braked at the bottom of the hill and expertly popped the curb to reach the parking lot. At the bike rack. Talia took off her bike helmet and shook out her hair, her locks spilling to her copper shoulders and green tank top. Thomas stayed outside to lock their bikes as Talia entered through the automatic double doors. She looked back through the tinted glass to see Thomas standing at the curb, talking to a scraggly young kid with a guitar and an open case. Thomas shook the youth's hand and gave him some money before heading into the store.

When Thomas entered, Talia was staring at him, smiling and shaking her head. "Didn't you tell me just this morning that your fridge was empty?"

He scowled, caught. "It wasn't anything," he grumbled. "Besides, I still have plenty of peanut butter."

"But no bread," she laughed as they moved across the tiled entryway.

"Tortillas," responded Thomas. "Come over tonight and I'll serve you a dinner fit for a queen."

"Burritos? I'd rather lure you over to my place again tonight," she countered. "How about pasta carbonara, sautéed spinach, and a little fruit of the vine?"

"Grape jelly? I have that at my pad."

"Merlot," she said, laughing. "After practice, I'll be ready to relax and have a glass of red with you on the back patio."

"Shower first?" Thomas asked mischievously.

"What else does a hot and sweaty girl do after Ultimate Frisbee?" Talia responded with a raised eyebrow.

"Now we're talking," He grabbed a metal shopping cart and the pair headed deep into the cavernous store. "You know, I could get used to being your house boy."

Passing the manager's kiosk, Talia nodded a greeting to the store owner. "Hi Dan, how's it going?" she called. The whiskered hippie behind thick glasses gave a silent nod back, his blond dreadlocks poking out from under a psychedelic bandana. Thomas couldn't help but note the man's hair looked astonishingly similar to a bale of hay.

"So how much did you give away this time?" Talia inquired as they moved down the aisle, jerking a thumb back in the direction of the kid outside on the curb.

"Whoa, I didn't know we were married yet, Simmons." Thomas dodged her playful punch, cracking up at the look on her face. "What, you're managing my bank account now that I broke your boyfriend record?"

"Touchy, are we?" she said with a smile. "I'm just saying you give to so many people, you don't leave a lot for yourself." They moved down the main aisle, metal bins of bargain merchandise looming on each side. "Nobody else I know does what you do."

"What's that?"

"Just gives," she said quietly. "Like, you don't care if it's a runaway kid or a crazy vet or a meth addict."

He stopped. "Should I?"

"Well, what if--" She stopped herself and laughed softly. They came to a section labeled *Camping & Survival Supplies*. "I guess not. Me, I guess I'm too full of 'what if's'. My questions stop me every time."

Thomas looked up from a bin of merchandise. "Like what?"

"Like what if he uses my money for drugs? What if the guy's all creepy and follows me? What if I don't have enough cash at the end of the month to pay rent?" To her words, Thomas just nodded. Her questions hung among the towering bargain shelves above.

Talia spotted mosquito netting high on an upper shelf and grabbed a nearby stepladder. "Silly things to stop me, I know," she said. "But they do." She lightly scaled the three steps and examined the bug protection options. "But you--you only have peanut butter and you still give money away."

"And all this time I thought you liked me for my big bucks."

"I like you for your big heart." Talia reached up on tiptoe to pull down a box of green mosquito netting. When she turned to look down at him, she was caught in a shaft of sun coming through the store's skylight. Her honey-colored hair shone and her strong shoulders gleamed, and Thomas almost forgot to close his mouth.

18

"You know what else I like?" she said, hopping down to the cement floor and grabbing his waist. "I like that you don't care about my big nose or that I eat like a horse. You take me just as I am." She looked down at her feet. "Not used to that." Talia broke away from the embrace and held up the bug netting. "Only $6.99. Will this one do?"

"This one will," Thomas said quietly. He pulled her in for a long kiss, jeans against jeans. "This one's doing just fine." He grabbed the mosquito netting from her hand and tossed it into the cart without a glance.

"Later, house boy, after practice," Talia smiled, extricating herself. "Next stop: water purification," she said over her shoulder, directing the search further along the gray aisles jammed with bins of merchandise. "Should be down here somewhere."

You take me just as I am. Her comment echoed in Thomas' mind. *Do I really?* He watched her graceful, powerful torso reach up for another bin. *In many ways, yes.* Thomas considered. *Probably too much. I love her personality and the way she laughs out loud. I love the way she listens. Man, she's right, I even love the way she eats. I love being around all that life.*

Suddenly a different voice rose up in his mind: *Why, Whidman, you're in love with a heathen!* His cheeks flushed at the realization. He'd told himself three months ago she might become a Christian if he got to know her better. *How's that working out?* The voice questioned. *Is she closer to Jesus now that you're sleeping together?* He remembered one morning, when they were cuddling, he'd suggested that she ask Jesus to come into her life. She'd just laughed and said God was already there. Thomas had no words to respond. *Who's soul needs saving anyway, Whidman?*

- - - - -

He caught up with her a few yards down the next aisle. Talia was facing a wall display labeled *Water Purification & Treatment*. "Found it," Talia said as Thomas arrived. "So many options to choose from." She chewed on her lip. "And all out of your price range."

She wasn't kidding. Displayed before him were about a dozen different products--tablets, filters, drops, and bottles – all expensive. Thomas did some quick calculations in his head and frowned. His face fell.

"Why don't you just take some of my iodine for water treatment?" Talia suggested. "I've got a bottle in my med kit. Outward Bound will resupply me before I go."

Thomas' eyes went huge. "You trying to kill me?"

"Trying to save you money, squid," Talia laughed. "Who's the wilderness guide here?"

"Iodine's poison, Tal. Skull and crossbones."

"It's an antibiotic, lame brain."

"So you admit it kills things." His eyes were narrow, joking but not joking.

"Well, of course. It kills bacteria." She threw up her hands. "Just trying to help a desperate man."

"I want to believe you," Thomas said playfully. "But I have trust issues. Is the offer still open even if I phone a friend first? Just to make sure?"

"Rock on," Talia said. "You go, boy. Talk to whomever you want. This'll be interesting."

- - - - -

When Thomas and Talia found Dan the store owner up at the front of *Peace Surplus,* the old hippie was scuttling like a spider among newly-arrived boxes, unpacking his fresh inventory. Oversized headphones arched over the plump muffin of his blond rasta braids. It took a few moments to get the man's attention, but finally they gained permission for Thomas to use the store phone.

"So who's your life line?" Talia inquired as Thomas picked up the receiver at the manager's desk.

"One of my old friends from college," he replied. "The one who's visiting soon."

"Ed, the wandering soul?"

"Bingo."

"Looking forward to meeting him," she smiled. "From what you tell me, he seems pretty different from you."

"Yin and yang, that's for sure. Mike and I being freshman roomies with Ed was odd at first, 'cause the two of us seemed so opposite from him, but then we bonded together over the bakery project."

"The Rubber Biscuits thing? Sounds like you had a really great time baking some really bad bread."

"Yeah. We've been buds every since. He's the man I need to call." With that, Thomas dialed 1-800-TAOS-BOX.

"Hello, nothing rocks like the Taos Box," answered a bright, professional male voice. "The river is high, the sky is blue and the sun is hot. Can I schedule a trip for you today?"

"Gimme five pepperoni pizzas ta go," Thomas mumbled in a thick Mafia accent, winking at Talia. "Heavy on da sauce."

A brief pause. "Um, sir, this isn't a restaurant. We run river trips."

"Not a restaurant?" Thomas exploded. "You don't serve meat?" He grunted, still sounding like a 350-pound Italian crime boss. "Then why you talkin' to a meat head like me?"

"Thomas, you ignorant slut," came Ed's voice, cracking up. "Why the fuck would you be crank calling me in the middle of this fine day? Seminary a little too tight-ass for you? You need some entertainment?"

"I'm on summer vacation, Ed my man," Thomas grinned. "No entertainment needed. But this isn't just a joke call, brother. It's a matter of life and death. Right now I need serious advice. I told you I'm going to Guatemala in a month, right?"

"Sounds like you called the right *muchacho*," Ed Chapman replied from a worn wood-paneled desk in Taos, New Mexico. "Been traveling south of the border for fifteen years. Hey, wait just a sec." Thomas could hear his friend lay his phone down for a moment to punch a few buttons. "Okay, I'm back. The other line is flashing, but the boss isn't here, and this sounds much more interesting than booking another daily. Where were we? Oh yeah, life and death. Give it to me."

"Our trip leaders say they're taking care of everything. We're supposed to drink bottled water for the whole two weeks, so we're not bringing anything to treat the water."

"What, they keeping you on a leash?" Ed exclaimed. "Where's the adventure in that?"

"Exactly," Thomas agreed. He remembered Paloma's encouragement to get adventurous. "Their plan is for us to stay in this tiny village the whole time and build a community center. Me, I want to get out a little."

"*Aproveche la situación,*" Ed advised.

"Come again?"

"Take advantage of the situation, man. You're going to be in fucking *Guatemala*. Mayan ruins, villages, jungle treks. Don't get stuck doing construction the whole time. Get out and see the country. See how people are really living."

"My thoughts exactly," Thomas said. "So now to my life and death advice. I know I might get killed by bullets in the jungle. But I don't want to get killed by bad water if I don't have to. What kind of water purification do I bring?"

"There's lots of options," Ed began.

"No kidding," Thomas responded. "Right now I'm in a store full of water pumps and treatment tablets. All pricey, and me with not enough money. Talia's right here next to me, telling me to forget all this expensive crap. She's got iodine I can borrow."

"For free," Talia said loudly toward the phone.

"Listen to your girlfriend," Ed said from his end. "She's the Outward Bound instructor."

"But isn't iodine *poison?*" Thomas blurted. "The red stuff with death warnings on it?"

"Yeah, but--"

"My mom put it on cuts when I was a kid." Thomas didn't remember a lot about his mother. An auto accident took Jill Whidman's life when Thomas was eight, so when he did have a specific memory, he held on to it. "She didn't tell me to drink it!"

"Life and death, life and death," Ed chuckled. "Now I see your dilemma. Which is more deadly: ignore your mom's advice and drink the poison, or ignore the wisdom of your hot new girlfriend who's leaning over your shoulder?"

"I knew you'd get it." Thomas breathed. "That's why I called my trusted friend."

"Drink the poison, holmes."

"You're kidding."

"Your girl knows what's up," Ed explained. "Iodine's a cheap antibiotic. Not so great for your thyroid, but only a poison if you chug a bottle. A few drops in your canteen will kill most germs without killing you. Take it. Then you can ditch out for an adventure whenever you want."

"Cool, man. It's not like I ever doubted either of you," Thomas said, projecting his voice at Talia with a guilty smile. "I just trust warnings on bottles, too. Now I'll just plan on bringing some iodine and not tell Uncle Ben until I have to. I--"

"Wait just a minute," Ed interrupted. "Ben? I thought this gig was through your seminary. You're saying your scary uncle's in charge?

23

"Come on, Ed. Ben's not that scary."

"Maybe not for you, Christian. I only met him twice, but I've seen how he looks at me with those glinty eyes and his slick black hair. Like I'm another recruit for his cult. So why's he organizing this trip--to save the souls of savages in the jungle?"

"For Ben, yeah, probably," Thomas conceded. "Back in high school Mike and I used to go on mission trips like this with him to Mexico. He'd always say the natives were poor in money but even more starved for Christ."

"I told you. Scare-e-e-ey," Ed sang in a falsetto.

"It was a little zealous," Thomas acknowledged.

"*He's* still more than a little zealous," Ed corrected. "Did I tell you I saw him last month?"

"Get out!" Thomas sat back in the chair at the manager's desk, stunned.

"Not joshing you, man. Saw him on the tube. I was up late one night watching TV with friends. We were flipping channels, and there he was, preaching on late night cable!"

"Ed, I haven't talked to him in a while, but I don't think he preaches on TV."

"I swear, hombre! It was his own show and everything! Insisting that the Bible's the only true Word of God. I tell you man, that guy is loco for the Lord. You, you only froth at the mouth a little bit." Ed's voice softened. "Your faith I even admire, misguided as it is."

"Thank you. I think."

"Serious, Thomas. Remember who you've become: an open-minded, compassionate dude who is still for some reason into Christianity. That's the Thomas I know. And love. Don't get sucked back into your uncle's spell. That's a dark space."

"Fat chance," Thomas gave a bitter laugh. "I stopped being his golden boy a long time ago."

"Halle-fucking-lujah for that," affirmed Ed. "I don't think I could've survived being roomies in college if *both* you and Mike handed out pamphlets in the dorm. But Tommy, if you're not into saving souls, then why are you going with your uncle's church?"

"Ben and Mike can preach all they want. I'm not going for their reasons. I'm going for mine. I need to get out of the U.S. again and-- "

"Wait just another freaking minute! Am I hearing things? Did you just say *Mike* is going on this trip, too?"

"Well, yeah," Thomas said, face reddening. "Mikey wants us together again. We've been growing apart since high school, he said, and he..."

"Of course you have! You've escaped the Orange County cult, that's why! You hang out with normal people now, like me." Ed paused. "Tommy, don't get pulled back into that."

"Don't worry." Thomas halted. Dan, the hay-haired owner of Peace Surplus, was making a beeline for the couple using his phone. One baleful eye glared over the top of his thick coke-bottle glasses, and his stubbly jaw twitched in a decidedly unpeaceful manner. Talia, seeing the incoming danger, smiled winsomely and moved to intercept.

"Look Ed, I gotta go," Thomas said curtly. "I really just called about the iodine."

"I'm just telling you, don't let your uncle draw you in. Dark space."

"Don't worry about me, boyo. Like I said, Mike and Ben can save all the souls they want. Me, I'm going so I can see how the rest of the world really lives." The store owner was now two feet away, glaring at Thomas. "Hey Ed," Thomas said, "I really have to go."

"See how the rest of the world really lives," Ed repeated. "Now that's the wild man I've come to love. And hey, remember: that's what your boy Jesus did."

"Huh?" With his eyes on Dan, Thomas had a hard time following Ed.

"Jesus, bro. He showed up at people's villages, gave what he could, and ate whatever they offered him. He got out there. You get out there too, man. Have a good trip."

"I'll tell you all about it when I get back. Or better yet, over a couple *Negra Modelos* on my front porch. Still coming out to repaint my apartment?"

"Count on it, holmes. Probably in late August, after the rafting season slows down. Then I'll be free to hit the road." On the phone, Thomas heard the buzzing of an incoming call, and the sound of Ed pushing some buttons. "Well, Tommy boy, may your time in Guate be awesome. Take a lot of pictures for me. And T, remember: trust the hottie. Drink her poison."

- - - - -

A few minutes later, Thomas and Talia were in an aisle filled with bandanas, shirts, wool hats and scarves. Several customers were examining merchandise in the long aisle. Color after color of bandanas were stored in a long row of round bins, like root beer barrels in an old-tyme candy store.

"That was a wild phone call," Thomas reflected, running his hand absently through a bin of scarves. "Suddenly made my trip feel a lot more real."

Talia turned. "Nervous about what might happen?"

"Not really," Thomas muttered. "If you both say use it, I'll use it. Save some money."

"I didn't mean the iodine, squiddly," Talia snorted. "I mean what you said in class the other day with Paloma. Nervous about your uncle?"

"Yeah," Thomas admitted. "Him, and Mike too. Talking about those guys kind of got me jangled."

Talia nodded. "Yeah, I learned a lot just listening in." At Thomas' quizzical look, Talia kept going. "I mean, I knew you and Mike and your uncle were tight when you were younger, but I heard things that kind of surprised me.

About who you used to be. Stuff I didn't know."

"Sorry about that, Tal." Thomas looked at her. "I haven't been hiding anything from you" He shrugged. "It's just that the person I was in high school isn't interesting to me anymore."

"But he is to Ben and Mike?"

Thomas gave a single laugh. "You could put it that way." He moved down the line of scarves. "Mike wants the three of us to be like we were ten years ago, when Ben was our youth pastor and we were his anointed ones. But I can't go back." He shook his head. "He was the center of my world since I was young. Studying Greek, youth group pizza nights, campfires at the beach. He even came to my basketball games."

"You obviously meant a lot to him."

"Seemed that way," Thomas agreed. "Up 'til senior year."

Talia hesitated. "What caused the split?"

Thomas gave a sharp laugh. "Guess he taught me to read the Bible too well."

"Oh?"

He looked at her skeptically. "You really want to hear this?"

"Hell yeah, I want to hear it. Pull up a seat and tell your tale."

"Alright, you asked for it," he said, laughing, amazed at how easy it was to talk to this woman. He hopped up on the bin. "Way back in our senior year, like ten years ago, my uncle took Mike and I under his wing."

"Your uncle has wings?" Talia joked.

"It was a mentorship thing," Thomas explained. "Training us to be holy men of God. He gave us twelve weeks to read all the books in the New Testament. Mike breezed through it and focused on Revelation, just like Ben told us to."

"And you?" Talia inquired. "Not so breezy?"

"Me, I got derailed." Thomas looked at her. "The *Letter of James* grabbed me and never left."

"How so?"

"*James* broke open my world, Tal." Thomas held up a finger. "One line, actually." The opening words of the phrase in Koine still burned in his mind: *Threskia kathara*, true religion.

"You remember it? The line?"

"Sure." He balked when he saw the look on her face. "What, you want me to recite it?"

"Changed your life, didn't it?" Talia's eyes narrowed. Her smile threw down a challenge. "Yeah, I want you to recite it." She pointed to the customer coming at them down the aisle. "Time to practice your skills, preacher man."

"You asked for it." Thomas hopped up off the bin and stood tall, right in the center of the aisle. A hunched woman in a flowered dress was coming his away.

"'True religion is this,'" Thomas shouted, startling the oncoming woman. She stopped moving, and stared suspiciously. He stood to the side with the flourish of a bullfighter. "'To look after widows and orphans in their distress.'"

"That'd be nice," the woman said, her back bowed from time. "Being looked after. I could use somma that." She came closer, and cocked her head to look up at Thomas with one eye. "How about getting me one o' those red wool scarves way up there?" When he reached up to acquire one for the bent woman, she patted his hand. "Thanks, sonny. One thing, though. You ought to stop preachin' in discount stores. You might get slapped." With that, she waddled off down the aisle.

The pair waited until she turned the far corner before collapsing into hysterics. "That almost made me believe in miracles," Talia said, wiping her eyes. "Where were we? Oh yeah, the *Letter of James*. Getting derailed."

"Yeah." Thomas became somber. "My uncle always said the heart of Christianity is *belief*. So it blew me away when James asserted the heart of Christianity is *action.*"

"Believing versus acting," Talia mused. "I get the tension. Did you just part ways, or was there a showdown?"

Thomas swallowed. "Showdown." From ten years ago the scene came fresh to his mind, as did the Greek words he'd been reading that night. It was a February evening in his senior year, and a chilling rain beat on the roof of his car as he read under the glow of a street lamp in the church parking lot. Now that he was in training to be a man of God, he made it a habit to read Scripture daily. He'd taken to coming early and alone to youth group on Saturday nights and sitting in the parking lot while the others trickled in, teasing apart the Greek text like a solitary monk in his cell. This particular night he'd been reading deeper into the *Letter of James*, and the writer was urging his flock not just to be listeners but to be *poietai*—doers, makers, poets. Those who carry out. Those who make real. Thomas' nose was buried in the text when an urgent knock on his windshield shocked him back into the wet night.

"Got some change for an old vet?" A rugged face above an army jacket loomed through Thomas' driver side window. Thomas' immediate panic subsided, replaced by a more rational mind that took in the man's rough beard, sandy hair, splotchy skin and dog tags dangling down to Thomas' eye level.

Thomas closed his Bible. Instead of mumbling an excuse like he would've another night, he took his key out of the ignition. Be *poietai*, James had said: be doers, those who make real. Thomas opened the door and stood on the wet asphalt.

"I'm Thomas." He held out his hand to the stranger.

"Bailey," the vet said, pointing to the name label on the chest of his fatigue jacket. "Like Beetle Bailey."

"Need some food, Bailey?"

"Yeah, sure would appreciate it. A burger and a few beers would make my night."

At least he's honest about his vices, thought Thomas. In fact, the man's whole being smelled like beer, and his sallow skin gave more proof. But Bailey's hunger was just as evident, and the pain in his eyes was profound.

"Well, Bailey, I'm not going to give you money or beer, but I can get you some hot food if you want it. Come inside. It's spaghetti night."

Within the large church kitchen, two long white laminate countertops under fluorescent lights had been turned into a buffet. A dozen high schoolers, including his best friend Mike Shaw, were milling around the institutional pots of spaghetti, metal bowls of green salad, and foil-wrapped loaves of garlic bread. Everybody stopped talking when Thomas led the stranger into the kitchen.

"This is Bailey, everyone," Thomas said, trying to sound casual.

"I'm just here for the food," the vet said quickly. He stepped up and put some steaming spaghetti into a Styrofoam bowl. "Thanks. I'll be on my way."

"No need to rush, Mr. Bailey." The figure of Reverend Benjamin Whidman came into the circle and faced the newcomer, eyes bright. "Any friend of Thomas' is a friend of ours, and you are most welcome. It's our custom for the youth to pray and then join together in fellowship."

"It's my custom to get some food and go," Bailey said, yellowed eyes darting for an exit. "I didn't come here to get saved. Now get out of my fucking way." The man elbowed through the kitchen doors.

Reverend Ben turned back to the circle of youth and shook his head sadly. "How many sheep gone astray still do not return to the Shepherd?" He looked at Mike and Thomas. "That's part of this week's Scripture for you two. Check it out. First Peter. Okay, everyone, let's get our food and begin."

Hesitantly, Thomas followed Mike into the buffet line. Ben was doling out a large portion of spaghetti onto Mike's plate when Thomas murmured, "'Suppose a brother or sister is without clothes or daily food.'"

Pastor Ben looked up from serving, his dark eyes searching those of Thomas. "Still reading *James* are we, nephew?" Mike glanced sideways, confused, and saw Thomas blanch under his uncle's scrutiny. The preacher scowled and plunged the spoon back into the spaghetti. "Like Martin Luther himself said, the Letter of James is an epistle of straw: thin, empty, and totally lacking in nutrition." Ben scraped up another portion and spoke with quiet authority as he handed full plates to both Thomas and Mike. "Stop lingering in that dusty book and get up to speed on your reading, Thomas. Ever since you used to sit on my knee, I've known you're gifted. You're one of the most promising Greek scholars I've ever encountered. The Lord has big plans for you. You and Mike both. But lately you've been different. You're not applying yourself. We're supposed to be in First Peter." Uncle Ben looked to Mike, who confirmed with a nod. "'Like living stones,'" the preacher quoted from this week's text, "'You are being built into a spiritual house, to become a holy priesthood.'" Ben put a hand on Thomas' shoulder. "A holy priesthood, Thomas. Not a target for drunkards on the dole."

Fuming, Thomas followed Mike toward a plastic table for dinner. Always before when his uncle chastised him, Thomas had backed down. But not this time. He turned, his face hot. The rest of the passage from *James* came unbidden in his raised voice. "'If one of you says to a brother, 'go, I wish you well; keep warm and well fed,' but does nothing about his physical needs, what good is it?'" Thomas stared right at his uncle. "'In the same way, faith by itself, if it is not accompanied by action, is dead.'"

Silence reigned in the room. "Are you defying me, my young scholar?" Ben's voice was playful, but his eyes were hard.

"No, sir," Thomas said, aware of all eyes upon him. "Just quoting the Word of God."

In *Peace Surplus,* Talia had been listening intently. She waited as Thomas lapsed into silence. "Wow. You weren't kidding about a showdown."

"That was just the beginning," Thomas mumbled. At an encouraging look from Talia, Thomas continued. "I figured I'd never see Bailey again since he took off that night, but the next morning he shows up for Sunday church service. Talking to himself in the back pew. Up front at the pulpit, my uncle's acting like everything's normal, but inside he's having a cow."

"Did they kick him out?"

Thomas laughed. "No, that would be too judgmental. Good church people don't do that. Everyone was just squirming, like polite people do, pretending the homeless guy wasn't there. Ben ignored him at first. But when communion came, Bailey walks up the aisle in his army jacket to get the bread and wine."

"No way." Talia eyes were wide. "What happened?"

"He just stood there, alone in a sea of people, everyone courteously avoiding him. I was staring at him when suddenly I start thinking about *James* again. Helping widows and orphans in their distress. Being a doer. So I walk up and stand next to Bailey at the front of the line."

"That took some guts."

"Bailey holds out his hand for the communion bread, but Ben doesn't give it right away. 'Surely you've been baptized,' my uncle says, like a statement that's really a question. Bailey doesn't say anything. Ben finally gives him the bread, but then holds the wine back. 'Surely Jesus is your Lord and Savior. Do you need to confess your sins?' The vet doesn't say anything and just reaches for the wine, but Ben raises the communion cup out of reach and keeps going with the ritual words. 'Just say the word, Lord, and we shall be healed,' At that, Bailey starts cussing him out—right in the front of the church and everything—but then he starts *crying*, Tal. Bawling. Ben's still asking him questions, and the old vet just turns and walks out."

"What'd you do?"

"I stared my uncle in the face for long time," remembered Thomas. "Then I walked out with Bailey. Mike tried to stop me, but I just kept going out of the church without a word."

"Wow. You weren't kidding about parting ways."

"In the parking lot, I gave Bailey some food money and bus fare, and tried to tell him not all Christians were like my uncle." Thomas barked a laugh and blinked his eyes twice. "Funny thing is, I'm pretty sure Ben still thinks he did the right thing."

Talia got up from her bin and turned to Thomas, resting her forehead on his. "I'm not going to complain about your big heart ever again." She kissed him on the brow. "You're a good man, Thomas Whidman."

4 BONEDIGGER

Paloma led the pair of archaeologists up the sandy wash of Wadi Musa toward the Cave of the Baptist and melted into the back of the crowd. The sun was just coming up, and all the other members of Leaven were looking up at the Shepherd high above. The trio's arrival was largely unnoticed, except by one who'd been waiting: a striking bald woman with lustrous dark eyes and olive skin. European in features, she dressed boldly in a black leather skirt and leggings. She came over and embraced the two archaeologists as old friends, then lingered with Paloma. "Welcome back, partner," she murmured, giving him a long kiss. "No problems with the Trials?"

The Zen teacher replied with a smile. "Angela and Ryan are back on the ledge. Everything's good."

"Good?" Simon Collister hissed in disbelief at Paloma's side. "Don't listen to your man, Magda! Government agents are about to catch us with our pants down!"

The quizzical expression that started in Magda's dark eyes didn't have time to grow into a question, because just then the ritual began.

"Welcome, brothers and sisters!" The Shepherd's voice resounded in the stone amphitheater, pouring down clear and strong as rain. A hush filled the dry *wadi* basin as the crowd craned their necks eighty feet above. "Two thousand years ago, John the Baptist emerged in this rocky place." She stood at the edge of the cliff. "He came eating honey and wild locusts and walking the Way."

34

Now that he could see better, Paloma was struck again by the Shepherd's vitality. Despite her years, she remained a lean piece of hardwood, just like the desert fathers and mothers of centuries gone by. In fact, if she replaced her beaten cowhide jacket with a robe of camel hair, she could pass for the Baptizer himself.

The white-haired crone raised her rod over her head, and the rising sun haloed her unruly mane in a ring of fire. "From here, the Baptizer called his people out of Empire," she cried. "'Come and be emptied,' he told them. 'In the wilderness be born anew.'"

"Tell it, Shepherd," murmured Magda crouched right beside Paloma, her shorn head and silver earbands flashing as the sun's rays began to reach the *wadi* basin.

"Don't encourage her, Magda," Collister groaned softly nearby. "Not today."

Despite himself, Paloma agreed more with his antsy friend than with his wife. He quickly reassessed his own inner state: *I'm getting as anxious as Simon,* he realized. Jeeps *could* show up at any moment, like Collister said. *What would we do then?* Paloma knew this much about his friend: although the high-strung Brit was often nervous, he wasn't often wrong.

Any other year, Paloma would be of a single purpose at this annual gathering. After all, he was the Preparer these days: now that Pater Theologos was too ill for the job, it was his task to watch over initiates during their desert Trials and bring new members into the body of the Called Out Ones. But today the Society of Leaven had even more important business: the Ossuary. Collister's concerns wouldn't just float away like boats down a river. What if he's right, Paloma thought, and in a few moments this whole place is crawling with Israeli bureaucrats?

"How are we going to get her attention up there?" Collister whispered in despair, echoing Paloma's worries. "The Shepherd needs to know, Stephen. She needs--"

"The Baptizer stood right here!" the Shepherd boomed from high above. Paloma watched as their spiritual leader took several steps down from the cliff top, moving to a ledge above the yawning cave mouth. Her sandals found purchase in two foot-shaped hollows in the tan sandstone, depressions made over centuries of use by Shepherds before her. She planted her legs like twin oaks. "We've stood here ever since."

"No more Mister Nice Guy," Collister whispered, fixing Paloma with a fierce gaze. "We don't have time for this! I'm going to send her a message she can see even from up there." Without another word, the burly archaeologist shouldered his way toward the front of the crowd. Intrigued, Paloma followed. It didn't take long for the diminutive archaeologist Adinah Sharon to trail in their wake.

Near the front, Paloma paused his motion, and watched as his friend beelined through the crowd toward a large rectangular packing crate situated in the first row. *The Ossuary*, Paloma realized. The man's heading for the Ossuary. As the archaeologist neared his destination, a new thought hit Paloma: *what's going to happen when Collister actually breaks his big news? Will Leaven love him for it, or crucify him?* Paloma shrugged inside. *We'll find out soon enough.*

Blatantly disregarding the solemnity of the ritual, Dr. Simon Collister scrambled up the side of the archaeological crate and sat down on top with a loud thump.

- - - - -

A minute later, it was evident to Paloma that his friend's stunt had failed to disrupt the ceremony. Though the Shepherd glanced down at Collister, she didn't seem the least bit interested in acknowledging him or his impatience. She didn't seem interested in stopping the ritual, either.

"One of those who came to join the Baptizer in the desert was a man called Jesus of Nazareth," the Shepherd boomed from above. "Our Master." As she stopped for a breath, Collister waved his hands frantically. Paloma looked on, somewhat amused. *What does he expect her to do, call on him like a third grader?*

"Our history tells us little about Jesus' life before his time in the desert at age thirty," the Shepherd continued. "Before the desert, what did he know of his true self? Was he unsure what he should do? What he should say?" High on the cliffside, she spread out her arms like a bird preparing to fly. "We don't know these things. But we do know this: when he returned from his Trial in

36

the wilderness, he was far more than a human being." Affirmations and amens rose from around Paloma in the crowd below. "He was calling the universe *Abba*, daddy. He knew with certainty that the kingdom of God was *here*, within reach. Jesus had become fearless, one with the Father. He gave his life to show others the Way. He offered his followers the Crown of Life."

"The Crown of Life," the members of Leaven repeated together. As a single body, the group bowed their heads to touch the intricate tattoos inscribed at the base of their necks. Stephen Paloma joined his brothers and sisters in the motion, touching his own with gratitude.

As the ceremony continued, Simon Collister gave up trying to derail events. He finally sat back on the crate, staring mutely at the sky. Paloma approached through the crowd. Collister's face was blank, though Paloma noted that other signs of nervousness remained. Finely tuned fingers drummed impatiently against the side of the archaeological crate that, Paloma knew, had become Collister's entire life in recent weeks.

"Hey, bonedigger," Stephen Paloma whispered. "Is this crate taken?"

"Plant your bum, chum." Collister moved over so Paloma could share the container. The Brit caught Paloma's sympathetic look and smiled weakly. "Not doing so well, am I?" The rising sun was already warming the surrounding desert, but Paloma knew it wasn't nearly hot enough to warrant the amount of perspiration trickling down his friend's neck.

"I thought this stunt would do it," Simon mumbled in frustration, looking down at the crate. "But the Shepherd's not stopping. Why should she? She probably just thinks I'm being my usual crazy self." The archaeologist laughed when Paloma didn't comment. "Isn't this when my friend Stephen is supposed to say, 'You're not crazy, Simon?" He looked around, toward the desert beyond. "At least I don't hear any Jeeps." The Brit's left hand fished around in his jacket pocket, eventually producing a half-eaten roll of Tums. He popped one and looked to his bald friend. "No time to lose, Stephen. But what can we do?"

"We?" Paloma whispered with a sly smile. He looked toward the cliff. "Don't know about we, but *you've* got another chance right now." He winked. *"Mano a mano."*

"Huh?" Simon glanced up. The Shepherd was no longer on the promontory, and all was hushed. "Oh, yes, jolly good. Up close and personal." In the new silence, a hopeful look came across Collister's face. The initiation ritual was in full swing, and now was the time the Shepherd climbed down to join the rest of the members of Leaven on the desert floor.

Soon, she'd be close enough to touch.

- - - - -

A familiar chorus rose from the throats of his brothers and sisters around him, and Paloma joined in. As he sang the words, he watched the Shepherd skillfully descend the cliff face, placing one leather sandal after the other in a series of narrow footholds.

"That woman is hardcore," Collister whispered to Paloma, for a moment forgetting his own urgent agenda. "Can you bloody believe it?" he said, watching her. "She's still got that one pair of Birkenstocks. Nothing else. That one pair."

Paloma nearly burst out laughing. Last year at this time, the two of them had decided that the only significant difference between Sofia Kazantzakis and the two thousand years of Shepherds before her was the pair of Birkenstocks she'd purchased for her splayed, calloused feet. Machine-made sandals, her one concession to the modern world. But from the ankles up, for the last thirty years she'd been living as the old Shepherds of Leaven had. Ever since she took on the mantle, Sofia Kazantzakis dwelled in the same unheated cave, practiced the same desert disciplines, protected the same sacred texts. Hardcore, no exceptions. Just the sandals. As Simon had joked, she probably didn't give a flying fig whether it was *92 A.D.* or 1992 A.D.

The Shepherd was close, and Simon's moment was almost here. But when their leader came down from the cliff just three meters from where they sat, the archaeologist lost all resolve. "Stephen, I can't!" Collister whispered. A new idea sprung into his eyes. "You do it. *You're* the one who should talk to her!" he hissed. "She listens to you. Tell her to bring the Ossuary to the Cave now, before we do anything else, and we'll--"

"Behold!" The Shepherd's voice killed any further words. She was staring

right at them. *"I am doing a new thing!"* The crone's weathered voice was not her own, and her eyes were milky. Paloma recognized she was channeling the ancient prophet Isaiah, their first father, he who led water rites in this Cave seven hundred years before the Baptist ever did. *"'Now it springs forth,'"* her voice cried, exulting, pleading, her body right next to them. *"Do you not see it?"* After the keening cries, the softness came as a surprise: "Do you not see it?" she whispered, swiveling from the archaeologist to direct her full gaze on Paloma. "I am making a Way in the desert."

"A Way in the desert," Paloma echoed the ritual words with the rest of the crowd, his eyes now inches away from hers, ancient milky pools of wisdom pouring into his soul. The old woman's impossibly lined face, possessed by Isaiah, abruptly moved away, and then she was the Shepherd again, walking slowly with her staff among the seated members. Her voice lifted over the crowd.

"Over the centuries, thousands have come here seeking the Way, seeking freedom from the chains of Empire." The Shepherd gave a wily laugh. "But freedom does not come easy, does it?"

"Amen," Paloma heard Magda's voice shout from the back, along with a few others.

"Ever since the time of the prophet Isaiah, our spiritual ancestors have faced their Trials out there," the Shepherd declared, her staff pointing like a serpent over the vast expanse of desert. "They experienced the emptying, and the Spirit came to fill them. Just like the Spirit came to fill each of you." Murmurs from all around Paloma rose like prayers. "Just like the Spirit has come to fill our new initiates who return from the wilderness today."

At this cue, the crowd turned around, like wedding guests watching for a bride. A figure clad entirely in black unfolded from his sitting position at the rear of the dusty basin and stood tall, a bearded sinewy man wearing the robes of a Greek Orthodox monk. The grand old man of the mountain, noted Paloma, turning his neck with the others to see. The *podhviznik* himself, Pater Theologos of Athos. Preparer of all preparers. *My mentor.* Tinted aviator glasses protected the monk's now-frail eyes from the sun, and an impressive white-gray beard tumbled down from his cheeks to his waist.

"Was he *really* a professional surfer when he was young?" Collister whispered into Paloma's ear as they sat together on the crate.

"That's what he told me," Paloma replied. "Hard to imagine, but true." Actually, not so hard. The elder statesman of Leaven moved with a fluid grace that belied his age. Reverent hands reached out to touch the hem of his dark robe as he slowly picked his way through the crowd.

Theologos neared the front of the sandy basin. Paloma started when the old man paused at the crate he and Collister sat upon. "Worry not, my British friend," the old monk murmured, placing a wizened hand on the archaeologist's shoulder. "God is somewhere in all of this."

Collister opened his mouth to reply, but the Preparer had already moved on. Collister's eyes darted to Paloma. "How the blazes did he know I was worrying?" In his friend's shocked glance, Paloma could see surprise, but also the ebbing of panic. Looking inside himself, Paloma noted his own anxiety fading a bit, too. *God is somewhere in all of this.* "Maybe he saw the Tums," Collister muttered, the roll of antacid still in his hand.

Pater Nicodemus Theologos, sage monk and unrepentant prankster, stood next to the Shepherd in the natural amphitheater formed by the band of sandstone cliffs. He turned his strapping frame to face the crowd, colossal beard flowing, lenses flashing in the sunlight. The loose black sleeves of his robe flew high as he raised his arms wide. "God is good, my brothers and sisters!" he bellowed in his rough Greek accent.

"God is good!" cried the crowd.

"Two more initiates have stood the Trial and returned to us. Two more *bar enasha* are added to our number this day. Our brother Stephen Paloma has been preparing them. Stephen, my friend!"

Paloma hopped off the crate, catlike, and joined his mentor at the front of the amphitheater. His dun-colored robe, shaved head and compact, gymnastic build were a marked contrast to the sprawling and furry Theologos, dressed all in black. The Zen teacher smiled and looked out over the gathered brethren. "Angela Martinez and Ryan Walker, you who have died and returned from the desert, come forth." His calm, clear voice washed over the seated crowd and rolled down Wadi Musa.

In the following hush, Paloma breathed deeply, noticing his calming heart rate, and took in the fragile beauty of the moment. *Maybe in a few minutes we'll be invaded by Jeeps,* he mused. Maybe this is the last time we'll ever meet in this place, below this Cave, under this sky. *But this is what's needed now.* An initiation ceremony, not a frantic discussion about the Ossuary. The heart of Leaven—the thing, the *only* thing that made all the difference—was its radical insistence that initiates undergo a Trial in the wilderness to experience the *kenosis,* the emptying. Christendom had abandoned the practice more than fifteen hundred years ago, when Constantine had offered it a soft bed with all the comforts of the Roman Empire. But the Society of Leaven had remained steadfast. Hardcore, like the Shepherd herself. *Good thing, too,* thought Paloma. *The desert Trial's what's kept us sharp for times like these.*

As Paloma watched, the small crowd parted, and his two initiates came forward. Dust-caked in their desert robes, Ryan and Angela came to stand next to their Preparer. Theologos and the Shepherd joined Paloma and his charges and took their outstretched hands, making a circle.

"Welcome," the Shepherd said. She smiled warmly at the pair. Ryan and Angela returned her greeting with broad smiles of their own. "Our Master said, 'The kingdom of God is like leaven, quietly spreading through the loaf until the whole has been transformed.'" The Shepherd put a hand on a shoulder of each. "Ryan, Angela, turn and meet your sisters and brothers in Leaven."

Both initiates turned to gaze around the circle at their new companions. Though weeks of desert living stained their robes and salty dust lay deep in the creases of their sun-ravaged faces, they were not beaten. They had passed through the desert. They were family now.

A massive gurgling noise suddenly erupted from Angela's stomach. "Need some Tums?" Collister chortled from the front row. Warm guffaws, hoots and clapping burst from the crowd.

"Sounds like you're ready to break your long fast," the Shepherd chuckled. She raised both their arms to the crowd in celebration. "Come, all you of Leaven who have dared the desert and died. Come and be witnesses as these two die and are born anew in the Drowning Pool."

Paloma, along with the two initiates, followed the Shepherd as she led the entire crowd up the goat trail in the cliffside, making a zig-zagging pilgrimage to the Cave of the Baptist above them. Midway up the climb, the Zen teacher heard noises and turned to see Collister scrambling past his peers, dislodging rocks in a frantic attempt to reach the front of the line.

"Stephen!" the archaeologist huffed, drawing near to Paloma. "Now's the perfect time to get her to stop! We can still do this before the Drowning Pool! We have to--"

"Enough." With one word Paloma halted the Brit's forward motion. Together they stepped out of line to let others pass by. "Simon, the Shepherd knows what she's doing," he breathed into his friend's ear. "That's why she's our spiritual leader and you're our archaeologist."

Caught up short, Collister laughed, the first real laugh Paloma had heard from his friend all day. "I'm incorrigible, aren't I?"

"With a capital 'I, '" Paloma said, putting his arm around Collister's shoulders. "The bones have been hidden for two thousand years, Simon. They can wait a few minutes longer."

5 PEREGRINOS

Thomas glanced up from his station of black beans, alert. He couldn't identify how or why, but something just changed in the festive mood of the food line. Over the last four days his construction brigade had worked with the villagers of Todos Santos in the Peten region of Guatemala to raise framed wooden walls and complete a rough floor for the new community center being built next door, and spirits were high. Reverend Whidman's group from Church of the Harvest in Orange County had taken over the interior of the little village church for most of the week, and were now hosting a grand lunch for the community to celebrate a job well done. The feast had been going great, but Thomas no longer felt like celebrating. Something had just changed. The smell of fresh sawdust from next door was the same. The indigenous *campesinos* passing in front of him still wore the same bright weavings as those who passed through the line moments before. But this new group exuded an emptiness. They filed silently by, solemn ghosts.

Kind of like a parade of the dead, actually, Thomas couldn't help thinking. He glanced up. Down the serving line, Uncle Ben and Mike didn't seem to notice anything different.

A wrinkled Mayan woman with a gold tooth now stood directly in front of Thomas, head down. Stoic, she held out her tray to receive whatever food the North American might dole out. On her back, she bore a load bound in a colorful woven *huipil* like many mothers half her age. But Thomas noticed something odd: it wasn't an infant in her pack; instead, she carried picture frames. Four gold-painted wooden frames of various sizes—the kind he'd seen bordering images of *santos* on the walls of Catholic churches in

43

Mexico—were carefully wrapped up in the colorful cloth.

"Con permiso," began Thomas. The woman looked up, years etched into her face. *"Me llamo Tomas. Como se llama?"*

"Juanita. Me llamo Juanita." She tried to give a weary smile, the gold tooth glinting. *"Con mucho gusto, Tomas. Gracias por la comida."* Her companions murmured the same.

"Disculpa me, pero..." Thomas' voice trailed off. His command of Spanish ended soon after *what is your name* and *excuse me.* Thomas looked around and caught the eye of Arsenio, the gregarious pastor of the local congregation who'd been their construction supervisor and host throughout the week. The stout middle aged man came forward cheerily from the kitchen door. "Need a new pot of *frijoles, Señor Tomas?*"

"No thank you, Arsenio. Something else." The Guatemalan pastor looked into his eyes, questioning. "Please ask this woman why she is carrying those picture frames."

A forced smile came to Arsenio's lips. "Oh, *señor,* I don't think that would be appropriate. These people are just passing through. *Ellos estan peregrinos.* Not part of our community." When another woman, much younger but with similar red eyes, passed woodenly through the line, Thomas suddenly noticed Juanita was not alone in her strange burden.

"Arsenio, why are *all* these women carrying picture frames? Why are they so sad?"

"Perhaps they are going to a funeral," said Arsenio. "But it would be rude to ask them." He took Thomas' pot, though there were still several spoonfuls left. "Let me get you some more beans."

6 THE FIND

"Three weeks ago our Wadi Suba dig team excavated this object. It's been to my lab in London and back. It appears authentic." It was a few hours after the initiation ceremony had ended. Dr. Simon Collister stood next to his precious crate in the Cave of the Baptist, like he'd been begging to do all day. But now that he was in the spotlight, the archaeologist didn't look so happy about it.

Paloma guessed Collister's unease was not just due to his fear of public speaking. Perhaps Collister was also realizing that the phone call he made to Dr. Adinah Sharon yesterday might make him very unpopular with his friends. Revealing that he'd discovered an ancient artifact would be news well-received; revealing that he'd carelessly leaked the discovery to the Israeli government, not so much.

Collister stood in the center of a large ring of Leaven members seated on the cavern floor, his face pasty in the orange light of mounted torches. Somewhere in the back of the cave, water dripped. The living rock, flickering firelight, and the circle seated around the storyteller gave the gathering a primordial, timeless feel. *This gathering feels timeless*, Paloma thought, *but Collister's all too aware of time*. It was killing him. Paloma watched the archaeologist's breathing, observed the nervous sweat trickling down the man's neck, and knew Collister was feeling pressure: pressure of minutes passing, of forty sets of eyes on him, of the Israeli Jeeps that could ruin everything. Paloma could almost smell the man's fear. "Everyone feels fear," Pater Theologos had told Paloma before his own Trial, so many years ago. "Even the Master had fear," the old monk noted. "The question is: are you going to let it win?"

45

What about you, Simon? Paloma wondered, looking at his sweating friend on center stage. *Are you going to let it win?* To better the odds, Paloma decided to help his paralyzed friend. "Dr. Collister, tell us more," he urged from his place in the circle. "Where was it discovered?"

Emboldened, the archaeologist continued. "Our team found it buried in a shallow niche in the sandstone, about two hundred meters down that tunnel." Collister pointed toward his left, indicating a cave shaft snaking away from the main chamber. In the torchlight, Paloma could see the man's hand was trembling. But the Spirit was moving, and Collister was being swept along. *God can use even the most broken of tools,* Paloma recalled from *The Theologos Commentaries.* Indeed, what else has God ever used? Paloma hoped the portly archaeologist remembered, too. *Come on, Simon. Time to be used. Time to be a tool.*

"Let's take a look at it, then," the Brit said finally, rubbing his palms together. "Dr. Sharon, lend a hand, won't you?" Dr. Adinah Sharon stepped forward. She wore a government-issue Israeli field jacket and carried a cordless screw gun. Small and efficient, she placed a calming hand on her colleague's shoulder and the team got to work. With practiced ease they unscrewed the sealed lid of the crate, removed some foam casing, and then carefully lifted out a heavy, oblong object encased in sawdust and bubble wrap. The duo set it on the cave floor.

"I'm still reeling from the implications," Collister muttered as he lightly touched the mysterious rectangular package.

"How about letting the rest of us reel, Simon?" Magda remarked from her seat in the circle, her black motorcycle boots drawing dust lines in the cave floor. "I've been hearing about this bone box for months."

Reverently, Collister meticulously removed the multiple layers of bubble wrap, and stepped back. Dr. Sharon pulled out a full-spectrum hand spotlight. There, illuminated in the center of the cave floor, sat a curious, rectangular stone box.

Even though Collister had described the ossuary to him, Paloma had not seen it first-hand until now. The box was fascinating in its simplicity: rectangular, white, with a heavy stone lid. Etched lines stood out just below the lip, but other than that, it seemed unadorned. It was the size of a large toolbox--a foot tall and a foot wide, while its length fit a human thigh.

"Cool!" Magda crawled forward in her leather skirt and leggings to peer at the relic. "So this kind of box was made by ancient Hebrews specifically to hold human remains?"

"Yes. Ossuaries were usually carved from high-quality stone, like this one, to contain the bones of someone of high repute."

"Are the bones still in there?"

"Erm. Yes."

At that answer, a dozen members of Leaven joined Magda around the relic. Their curiosity was contagious, and soon most members of Leaven were pressing in close to get a good look at the object. "Easy, it's fragile!" Dr. Collister exclaimed. "No touching! It's an ancient bone crypt. Nearly two thousand years old!"

"Why does he say things like 'it's an ancient bone crypt' and then expect us *not* to touch it?" whispered Magda as she crouched next to Paloma, their heads just a foot away from the ancient stone container.

"Behave," responded Paloma, "or he'll make you sit outside."

Collister resigned himself to the sea of people surrounding him. "This ossuary is of limestone," he informed them. "Many Jews in Jesus' time would initially bury their dead in human-sized niches in cave tombs all around Jerusalem. But after a year, when the flesh had desiccated, the bones of the deceased would be placed into an ossuary like this, for long term storage."

"So then, let's get to the important question," a deep fluid baritone said from near the cave entrance. Professor Clarence Washington rose from the Elder's Bench and approached the archaeologist, animated in his blazer and khakis, his reading spectacles dangled in his hand. "The secret you've been holding from us. Exactly *whose* bones did we travel this far to see?"

"Let's first identify the time period," Collister responded, rubbing his hands together, excitement overcoming anxiety for the moment. "Jews only used this type of limestone ossuary for a period of about a hundred years. We can pinpoint the time window fairly precisely: the use of ossuaries became widespread about 25 BC, but when Rome destroyed Jerusalem in 70 AD the practice abruptly stopped. It seems that--"

"There's an inscription!" Magda shouted, eyes fixed on the etchings. "Two lines."

"Why, yes there is," Collister said, gleeful. "Take a look. But carefully."

Magda lay prone with her chin on the rocky floor. Paloma rested his shorn head on her shoulder for a better view. The angled, flowing text was engraved into the rim of the box. "Appears Aramaic or Semitic," guessed Paloma. "But I'll leave it to the experts. Clarence?"

Magda and Paloma made space near the artifact, and Clarence Washington came in close. Lauren Makwela, Angela and Ryan peered at the foreign writing as well. Fascinated expressions danced in the torchlight.

"'Ya'akov,' whispered Clarence from his kneeling position right in front of the ossuary. "I can make out the name 'Ya'akov.'" The elder's tortoise-shell glasses gleamed in the torchlight, individual fires contrasting with his round, chocolate face and graying sideburns. The former professor glanced to Dr. Collister. "It's first-century Aramaic, yes?"

"Spot on, Clarence," Collister grinned, then spoke to the crowd. "My friends, in English Ya'akov is usually translated as James. Ya'akov was a very common Hebrew name in the first century." The Brit then turned to his diminutive Israeli colleague. "Adinah, a little background, please."

Dr. Adinah Sharon smiled politely behind her sensible glasses. "Roughly 900 ossuaries of this type have been excavated and cataloged since Israel's Department of Antiquities was formed in 1948," she reported to the group. "They've been found in the catacombs under the Holy City, as well as in hundreds of smaller locations like this, other caves that honeycomb the Judean countryside. Remember, Leaven emerged from the Ebionites, and our ancestors weren't the only ones who made homes out here—the Essenes and other ascetic groups were practically our neighbors. And we weren't the only desert dwellers who buried our leaders' remains in labeled ceremonial boxes, either. Out of the 900 ossuaries cataloged so far by the Department, about 250 bear written inscriptions like this one. They provide lineage and identity to the bones within."

"The first line does indeed seem to be genealogy," Clarence concurred. The Old Testament scholar crouched closer to the limestone inscription, his horn-rimmed spectacles alive once more in the torchlight. *"Ya'akov bar Yosef..."* His dusky finger trailed the Aramaic script from right to left as he read the symbols. Suddenly, Clarence looked up to Dr. Collister, and whipped off his reading glasses. "Simon, it's not... *Ya'akov bar Yosef achui'd Yeshua?"*

Leaven's chief archaeologist was giddy. "That's how I read it too, old friend!"

"Gentlemen!" interjected Magda from where she squatted in the circle. "For the sake of the rest of us, let's put the Aramaic on hold!"

"I agree with Magda," Paloma cut in. "I think we're ready for the translation. Simon?"

"Well. Ahh." Collister glanced nervously at Clarence, who gave a silent nod of affirmation.

"Not the best time to be reluctant, Simon," Paloma said. "Remember, we might have visitors."

"Visitors?" interjected a startled Shepherd from the cavern entrance.

"Tell us what the writing means!" Magda blurted. "Tell us!"

"Alright!" sputtered Dr. Simon Collister. All forty sets of eyes were once again upon him. The archaeologist cleared his throat. "As far as I can tell, the first line reads, 'James, son of Joseph, brother of Jesus.'"

"James?" Magda questioned. "*Our* James?"

"I...think."

"And the second line?" Paloma encouraged, eyes alight.

49

Collister looked straight into the eyes of Clarence. "Tell me if I'm wrong, but I believe it says 'one of the *bar enasha*.'"

"One of the..." Clarence Washington was no longer able to speak. He stared at the line of Aramaic characters. "He's right. The sentence structure connotes the plural form."

"What did you say?" The strapping elder monk Pater Theologos strode to the center of the circle and crouched at the ossuary. "But that would mean..." His lips moved silently as he read the inscription on its lip, and his hand pulled at the white and gray forest of his beard. He looked up at Leaven's head archaeologist. "Simon, the term *bar enasha* hasn't been found inscribed on any other artifacts, has it?"

"Not yet. I certainly would've heard about it." Collister ran his fingers through his red hair with an impatient hand. "That's why this find is so stunning. I mean, Jesus himself used the phrase often, but no one else in the Bible did. So who could've engraved such a sentence?"

"Only someone very close to Jesus," Clarence responded. "Aramaic became a dead language when Jerusalem was destroyed."

"Hold on, History Channel," Magda interrupted. "Rewind. With details this time." She looked around, aware of the international character of the gathering. "In English, and maybe a lot of other languages, too. This sounds too important to misunderstand."

"That's a good idea, Simon," Lauren Makwela echoed. "As a journalist, I'm used to processing complex information rapidly. But I need to hear this again."

"Right you are." The Brit took a deep breath. "Here goes. When Rome destroyed Jerusalem in 70 AD, the original communities of the Jesus Way scattered. Our ancestors the Ebionites were the only ones who stayed in these caves. The other communities fled to Rome, Pella, parts of Egypt. And when they fled, they left the Aramaic language behind."

"Why?" Magda asked Collister. "Aramaic wasn't so popular in the larger Roman Empire?"

"Right," he responded. "Greek was. *Koine,* the common language of the Empire. And Jesus' rich Aramaic phrase *bar enasha*--his vision of a new kind of God-filled human--got butchered. When he used it, he used it in different ways: sometimes he meant himself, sometimes he meant himself and other people. But out in Greek-speaking Empire, Roman scribes who didn't understand Aramaic translated it in every case as *ho huios tou anthropou*— literally, 'the son of the man'."

"Crap translation!" blurted Theologos in a thick accent, now towering in the center of the room.

"Our unorthodox monk is coarse, but accurate," Simon Collister muttered to the assembled group. "The early scribes were translating a nuanced phrase they didn't undersand."

"You mean the scribes who were helping Paul send letters all around the Mediterranean?"

"Exactly those people." Collister nodded. "By 70 AD, only forty years after our Master's death on the cross, the core of his message was already being radically misunderstood even as it was being radically spread. Nobody was writing in Aramaic anymore—remember, it was a dead language for a culture that had just been demolished by Rome. I'm fairly certain cave-dwelling Jewish Christian sects--such as our ancestors the Ebionites and the community at Pella--were the only ones using *bar enasha* anymore to refer to a group of people. All the other early Christians—those who'd fled and assimilated into the Greek speaking world—had dropped Aramaic and were solely understanding it as an exclusive title for Jesus the Christ." Collister rubbed his ragged red head and wagged his finger at the ossuary. "That's why this is discovery is...so..." He finally gave up trying to make a coherent point. "This changes everything."

"So that's why this James is almost certainly our James." Magda sat back on her heels, stunned, and stared at the box. "James the Just, the first Shepherd of Leaven, *one of the bar enasha.*" She looked at Collister for confirmation, who nodded yet again. "Now I *am* reeling."

Silence reigned. In the stillness, all members of Leaven stared at the ossuary. Paloma became aware he'd been holding his breath. *Collister was right,* Paloma thought, like he so often was: *this find changes everything.* Stephen Paloma watched the forty faces of his brothers and sisters come to the same conclusion. The unbelievable stood before them on the cavern floor: a two thousand year-old bone crypt bearing the inscription '*James, son of Joseph, brother of Jesus.*' One of Jesus' *bar enasha.* One of the new humanity.

"Glad we know the signicance of what's in front of us," the Shepherd said loudly, silhouetted in the cave entrance. She stood gazing out through the opening and into the desert. "Because unless I'm mistaken, I think I see a half dozen vehicles coming our way. And I doubt they're lost."

7 VAYA CON DIOS

Arsenio hurried away with the semi-empty pot of beans through the doors leading to the church kitchen. Thomas, temporarily jobless in the food line, used the moment to take in the whole scene.

Five days ago, when his construction brigade arrived at *Asamblea de Dios* nestled in the tiny jungle town of Todos Santos to build a new community center next door, the small Pentecostal church had been orderly and neat. Now the pews were pushed back to the whitewashed plank walls, and the barn-like building had become a combination of catered party, tool shed, flophouse and camp meeting.

As Thomas watched from the food line, Anglo volunteers and indigenous Guatemalans seated themselves around cheap plastic tables to eat the hot lunch of black beans, tortillas and *caldo de pollo*. Around them the church interior was crowded with boxes of power tools, flats of bottled water, colorful backpacks, and stacked bedding. Each morning, the American volunteers rolled up their sleeping bags, cushions and air mattresses in an attempt to make room for the usual daily functions of the church. It was a bit of a zoo, but it worked.

Arsenio still hadn't brought a new pot of beans, so Thomas watched gold-toothed Juanita and the other sad-eyed women shuffle farther down the line. Thomas noticed again how each woman carried a colorful back bundle of gilt-edged picture frames, the gold corners protruding out of the pouch like square, flat children. As Thomas watched the women move through the line to the soup and tortillas, his gaze fell on Uncle Ben. Pastor Benjamin Whidman stood at the end of the food line in slacks and a navy blazer over a pale blue shirt, handing out handmade sweets and blessing each passerby.

"Vaya con Dios!" Ben said earnestly to each peasant as he handed out his treat. He'd learned that much, thought Thomas. Ben's oiled black hair made his dark eyes bright in contrast to his pale skin, and his white teeth sparkled above his trim black goatee. He still didn't seem to notice the pall of sadness that Thomas felt so strongly, the wave of darkness that followed Juanita's group as they traveled down the food line. Pastor Ben looked up unexpectedly and caught his nephew watching him. "The Lord has done so much this week, Thomas!" Reverend Whidman exulted from across the room.

Thomas couldn't deny it; his uncle was right: The Lord *had* done so much this week. Mike had been right, too: the trip had been a good way to reconnect. Years of distance and alienation had melted away, and being around Mike and Ben was beginning to feel natural again. In just four days, their construction brigade had framed out a community center for this humble Guatemalan village at the edge of the Peten jungle. The reverend had been productive spiritually as well. Like Ben was fond of saying, the natives might be hungry for resources, but they were starving for the Lord. In addition to food, Ben had provided evening worship services, baptizing more than a hundred souls. Thomas looked again at his uncle, enthusiastically doing his job at the end of the food line. The Lord had indeed worked wonders, thought Thomas. His mind flashed to Bailey, the homeless vet that showed up at youth group ten years ago, and he sent up a silent prayer. *Bailey, wherever you are, I wish you could see this now:* Uncle Ben actually providing food to people without interrogating them. Maybe he and Ben *could* find some common ground again.

"Just like old times, hey bra?" Mike Shaw's large blond head popped up from the vast pan of rice he was distributing midway down the line. His meaty forearm handled the heavy serving spoon like a toothpick, and a contagious grin spread across half his face. A silver cross dangled across his broad chest.

Not quite, Mike, but it's sure been good, thought Thomas. Mike had been Thomas' best friend since they met in 9th grade youth group at Church of the Harvest. In high school, they'd been inseparable—both taking AP classes, both forwards on the varsity basketball team. Thomas took the outside shot while Mike bulled his way into the key; together they made a formidable duo.

Even more than academics or athletics, the pair revolved around Reverend Benjamin Whidman. The boys were potent allies for the pastor: Thomas suggested nuanced translations of Koine Greek to help his uncle's sermons, while Mike's charisma brought scores of young people to the church for Ben to baptize. Mike and Thomas were Ben's chief lieutenants on a number of mission trips to poverty-stricken regions south of the border, serving food, handing out Bibles and saving souls. It was only a slight surprise, then, when Ben selected both Mike Shaw and Thomas Whidman to receive 1981's Promising Young Pastor Award, an annual scholarship bestowed on a highschooler by the Church of the Harvest Foundation to fund three years of seminary tuition after college. The award formalized the boys' role as pastors-in-training, young men of God whom Reverend Whidman would train in the deeper mysteries of the Word.

Then James happened. The Koine that Thomas read in the Letter of James grabbed him, pulled his soul away from the Church of Ben and challenged him instead to be a *poietis*—a doer, one who makes the love of God real through action. Everything changed. *Just like old times, Mike?* thought Thomas. *It hasn't felt like old times in years.*

His musings were cut short when Arsenio brought a second pot of beans. Thomas spooned portions into the bowls of the last *campesinos* in line, then he and Mike and the other volunteers filled their own plates.

"Hallelujah!" Pastor Benjamin Whidman wiped his hands on his apron and walked to the center of the room, followed by Arsenio. "What a glorious week so far, praise God!" He paused briefly to let Arsenio translate to the mixed group. "All have been fed, body and soul! A new community center is almost done. We've had a week of song and worship. More than a hundred souls came to Jesus! New friendships have been made across borders. Take a moment to pass the peace of Christ to your neighbor."

Around tables, gringos in t-shirts shook hands with traditionally dressed villagers and exchanged words of blessing. Hugs were awkwardly shared. During the interruption, Thomas noticed the old Mayan woman Juanita and her group of indigenous peasants grab their food bowls and head straight out the double doors of the church entrance.

Ben continued his afternoon sermonette. "Our God is a gracious God, showing his mercy to those who walk in the path of righteousness. Who would like to receive a brand new Bible this afternoon?" After Arsenio translated, a score of local villagers stood to form a solid line, and Ben invited Mike to join him at the front of the church.

For a moment, Thomas watched while the two of them handed out gilt-edged volumes bound in faux red leather. Then he darted past the pews along the right side of the church wall, opened the double doors where Juanita's group had gone, and slipped unnoticed outside.

8 EVERYTHING'S BLOWN WIDE OPEN

"Vehicles are definitely coming this way," the Shepherd confirmed from the mouth of the Cave of the Baptist, looking into the distance with binoculars. "Not making a secret about it. Still far away, but you can see the clouds of dust."

Jumping up, Simon Collister joined the Shepherd at the rocky opening. After one glance, he walked back into the cave, all business. "They're coming. Adinah, Stephen, help me get the ossuary back into the crate. We mustn't let them see it."

The rest of the members of Leaven came to the lip of the cave now, looking out. Ryan, wearing a Red Sox ballcap after the initiation, asked the Shepherd for the binoculars. "Five of 'em, judging by the dust plumes," he said with an unmistakable Boston accent. He turned to shout back into the cave. "Don't you think they're probably just recreational vehicles way off course?"

"Those aren't dune buggy drivers," Collister said tersely from deep in the cavern. "They're bloody agents from the Department of Antiquities." He was scooping packing sawdust from the cavern floor with his bare hands, attempting to pour it back into the crate between the bubble wrap and the limestone ossuary. "Hand me that screw gun, would you, Adinah?"

The Shepherd left the cave entrance to stand next to Simon. "Why are you so sure they're agents?" she asked the back of the archaeologist's head. Collister, working, didn't meet her gaze. The Shepherd grabbed his startled shoulder and turned him bodily. "Simon Collister," she called out, her white hair and milky eyes wild in the torchlight. "*What have you done?*"

The Brit slumped to the cavern floor, head in hands. "I've ruined everything!" His face twisted in a spasm of guilt. He looked up, voiceless, into the eyes of Leaven's spiritual leader. "I told you I'm no good at keeping secrets!"

The Shepherd waited for her answer. Adinah Sharon came to kneel at her colleague's side. "Yesterday he telephoned me about the dig," she explained. "While I was at the lab."

"When you were working?" asked the Shepherd, aghast. "During office hours?"

"It surprised me, too," Adinah confessed. "I didn't handle the call well. I thought I was alone, and Simon was so anxious, so I talked to him."

"I thought she was traveling!" Simon wailed. "I didn't know she was working at the lab!"

"I took the call and tried to calm him down." Adinah's eyes looked afraid. "It was only two minutes, tops. But my co-worker was under his desk fixing a computer cord, and he heard me speaking in English about a dig he'd never heard of before. When I hung up I tried to pretend it was a site he already knew about, but I'm not a good liar. Once he started asking questions, I had to tell him *something.*" Adinah looked down, ashamed. "I should've known better than to take the call at work."

"It's my fault, not yours," Collister said softly. "I'm the one who called *you.*"

"What's done is done." The Shepherd took a breath, centering. "Adinah, what exactly do they know?"

"Bits and pieces," Adinah replied sullenly. "I tried to keep it vague, but my co-worker was jealous. He knew I'd filed exploratory permits for the Wadi Musa sector last year, without asking him to be part of it." She shrugged under the Shepherd's scrutiny. "Specifics? I'd say they know where this dig is and that we found something of significant interest. During the phone call, my colleague overheard we discovered a relic several weeks ago and packaged it for safekeeping."

"What's the crime in that?"

"I didn't file a report. Policy states we must report all new finds to the Department of Antiquities within 24 hours of initial discovery. To prevent further unsupervised excavation or unauthorized removal." She swallowed. "Which is what we were doing."

A deep voice like the sea broke into the conversation. "So your colleagues are coming out here expecting to bust one Israeli archaeologist about an independent dig." At the cave entrance, black-robed Theologos scratched his beard, and glanced out at the advancing dust plumes. "But when they get here, they're going to find something very different. They're not going to know what to do when they come upon an international group of forty unwashed tourists huddled in a cave around the bones of Jesus' brother." He gave a loud guffaw.

"This isn't a laughing matter!" Collister bellowed, red-faced.

"Everything's a laughing matter," responded the old monk with glee.

"They're fifteen minutes away, you nutjob!" The Brit exploded. He ran his hands through his sweaty red hair and sat heavily on the crate, looking around at his brothers and sisters. "We've got to get this hidden, everybody. If even one of them finds out about the Ossuary, it will be the end for us! Archaeologists all over the world will demand provenance."

"Provenance?" Magda asked. "What does that mean?"

"Sorry." Simon took a big breath, and regrouped. "They'll demand to know the context in which it was found," he declared. "Archaeologists will be crawling all over these bloody caves. For years."

"Mierde, my son, *everyone* will want to know where it was found. It'll be like flies on *skata."* Theologos' coarse Greek words emerging out of the darkness elicited more than a few chuckles.

"Crude, but the monk's simile makes my point." Collister's eyes were fierce. "Say goodbye to our secluded haven in the desert." He hopped up again. "Let's get this hidden!"

"Son. Be still." The Shepherd's tone was light, but it carried an edge. Conflicted, Simon stopped and listened to Leaven's leader. "Sit," she said, smiling. "Let's think this through before we do something rash."

"Sit?" Magda questioned. "Shepherd, sorry to object, but I'm with the bonedigger. Trust me, you don't want to sit when authorities are on your tail. I say we pack it up *now*. If we don't, these caves will be crawling with once-borns for the next fifty years."

Magda started to rise, but a commanding look from the Shepherd pinned her in place. "That's your instinct talking," the crone counseled. "The urge for self-protection. We need to think this through a bit more. Together."

"What's to think?" barked Collister. "Let me lay it out for you." He faced the Shepherd boldly. "Archaeologists will come first," he predicted tersely. "By the truckload. Then journalists. Then mid-level officials."

"Then tourists," Magda joined in. "Taking pictures of everything. Leaving their trash." She moaned. "This place will turn from our proving ground into a public museum."

"True that," Ryan added, his Boston accent identifiable even in the darkness. "No more changing lives; just charging admission." He shook his head. "Can't run desert Trials when they'll be serving popcorn at every corner."

"Aaagghh!" Simon groaned, head in hands. "And once the archaeologists see the Cave, they'll figure it all out."

"All of what, Simon?" the Shepherd inquired.

"Us," the archaeologist muttered. "They'll see the Drowning Pool. They'll count the steps." Collister aimed his flashlight to shine on the rear wall of the cave, where water seeped. "They'll see the carvings." There, high above the dripping pool, two ancient carvings were etched into the sandstone walls. The first was a crude outline of a wild-haired, bearded man grasping a wooden staff and wearing a robe of skins. On the opposite side of the pool was the same man's decapitated head on a platter.

"The clues are all just sitting here," the Brit despaired. "They'll see the images of the Baptizer, carved right here in the walls above the ritual pool he used for the life-change. They'll do the proper dating. Even a bloody amateur could figure out this was the cave of John the Baptist."

"Dr. Collister?" Adinah Sharon, the soft-spoken Israeli field archaeologist, entered into the conversation. "Remember that these caves are also littered with buried potsherds from the Iron Age. We've excavated test trenches, but the majority of specimens remain in the pool. Proto-Isaiah. Dated to 700 BC."

"Gads, you're right!" Collister wailed in the dark. "They'll only have to dig a few inches in the mud before they link this place back even farther, to the schools of Isaiah himself. Once that happens, they'll realize how ancient our tradition really is." Murmurs rose around the circle as individuals processed this new information. "Bureaucrats will start up an investigation, and demand to know all about our membership, our connection to this cave and our current practices. We'll look like a cult. Be on bloody talk radio. Laughed at by Rush Limbaugh!" Simon Collister cried. "Exposed on bloody Oprah!"

The crowd in the cave erupted. Forty people were now talking, shouting, trying to listen.

"Is that so bad?"

The unexpected question quieted the din. All heads turned to follow Paloma's voice.

"Is this our time to rise?" In one fluid motion, Paloma leaped to stand on top of the packing crate. His bare head gleamed in the beam of Collister's flashlight. "Just because we've kept ourselves secret for so long, it doesn't mean we should keep doing so." He spoke in a voice that carried to the edges of the cavern. "This generation might be ready for a kingdom revolution."

"That's how I see it, too, folks." The silhouetted figure of Clarence Washington came to stand next to Paloma in the center of the circle. "The signs are too strong. If this isn't a nudge from God, I don't know what is."

"Nudge from –!" Simon blurted in disbelief. "You're barmy, the both of you!" With uncharacteristic violence, Collister elbowed Clarence Washington out of the way and pushed at Paloma's legs. The Zen teacher toppled off the crate, startled. The rest of the group was in shock, too. Neither the Shepherd nor Theologos moved, though the old monk looked amused by it all.

"Listen," Collister said authoritatively to the ring of startled faces. "Unlike these two, I think most of us agree we can't let them find out about us. Leaven, in the tabloids? It would ruin everything we've protected for thousands of years." A few murmurs of agreement came from the crowd, so Simon continued, emboldened. "Now, I got us into this mess, and I've got a plan to get us out." Resolve formed on the archaeologist's face. "But we've only got a few minutes."

Paloma stood with regained balance at Collister's side. *This is your moment, Simon, and you're being mightily used,* he thought. *But are you being used by a spirit of wisdom, or of fear?*

"Magda and I will take the crate out the back way," Collister explained to the forty sets of eyes glued on him. "Adinah, everyone else, grab some of the excavated potsherds and then sit around them in a circle. Hum something. Kumbaya, perhaps. When the government agents show up, you tell them you were charging people for a vision quest. You know, one of those Holy Land experiences for tourists." Collister's eyes were filled with desperate enthusiasm, caught up in his own plan. "Adinah, the Department just might buy that, and give you a slap on the wrist for profiteering. Meanwhile, by the time they get back in their Jeeps, Magda and I will make sure the box is long gone." With new energy, he began fastening the waterproof lid.

"Stop."

"Magda, give me a hand, will you?"

"Stop, Simon, stop. Just stop." It was a command, but not without kindness, and it came from the Shepherd. "But I do like your idea of sitting in a circle singing Kumbaya."

"I know, brilliant, isn't it?" A gleam shone in Simon's eye. He glanced from his end of the crate to the wild-haired woman standing in the torchlight. "In fact, with the way you look, Shepherd, we could pass off this gathering as an Old Testament vision quest for tourists!" He looked to his moving partner.

"On three, Magda. Lift from the knees."

"No Simon," the Shepherd said softly. "No. We're going to sit together. For real."

"Sit? At a time like this?" The Brit desperately looked around the group for hints of shared sentiment. He found some. "Are you stark raving mad?" Collister laughed at Leaven's leader. "First Paloma and Clarence, and now you. They're almost upon us, Shepherd! Now this *is* a laughing matter, because it's time to pack up, not sit down. You three are being absurd."

"Sit. Down. Now." The Shepherd's eyes blazed, and the whole cavern stilled at her words. Simon stepped back, stunned at his own temerity.

Paloma took the moment to push down with sudden force on Collister's shoulders while giving a deft foot tap to the back of the man's legs. The Brit's knees buckled. In a few giant strides, Theologos was across the cave floor and sitting next to the astonished archaeologist, his long monk's sleeves around the man in a containing embrace. "You heard the Shepherd," the old Greek exhorted the rest of the group in his rough accent. "Don't just do something; sit here."

Collister, dumbfounded, began to struggle in the monk's arms. "But--"

"Butts are for sitting, not sassing," the monk replied, wrapping the stocky archaeologist even tighter.

Many members of Leaven remained standing near the cave entrance, torn. The dust plumes were much closer now, and everyone knew it. "Looking at those Jeeps coming isn't going to make them go away," Clarence Washington said loudly, coming to the cavern lip. "We can't run, so let's be together while we still can." He and Lauren ushered many of their brothers and sisters back into the heart of the cave to sit in a ring around the crate.

Magda, grumbling, took a last look at the approaching dust trails and then pulled the last members of Leaven from the cave entrance. "Come on, my friends, I'm not liking it either," she said, rounding up the reluctant like a mother hen. "But the Shepherd has asked for a circle." When she came to the circle, Magda sat on her haunches next to the old monk.

"*'Butts are for sitting, not sassing?'*" she murmured out of the side of her mouth. "Where *do* you get this stuff?"

"*Phrasebook of American Slang,*" Theologos whispered proudly, patting a huge pocket of his monk's robe. "1986 edition. You like?"

Magda rolled her eyes. "No comment."

Soon, all forty members were seated, albeit with some grumbling. Tension gripped the cavern.

"Okay." The Shepherd let out a large breath. "Here we are." *Good idea,* thought Paloma, breathing to center himself as well. *For all of us.* With the group quiet, he became aware of the low thrum of distant engines. *Already?*

In the semi-darkness, the Shepherd spoke. "Magda, my dear girl, please put out the torches."

The younger woman rose from her crouch, a bit unsure. "Total darkness, Shepherd? But – "

The wizened head nodded. "Darkness often brings out the truth." At those words, Magda hopped to her feet and began extinguishing torches, one by one. Paloma watched as his partner moved purposefully about the perimeter of the large cave. Her large, liquid eyes and silver ear bands glinted orange as she smothered each torch. Then she would vanish, only to reappear in the next pool of firelight. Soon the cave was plunged into darkness.

"We're all nervous," the Shepherd spoke out of the black. "But go past your anxiety, my friends. Find your real fear." As Paloma's vision adjusted, the cave opening sixty feet away glared like a giant bright eye in the gloom. By the way people glanced toward the entry, he could tell others heard the whine of several engines echoing up Wadi Musa as well. *Time to spread calm.*

"One moment, everything's secret," said Paloma in the new darkness. "The next, everything's blown wide open." In the murk, the crate in the center of the circle loomed pale and large. "This ossuary is now part of our lives. So are the visitors that are approaching our cave. We can't erase what's happened. We can't put it back in a box." He paused. "Do you understand?

This isn't going to be our cave anymore. Won't be our desert anymore."

"But this place has always been our heart," Magda said, eyes wet. "We can't just leave!"

The Shepherd nodded. "Trust me, child. I know the feeling. Where am I going to get sunrises like this?" The old woman spread her arms with a sad smile. "Thirty years it's been. If you guys put me in a house with plumbing, I won't know what to do."

"It just isn't right," protested Magda. "We've got to do something, and Collister's the only one suggesting anything."

"Don't be such a drama queen," said the old monk next to her in his thick Greek. Laughs erupted despite the tension. A smile of white teeth flashed at Magda. "Is that how you say it?"

"That's how *I* say it," she said dryly. "Hearing it from you is just wrong."

"Your *mama's* wrong."

"Somebody stop this man!" Magda said, throwing up her hands. "I can't believe this is happening!"

"Me neither, child," said Theologos, suddenly serious. He unwrapped himself from Collister and looked around the group. "None of us can believe this is happening, can we?" Anxious eyes from all around the circle nodded back at the monk. "My soul grew up here," he said. "So did most of yours. It's been our secret home forever. But we can't hold on to it anymore." He took sand from the cave floor, and let it run through his fingers. "We simply can't."

"But--"

"But nothing, Magda." The Shepherd's voice was gentle, but firm. "The engines of change come even now. We can scream if we want, but this little patch of desert is no longer our playground. Remember, my children, we're the followers of a homeless man. Like the Master said, 'The fox has its hole, the sparrow its nest, but we *bar enasha* have no place to lay our heads.'"

With those words, the spiritual leader of Leaven slowly rose to her feet. Theologos did too. He struck a match in the cavern darkness, and in seconds the torch in his hand illuminated his craggy face. "We've run Trials elsewhere, brothers and sisters. We'll do it again." He smiled hugely, his monstrous grayish-white mustaches spreading wide. "God is bigger than this desert."

Just then, the approaching engine noise turned into a chaotic roar as five white government Jeeps burst around the last bend of Wadi Musa. They circled the basin in a billowing dust cloud, their engines echoing around the amphitheater below. Inside the cave, Paloma and the others heard vehicles braking, doors slamming, a dozen people shouting in a number of tongues. The circle of Leaven panicked.

"Stay where you are!" the Shepherd commanded, holding the circle together by just a thread. "Master your fear. Things are going to get crazy in the next few minutes," she predicted. "Only God knows when we shall meet again, or where."

Massive audio feedback split the air as an amplified bullhorn came to life in the sandy basin below. "*Attention all persons,*" an Israeli voice boomed and crackled in broken English. "Attention all persons. We are officers from Israeli Department of Antiquities, and you are in suspected violation of national policy. Come out of cave immediately, all persons. Have nothing in hands. Have nothing in hands."

"Bullocks to their bullhorn!" Dr. Simon Collister stood arms folded, square-jawed. "Those bloody bureaucrats aren't going to tell us when to stop. We can block the entrance to the cave with our bodies if we have to!"

The Shepherd stared at the archaeologist, speechless.

"Yes, Shepherd, you had to tackle me to start this circle, and I sat through it. But now we've finished our sitting, and I'm still ready to act. We might lose this desert, but I'm not going to let us lose the Ossuary of James." Quite a few heads nodded in agreement. "So who's going to help me hide this bloody box?"

"Count me in," said Magda. She and several others moved toward the Brit.

"Beware, Simon Collister!" At the Shepherd's icy words, people halted.

"What am I missing here?" the archaeologist responded, pulling at this hair, looking wildly around the circle. "If we hide the bones, they only find out about this cave. If we show them the bones, they discover our whole history!"

"Perhaps this is the moment we've been made for." Paloma's voice rang clear into the brief silence.

"Blazes, Stephen, I used to think you were rational," Simon cried. "Are you potting mad?"

"No, listen to him, Simon," the Shepherd declared amidst the chaos. The bullhorn continued to squawk below. "This invasion is coming at us fast, and we're torn. I'm torn. Is this the time for Leaven to bubble up once more into the world?" Her milky eyes looked to the whole group, questioning in the firelight. "Or is it our job to hide the Ossuary from prying eyes?" She looked to her old friend Theologos. "I wish I could have some time," she sighed. "Just a little more time."

"As do I, Sofia," Theologos confessed. "But we both know that's something we don't have."

The Shepherd looked up at the tall monk, suddenly small. "Where's the divine breath blowing, my friend?" she asked plaintively. "The way is dark to me."

The Shepherd, unsure? Mutters erupted around the circle, echoing Paloma's own thoughts. In the face of their leader's confusion, the fragile circle threatened to drift apart.

"Hear me now, people of Leaven!" The sea-blown roar of Pater Theologos' voice filled the cavern. The man was suddenly huge, bringing the circle together again by sheer force of will. "Hiding. Discussing. Running," he bellowed. "These are sensible actions. Human-sized actions." The old man's broad, rough hand was warm and strong in Paloma's own, and his vitality was a living thing. "But have a care, my friends," he said, softer. "If we devise our own well-reasoned human plans, we may misjudge the best opportunity God

has put in front of us in five hundred years."

He stopped. The cavern was utterly still. All eyes followed the monk. Without warning, Theologos burst out laughing. "Do you feel it?" he hollered. He turned to the Shepherd, black robe whirling. "Don't worry about getting in touch with the Spirit, Sofia!" The towering monk opened his dark wings wide and stared at the Shepherd with eyes on fire. "It's already here, surrounding us, no question. The question is: are we going swimming, or not?"

The Shepherd locked her eyes with those of the old monk for a long moment, indecision battling across her face. When she turned back to face her flock, it was with new clarity.

"Excuse me a minute," she said to the group, businesslike. "Stay here, will you?" Taking Dr. Sharon in tow, the Shepherd strode out the cave opening to look down at the Jeeps in the amphitheater, eighty feet below.

"What the blazes are you doing?" Collister shouted. "Don't –"

"Greetings, gentlemen," she cried down to the milling officials. The bullhorn stopped. She cupped her hands around her mouth to shout her message. "We are conducting a legitimate archaeological dig for the nation of Israel, but Dr. Sharon here has been tardy in her paperwork. So sorry. However, she has found something of great interest, and she'd like you to see it."

9 WE TRAVEL WITH THEM NOW

Thomas emerged from the whitewashed plank church in the village of Todos Santos, and the glare of the afternoon sun temporarily blinded him. After a moment, he located the group of Guatemalan *campesinos* sitting under a few scraggly shade trees in the earthen hard pan courtyard. Gathering his courage, he walked over.

Unlike Reverend Ben's scene inside, no one was preaching. No one spoke, even. The group—maybe thirty in all—simply ate their food in heavy silence, gazes averted. Thomas wanted to kick himself. *Why'd I think I could just follow them out here?* He turned to go back inside when his eyes met those of Juanita, the Mayan woman he had spoken with in the food line. She patted the ground next to her and motioned him over with a kind smile, her gold tooth showing. He sat down, in the place she offered.

"Mi hijo, Tomas," she said softly.

Is she calling me her son? Thomas stared at her, puzzled. No, she was indicating a large picture frame she held in her hands, one of the many she'd carried in her pack. She gently held the picture in her lap and showed him. It was a photo of a young man who must be her son: a handsome high-school age soccer player, posed kneeling with a ball on a green field.

"Tomas Antonio." The old woman's voice cracked with pain.

"Lo siento," Thomas said. He had no idea what was wrong with her son, but *I'm sorry* seemed okay to say.

"*Consuelo Luz y Edgar Ruiz,*" said a voice next to Juanita, coming from a much younger woman. From her colorful *huipil* wrap, the young woman pulled a gaudy bent gilt frame and thrust it out at Thomas, who instinctively took it in his hands. The poorly printed photo displayed a dated image of what might have been a prom picture of a young couple in front of a backdrop of a fake sunset. The woman wore a short white dress, the man a tuxedo. "*Tuvieron cinco niños.*"

"*Como?*" said Thomas, uncomprehending. He became aware of many Mayan eyes resting upon him. "I'd like to understand, but..."

"They had five kids," interjected a small wiry boy Thomas hadn't noticed before. The boy squatted next to a sharp-eyed old man at the base of a shade tree. The old man kept his milky gaze fixed at a distance, vigilant for something far away, but the boy was looking right at Thomas.

"You know English," Thomas said. It was both a question and statement.

"I learn in school," the boy explained. He was maybe eight years old. "My name Miguel."

"*Me llamo Tomas.* Listen, Miguel, can you tell me what--"

"*Vamanos!*" the old man croaked, rising. He pointed. "*Estan aqui.*" The rest of the group picked up their things and hastily stacked the plastic bowls from lunch. Thomas scooped them up. Softly, and getting louder, Thomas heard the sound of a sputtering engine.

"Who's here?" Thomas looked to the boy as the rest of the group prepared to depart. "Why do you need to go?" Without warning an old red Nissan pickup burst out of the lush canopy of the jungle. It traveled a rutted dirt road, bearing a comically tall load covered by a bulging, blue plastic tarp. Its bald tires struggled in the mud, but the sheer weight of its mountain of baggage kept the truck moving forward, albeit slowly. Flanking the aged vehicle came several Guatemalans on foot and burros, loaded down with possessions. Two men in saddles cradled rifles.

"The other *pueblos*," the wiry boy responded. "We travel with them now. Safer."

Small boys ran alongside the red pickup, throwing sticks under the muddy tires, helping it gain traction during rough spots. As the truck and its retinue moved closer and into a clearing, Thomas' eyes went wide: dozens, maybe hundreds of indigenous villagers were emerging out the jungle behind the vehicle, following by foot in the truck's wake. Thomas had never seen a pilgrimage like this. Countless dogs trod at the villagers' heels, ranging out on both sides of the muddy track.

As the train of people progressed, Thomas saw pigs on leashes, goats on lead ropes, and a heavy-set woman leading six hens and a rooster by a string. Whether young or old, all the travelers carried burdens, household possessions bound up in colorful cloth bundles.

"Where are you all going?" Thomas whispered to the boy next to him.

Miguel pointed farther down the dirt road. "Into the jungle. To find a new home."

Juanita's group of *campesinos* under the shade trees was moving out. Two men pushed wheelbarrows loaded with plastic bags of handwoven blankets, and the group moved to join the steady stream of pilgrims.

Suddenly Juanita was at Thomas' side, touching his elbow. *"Ven conmigo."* Her deep-set eyes, buried in wrinkles, gave the American a searching look. *"Ven y ve, Tomas."* They both stopped walking, as did the boy Miguel. The endless train of travelers flowed on, a river around a log.

"What did she say?"

"She says to come with her." Miguel hesitated. "She says come and see."

Thomas laughed, startled. "That's sweet, but I can't," he began, shaking his head. "Miguel, tell her my group's leaving for California in a few days."

Juanita began to move with the group around her. *"Adios, mi hijo Tomas,"* she said with a sad smile, looking back at him. *"Gracias por la comida."*

Thomas felt paralyzed as she slipped away. He wanted to say something comforting about her son, like pastors do. If she spoke English like Miguel he'd say, 'Remember, God never gives us challenges we can't handle.' Or if she knew even a little he might say something simple, like 'God never fails.' Instead, he gave the only blessing he could. *"Vaya con Dios,"* he called.

"Vaya con Dios," she responded, drifting away in the crowd. Abruptly she stopped, a rock in the flow of pilgrims, and looked right at him. She held the large framed photograph of her son tight against her chest. *"Lo espero,"* she said earnestly, then disappeared into the sea of travelers.

"What'd she say?" Thomas looked at Miguel, who had remained at his side.

"Go with God."

"I know what *vaya con Dios* means," snapped Thomas. "What'd she say after that?"

"Lo espero," the boy said. "It means 'I wait for it.' Or..."

"Or what?"

"It also means, 'I hope it's so.'" With that, Miguel ran to join the rest of his villagers.

I hope it's so. I hope I go with God. Thomas took a long look back at the double doors of *Assemblea de Dios,* a courtyard away. Most of the travelers had passed him now, just a few stragglers still walking by. His hands instinctively felt under his shirt and found the hidden pouch that contained his passport, some money and Talia's iodine. He looked back at the church once more, his group inside.

Then he ran to join Juanita and Miguel, joining the mass of campesinos trudging into the Peten, wandering through the jungle in search of a place to call home.

10 ARRANGEMENTS ARE BEING MADE

Two minutes after the Shepherd shouted down her announcement, a swarm of Israeli officials entered the Cave of the Baptist. Paloma observed that this squad seemed specially trained for this kind of work. Probably very needed, he reflected: the Israeli government was continually busting enthusiastic pot hunters who found ancient artifacts and began digging without government approval.

While the members of Leaven watched, Israeli officials began to systematically catalogue the cavern complex. The lead official, a keen-eyed officer with a drooping black mustache by the name of Kartouf, explained it was their usual routine when encountering an unsanctioned and possibly unstable dig.

For a precautionary first step, all unauthorized personnel—meaning all of Leaven—were searched. Paloma, Magda, and the rest calmly stood against the cave wall while their bodies and clothes were examined for weapons and stolen artifacts. The old monk Theologos giggled when Kartouf frisked his large frame.

"What is this?" Kartouf pulled a dog-eared *Phrasebook of American Slang* out of the monk's voluminous robe, 1986 edition. The Israeli's sharp eyes scanned the pages, puzzled. "I not understand this book."

"Keep it," Magda said firmly, pre-empting any comment from Theologos. "It's a compilation of rituals he was conducting without your government's permission. Without anyone's permission." Confused, Kartouf handed the book to his assistant. Theologos just laughed all the harder.

After an initial site assessment was completed, Kartouf released most of the group, keeping only those who were responsible for the excavation: archaeologists Simon Collister and Adinah Sharon, and their leader Sofia Kazantzakis. The rest of Leaven were ordered to disperse. Despite the directive, Paloma, Magda, and Theologos lingered in the cave to watch the officials continue their inspection of the site.

The government workers were deeply engaged in their routine—cataloging artifacts, analyzing the disturbed soil stratigraphy that was so crucial to determining context and provenance, interviewing the rogue archaeologists who'd initiated the dig--when a few things about this excavation caused General Kartouf to stop short.

First of all, the violator was one of their own: Dr. Adinah Sharon, a respected colleague at Israel's Department of Antiquities. Second, Dr. Sharon's strong professional opinion was that this primitive site had been continuously occupied since the time of John the Baptist by religious hermits, and to this day was still used for ceremonial purposes. But it was the third thing that caused Kartouf to halt all work: Dr. Sharon had just asserted that the crate in front of them held the bones of Jesus' brother, found in this very cave.

Officer Kartouf stared at Adinah Sharon, and commanded his team to wait for additional experts. Sensing it was the right time, Paloma, Magda and Theologos quietly exited the cave and started down the short but steep goat trail leading to Wadi Musa basin and the world beyond.

"Wow." The simple word escaping the old monk's mouth spoke volumes. "Well, that settles it. The Shepherd made us all start swimming." Theologos chuckled as the trio descended the dusty trail. "If you're going to go, go big." When Magda glanced over her shoulder at him with a look of exasperation, he winked. "This is how you say it, *neh?*"

"That *is* how I say it," Magda replied, laughing. "And, yeah, it's what we're doing." She grabbed Paloma's hand just ahead of her on the trail. "Leaven is rising, Stephen. Let's hope it's not a bad thing."

Paloma turned to respond. He jerked his thumb at Pater Theologos. "This old monk said God is in this somewhere. I'm counting on that." After a few switchbacks, they reached the sandy basin below. Passing officials and Jeeps, they began the long walk up Wadi Musa back to their vehicles.

"Hey, wait up for an old man!" The voice came from high above. The trio at the bottom looked up to see Clarence Washington halfway down the cliff trail, cruising along at a rapid clip in his blazer and black t-shirt. He stopped at a switchback to catch his breath, and pointed above him. "The Shepherd wants to talk to you."

Eighty feet above, the Shepherd was standing at the lip of the cave.

"Hello, my friends!" she called down, cupping her hands to shout. "Remember what I said about not getting too comfortable?"

The three in the basin looked at each other. "Uh oh," Magda muttered with a dark smile.

"What are you getting at, o' Shepherd my Shepherd?" Paloma called back.

"Looks like Adinah is hammering out a proposal," the Shepherd shouted. "Thought you might want a heads-up."

"Proposal?" Paloma ventured, craning his neck.

"She's on the satellite phone with the head of Israel's Department of Antiquities," the Shepherd reported. "Certain arrangements are being made."

Magda looked skeptically at Paloma and Theologos. "And how will these arrangements affect us?"

"Glad you asked, my child. Adinah says we have some significant leverage in our negotiations because of our special knowledge of the site." The Shepherd chuckled. "We might actually get what we want. Which means we'll be leaning on you two."

"To do what?"

"Sounds like Adinah is persuading them to hold the worldwide premiere of the Ossuary of James six months from now in the San Francisco area," the Shepherd stated matter-of-factly. "Berkeley, in particular. The venerable

Museum of Man."

"You're kidding." Paloma and Magda weren't smiling. But Theologos was.

"Not in the least," grinned the Shepherd. "I want you two to orchestrate the public opening and reveal Leaven to the world."

"Us?" They looked at each other.

"Yep." The Shepherd nodded. "Clarence will help you from Portland." Her attention was drawn by something going on behind her inside the cave. "Well, my friends, the officials are calling. Berkeley. Six months. We'll talk later." With that, she disappeared into its dark mouth.

Clarence Washington, the former Old Testament professor, adjusted his tortoise-shell sunglasses as he caught up to the other three at the basin. "Magda, Paloma, I'm at your service, as always. Sounds like we have a job to do."

"Yeah, *we* do. In Berkeley," mumbled Magda. "I love you dearly, Clarence, but remember, you live in Portland."

"No worries," Clarence said as they walked together. "I still keep busy at the Catholic Worker, but now that I'm retired, I skip town a lot. I'll come when you need me."

"I've never done anything like this before," Magda grumbled. "I've got no clue."

"When has that ever stopped you?" asked Theologos merrily from behind. "The Spirit's moving, my dear. Like the apostle Peter, you're being led to places you'd rather not go."

"Isn't that a scripture foreshadowing his death?" Magda asked. At Theologos' nod, she grimaced. "Note to Theologos," she said dryly. "Next time you want to encourage someone, don't compare them to a man who was crucified upside down."

"Get over your bad self, girl. Your small self, that is." The old monk chuckled. "The one that worries. The Spirit's spilling all over this one, Magda, the swells are forming, and it looks like it's headed toward Berkeley. You and Paloma just need to either get on board or get out of the way."

Clarence Washington put his arms around Paloma and Magda as they walked. "We've never done a museum opening before. It'll be fun." He breathed a big sigh. "But there could be resistance."

"*Au contraire, mon frere,*" corrected Paloma. "There *will* be resistance." He'd been silent, thinking of all the changes looming for Leaven. "The bones of Jesus' older brother will rock more than a few theological boats. The agents of Christendom will use all the resources of church and state to protect the industry that Christianity has become. Playing the game on their terms will be pointless." He gave a mysterious smile. "We'll have to get creative. Subversive."

"How so?" Magda and Clarence said in unison. Theologos, too, gave Paloma an inquiring look.

"My specialty," he said, clapping his hands. "Time to brew up a little holy mischief."

11 MAYBE

These days, Thomas loved Saturday mornings. Since his return from Guatemala three weeks ago, life felt fragile. So he cherished moments like this. He loved watching Talia get ready for practice after she slept over on the weekends: shaking out her wet hair fresh from the shower, changing out of the oversize Oxford she'd borrowed to sleep in, and sliding a sports bra over her trim, firm breasts. Especially that part.

He sat on the carpet leaning against the futon with a steaming cup of coffee and felt warmth infuse him. *Can I trust this?* He used to. But now he knew how peace could be shattered in a moment. He watched as she went about her morning tasks, her lean body working with a languid efficiency, slow but sure. Over her bra she threw on a Bay Area Breakers t-shirt, representing the Ultimate Frisbee team she'd captained to first place in regionals last year. With practiced ease, she gathered her tousled mane of blondish hair into a ponytail.

"Will your homie Ed make it here in time for meditation tonight?"

"Maybe. Depends on how fast he's driving." Thomas laughed. "I know he left Taos yesterday on his Harley, but that's it. Maybe he drove all night and is sleeping in the front yard with Agnew right now."

"Sounds like a free spirit." Talia slipped on a pair of nylon running shorts. She dropped to the floor and began doing hurdlers' stretches. "Is he a flake? He sounded like someone you could count on when you called him about iodine. Sure about things."

"That's because he was talking about *my* life. His own's full of maybes."

"What do you mean, maybes?"

"Like maybe he's already here, or maybe he got waylaid at the Arizona border by a pipe smoking shaman and he's passing the peace in one of those metal roadside tipis," mused Thomas.

"The kind of guy you count on for adventure."

"That's for sure. But he's deep, too. Not just Mr. Fun. I think you'll dig him, Tal, once you know him."

"Glad I'm getting the chance." Talia glanced at her watch. "Yikes. Gotta go."

Thomas tugged on her graceful, athletic leg as she stood up to leave. "C'mon, you can fudge. Don't you want more coffee?"

"Sorry, no fudging for the captain. Not today." She extricated herself from his grasp. "We've got regionals coming up, and while I've been out backpacking the team's gotten lazy." She wheeled her road bike across the hardwood floor to the front door. "So when am I going to see you next? Right before Paloma's class?"

Thomas nodded. "Seminary bike rack. Ten minutes 'til. Then we can breeze in to class together. Maybe Ed will be here then."

"Ed or not, let's make it the bike rack, but at twenty to five," Talia responded, heading out the door to the front porch. "First meditation class after summer break, and I'm rusty. I'll need to change into my *gi* after practice, and I don't want to be late. And hey, I have a meeting with my supervisor later tonight to get ready for a federal grant report. Maybe we can catch a quick dinner beforehand."

Thomas joined her outside as she wheeled to the front gate, following her down the cement walkway through his untamed front yard. "No Harley visible," she said, scanning the street in front of the sidewalk. Talia looked around in the tall grass. "No sign of Ed bedding down your yard, either." She shouted into the doghouse: "Agnew, anyone in there with you?"

At the sound of his name, their Great Dane came bounding out to Talia, slobbering on her hands. She peered in the empty doghouse. "So I'm guessing he didn't drive all night."

"Maybe he got held up searching for wild mushrooms somewhere near Mendocino." Thomas grabbed Agnew's collar to keep him from running while Talia opened the front gate and pulled her bicycle out onto the sidewalk.

"See you in a few hours, lover boy." Talia began pedaling away but turned. "Make sure to finish your homework!"

"Shit! That's right!" Thomas brought his fist down hard on the top of the chain-link fence. "Damn!" he exclaimed. An angry red line of blood welled up on his palm.

Talia stopped in her tracks. "Thomas, what's wrong?" She circled back and got close. "Why's this so hard for you?"

Thomas stuck the fresh gash in his mouth. "I've been wanting to talk to you since I got back, Tal, but with all your trips, it never felt right."

She ignored the blame. "You've been different since you left," Talia stated. "Harder. Less happy."

Thomas didn't answer. "We'll talk later, Tal. You're gonna be late." He moved toward the house.

"Something broke inside of you during that trip, didn't it?"

He turned. "I guess you could say that." He looked at her across the waist-high fence. "I haven't known what to say, Tal." He shrugged. "So I haven't."

"Well, it's weighing on your soul like a stone." She paused. "Whatever happened, Thomas, you can tell me. Or tell Ed, if you like. But you *need* to tell someone. Get it out." Talia gave him a kind smile. "Maybe putting it in writing for Paloma will help."

"Maybe."

"C'mon. Grab a pencil and try."

"Right now?"

"Right after I leave. Promise me."

"It's not that big of a deal, Tal. I'll get to it."

"Not a big deal?" Talia gave him a look. "Come on, lover. You just smashed your hand on a fence."

He picked at his wound. "You don't let people off the hook, do you?"

"Nope. Guess that's why they like me for wilderness challenge trips." She flashed an evil smile.

"Okay," he said, surrendering. "I'll write. Maybe it'll help me find words."

"Maybe," Talia agreed. With one foot, she pushed off and started coasting slowly down the street, still looking at him. "Thomas, I know it's hard to dig into painful things. Maybe you're not ready yet. But I'll be there when you are." She gave him a little wave. "See you soon."

Thomas waved with his good hand as his girlfriend vanished down the street. Then he banged back in through the front porch screen and stalked to the fridge. From under a magnet, he pulled the letter from Paloma, laid it out on the kitchen table and tried once again. He grabbed a pencil.

"332 people massac--"

Thomas crossed it out. *No way. Not like that.* He stalked back to his bedroom, kicking his scattered laundry into a pile. Paloma, his meditation teacher, had mailed a note to all students two weeks ago, requesting a short writing assignment due when the group resumed August 14. Today.

Writing? Thomas fumed. *For a non-credit class? Who does Paloma think he is?* How about the real question, Thomas thought. *Who do I think I am?* Here it was, a few hours before class, and Thomas was blaming the teacher because he didn't know what to write. *Lame.*

Thomas looked at the note again:

> Warm greetings, my students! Over the summer I've realized
> something about our sangha that I want to share with you. A
> Zen meditation course at a Christian seminary in the Bay
> Area is a unique space: our class combines cosmopolitan
> diversity, monotheistic theology and Western attitudes with an
> Eastern form of focused attention--which could be called prayer.
> Our sangha includes grandmothers, professors, housewives,
> plumbers, seminarians, activists, cafeteria workers...seekers all.
> This is a richness to celebrate.
>
> I hope your summer has been full of travel, discovery and
> rejuvenation. Mine certainly has—my trip to Israel was just
> what I needed, and set me on some new paths. We'll be starting
> back a few weeks before regular seminary classes resume
> September 1, so be prepared! Two requirements as you come to
> our first class of the semester, August 14: wear your gi or other
> loose clothes, and write a summary of your current spirituality,
> no more than a paragraph. Entienden? No more than a
> paragraph . Let's discover the inner richness we have together. --
> Stephen Paloma

Current spirituality? After his time in Guatemala, all Thomas wanted to bring was a blank sheet of paper. As in empty. No, there was a lot more than emptiness: there was rage. He grabbed a black Sharpie and scrawled on the back of Paloma's letter:

> MOST OF US DIE STILL BELIEVING THAT WE'RE
> PROTECTED BY A LOVING GOD.
>
> BUT SOME OF US FACE TERROR AND SEE THE
> REAL TRUTH: THE UNIVERSE DOESN'T CARE.
> AND NOBODY'S DOING ANY RESCUING.

Well, you wanted it, you got it, thought Thomas. *Here's my inner richness.*

He put the note in his pocket, then reconsidered. *No way. Paloma's gonna share these with the whole damn sangha.* Thomas crumpled the paper and tossed it out the open screen door.

"Incoming!" a voice on the porch said in surprise, caught off guard by the missile. A short, muscular man with dark hair and a goatee stood in Thomas' doorframe, attired in a black leather jacket, ripped Carhartt pants and snakeskin boots. "Well, *buenos dias* to you too, *hermano*."

"Ed my man!" Thomas exclaimed, abashed.

The newcomer juggled the ball of paper as he strode into the living room. "What's this—our paper anniversary, T? How sweet. You shouldn't have." Smiling wickedly, he started to uncrumple it.

"Dude, I didn't...hey, wait, that's mine!" Too late. Thomas tried to snatch the paper out of his friend's hands, but Ed opened the note and dangled it out of his friend's reach.

"What is it, a love letter to your hottie?" Ed taunted. But when he saw the writing, his smile vanished. "Fuck me, man. This is some serious existentialist shit." He carefully recrumpled the note and handed it back to Thomas. "Seminary's been rough, huh?"

"Seminary's got it's problems," Thomas muttered. "But this is bigger."

"What is it, T?"

"Something happened in Guatemala."

Ed took a step closer. "Want to talk about it?"

"No," Thomas growled. "Maybe tomorrow after a couple of beers." He enveloped his smaller friend in a huge hug. "You smell like a freaking peace pipe. Let's get your stuff."

12 A BOX OF BONES

"Think I'm in heaven, *amigo*," Ed howled into the wind an hour later, cruising down Claremont Avenue on his Harley with a big grin on his face. He took in downtown Berkeley with delicious slowness, his motorcycle keeping pace with Thomas' pedaling.

Thomas had to admit: Ed fit right in. He could pass for a local riding his chopper with his silver earring, red bandana, unruly black hair, braided goatee and wraparound Ray-Bans. They'd left the sprawl of UC Berkeley a few blocks ago on their way to meditation class at the seminary. Now they were passing a riot of eclectic businesses: ethnic restaurants, second hand stores, coffee shops, copy centers, bagel stands, veggie markets, alt-boutiques and lefty bookstores competed for space along both sides of the busy street.

When Claremont crossed Mason, though, things changed. They now rode through the domain of museums and seminaries; bustling retail gave way to brick quads. Open plazas for the learned hugged the road with manicured lawns, wrought-iron benches and shaded walkways. Huge ancient oak trees presided over the plazas and gave each an air of eternity. Gnarled roots broke through brick and cement alike.

Thomas signaled left off of Claremont, and the pair turned in to the broad circular driveway that marked the entrance to the Bay Area Theological Union. At the back of the driving circle, Thomas picked his bike up over his shoulder, while Ed deftly hopped his chopper up over the curb and wheeled a short distance across the sidewalk to the seminary's bike rack.

"So this is where we're meeting the titillating Talia?" said Ed expectantly.

Thomas shot him a warning look. "You better be cool," Thomas muttered. He connected the back wheel of both bike and motorcycle to the rack with a long chain. "If you start pulling that Shakespearean pirate shit like you do, I'm leaving. With Tal. Without you."

"Touchy, aren't we?"

"Just don't embarrass me." He closed the lock with a click. "I want you guys to like each other."

"Watch how likable I am. I'm Señor Likeable." Ed gave a huge smile behind his Ray-Bans.

"That's what I'm worried about. Just keep your eyes open."

"What am I looking for?" Ed said, scanning the grassy quad.

"A tall blonde with a long nose, sporting a great smile and running shorts. Or maybe a karate outfit." Ed shot Thomas a quizzical look. "Depends if she's changed already," Thomas explained. "Our teacher wants his students to wear a martial arts *gi* to class. He thinks it helps you get in a more ceremonial attitude. Helps you meditate."

"Like what, a spiritual warrior?"

"I guess." Both men looked around the quad, searching for Talia. While they waited in the warm sun, Ed took off his jacket and boots, and began to run through some basic Tai Chi forms in ripped jeans and a sleeveless t-shirt, the tight black curls of his armpits on stage. Thomas rolled his eyes, and hoped nobody he knew was walking by this afternoon. His gaze traveled across the street to the old museum he loved visiting.

Across from the seminary campus, set behind a giant fountain, stood Berkeley's fabled Museum of Man, a venerable institution that had been for over a century a premiere showcase for some of the world's greatest discoveries in anthropology and archeology. In recent years, it had beaten out top-notch institutions in Los Angeles, Seattle and San Francisco to be the first museum on the West Coast to display the traveling collections of King Tut's Tomb, frescoes and gold filigree found at Knossos, and some exquisite porcelain crafted by master ceramists of the Han Dynasty. It was always showing some exhibit that blew his mind.

As he gazed, Thomas noted a new billboard going up in front of the museum, directly facing the seminary. Two men were plastering the fresh billboard into place. They'd started with the top, slowly unrolling and pasting the huge new poster as they went. So far the top right corner was visible:

A BOX OF BONES?

"Check it out," said Thomas. Ed, slowly rolling into his next Tai Chi move, followed his friend's eyes to the billboard.

"Looks like the museum's going to be showing a box of bones soon," said Thomas. "How much you wanna bet it'll be the Ossuary of James?"

Ed's face showed no sign of recognition. He stood balanced on one foot, arms raised.

"I forgot—mainstream media is so below you," Thomas remarked. "Take a look at *Time* magazine lately? *Newsweek*?"

Ed remained unresponsive as he moved to a crouch in slow motion, a heron seeking a frog.

"James was Jesus' brother," Thomas explained.

Ed looked up. "Jesus had a bro?"

"Several, actually. Sisters too."

Ed came to standing and glanced at the sign going up across the street. "And I gather you're telling me somebody found the man's skeleton."

"The story was all over the news last month," Thomas explained. "Right when I got back from Guatemala. What is it, mid-August? Just about a month ago, some archaeologists near Jerusalem found a bone crypt in some desert cave. The crypt had an inscription on it, something like, 'James the Just, son of Joseph, brother of Jesus.' Many scholars think James was Jesus' *older* brother. Mary's first son."

Ed paused in mid-form, one leg raised at the knee. "Doesn't that mess with the whole eternal virgin thing?"

"Exactly." Like most waking moments, ancient Koine was not far from his mind. "Of course, the Greek word *kore* that the church has translated as *virgin* also means *maid* or *young woman.*"

"Rahhhrr," Ed growled sensuously, one paw scratching the air. "Speaking of young maids, I think the one we're looking for has arrived." Talia, still in her shorts and t-shirt from Frisbee, was pedaling up in sunglasses and backpack, hair flying, face beaming, her body alive and flush from her practice.

"Is this who I think it is?" Talia grinned, coming to a stop. "Ed the river guide and poison consultant, coming all the way out here from Taos? So great to finally meet you."

"*Igualmente,* darlin'," responded Ed, making a quick bow with his palms pressed together. "What energy you have! Thomas has been telling me about you, but now I see for myself why he's happier these days."

"Wow!" Talia laughed aloud, genuinely pleased. She dismounted from her bike and kissed Thomas on the lips. "You can introduce me to all the old roomies you want, as long as they're as nice as this guy." She looked back at Ed. "That was sweet to say."

"Believe it," Ed responded. As Talia crouched to lock her bike to the rack, Ed caught Thomas' eye, pointed to himself and mouthed *Mister Likeable.*

Thomas glanced over at the seminary's clock tower. "Well, we still have a few minutes. I wonder if we should--"

"And is *that* who I think it is?" said Talia, rising up from her bike wheel and looking up across the street toward the museum.

"Sweet Jesus," muttered Ed, looking. "It's a freaking sign from God. And he's talking to you, T."

"What are you--?" Thomas turned. And nearly shat his pants. There, in front of him, twenty feet high, was his uncle Reverend Benjamin Whidman.

An image of him anyway, plastered larger than life on the new billboard. Dressed in a pinstripe suit, Ben's arms were spread wide. His eyes were ablaze, one hand holding the Holy Scripture and the other wielding a long bone. Above his head, a huge banner headline read:

WHERE DO YOU FIND TRUTH: THE BIBLE, OR A BOX OF BONES?
Come Defend Your Faith With Rev. Benjamin Whidman

And in large text below his feet:

Be Part of Reverend Ben's "Bible Before Bones" West Coast Tour
Los Angeles Sept. 30th   Portland Nov. 26th   Berkeley Jan. 15th

A *Millennial Harvest* Stadium Event

"I can't believe it!" moaned Thomas.

"I can," Ed remarked. "*Mega-Harvest, Millennial Harvest,* whatever. I *told* you I saw him on late night TV! I *knew* I wasn't dreaming. Your uncle, he's one crazy zealot."

"And he's *my* crazy zealot!" Thomas wailed. "Related to me, and always pulling these kinds of fundie hellfire stunts!" Thomas grabbed his head and wheeled on one foot, throwing his arms out in exasperation.

"Hold it. Right there." Ed held Thomas' open arms slightly wider and eyed the billboard looming behind his friend. Ed looked over to Talia. "Yes? Do you see the family resemblance?" Talia's laugh twinkled in the air, making Ed beam. "All you need to do, T, is glare more and wave a bone around."

"Quit it," Thomas growled, dropping his arms. He turned around to take in the billboard again, his uncle towering. The seminarian shook his head. "I can't believe I actually wanted to be like that guy."

"Makes sense," Talia said. "He's impressive. And he gave you answers when you needed them."

"Yeah. Answers that don't work."

"Give yourself a break, Thomas," she said softly, holding his hand. "Give *him* a break. He's your *uncle*. He loved you, in his own way. Spent more time with you than your dad did."

"You're related to that man?"

The question came from a newcomer approaching the trio along the brick walkway: a middle-aged lean man dressed in a black t-shirt, jeans and a close fitting black knit cap. Though he had chiseled features and a salt and pepper goatee that made his face serious, he had an amused light in his eye.

"Paloma!" Talia said, springing forward to give a big hug to their meditation teacher, who gave a deep, startled laugh. "Sorry, I hug everybody," she gushed. "I'm just glad to see you after the break."

"I'll take a welcome like that any day," the meditation teacher said with a huge smile. "Surprise me any time you want."

"Hey, teach," Thomas said, waving and coming close. "Long time no see."

"Good to see you, Thomas," said Paloma warmly, shaking his hand. Seeing a new face, he introduced himself to Ed, then turned to Thomas once more. "So how was your trip—a building project in Guatemala, right?"

"It was okay," Thomas mumbled, looking sideways at his friends. "Tell you later, alright? I want to know about your trip—how was Israel?"

Paloma gazed intently at Thomas for a second, then answered. "I came back to the States a month ago, but I can't stop thinking about my time there. Huge deserts, old friends, ancient sites, new ideas. All I discovered, all I got to experience. I'll tell you guys more about it sometime if you're interested. Maybe over tea?"

"Cool," said Talia. "I'd like that."

"What about this crazy thing?" Thomas pointed at the billboard. "Did you hear about the Ossuary of James while you were in Israel?"

Paloma chuckled. "I guess they discovered it in some caves quite near me while I was sightseeing near Jerusalem, but I didn't read about it until I came back to the States. James is my favorite."

Thomas was startled. "Mine, too." He raised an eyebrow at Paloma. "A Zen meditation teacher has a favorite book of the Bible?"

"Sure. The Bible's Judeo-Christian. Me, I'm Budeo-Christian."

Thomas wanted to follow up on that comment, but Talia was still thinking about the Ossuary. "It's ironic," she said. "Paloma, you were in Israel right when they were making this discovery, but you traveled thousands of miles before you read about it. Funny how we sometimes miss something huge even when it's right in front of us."

"Like this," said Paloma, pointing back to the billboard. "If I hadn't heard you talking, I wouldn't have made the connection that this was *your* uncle, Thomas. I had no idea you were related to someone famous."

"More like *in*famous." Thomas looked up and scowled at his uncle waving a bone. "He's everywhere. Defending the faith, getting America ready for the Second Coming."

"I tell you, he's following you," commented Ed. "In a creepy way."

"Following you?" asked Paloma, eyebrow cocked at Thomas.

"Uncle Ben leads the *Millennial Harvest* movement," Thomas said darkly. "Heard of it?"

"It's been around for a few years, right?" Paloma asked. Thomas nodded. "They run those end-of-the-world stadium events."

"Bingo," said Ed. "Jesus is coming back to kick ass, so you better join the club."

"Uncle Ben started doing them in Orange County, when I was still in high school," explained Thomas. "Back in our zealous days, my buddy Mike and I would pray out loud on street corners and pass out flyers for Ben's events."

"A very dark space," Ed commented. "But then you went to college and started hanging out with sane people."

"You went away from your uncle for college, I'm guessing?"

"Yeah, Portland. Mike and I both went to Lewis & Clark, where we met this guy"--he jerked his thumb at Ed—"and we all became roomies."

"Enter the stalker," joined in Ed. "Ben missed you too much to stay in Orange County."

At Paloma's raised eyebrow, Thomas explained. "Just a few months after we moved there, my uncle expanded his operation to hit all the West Coast. Started running big *Millennial Harvest* events in Portland." He shrugged. "It did feel a *little* like he was following me."

"Stalking you," corrected Ed, eyes slitted. "Say it."

"At the time, freshman year, I'd already walked away from Ben's brand of Christianity," Thomas recalled. "But I still thought it was pretty cool that my relative was the star of these huge stadium events. I didn't like how he focused on the afterlife, but I still was into his main message."

"What was that?"

Thomas laughed darkly. "If you ask Jesus into your heart, God will watch over you, like a shepherd watching his sheep. He'll deliver you from evil." Thomas shook his head. "Can't believe I used to believe all that crap."

"You no longer believe God watches over you?" Paloma stepped back, looking keenly at the younger man. "That's not the bright young seminarian I knew a few months ago. He was a true believer, like his uncle."

"Yeah," Thomas admitted. "Ben sure taught me how to believe. And I did, with all my heart." Thomas' face darkened. "But that was before this summer."

"What happened, Thomas?" Paloma asked gently. Ed and Talia watched intently.

"We better get to class." Thomas left the bike rack and started off at a brisk walk.

Ed, Talia and Paloma just looked at one another. Shrugging, Ed stood up barefoot to brush the grass off his jeans. "Guess that's our cue to follow."

The trio caught up to Thomas halfway across the brick quad toward the seminary's student union.

"You've changed. Did your uncle change too?" Paloma asked, joining the younger man.

"My uncle, change? Don't think so," responded Thomas cynically. "It's still about correct belief. He's probably rallying this *Bible Before Bones* thing just to make sure his followers don't get led astray by facts before the end of the millennium."

"Ben Whidman seems like an interesting bird." Paloma turned to Thomas as they walked. "He sees himself as much more than just a preacher, doesn't he? More like there's an eternal battle going on against the agents of darkness, and he's God's chosen protector of the true faith."

"Uncle Ben was born to defend the Bible from darkness," Thomas said. "He told me once about a dream he had all the time when he was a kid."

"Really?" Paloma cocked an eyebrow. "Tell me."

"Let's see if I can remember," said Thomas, recalling as he walked. "He said he'd be riding a horse among millions of little people, and a double-edged sword would come out of his mouth. He'd attack threatening beasts."

"Like in Revelation?" Paloma's eyebrow went even higher.

Thomas nodded, intrigued again by his Zen teacher's knowledge of Christian scripture. "Ben says that's when he knew it was his mission to defend the word of God." The young man threw Paloma a look. "Why so curious about my uncle, anyway?"

"Hmm. I guess I want to understand a mind like that." The four of them arrived at the student union, and Paloma opened the main door for the group. "Who knows? Maybe someday I'll need to convince someone like him that we're on the same side."

"On the same side! Fat chance of that," Thomas scoffed as their group walked down a hallway crowded with other seminarians. "Not to get all Buddhist, but you two are definitely yin and yang."

Abruptly, the group found itself at the classroom door.

"While you all meditate, I think I'll check out the campus," Ed said. "Stretch my legs after twenty hours on my Harley." He started walking away, and only now Thomas noticed Ed was still barefoot, his feet slapping the hallway tile. "See you in an hour or so," Ed waved.

"And I'll see the two of you in class in a few minutes," Paloma said, approaching a side door. "After being gone so long, I need to remember where I put my *gi.*"

13 THIS CIRCLE IS FOR EMPTYING

Minutes passed. A cough. A squirm. The previously motionless sangha became a *somewhat* motionless sangha as the effects of summer break caught up with the group. Students who last spring were sitting in the lotus position during meditation now found themselves squirming, painfully out of practice. Thomas was no exception.

Breathe. Relax, Thomas told himself yet again. *My foot's falling asleep. Man, it's hot in here. Detach the mind from all arising thoughts. Let them drift away like boats down a river. I wonder what Paloma thought about my inner richness?*

Thomas did his eye-cracking trick to see Paloma serene, unmoving, in the center of their circle. All was silent except the sound of breathing. Nothing seemed different than the previous time Thomas sat here, the last day before summer. But everything was.

Paloma sure asked a lot about my uncle, Thomas mused. *But who wouldn't, after seeing him on that billboard? Ed's right, maybe Ben is a stalker. Why else has he been calling me every week since Guatemala? Why doesn't he just leave me alone?* Thomas knew that last thought was unfair. *You know damn well why,* he told himself. *You still haven't told Ben what really happened. You just took off with those villagers into the jungle and--*

Too late, Thomas realized how distracted he was from the task of meditation. *Focus, Whidman. Remember, let thoughts go like boats down a river.* He began to recite the ancient, rich words that he loved. *Hesychia,* stillness, to be at rest. *Pneuma,* breath, or spirit. Eventually, the familiar practice of Koine began to calm Thomas' mind, his emotions settled, and his breathing took over.

Out of a pool of deep stillness, Thomas heard the gong sound for a second time. He wasn't sure how long he'd been meditating, but it must have been a while. The session was already coming to a close.

"Welcome back," Stephen Paloma said in a soft but resonant voice as his students brought their consciousness back to the room. "It has been some time, has it not? I look forward to catching up with many of you and hearing about your summer adventures." The teacher paused to look at the eager faces around him. "Many of you might feel ready to talk, but that will have to wait. We are a raw and unrefined vessel. At the risk of sounding like something from a bad kung-fu movie, remember: bamboo must first be cut, dried, hollowed and emptied before it can become a flute. Talk all you want outside of this room, but this room is for emptying. Emptying: that's our shared work.

"To those of you who recently joined our community a few months ago"-- and here he smiled and indicated to Talia and two other women--"I bid you welcome again, and hope that you learn to find more of your true self in our sangha." He paused, and let silence enter into the circle.

"A new semester is a time for new beginnings. Although each of you may feel that you know me, I would like to reintroduce myself. My name is Stephen Paloma; if you would like, you may simply call me Paloma. Initially, many students find my manner at times to be disconcerting or disagreeable. This may be because I am sometimes an asshole."

Chuckles arose several of the veterans, including Thomas.

"It also may be because Americans generally place great importance upon individual wants and opinions. This may come as a shock to you, but my job is not to care about your feelings, your opinions, what you think about this or that. All of that is merely distraction from discovering the true self. And *that* is what we care about: finding the true self, the diamond that has been buried under layers of distraction and ego. That is why we are here. We practice in order to reveal the inner self."

Paloma pulled an embroidered pouch from within his scarlet *gi*. From it he removed many slips of paper and placed them into a carved wooden box in front of him. "I gave you all an assignment for our first class, and I've read your homework." He held the box aloft.

Thomas came to full alert. *Damn!* He blanched. *He's going to read 'em right now!*

"Each of you shared with me your current spirituality," Paloma continued. "These summaries are rich, very rich, and full of wisdom and wonder, joy and pain. Yet they are merely beliefs. Opinions. Boxes. Even for those of you who stated that spirituality is just an illusion, these are the containers which define us. These are the stories that make us who we *believe* we are."

With that, Paloma closed the wooden box with a snap. "I ask you to leave your thoughts and beliefs here inside this vessel. Separate yourself from your beliefs for a while. If you can, you may find a bigger truth than you've ever known." He set the container down behind him. "Then you can think outside the box." He clapped, ending the session. The students stood to depart.

Thomas wanted to leave his current beliefs here. He wanted to walk through this semester with new eyes, more than Paloma would ever know. But painful images flooded Thomas' mind—Guatemalan children broken like dolls on the cobblestones, men and horses trapped alive in a burning church--images he was unable to exorcise. Thomas grabbed Talia as the class filed out through the narrow door. "You said you'd be there when I'm ready."

Talia turned, startled. "You mean about Guatemala?" His disturbed eyes gave her the answer. "Okay, then," she responded. "Here I am. Let's go."

Arm in arm, the pair pushed through the cluster of other students putting on their shoes in the foyer, and burst into the hallway beyond.

"Hola, *compañeros!*" Ed saluted from out in the student union hall, cross-legged on the floor. He closed his copy of *Chopper* magazine and hopped up, still barefoot and sleeveless. "Where shall we chow? I'm famished!"

"Me too," said Thomas. "But food's going to wait. Remember that talk we were going to have tomorrow over a couple of beers?"

"Yeah," Ed nodded, puzzled.

"Well, we're having it now."

14 LAZYBOY

It was an odd choice, but Thomas knew just where he wanted to talk. He led Ed and Talia to the cement garage attached to his apartment: his private lair that consisted of a ripped pool table, two metal stools, and a green, duct-taped Lazyboy under a flickering fluorescent.

Ed and Talia sat on stools, pale under the bad light. Curious. Waiting.

Thomas blew out a sigh and sunk into the Lazyboy. He'd grabbed a Guatemalan belt that had been hanging over the chair, and now it lay on his lap. "Down to the last seed."

"What's that mean, Thomas?"

"I'd have to agree with Talia on this one, holmes," Ed added. "We'll need more than that. I'm guessing this has to do with the wad of paper you threw at me when I first arrived."

Thomas nodded. "Paloma was right—something happened over the summer. Haven't talked to anyone about it yet." He looked at his wounded hand. "But like you said, Tal, I have to talk to somebody, 'cause it's eating me alive." Thomas looked up with a grim smile. "I guess you two are my somebodies."

"Wouldn't have it any other way." Ed leaned forward on his stool. "What did you mean, 'down to the last seed?'"

"I shouldn't start with that," Thomas muttered. "I need to start at the beginning."

"Take your time," Ed said, playing with a pool cue. "Got nowhere to go."

Thomas let out a big breath. "So you both know I went as part of a construction brigade with my old church," Thomas began. "Mike had this idea that if we went with my uncle on this trip we'd reconnect like old times."

"You weren't so sure," Talia prompted.

"I knew it wouldn't be," Thomas agreed. "But, I went anyway. In college I'd heard about Rigoberta Menchu and the struggle of indigenous people in Guatemala, and I wanted to see what was really going on. It was a two week trip: one week driving there and back, and one week building a community center. About a dozen of us in three trucks took off from Orange County and headed through Mexico on the Intercontinental Highway, bound for Todos Santos in the Guatemalan highlands."

"That's the village?"

"Yeah. A new plank-board town, on the frontier of the jungle before you enter the Peten. We got there fine, and the week went well. Ben and I even got along well. But near the end of our time there, some strangers from another village passed through the lunch line we were serving. They weren't from the area. They'd been traveling for days. There was something haunted about them." Thomas' gaze clouded, remembering. "They were like ghosts. I don't know what got into me, but while Uncle Ben was handing out Bibles after lunch, I followed them out to the courtyard. Just bolted. Without telling anyone." He paused. "I *do* know what got into me, actually," he responded, eyeing Ed. "You did. You'd told me to get out there like Jesus did, hang out with people and eat what they offer."

"Proud of you, man."

"I thought I'd just hang out with them for lunch," Thomas said. "But as we were eating, this old Guatemalan woman told me their group was traveling deep into the jungle to find a new home. She asked me to come with them." He shrugged. "So I did."

"You did what?" exclaimed Talia. "I didn't know this!"

"I just started walking with them in the jungle, Tal. For a few days."

"Without telling anyone?" Ed asked. Thomas nodded. "That's ballsy, bro."

"That's stupid, bro," remarked Talia. Then a small smile emerged. "But probably mind-blowing."

"Yeah," Thomas reflected. "Both."

"How did Mike and Ben react?" asked Ed. "They freak out?"

"More than a little bit," admitted Thomas. "That first evening when I walked with the *campesinos*, a young kid helped me find a phone at a little muddy *tienda* along the way. I called the church where we'd been staying in Todos Santos. Mike and my uncle were leading the group in prayer, certain I'd been kidnapped, when the phone rang."

"Sign from God if I ever heard one," Ed said dryly.

"That's actually what they thought," Thomas said, a smile forming for the first time. "Uncle Ben told me to come back right away, but we weren't scheduled to leave for three more days. He told me it wasn't safe. I told him to find another volunteer to serve the beans."

"Definitely not just like old times." Ed shook his head admiringly.

Thomas shrugged. "Something told me I had to keep walking with these people."

"I still don't get one thing," Talia said softly. "Why they were looking for a home?"

"This kid Miguel told me their entire village had fled north to Mexico when he was tiny, and were returning to their home country for the first time in years. They were part of the thousands of Guatemalans who'd fled for their lives over the years, and now they were daring to trust the government and come back."

"Why'd they flee in the first place?" Ed asked. "The army?"

"Yeah. For decades villagers like them were harassed and terrorized by the paramilitary. They had to leave if they wanted to live."

"I read a big article about that a few years ago," Talia added. "It made me sick to know our government supported that kind of terror for so long."

"Me too. I thought I knew all about it." Thomas shook his head. "But meeting the people who suffered was a lot different than hearing about it on the news."

"Is that what this is about?" Talia asked softly.

Thomas nodded. "There was this old woman, Juanita, the one with the gold tooth who'd invited me to join them. She'd had a son whose name was Tomas, too. When I walked with the village, she stayed at my side, holding my hand and talking to me in Spanish the whole time. I didn't understand much at all. She kept saying *la semilla última, la semilla última.* So I asked the kid about it."

"The same kid?" Talia asked.

"Yeah, skinny little guy with glasses named Miguel, with a bit of a club foot. He tagged along next to us, and knew some English from school. Turns out the old lady was his grandmother. He told me *la última semilla* means 'the last seed.'" Thomas looked down. "That military came eight years before to destroy their village down to the last seed."

"War always hits the poor the hardest," Ed said. "That kind of thing happens a lot."

"That's what I told myself, too." Thomas twisted the Guatemalan belt in his hands. "Thought I was prepared for it. But then they started showing me the pictures."

"Photos?" echoed Talia.

"Everyone was carrying portraits. You know how Guatemalan mothers carry babies in those backstraps they wear?" Talia and Ed nodded. "Well, these women weren't carrying babies. They were carrying photos in big gold frames into the jungle. Hundreds and hundreds of photos, young people, old people, pictures of whole families."

"Who were they?" asked Talia. "Loved ones in Mexico?"

"People they'd lost. That first day, people would come and show me a photo, whisper a name. Pretty soon I realized that all these people were dead. My hair started sticking up. It felt like we were carrying a train of ghosts."

"Creepy," said Ed.

"Not so creepy," countered Talia. "It's sad, but also fascinating. They were carrying their loved ones to their new home."

"Yeah, at first I thought it was kind of neat, too," Thomas remembered. "Bringing your ancestors with you to start a new life." His face darkened. "But then Miguel told me they all died on the same day. 332 people."

"Whoa."

"Yeah. During those bad years the Guatemalan military treated the indigenous people like livestock. Animals. In 1983 Miguel's village was suspected of harboring rebels, so guess what happened?"

"Bloody chaos, I'm betting," said Ed.

"Not at all," Thomas said. The other two looked up, surprised.

"It was systematic. Juanita told me all the details, and Miguel translated. The soldiers came in helicopters, and had the town surrounded in minutes. They herded the women and children into the courthouse, and the men into the church, along with the horses and chickens. The officers asked for confessions. They were sure the village was hiding communist guerrillas. The officers told the villagers they would get one chance to confess. None of the villagers were communist rebels, so they didn't confess." Thomas looked right at Ed. "So guess what the soldiers did?"

"Something very ungood," Ed guessed in a quiet voice.

"Juanita said they barred the doors of both the buildings. She'd been going to the bathroom with two-year old Miguel in the bushes when most of the other villagers were corralled. She saw the soldiers take the women out of the courthouse a few at a time and rape them in the town square, right in view of the men trapped in the church. When the soldiers were done with each woman, they'd gun her down in the street. After the day was done and Juanita crept back into the village at night, she found her three daughters with their skirts still up around their waists. In the mud."

"Her own girls," Talia whispered, hand to her face.

"Then guess what they did next?" Thomas' eyes were wild. "The officers told the soldiers to bring all the children out into the plaza, to get a good look at their mothers, dead in the dirt. And then the soldiers took the children and smashed their heads against the ground."

Ed's head darted up. "That really happened?"

Thomas nodded. "I had to ask Miguel three times to make sure I understood. While we walked together, Juanita said she saw all this happen to her loved ones. First-hand."

Ed avoided his friend's gaze. "I get the picture. You don't have to keep going."

"Yes I do. I need you both to keep listening. Please."

Talia didn't waver. "You have to tell it, Thomas. Go on."

He drew a breath. "The men of the village were crazy with rage, trapped in the church. They wanted to die. But it wasn't their time yet, because the soldiers took a break. The massacre was a lot of work, Juanita told me, and took hours. So after they killed the children, the officers told the soldiers to rest. They sat on the steps of the courthouse, chatted, played guitar, rolled cigarettes. During the break a few soldiers broke down, started to cry. Two tried to run. The officers knocked them down with the butts of their rifles and commanded everyone to get up and keep working, reminding them they were fighting communism. These villagers were supporting guerrillas, they said, and so had to be destroyed down to the last seed. *La semilla última.*"

"So what happened to the men inside?" Ed asked, his face clearly not wanting an answer.

"Whenever the Guatemalan military handled a troublesome village, dealing with the men was always the last step. They made a science of it. When the break was over, the officers asked the men in the church one last time for any confessions. No one admitted anything from inside, they just kept screaming with rage. So the soldiers poured gasoline over the whole clapboard chapel and lit the fucking thing on fire."

"With the men inside?" Ed said, disbelieving. "Alive?"

Thomas nodded. "They shoved gas and torches through the vents. Horses, men, dogs, boys, all screaming. All the creatures started clawing at each other, frying. Anyone trying to break through the windows was shot by the soldiers as a rebel."

Thomas leaned back in the Lazyboy and rubbed his face. "I was walking with hundreds of survivors in the jungle, and once they knew I understood who was in their photographs, they wouldn't stop showing me their pictures. By the second day of walking, I just wanted to find a bus back to Ben and Mike and the group, get out of there, get out of Guatemala. But people kept coming up to me and handing me those damn photos with their big gold frames. They needed to tell me the stories. Miguel translated for everybody, and told me the people journeying with us were the lucky ones—they'd been away from the village at the time, or they'd hid like Juanita before the soldiers could corral them." Thomas smiled grimly. "Lucky, he called them. Their brothers and kids and husbands and wives were trapped, and they could only watch helpless. 332 souls, raped, butchered, and fried alive."

"What kind of government would do that to their own people?" Ed said, dumbfounded.

"I don't ask that question anymore," responded Thomas. "That's easy: a human one. With our help. At first I was raging at America and Guatemala, but then I started raging at more. We humans have been doing this for so fucking long it feels like we're permanently broken."

"I know," Ed said. "You just saw one chapter of our never-ending need to

103

torture each other."

"'Go with God,' I'd told Juanita that first day. She'd responded, 'I hope it's so.'" Thomas shook his head. "She held my hand the whole time we walked, saying my name. I kept watching her eyes, and knew she'd seen her daughters raped, her son burned alive. I couldn't talk to her directly, but we both were asking the same question: *What kind of God could let this happen?*"

Ed let the silence linger. "That's an important question for you, isn't it?"

"Damn right it is," barked Thomas. "In case you haven't noticed, I'm in fucking seminary!"

"Training to speak for a God that lets his people burn alive," Talia said out of her silence.

"Exactly," Thomas said, collapsing back in the recliner. "How can I follow a God like that?"

"Relax, Tommy!" With a grin, Ed abruptly yanked on the lever of Thomas' Lazyboy. Thomas flailed. His chair back plunged downward and the footrest popped out, flattening his body in a prone position. "Get comfortable," Ed said, leaning over the helpless Thomas. "You should be happy."

Thomas glared up at his friend, uncomprehending.

"Happy in a kind of twisted way, at least," Ed continued. "Welcome to the human race." He rested his braided goatee on the armrest of the Lazyboy and looked at Thomas with big eyes. "Congratulations, Whidman. You're finally free of that Christian delusion of an uber-God in superhero tights."

Talia snorted out a laugh, much to Thomas' surprise, considering how somber she'd been. "He actually has a good point," she noted. "Unorthodox delivery, but good point." They looked at Ed expectantly.

"Your Uncle Ben taught you to believe in a God who's some kind of super hero," Ed explained. "Like God's just waiting to jump in and rescue good people from harm if you pray hard enough."

"But Ed, I'm not like my uncle anymore."

"Sure you are. You're no longer in his cult, true. But you've always believed in being rescued."

Thomas started to respond, but Ed cut him off. "Congratulations. Now you know there isn't a God who saves good people from bad stuff." He shrugged and sat back on his stool, satisfied. "Never has been. Welcome to the real world."

Thomas looked to Talia.

"Got to say, he's got a point," she shrugged. "Insensitive delivery, but solid content."

"Tough life lesson, yes," Ed continued. "A shock, even. But a big deal? Not at all. No reason to leave seminary, even." He cracked his knuckles and rose. "You just gotta relax into a new way of thinking." He patted Thomas on the shoulder. "Stay in that Lazyboy a little longer and let it sink in. I'm going to get you a brew."

As Ed left, Thomas looked over into Talia's kind eyes, speechless.

"Still have a stone on your chest?" she asked.

"It feels better, just letting it all out." Thomas blew out a breath. He held up his wounded hand. "Thanks for pushing me this morning."

"Pushing you?" His girlfriend laughed. "That was nothing, sporto. You should see me when I *really* get in somebody's face. All you needed was a love tap." She turned somber. "That wasn't an easy thing you just did, Thomas. And the next part isn't going to be easy, either."

"What? Learning to smile in a world that lets good people be burned alive?"

"Well, yeah," Talia said. "I think that's what I mean." She paused. "You wrestle with things that I don't, Thomas. You try to understand God and the world and have wise answers to life's big questions. That's why you want to be a pastor, I think." She shrugged. "Me, I just try to live the best I can in the midst of a life that doesn't usually make sense." Talia paused. "A lot of your boxes have broke wide open lately, Thomas. Now comes the tough part of growing into something bigger." She smiled. "Don't worry. It'll happen."

"I hope so," Thomas sighed. "Right now I just feel broken."

Talia stood, and kissed him on the forehead. "I've got to go. Can't leave my boss alone with all the case files. Should I come by later, or leave you and Ed to your own devices?"

"Come by." Thomas let go of her hand regretfully. "I'll need somebody to hold me tonight, and I want it to be you."

- - - - -

As Talia departed, Ed returned with three Negra Modelos in hand. "That *chica* is righteous," he commented with admiration. "Where's she headed?"

"Evening work meeting," Thomas replied. "Her boss is running late on a federal grant report."

"More *cerveza* for us," Ed shrugged. "I can't believe she'd choose responsible work over the passive imbibement of empty calories and fermented grains." He tossed a beer to his friend in the Lazyboy and gave him an inquiring look. "So, T, you doing okay with this?"

"Yes." Thomas rubbed his face. "And no. What am I gonna do, Ed? I've just wasted two years of my life studying a superstition."

"No you haven't, holmes." Ed handed the opener to Thomas.

"What do you mean? You just said studying Christianity's a crock."

"Forget Christianity," Ed said. "Why don't you change to a Master's of Ancient Greek? You're awesome at that shit. What about Greek philosophy? You could switch over to another track and become a professor teaching Homer and Aristotle."

"Nice idea. But can't do it here. The only degree my seminary has like that is

Biblical Languages. All they focus on is the Greek found in the Bible. After Guatemala, I can't imagine taking that book seriously." A Koine word floated to his mind: *pseusmata*, a bundle of deceits.

"Okay, then, no Bible for you," Ed said. "What else might you study?" He took a swig and paced the room. "Got it!" With a pool cue he pointed at Thomas. "Comparative Religions. Get away from Christianity as far as possible. Yesterday I checked out the course catalog. Bet you can transfer from a Divinity degree to Comparative Religions, no prob. You've only wasted your life if you quit."

"But--"

"But shit, T. Change your program, man, change your perspective. Change your religion, since your uncle's isn't working for you. Change your diapers, and stop being a spiritual baby. It's a big world out there, with a lot of traditions. You'll find your answers somewhere."

"Answers? Nah." Thomas sighed. "Not interested in answers anymore."

"Bullshit," Ed replied with a smile. "You're just tired of freeze-dried Christianity. You grew up with answers before you ever asked the tough questions."

"That's the truth." Thomas sank back even farther in the Lazyboy. "Ed, thanks for trying to give me options. But I'm done with religion."

"More like you're finally beginning. Not all religions say there's a superhero God who takes sides in wars and rescues us from floods and casts bad people into hell. Take Buddhism, for example."

"It's not even a religion."

"Don't be a dick," said Ed. "I know, it's a philosophy. One you should study, by the way. The first lesson of the Buddha is that life is suffering, dude. People get shafted all the time, be it rape or burning or genocide or even indigestion. For some reason suffering's part of it all, man. Once you learn that, you're on your way to truth."

Thomas leaned back and stared at the ceiling of his garage, mind whirling. Then Ed went for the clincher. "Beside all this spiritual crap, you've got an even better reason to stay in seminary."

Thomas brought his recliner back up to the sitting position. "What's that?"

"Your new girlfriend thinks you're the shit."

"Talia? How do you know? You've only spent, like, four hours with her. You can't--"

"I can," Ed countered. "I see how cool it is between the two of you. You got something going with her, better than anything else you've had." He pointed his beer at Thomas's face. "You'd be an idiot to leave that awesomeness."

"Talia doesn't have anything to do with seminary."

"She's part of the life you got here in Berkeley." Ed waved off Thomas' protestations. "Shut your trap and hear me out." He took a big slug of his *Negra Modelo*. "Too many men focus on school and career and then they're fifty, balding and alone. Or worse, they wake up with a wife they can't stand. They'd give their left nut to be in your shoes right now."

Thomas spun the Lazyboy in a slow circle and let his friend's words sink in. Talia *was* the best thing in his life right now, by far. He didn't have to leave seminary or the Bay Area. Maybe he *could* switch gears at BATU and salvage a degree without having to get near another Bible. Without quitting. Without having to leave Talia. The relationship was pretty new, but when Talia was around, the world felt right. She felt a lot more trustworthy than God did.

As Thomas considered, Ed held out his half-empty beer. "Come on, T, gimme a toast. Sometimes where you are is just where you're meant to be."

"Edward Chapman, you're a total new-age cheese ball," Thomas growled, clinking bottles. "But you're absolutely fucking right."

15 REQUIREMENTS

"It's a bit on the greasy side, but hey…that's part of its allure," Thomas remarked to Talia as they hopped down from his old VW bus and strode across the cracked asphalt of the parking lot to the Oakland diner's back entrance.

A blend of coffee, steam, rapid Spanish, and the aroma of fried eggs billowed out at them through a flapping screen door at the rear of the kitchen. Silverware clattered from within, followed by an undecipherable curse. "I saw an ad in the Pennysaver. Think we'll like it," he said, opening the rear screen door with a squeak. "Lots of high-fat dishes."

Talia grinned. "My kind of place."

Entering the restaurant, the couple found themselves a table in the corner and decided upon *huevos rancheros*, potatoes and *chorizo*. Although they both ate vegetarian most of the time, they'd given each other permission to eat questionable, greasy meat of any kind when going to diners for breakfast.

After placing their orders, a comfortable silence fell. Thomas realized this was the first truly private time they'd shared since Ed arrived a week ago. That first day they'd had the big talk, and then the rest of the week the two college friends had repainted Thomas' apartment while Talia commuted daily to her job in Oakland and prepared her Frisbee squad for regionals.

Yesterday, Friday, marked the end of Talia's work week and the culmination of the painting project. By the time Ed and Thomas rolled up the tarps, mopped the whole apartment, and replaced all the furniture, it was already evening. Exhausted and fuzzy with paint fumes, the two went to Talia's and ordered a late-night pizza. No one wanted to wash any dishes, so the three of them celebrated Ed's last night in the Bay Area by eating slices straight out of the box and wine straight out of the bottle. To Thomas, the evening felt a lot like a junior-high sleepover: three friends on a futon laughing and eating, fighting for pillows and telling jokes. They drifted off to sleep sometime after midnight.

When Thomas and Talia finally rose this morning, the sun was streaming in the window. Ed was gone. They found a note on the kitchen table saying he'd snuck out early for the long ride back to Taos. Hungry, they ventured out to try a new diner.

The breakfasts came, as greasy as they'd hoped. After gulping some *chorizo,* Talia spoke. "You were right about Ed. He's a wild one, but I like him. I think you needed his energy more than you knew."

"Yeah." Thomas downed some coffee. "He helps me out of dark spaces."

"Yeah. You were in pretty deep. He helped you see some new possibilities. By the way, what's new in the world of 'As the Seminary Turns?'"

"Some good news. Some bad."

"Shoot. Good news first."

"The good news is that Ed was right. I transferred to Comparative Religions without losing many credits. It's what--only a week before classes start-- but they let me re-register. I contacted a professor named Dr. Horace Cavanaugh, Head of the Comparative Religions department, who might be my new adviser. Turns out most of the courses I've taken so far can apply to the Comparative Religions Master's program."

"And the bad news?"

"Serious thesis requirement." Doing his best impersonation of Professor Cavanaugh's western drawl, Thomas repeated his adviser's words: "'Since you are asking to join our program as a transfer, son, I'm sure you've done your homework and are familiar with our requirements.'"

Talia looked up, mouth full. "How'd you respond to that?"

"What else could I say?" retorted Thomas. "'Uh, yes, sir, quite right sir." He then moved back to Cavanaugh's drawl: "'Then you surely know, Mr. Whidman, that all our Masters candidates are expected, at the beginning of their third year of study, to start their thesis preparation in earnest?'" Thomas paused for a big bite of his home-fried potatoes.

"You told him, of course, you'd been thinking deeply about it."

Thomas nodded, chewing. "Everything was going fine until he said, 'So what topic did you have in mind, son?'"

"Gulp."

"Exactly. What the heck was I supposed to tell him?" He dug into his potatoes. " 'Frankly, sir, my head's up my ass and I have no idea?'"

"Keep it real," Talia laughed. "That would've been a strategy. A sucky one. What'd you do?"

"I said I was considering several topics, but that I wanted to discuss them face-to-face when I had my notes in front of me."

"Decent cover," Talia said. "Did he buy it?"

"I'm pretty sure he knew I was buying time. He's probably used to excuses like that from transfers like me. Cavanaugh said I still had some weeks to decide on a topic, and then suggested, a little too firmly, that he be my adviser. He said it made sense because I'll be taking at least one course from him this semester."

"Sounds logical."

"Yeah. But I think he wants to be my adviser to see how lame I am. Whip me into shape. It was just a phone call, but he sounds like a cowboy, Tal. Like a guy who wears snakeskin boots."

"Your own personal trainer." Talia chewed, amused. "So you said yes?"

111

"What else could I do? I don't even know the *names* of the other professors in the department." Thomas shook his head. "So for better or worse, Professor Cavanaugh's my adviser, and I'm studying Comparative Religions."

"Here's to small victories," Talia said, and took anther huge bite of *chorizo*. Like she said, eating was her favorite sport, even more than Ultimate. Now that he was done telling tales, Thomas joined in, setting to his own food with a vengeance. The *huevos rancheros* were divine, still soft even after the bout of talking. Looking up, he marveled at how right he felt with this woman across the table from him. He liked the feeling he had in his gut whenever he was around her. Like now.

"Good call on the restaurant, lover. This place is first rate." She mopped up the yolk and sauce of her *huevos rancheros* with a tortilla. "So now that you know you have to write a thesis, any topic caught your interest?"

"Interest?" Thomas laughed blackly. "I wish. Right now religion's about as interesting as failed campaign speeches. And about as true. Let's drop it, okay?"

He looked over his coffee to see a look on Talia's face he hadn't seen before: surprise, and hurt. "Sorry, Tal. I didn't mean to shut you out," he said. "I just don't think I'm going to find a topic I can believe in." He gave a single laugh. "Figuratively *or* literally. And I have a few short weeks to choose one before I'm totally screwed."

16 THE HUMAN MIND CAN CONVINCE ITSELF OF MOST ANYTHING

Fall had come in earnest to the rolling green campus of the Bay Area Theological Union. Strewn maple leaves filled the walkways as Thomas traversed the grassy quad. The leaves underfoot sounded eerily like the cockroaches Thomas squashed in the corner of his apartment.

Thomas paused to look back as he left the busyness of Claremont Street. Ben was still there, looming larger than life and wielding a Bible in one hand and a bone in the other. Thomas turned toward the seminary again, heading to class. It had been three weeks since courses started, and he was still play-acting. Pretending he was someone who cared.

The campus felt different this fall, but he knew it would. Gone was the sense of rightness that had infused his life a few months ago. Gone was the feeling that all roads had led to this one, that God was guiding him on a special path. Replacing this was a growing certainty that the human mind can convince itself of most anything that makes it feel secure and special.

Two months ago, in late July, he had returned from Guatemala a wrecked man. Seminary became a sad joke. With gusto, he'd hurled a monogrammed plate—a platter Ben gave him back in high school with the title "Promising Young Pastor" emblazoned upon its face—shattering it against his garage wall. He was through.

But then thirty days ago Ed's pep-talk convinced him to make a change. By switching programs after his second year, he planned to salvage at least *something* of value from seminary. To get a degree in Comparative Religions, all he needed to do was pass a few courses covering the major Eastern traditions—Hinduism, Taoism, Buddhism—and a course called *Faith & Fanaticism*, taught by Professor Cavanaugh himself. That, and complete his thesis. Once those requirements were met, he could walk away this May from seminary with a Master's and never look back.

Of course, an advanced degree in Comparative Religions wasn't exactly setting him up for a booming career field. But at least it wasn't boring. He had to admit Ed had been right: he wasn't done with religions, only freeze-dried Christianity. Some part of Thomas still had a sick fascination with the variety of illusions that the human race had developed over the millennia to let them sleep at night.

Thomas' journey across the leafy quad terminated at a low-slung brick and glass building. The cluster of small classrooms were designed to hold a dozen students each, an ideal number for upper level graduate seminars such as his.

Speaking of illusions, he thought, going inside. Time for *Faith & Fanaticism* with Cavanaugh.

- - - - -

"Isn't it obvious?" Thomas barked. "Their religious language is just a thin veil for a secular Marxist agenda,"

"Mr. Whidman speaks once again on the side of cynicism," drawled Professor Horace Cavanaugh from his point in the circle, surrounded by third year seminary students. The white-haired, large-limbed man dominated the room, even though he was seated in the round. The lanky, creased legs of his dark-blue Wranglers were crossed, ending in shiny cowboy boots. "Anyone else care to voice an observation about our visit to the Bay Area Catholic Worker?"

"That woman didn't seem Marxist," ventured a reddish-haired young woman from the other side of the circle, looking sideways at Thomas. "And she didn't seem to be hiding an agenda, either. On the contrary, she exposed things. Exposed our consumer culture for what it is, conventional Christianity for what it is. She told the truth." The woman gathered a little more courage. "To be honest, by the time we finished our visit, she didn't seem very extreme anymore." A few other seminarians nodded in agreement. "And her religious identity wasn't some veil. It seemed authentic."

Thomas bit his tongue and slunk deeper into his chair. *Nailed,* he thought. *Why'd I have to go off like that?* The redhead had spoken truth, while he'd just spewed some crap. She was right: the Catholic Workers they'd visited last week *did* have a light in their eyes that wasn't just some Marxist axe to grind. In fact, they'd impressed him. Where'd they get their strength, their easy laughter? He would've burned out long ago if he lived in the trenches like they did, month in and month out. They were what he'd aspired to be ever since he'd read the Letter of James: they were *poietoi,* doers who took care of orphans and widows and the broken ones in downtown Oakland, providing hospitality to addicts and prostitutes and families living on the streets.

How did they keep believing in a loving God when nothing changed? In his seat, Thomas gripped his pencil like a vise. *Can't they see that God isn't in the rescuing business?* He recalled something else about the Catholic Workers that would've been laughable if it wasn't so sick: they said God was always on the side of the poor and downtrodden. *Right,* thought Thomas. *Always.*

He remembered another thing that struck him during the visit. Cavanaugh had made a good choice with this one; these guys were extremists. They didn't even want to be called Christians. What'd the woman say they call themselves? *Followers of the Way,* that was it.

"What causes us to live with the poor, to refuse the war machine, to go to jail?" their spokeswoman asked Cavanaugh's class after the students had toured their gritty neighborhood. "We choose these things because we try to walk the Jesus Way." Thomas pictured the woman now, seemingly their leader, a striking, articulate woman with a shaved head and dark eyes. Her accent and attitude made Thomas think she was an anarchist from Eastern Europe.

Someone had asked her about the Jesus Way and how it differed from the Christianity promoted by most churches. "It's a way of life more than a belief system," the woman said simply. "We don't worry too much about beliefs that keep certain people in and others out. The Way is about deeds more than creeds." As Thomas left Catholic Worker house with his hands full of flyers about upcoming protests and petitions, He saw a message inscribed in block letters above the kitchen door: "Christ has no hands but yours."

"Any other observations?" Professor Cavanaugh asked the class, bringing Thomas back to the circle. After nobody jumped in, Cavanaugh glanced at his watch. Their allotted time was nearly up. "Okay, let's talk about the broader assignment for the semester," he drawled. A toothpick dangled from his lip. "During these first weeks of our course, we've observed firsthand three very different faith communities that modern America considers extreme: first the Buddhist Reconciliation Fellowship, then the Muslim private school, and now the Catholic Worker. Remember these visits well, folks, because at the end of the semester, your final assignment will be to go undercover on your own and compare."

At this the students perked up. The nervous ones gripped their desks a little harder. *Undercover?* That got Thomas' attention. Cavanaugh grinned, a bit too mischievously for Thomas' liking. "That's right, undercover. Time to step out of your comfort zone, ladies and gents. You'll need to join an extreme faith-based event of your choice, and then write about it. Folks, you can't just study religious extremism to understand it; you gotta feel it. We'll discuss this further in upcoming days. Class dismissed." Questions exploded from the circle of students.

Cavanaugh held up his arms to fend off the flurry of hands. "Don't fret, people," he said with a toothy grin, donning his cowboy hat and denim blazer. "Lots of time, lots of time. Just wanted to let you know what the future holds. Relax, you've got two months to figure something out."

17 THE RIGHT TRACK

The bell of mindfulness sounded again, and the students' rustling began to cease. By the time Paloma struck the gentle gong the third time to commence the session, absolute silence reigned. Thomas loved to follow the clear sound as it lingered, rolling in waves around the dojo before finally disappearing from awareness.

Thomas and Talia meditated next to each other now. Not touching, but not exactly apart either. He was fully aware of Tal's presence, but it wasn't distracting. Rather, it was more a familiarity, like two cats contented in the sun. Both were conscious of the other, but neither lost focus. Neither felt distracted with a need to *do* anything. This week, as Thomas settled in for the hour-long sit, he noticed Paloma observing them. Before turning his gaze, their teacher gave a small nod, recognizing the new depth of the relationship.

Today Thomas went deep. When the ending gong sounded, he came out refreshed. He checked his watch. He was just realizing the session ended early when Paloma broke the silence.

"We're going to talk a little more than usual today," Paloma said from the center of the circle. "At the end of summer, I asked you all to complete a writing assignment, which told me a little bit about each of you. Some weeks ago I told you a little bit about me. This week I'd like each of you to share a bit about yourself with the rest of the sangha. Starting with Sarah, please introduce yourself and tell us why you come to this group."

The stringy-haired librarian smiled, the one who'd been oil painting this summer, and said she came to get in touch with her intuitive intelligence.

Soon everybody was sharing their reasons for joining the meditation class, taking turns in a circular fashion. Each student said his or her piece; Paloma in turn nodded in recognition, and expressed his thanks for attending. And so it went.

When Thomas' turn came around, he too gave a thumbnail sketch of his background and interest in the sangha, mentioning he was starting his third and final year of seminary. He finished, and turned to listen to Talia on his left.

"Are you a believer?"

The question came from Paloma, who was not nodding politely or expressing thanks. Instead, he was staring with curious and burning eyes directly at Thomas.

"In what?" Thomas wanted to yell. No one else in his past two years at seminary had asked him that. Flustered by the complexity and the simplicity of the question, Thomas balked. "I think I'll pass on that one."

The room was silent. A person coughed across the room. Thomas expected Paloma to move on, or say something to cut the ice like a normal person. Instead the teacher simply waited. Same eyes, same gaze. *Now I know why some say you're an asshole.* The attention of the entire room remained on Thomas.

"I don't know," he finally said. "A lot of what I once believed isn't true anymore."

"You don't know. Good for you." Paloma smiled that maddening half-smile. "You sound like you're on the right track." He nodded at Thomas, expressed thanks for speaking, and moved on to the next student.

18 PROPHETS & RUBBER BISCUITS

The late September rain came down hard, turning a nice day chilly. *So much for a romantic picnic,* Thomas thought as he and Talia scrambled up to put their gourmet spread back in their cooler. He tried to make a tent out of the newspaper they'd been browsing, but failed miserably. Laughing, Talia dragged them into the enclosed patio of the nearest street cafe. *Tolstoi's Tea House,* a tiny bronze plaque proclaimed at the front of the small Victorian foyer filled with plants.

"I think I've walked by a million times and never noticed this place," said Thomas, drenched.

"I know," Talia said, dripping. "I always thought it was an old person's book store." The pair shook like dogs, casting a shower of rainwater from their clothes and hair.

Too late, they turned to see they'd sprayed two people at a nearby patio table. "Paloma!" Thomas exclaimed, taking in his meditation teacher and the woman seatedwith him. "Oh my God, I am so sorry!"

The seated pair, though damp, just laughed. Waving off the profuse apologies, Paloma stood. "Sit with us!" He pulled out a chair. "If you have to wait out a storm, might as well enjoy doing so."

Grateful, the newcomers found seats. Paloma made introductions. "Talia, Thomas, this is my wife, Magda. Talia and Thomas are two of my regular meditation students."

Paloma has a wife? Prior to this moment Thomas had never thought of Paloma as being part of a relationship. Part of *anything*, really. Paloma was an isolated pillar, an island sitting alone in a sea of meditation mats. How old is he? Thomas started to wonder. Does he have kids and a dog? What did he do before being a meditation teacher? *There's a whole world I don't know about Paloma*, Thomas realized.

Magda, Paloma's wife, was a fit, healthy-looking woman of indeterminate age, angular and tan as if she worked outside a lot, like a landscaper or something. She wasn't exactly small, Thomas noted. More like concise. Compact. Her dark pea coat, scarf and wool cap made her look ready for an ocean voyage, and definitely better prepared for a September downpour than either Talia or Thomas. Something about her seemed familiar.

"Nice to meet the two of you," Magda said in a gracious and melodic voice. Intelligent, dark eyes gazed out of a sculpted face. She reached across the table to shake hands.

"Wow, cool tattoo!" Talia indicated a delicate braided design encircling the other woman's wrist.

"Why, thank you," said Magda, covering it up with her jacket sleeve. "Sometimes I almost forget I have it."

"Matching, isn't it?" Talia inquired. "How romantic." Magda shot a quick look at Paloma, who simply nodded with a smile and pointed at his left wrist, which was covered by his sleeve. "Probably has a good tale behind it," Talia commented, fishing.

"You have to earn that story," laughed Paloma. "You only get to hear it when we invite you over sometime for Magda's famous lasagna and a couple of glasses of wine."

"Deal," said Talia, sitting down.

"More rain than fog lately," Magda noted, looking outside at the downpour. Now that he heard her voice again, Thomas knew he'd heard her accent somewhere before. It was European of some kind. The woman turned to Paloma and murmured. "Reminds me of Portland."

Talia looked up from the menu. "You know Portland?"

"I lived there for a time," Magda replied. "I love the Bay Area, but I really miss that town."

"Me too," said Talia, including Thomas in her glance. "I grew up in the 'burbs outside the city."

"And I went to school at Lewis & Clark College," added Thomas.

Talia turned back to Magda. "When were you there?"

"Oh, quite a while ago now. In the late 1970s and early '80's. You were probably running around in diapers, I'm guessing."

"Not quite," Talia laughed, "but I'll take that as a compliment. I was probably in junior high."

"I was getting some education of my own," commented Magda. "I spent some time at the Catholic Worker house downtown on Vine and Fourth. Near the Burnside Bridge."

"Tough part of the city," Talia observed. "My folks kept me away from there."

Magda nodded. "That's why I went. I came there fresh out of high school, so full of angry judgments. Running away from who I'd been, so sure of who I thought I was." She laughed, remembering. "I thought I might spend a few months there over the summer, and I ended up living there for six years. Those folks turned my world upside down."

"How so?" Talia asked. "That is, if you don't mind a stranger being nosy."

"Not at all." Magda smiled graciously. "It's funny. Living there showed me that my precious opinions didn't define who I was. Instead, it was my actions in times of difficulty that showed my true nature. I learned pretty quickly that my creeds only mattered if they showed up in my deeds."

"That's where I know you!" Thomas blurted, leaning forward. "Deeds more

121

than creeds! That's what you said at the Catholic Worker house when we visited with my class!"

"Nice to know someone was listening," the woman across the table replied, eyes twinkling.

"I wouldn't be so rude to ask you to take your hat off. But if I did, what would I find there?"

Smirking, Magda slipped her wool hat off to reveal a sleek shorn head and delicate ears adorned with steel bands.

"Thought so," said Thomas. "I came with a seminary class visiting--"

"Extreme religious groups," finished Magda, nodding. "I know Horace well," she continued. "*'Faith and Fanaticism'* is the course, right?"

"Yeah." Thomas suddenly realized how that sounded. "I'm sorry, I didn't mean to judge."

"It's alright," said Magda. "No offense taken. We get it all the time. Horace brings student groups from the seminary to visit us like we're exotic beasts in a cage. Sad, but true." She shrugged, her voice calm and clear. "It's funny how anybody who seriously tries to help poor people is considered extreme."

"That's not *all* you do," commented Paloma at her side. "You Catholic Workers make the powers very nervous."

"True," she admitted. She looked at the young couple with a smile. "We run soup kitchens and bring food to shut-ins. Polite things. But we also resist war. We organize workers for better conditions. We defend human rights, for the poor, for the homeless, for the voiceless."

"Troublemaker," muttered Paloma with a smile. "Empire doesn't know what to do with you."

"It's like the former Archbishop of Brazil said," Magda commented. "'When I give food to the poor they call me a saint. When I ask *why* the poor are poor, they call me a Communist.'"

Talia jumped in. "I know this is a little personal, but it's not often that I meet a Zen teacher who's married to a radical Catholic. Seems like it could be challenging."

"Action and contemplation don't always cooperate together," Paloma responded. "But when they do, they really do. We've had to develop a new denomination. Budeo-Christian." He winked at Thomas. "So far it's a church of two. Want to join?"

"Maybe," said Thomas with a wry smile. "As long as I don't have to trust anything other than James." He turned to Magda. "I was pretty impressed by what I saw of your path."

"Oh?" said the bald woman, a look of curiosity on her face.

"Bread and debt—or rather, *sharing* bread and *forgiving* debt—didn't you say that those were two hallmarks of the Jesus Way?" Thomas said. Magda nodded, and he kept going. "Living the kingdom of heaven right here on earth, that's what you talked about. You said the institutional church spiritualized Jesus' message and focused almost exclusively on the afterlife."

"Wow," Magda said, throwing a surprised look Paloma's way. "Like I said, I'm glad someone was listening." She took a warming sip of tea, cradling her cup in both hands, and glanced back at Thomas. "Truly, what I recall most about your class was the glazed-over looks and the utter lack of questions. For a bunch of future leaders, you guys were pretty unengaged."

"Sorry," Thomas said. "Actually, I think I'll remember the visit for a long time."

"How so?"

Thomas sighed. "Let's just say I'm pretty down on Christianity right now. But I still care about doing the things that Jesus said to do. It seemed like you guys were serious about doing that."

"Wow, that means a lot," Magda said genuinely. She leaned back and nestled into her pea coat. "That's how I felt, the first time I ran into the Catholic Workers. When I woke up in Portland."

"Woke up in Portland?" Talia said.

"I was a runaway," Magda confided, meeting Talia's startled gaze. "I'd been on the street for a while, pretty strung out, and hitched a ride with a guy who was headed to Seattle. He promised to get me high. He slipped me something though, because when I next woke up, I was lying next to a dumpster near Burnside. Some street folks found me and brought me to the Catholic Worker house. In a shopping cart."

Magda sipped her tea. Talia spoke quietly. "Sounds like you found healing there, somehow."

"So broken inside. So angry outside," Magda remembered. "Couldn't believe these people were real. They weren't trying to change me, they just accepted me. Gave me a room. When I was finally ready for it, they helped me get my act together, turn my life around.

"After that, I lived and worked and ate and prayed and cooked and slept with that group of people pretty much every day for six years. College grads, old war protesters, drag queens, mentally-ill homeless guys, former communists, prostitutes, strung out street kids all living together, right in the midst of the hardest neighborhood in the city. Life in downtown Portland was crazy sometimes, but never boring. Changed my life, that's for sure."

Talia and Thomas just stared, amazed and humbled at how much power and light had just poured out of this calm, composed stranger. Paloma's wife. *Not only is this guy full of surprises,* thought Thomas. *So's his wife.*

Magda grabbed Paloma's hand. "Sometimes I miss that town terribly."

"Me too, though my experience couldn't have been more different," Talia confessed. "My mom took us downtown only on field trips." Suddenly, she remembered her plans. "Hey, Thomas and I are both visiting Portland in about a month!"

"Thanksgiving?" guessed Magda.

"First time for Thomas to meet the clan," Talia explained, nodding. "My mother will be checking him out. It's a little early for us, probably, but if my family's going to drive Thomas away screaming, it might as well be now. We'll be with my fam for a whole week over Thanksgiving."

"*You'll* be with them for the whole week," Thomas corrected. He turned to Magda and Paloma. "I'll be splitting my time: part of the week with Talia's family, and part with two of my buddies from college.

"But you'll both be in Portland the night *before* Thanksgiving, right?" Magda asked excitedly.

Thomas exchanged a glance with his partner. "Well, I'll probably be with my buddies, and she'll be with her folks, but yeah."

"Awesome! You should go to a big event my friends are putting on!" Magda said with delight. "It's called *Sharing the Table*. Free gourmet dinner at *Off the Vine*."

"Oh my God," Talia said, amazed. "That's my favorite restaurant! My parents took me there when I graduated high school."

"Best of Portland, eight years running," said Magda.

"*Love* that place," said Talia. "I'll be there."

"Me too, probably, with my college buds," Thomas said. "My friends tend to pay attention when someone puts the words *free* and *gourmet dinner* together." He looked over his steaming mug. "So what's the catch?"

"I think it's legit," replied Magda. "Just a big thank you to the city, funded by some anonymous donor." She took a sip of her tea. "So who are these friends you're meeting, Thomas? Old roomies?"

"Yeah, two of my very best friends," Thomas replied. "Mike and Ed. I grew up with Mike, and got to know Ed in college. Ever since we graduated, the three of us get together for a few days around Thanksgiving."

Talia chortled. "They do a serious man-gathering every year. Non-negotiable."

"Tal, don't start--"

"Oh?" inquired Magda, intrigued. "Tell us."

"They formed a club," volunteered Talia, ignoring Thomas' gaze of warning. "Guess what they called themselves?" Thomas tried to kick her under the table, but Talia dodged. "The Rubber Biscuits."

"Rubber Biscuits?" Magda and Paloma both said, laughing. Magda rested her chin in her hand. "Do go on."

"Well, Mike and Thomas asked to be roommates together freshman year, and Ed was tossed in with them. Mike's on the conservative side while Ed's sort of a new-age biker," Talia began. "Thomas was the man in the middle." She looked to Thomas. "Is that fair to say?"

Thomas crossed his arms. "So far."

"Well, it was a potent mix. The three would stay up late drinking beer, arguing about how to solve the world's problems. The arguments were good enough they'd often draw an audience, other people coming to watch their verbal smackdowns. They'd talk and talk, but never reach much agreement. Then one day they decided to stop arguing and do something positive together: they created a rebel bakery."

"Rebel bakery?" said Paloma, chuckling. "What in the world is that?"

"See?" said Talia to Thomas, vindicated. "That's what I said."

"The term made perfect sense to us at the time," explained Thomas. "Now, of course, years later, when we get together and think: a *rebel bakery?* What was that supposed to mean?" They all laughed. "None of us knew how to bake. Maybe that was the rebellious part."

"But that didn't stop 'em," continued Talia. "Didn't stop 'em from baking a variety of dark, lumpy baked goods. Didn't stop 'em from putting out a flimsy card table in the quad every week, trying to sell tasteless brown rocks made from only the healthiest organic ingredients."

"So not a real big hit?" surmised Paloma.

"Let's just say profits were secondary to our mission," stated Thomas dryly.

"They lost money every week!" exclaimed Talia. "Mike kept thinking he could fix things, since he was studying finance. But a lack of profit didn't deter them, anyway. The real goal was to *Educate The Public.*"

In the brief silence following, Paloma and Magda glanced at each other and burst out laughing, realizing they both had been leaning forward in anticipation. Paloma leaned back. "Well, I do believe you got us hooked, Talia."

"Me too," said Thomas. "I'm dying to know what's next, even though it's my life you're telling," he laughed. "Sounds like you talked to Ed while I wasn't around. He has a flair for telling stories. Do go on."

"Well I better order some tea, then, and y'all better settle in." She conferred with the waitress and soon a kettle was brought. She poured. "*Educating the Public,* their real mission," Talia resumed. "In addition to the lumpy baked goods, the Rubber Biscuits also peddled propaganda. Flyers, posters, that kind of thing. Hand drawn, right?" Talia checked with Thomas, who nodded confirmation. "Pamphlets crying out against the modern processed diet, calling for a mass return to whole grains."

Magda leaned back, impressed. "You guys were trailblazers, Thomas."

"Definitely ahead of our time," he nodded, accepting the compliment.

"What they didn't realize," Talia revealed, "was that if they'd baked whole-wheat cinnamon rolls that tasted like something other than hockey pucks, they could've converted many more diets than they did with their slogans."

"Slogans?" prompted Paloma.

"Slogans," confirmed Thomas.

"All movements need mottoes," Magda pitched in.

"Exactly what we said," agreed Thomas. "Gets their attention."

"This is where it gets really good. This one's my favorite," Talia spread her hands to frame a picture. "Imagine an eight-foot long bed sheet reading, *'Hey Whitey! Lose Your White Bread!'*"

"Ed painted it," Thomas mumbled. "One of our more controversial works."

"Ed said Lewis & Clark received complaints from *both* the NAACP *and* the national office of the Aryan Nations Youth Council on that one!" Talia loved the juicy details. "The Rubber Biscuits were banned from the quad for a month."

"What other propaganda did you peddle?" asked Magda.

"Well, our pamphlet entitled *'Wonder Bread is Not So Wonderful'* was the only piece we ever ran out of," Thomas added. "It seemed to be favored by some of the professors and young mothers."

"How boring!" Talia interjected. "Tell them about your best one."

"Zip it, Tal!" Thomas protested. Talia's command hung in the air, waiting. Thomas tried to backpedal, but seeing the expectant looks of Paloma and Magda, he knew his cause was lost. "I can't tell it," he said, hanging his head. "But you go ahead. Skewer me. Dredge it up."

Talia's eyes gleamed, and her words set the stage. "Picture Thomas Whidman a decade ago. Gawky, sophomore in college, so sure of himself."

"Don't forget cool. Uber-cool. And sexy."

"Thomas Whidman uber-cool and sexy, patrolling the quad, holding pamphlets and baked goods, wearing a sandwich board front and back, looking like one of those crazy guys on street corners who say the end of the world is near."

"The Whole Wheat Prophet," mused Paloma. "Unexpected. But quite imaginable."

"But the message Thomas proclaimed to the Lewis & Clark campus was more immediate than the end of the world," Talia said. "And far more personal." She paused, drawing in her audience. "The sandwich board screamed: *White Flour Causes Cancer In Your Butt.*"

Awkward silence wrapped the table like a blanket. Magda snorted with laughter and regained her tongue. "Did...did you ever think of just saying *'White Flour Causes Colon Cancer?'* Wouldn't that have been enough?"

"Mike suggested that once." Thomas shrugged. "He thought the banner was embarrassing."

"Slightly," concurred Paloma. The rest of the table nodded in agreement.

"Ed insisted that the banner remain that way," Talia said, regaining control of the story. "As uber-cool Thomas patrolled the college quad in his sandwich board, he'd attract attention and send a number of people to the table each week. They'd ask politely about white flour and how it encouraged colon cancer, but Ed was convinced that what drew people was not information about colon cancer--that could be found anywhere--but rather the words *'In Your Butt.'* People were fascinated, horrified. *Cancer in your butt?* They had to know more."

Talia took a final slurp of her tea and leaned back in her chair, stretching like a cat, breaking the spell. "This is a great little spot," she said, looking around the tiny plant-filled restaurant. *'Tolstoi's Tea House*, eh? I've walked by a thousand times and never stopped in."

"It's my favorite place to come and think. Or talk. Or just be quiet," explained Paloma. "They do a lot of things for the community other than serve hot drinks. I like their work."

Thomas called for the check. Paloma waved him off. "The least we can do, after such a fine tale, is pay for your tea," Paloma said, grinning.

"So that was the beginning of the Rubber Biscuits of Lewis & Clark," Magda summarized, learning back with a gleam in her eye. "Little did I know what I was getting into when I asked who you were seeing in Portland."

"Now Ed and Mike and I get together every year," said Thomas. "During the summer after college, the three of us stayed together in Portland. It was magic. We'd bake stuff, shoot hoops, bike around town and chew the fat of the universe. Then things changed. Mike moved back to Orange County to get married and to work at Ben's church. He and Mary immediately started having babies. Ed moved to Taos. I got serious with a girlfriend. After being so close, the three of us didn't see each other for a few years. Five years ago we had a Rubber Biscuits reunion, just before Thanksgiving. We've been doing it ever since."

19 KICKASS THE SECOND TIME AROUND

Thomas' old VW bus seemed stuck in a gigantic car wash as the rain came down in wet sheets, pounding the windshield. The frenzied wipers tried to do their job against the downpour, but all Thomas could see with certainty was the wet red halo of the stoplight shimmering through the glass at him, a floating neon sea anemone. That, and the vague outline of an aged Dodge truck that waited a few feet in front of him.

For one brief moment, the bumper sticker on the Dodge emerged clearly through the veil of water: *"GOD IS COMING. LOOK BUSY."* Talia and Thomas burst out laughing at the same instant, reading the rear-end revelation through the rain.

"Like to have coffee with whoever thought up that one," Thomas said. That creator had grabbed the pulse of modern American anxiety: fear of the future, fear of being judged, fear of a misspent life all in one little sticker.

After Guatemala, the idea of a God coming to end the world—coming to do anything, actually-- seemed absurd. A fairy tale to protect people from the void. Memories of the trek came back to him, walking along a rutted road with Juanita and her village, a train of *campesinos* carrying pictures of their massacred loved ones. *Was it just a hundred days ago I believed in a God who cared?*

The stoplight turned from red to green, and traffic began to move. Like a ship in rough waters, the VW bus lurched into the wet night, navigating through the slosh to the freeway on-ramp.

"Why do people always think God is 'coming,' anyway?" Talia mused.

"Beats the crap out of me." Thomas shook his head, baffled. "Seems to be our shared sickness, doesn't it?" He thought of people throughout history who'd proclaimed Armageddon, The End of Days, the Final Age, The Last Cycle. The van chugged onto the freeway, wakes of spray shooting behind. "Are humans just hard-wired to be anxious, guilty doomsayers?"

"Maybe there's a deeper reason," ventured Talia. "Maybe the idea of a god ending the world gives us meaning. Focus."

"How so?" Through the downpour, Thomas checked his blurry rear view to merge into traffic.

"Well, like the bumper sticker says, God showing up sure would get our asses into gear."

"Time for a little housecleaning."

"Exactly," agreed Talia. "If I knew God was coming next year to check up on us, I'd sure get busy. Get my values and actions straightened up, like Paloma talks about." Her face registered a new thought. "That kind of pressure probably works well for your uncle."

"I never thought about it that way, but yeah," Thomas said. "Back when I handed out flyers for his speaking events, Ben would tell Mike and me to get people thinking about their souls. Worrying about, more like. He'd pack the house, wherever he went. God's love and God's judgment are two sides of a coin, he'd say."

"You know a bit about that, yeah?"

Thomas gave a little laugh. "Around Ben growing up, a pissed-off God showing up was always a possibility. But he wasn't the only preacher doing that. Love is good and all, but most churches find that fear's a better motivator. It's been getting people through the doors for a long time."

"Not just churches," Talia added. "You Christians might be today's specialists, but the guys running temples, kivas, longhouses, mosques, stupas, and pyramids have done it too." She paused. "Now that I think about it, a lot of cultures have created end-of-the-world scenarios to get people motivated."

A red Porsche going about twice as fast as their VW cruised past them in the left lane, shooting a massive wave of water across Thomas' windshield. The van waded on, undaunted.

"I think the Aztecs used fear the best," Talia continued.

"Better than my Uncle Ben?"

"Your uncle's an amateur," she scoffed. "Check this out. The Aztec priests told their people that every 52 years the sun wouldn't rise the next day unless enough human sacrifices had been made to feed their gods, who lived on human life-force."

"Rise n' shine, y'all, time to go get some more enemies!" Thomas imagined. "Man, having to capture people to make the sun rise would get me outta bed."

"That kind of belief might've been the reason they became the mightiest Empire on the continent for a while," Talia said. "But their beliefs about the end of the world were their downfall, too."

"How so?"

"The Spanish *conquistadores* shouldn't have been able to conquer Mexico when they came in the 1500s," Talia explained. "Remember I told you I did a semester in the Yucatan my junior year?" Thomas nodded, and Talia continued. "My prof said the conquest shouldn't have happended. The Spaniards simply didn't have the people. They were totally outmanned."

"Didn't disease do them in?"

"Disease probably played a big role," Talia agreed. "But the Aztec's beliefs did too. The Aztec empire was old and decaying and spread out when the conquistadors came. Montezuma, their young king, was already superstitious and jaded, smoking a lot of herb and dreaming about prophecies. He and other leaders believed that their god Quetzalcoatl was going to come again. He'd return soon as a pale-skinned man, and he was going to end the world as they knew it. And then Cortez showed up."

"Good timing," Thomas observed.

"Exactly," said Talia. "When a few light-skinned strangers arrived from across the sea with powerful, strange objects like metal and horses and ships, the Aztecs saw their prophecies being fulfilled. Montezuma and other leaders basically opened the gates to their cities and laid their heads on the chopping block, ready for the god's judgment. With just a few hundred men, Cortez waltzed in."

In the brief lull, the only sound was rain pounding a relentless tattoo on the roof. After a moment, Talia ventured, "You know, Thomas, I don't know a whole lot about Christian beliefs, so this may be a stupid question..."

"There are no stupid questions, Talia. Only totally dorky people."

"You're so understanding," she said, smiling and punching him in the arm. "Here's what I don't get: if Christians believe God came to earth two thousand years ago as a non-violent hippie named Jesus, why do people like your uncle insist that God's going to be all violent and kickass the second time around?"

Thomas just stared at her for a long second. "That's a freaking brilliant question."

"Not so stupid now, eh?" she said proudly. "Hah! I stumped the religion guy."

"Seems like such an obvious thing, but I never thought of it before," he said. "It's what most Christians believe across America. But it doesn't make any sense. Not if God was love and mercy the first time around."

Emboldened, Talia went on. "The logic's always bugged me. I mean, wouldn't a violent second coming by Jesus make the whole first coming a little irrelevant? Like, 'Whoops, non-judgment and peace and sharing was a mistake. Forget that. This is what I really meant to do?'"

Thomas couldn't help laughing. "Yeah, it does." He shook his head. "Talia Simmons, you're good for me."

"Don't you forget it, Thomas Whidman," she replied, grinning. "Dinner's on you tonight." She glanced sideways at him. "My fee for helping you lighten your baggage."

Thomas careened off the wet highway at the next exit, twin plumes of spray trailing the VW bus like a lurching speed boat. They drove in silence a few blocks to the parking lot of *The Good Earth* restaurant, both alone in their own thoughts. Ideas raced through Thomas' mind—about Ben, about the Aztecs, about people obsessed by the end of the world.

By the time he ordered the vegetable lasagna, he was looking forward to tomorrow's meeting with Cavanaugh. He finally had a thesis topic he cared about.

20 I NEED MEAT

"Thomas Whidman. My favorite transfer." Dr. Cavanaugh's deadpan Texas drawl made Thomas squirm. He felt like he was in a back-roads police station, not an oaken-paneled academic office in downtown Berkeley.

"I believe I'm your only transfer, sir."

"You're a perceptive lad, Thomas. I like that about you." Cavanaugh lowered his reading glasses on a chain to rest upon his wide chest, barely contained by a faded denim shirt. Somehow, even after twelve years as the chair of the Comparative Religions department at BATU, Dr. Horace Cavanaugh still managed to look like a respectable New Mexican cowboy.

"I must confess, not many students switch degree programs in their third year," the professor observed. "Few and far between. Fewer still attempt to take other courses while completing a thesis."

Thomas sensed compassion in his adviser's comments. *He understands the workload I'm facing! I knew I'd get a cool adviser if I switched to--*

"Do you know *why* there are so few students in your position?" queried Professor Cavanaugh. The man rose from his chair, not waiting for a reply. "Because most students do something called *planning!*"

Thomas sat frozen, looking down at his thesis proposal on the desk between the two men. Dr. Cavanaugh had many physically imposing traits—a towering stance, a lantern jaw, a prominent nose, broad shoulders and a pot belly--but the one that troubled Thomas right now was the man's hairy ears.

He dared not look up. The lamp behind Cavanaugh was giving the professor's lobes an impressive aura.

"I understand I have a lot to do, Dr. Cavanaugh, but I believe I can do it," said Thomas humbly, deciding to fix his gaze on the bolo tie at Cavanaugh's neck. *Wrong choice.* More hair. White bristles rioted at the professor's neckline.

Mercifully, Cavanaugh sat again, rejoining Thomas at desk level. He pulled the hems of his gray Wranglers down low over his polished boots. "If you're determined to proceed, then so be it. Let's hear your research topic, son. Shoot."

Thomas was excited. "I've been thinking a lot about this, sir, and I think I have a good one."

"You've had five weeks, so it better be," said Cavanaugh, leaning on his elbows, templing his long fingers over the ten-gallon hat on his desk. "Out with it."

"Okay, here goes," said Thomas, taking a nervous breath. "How does belief in the imminent end of the world change a group's behavior?"

Cavanaugh nodded. "Pretty good."

Yes! I knew it would--

"For a seventh grader!" his professor growled. "This isn't a social studies book report, son. Let me guess: you intend to write a mishmash about the Aztecs and the Anasazi and Jonestown and some Christian fringe groups like the Shakers, and then in your conclusion you'll make some pithy comments about the traits they shared as they waited for the end of the world."

"No, not at all." *Crap, how did he know that?*

"This department doesn't need another analysis of the human condition from some twenty-something grad student, Mr. Whidman. If I want that, I'll read Joseph Campbell."

Cavanaugh grabbed his ten-gallon hat and stalked around the desk. "I want meat, son. Your thesis is supposed to be proof that you can conduct competent independent research. Kids like you transfer into my department all the time, thinking that Comparative Religions means that you don't have to do any real work. A Master's thesis in my department is the ultimate product of an individual's sustained and rigorous inquiry into a specific issue or population. Not a greatest hits of the human soul." He held open his office door. "Come find me when you have specifics."

21 SUDDENLY THOMAS WAS WIDE AWAKE

"*Ragnarok,*" Thomas entered into the keyboard at the seminary's library. In front of his tired eyes appeared seventeen titles related to the ancient Nordic prophecies detailing the final battle of the gods of Asgard and the giants of Frostheim at the end of the world. He laughed softly. Reading *Thor* comics as a kid was proving critical to researching his master's thesis. Three of those Nordic titles, including authors and call numbers, he jotted down as possible sources.

Specifics, he muttered to himself. He still liked his original thesis question: *How does belief in the imminent end of the world change a group's behavior?* But Cavanaugh had demanded that his research topic be rooted to one specific issue or population, so here he was. In the seminary library. Being rigorous, sustained and independent. At one in the morning.

He'd been at it all night. These days, he was a lot of things he wasn't proud of—cynical, angry, confused--but he wasn't going to let Cavanaugh add *quitter* to that list. The latest Nordic references gave Thomas a total of 142 titles to look up tomorrow, to see if he could find a specific topic worth researching. Roman imperial eschatology, John of Patmos, biblical Armageddon, Black Plague, Mayan calendar, Maccabbean revolt, Medieval apocalyptic poetry, Aztec eclipses, Nordic prophecies, Islamic Day of Judgment: he'd entered countless subject headings into the library data banks, and was running out of energy as well as ideas. *Time to call it a night.*

Thomas was organizing his mess of papers into a semblance of order when he noticed that one last topic remained to be entered. He was cooked for tonight, but the topic was a good one. He couldn't really go to bed without punching it in.

"Christian Millennialism." The words remained motionless on the screen for a split second as the card catalog's hard drive whirred. Then a list of 31 titles tumbled down the screen, neon green letters staring out at him from the blackness.

Thomas sighed, and rearranged himself back into the chair. *142 titles had been enough, hadn't they?* He'd been imagining himself next to Talia in a warm bed. Rubbing his eyes, he resigned himself to spend another twenty minutes copying down promising titles.

Suddenly Thomas was wide awake.

There in front of him was the most interesting item he had come across all evening. The title wasn't the intriguing thing; *"The Impending Kingdom"* sounded a lot like all the rest.

It was the place: published in Gilman, Arkansas, in 1919. His grandfather's hometown.

And it was the author: Josiah Adam Whidman. Somebody he'd never heard of. Somebody with his own last name.

Artifact # 1: Excerpt from Paul Silas' Thesis, "The Crisis of Faith of Josiah Adam Whidman"

A magnetic quality of leadership, masterful oratory, a keen mind and an organ-like voice assured Reverend Josiah Whidman of a following, despite a message that was sure to drive away the faint-hearted. An impressed church attendee, who nevertheless was not a resident of Whidman's "Faithful Remnant" apocalyptic community, gave this account in a 1921 radio show:

> I have heard a number of his sermons, yes. He is one of the most clever, one of the most affable fellows I've met, of such pleasing disposition. I'd dare say he's gifted with such oratorical ability as only one preacher in a thousand has. He has a deep voice like the sea, and is such a splendid singer that I've seen tears of rapture flow in the congregation.
>
> He is not addled in the head, no matter what those newspapermen from St. Louis say. Yessiree, he has one of the most wonderful intellects of any man I ever did talk with. Statistics and mathematical computations roll off of his tongue without any effort at all. When he was just a lad of 14, why he had the entire book of Revelation committed to memory! He attests this was the starting point of his studies of the Prophecy, and I believe him.
>
> He knew what he was meant for early on, that's for certain. Now he has near all the prophetic scriptures of the Bible memorized, including hundreds of chapters and thousands of verses, all tabulated out in his brain for ready reference on a moment's notice. He can quote dates and doctrines and revelations so fast and so right that I'd say he's the plumb equal to the fancy memory experts in those magazine ads. One smart man, that Josiah Adam.

--Excerpt taken from "The Crisis of Faith of Josiah Adam Whidman," Master of Divinity thesis written by Paul Silas, Bay Area Theological Union, 1985.

22 LIBRARY AVENGER

"So the next morning I go back to the stacks to find the book, and guess what?" Thomas slurped his coffee a bit too loudly in the quiet university café, but Talia didn't seem to mind. It amused her to see him foaming at the mouth like this, Thomas guessed. He felt like a kid working a crossword puzzle for the first time.

"The book I wanted wasn't there. I mean, it *really* wasn't there," Thomas carried on. "When I went to go check with a librarian, she told me her records indicated it was overdue. *Majorly* overdue. It was supposed to be returned seven years ago."

"Hate to see the fine on that one," murmured Talia.

"I know, huh? Checked out by a former divinity student named Silas. Paul Silas. I told the librarian I'd be a bounty hunter and track him down, if I got a good cut of the take."

"They could set a dangerous precedent with that one," Talia responded "You could create a new line of work. Library Avenger." She took a bite of her breakfast and then took on a gravelly voice: "'Hello, Mr. Silas...I know what you did seven years ago. Or, more accurately, what you forgot to do. And now you're gonna pay.'"

"Could've been a lucrative new niche," sighed Thomas. "But they didn't go for it. Instead, I did a system-wide search for the author Josiah Adam Whidman from the 1920s, to see if he'd written any other books. He hadn't, but guess what I did find?"

"No idea."

"Turns out a former seminarian wrote a thesis about him, seven years ago. The thesis was called 'The Crisis of Faith of Josiah Adam Whidman.' And guess who wrote it?" At Talia's blank look, Thomas plowed on. "The same Paul Silas, our library criminal. Coincidence? I think not."

"Spooky," Talia said dryly. "Maybe Silas was obsessed by the guy. Stole his book and then wrote his autobiography."

"Yeah, pretty weird," he agreed, plowing into his breakfast. As usual, they'd given him far too much pesto cream cheese on his bagel. He forgot to do any preventative maintenance before chomping into his meal.

"I was hooked by mystery, so I did what any aspiring Sherlock would do: I went in search of Silas' thesis." He wiped bits of bagel topping from his lips. "Now, you might think that it would be difficult to get your hands on a copy of a Masters' thesis written seven years ago, yes? Yes?"

"Sure," she played along. "Super difficult."

"Not at Bay Area Theological Union," said Thomas, wagging a cream-cheesed finger. "Many of our esteemed alumni become famous and influential members of the worldwide theological community. The library has kept a copy of each thesis since the inception of this fine institution. They devote an entire wing—the Hanselmann Wing—to the housing and preservation of said theses."

Now Thomas' upper lip was paying the price. Three significant gobs of olive-hued cream cheese clung tenaciously to his whiskers. What was formerly a well-tended beard now looked like someone's award-winning crustacean collection. The effect was disturbingly walrus-like.

"So to the Hanselmann Wing I went," Thomas continued, oblivious. "Armed with subject, title, author and year written. I promptly located the right row, yet when I came to its expected place on the shelf, the thesis was nowhere to be found. Nowhere on the adjacent stacks, either."

"More spookiness."

"Precisely, Watson." He listed the main points on his fingers. "First, the book missing for seven years. Next, the thesis not in the stacks. Both gone without a trace. Again, coincidence? I think not."

"We think not," Talia agreed absently, unfocused on his words. Usually, she kept eye contact with him when they talked; this time, however, her eyes were following the bobbing bits of cream cheese. "Thomas, you need to--" she made a wiping motion on her face, to no avail.

"I knew what I needed to do," he agreed. "I grabbed the closest librarian and we spent half an hour searching the area with a fine-toothed comb. Nothing."

"Nothing?"

"Nothing but more intrigue. The librarian told me three things could've happened to the thesis: first, someone could have swiped it. Second, it could have been misfiled. Or third, it may never have received endorsement by the sponsoring professor at the time of submission."

"What does that mean?"

"She told me that, typically, endorsement is just a formality. All completed theses arrive at the library desk and are taken to the Hanselmann Wing to be entered into the card catalog system, coded, and later shelved. A handful of theses come without a sponsoring professor's endorsement--due to the professor rushing off to an early sabbatical, or on maternity leave, or some such extenuating circumstance. The missing endorsement generally follows a few weeks later. In such a case the endorsement is added to the binder of the thesis and then shelved with all the rest, according to its catalog number. This librarian—with whom I had become quite chummy by this time—suggested that this particular thesis might have slipped through the administrative cracks: it may have been recorded in the card catalog, yet never received an endorsement and therefore never shelved."

"Where would they have put the actual thesis, then?

"My question as well. Was it placed under some counter? In the dumpster? Librarian Lady said that, after a few months, a thesis without an endorsement would probably have been sent down to the basement, to an area they call the

Labyrinth. She showed me the stairwell and gave me a wicked smile, saying, 'Enter at your own risk, honey.' Damn, she wasn't kidding. I felt like I was entering the library's emergency ward."

"Like the Island of Misfit Toys. But for literature."

"Yeah. All the castaways are down there. Books without spines, spines without books, incomplete theses, anthologies with their covers ripped off, impossibly oversized handwritten manuscripts from a century ago in big plexiglass tubes…it was all stacked together in a rough alphabetical order by author. It was like a haunted house down there, Tal. Thousands of theses, either incomplete or unendorsed, were mixed in with other damaged books, some more than two hundred years old. Shelf after shelf after shelf. I spent about three hours diving through the "S" and "W" sections, just to make sure it wasn't there."

"And I'm guessing it wasn't?"

"Indeed it wasn't," Thomas confirmed. "And when I finally came up for air and was about to leave, Library Lady told me about a retired prof named Moses who's pretty much the king of the Labyrinth. He's been volunteering forever in the Hanselmann basement, and he knows more than anybody else about what's down there."

"Going to pay him a visit?"

"Yeah. He comes in every couple of weeks to shelve new arrivals, shred some old documents to make room, conduct obscure searches, that kind of stuff. She said he'd be in next Thursday."

With globs of dairy bobbing up and down on his lips, Thomas looked so ludicrous that Talia became concerned for his reputation. After all, there could be influential professors or high-ranking deans witnessing this breakfast freak show. Engrossing as his story was, his visage was even more attention-getting than his words. Talia tried to make another attempt.

"The Iceman Cometh," Talia intoned, motioning to the pesto tailings on Thomas' confused face. "You've got so much cream cheese hanging from your lip you look like you're thawing out from the Ice Age." She tried to offer him a clean napkin. "Dressing up already? It's early for Halloween."

Thomas stayed just out of reach. Not moving a muscle, he turned a stone-cold gaze directly at her. "I like it there." Seconds passed. In the silence, a glob of pesto-infused cream cheese slid off his lip and fell to his plate far below, making a small splash. If Thomas noticed, he paid no heed. He kept his eyes fixed on Talia, unmoving.

"Don't be a butthead," Talia giggled, and kicked him under the table. "You look like someone attacked you with a pesto pie."

"It's my new look," Thomas said in a monotone, unmoving. "Why can't you just accept me as I am?"

"Alright." From her handbag Talia withdrew a fat black felt-tip marker and began writing deftly in big block letters on a paper napkin. Occasionally she would steal a quick glance at Thomas who continued to sit immobile, idiotic, cream cheese islands on a sea of scruffy whiskers. He was enjoying this.

"Well, Mr. Lobotomy, I simply must go freshen up. Thanks for the sparkling conversation and immaculate table manners." Talia rose and stuffed the napkin like a lobster bib into Thomas' still unmoving shirt collar. "I didn't realize up until now that I was dating an idiot savant, but without the savant." With that she turned and headed to the bathroom, laughing.

Thomas remained stoic, unblinking, until he was sure the womens' bathroom door had closed. Then slowly, ever so slowly, he lowered his gaze to the napkin she'd stuffed under his chin. Even upside down, the big block inscription was easy to read:

BRAIN DAMAGED

BEWARE: SUDDEN BOWEL DISCHARGES

ASSISTANCE IS APPRECIATED

She's good, Thomas thought, grinning. *Very good.*

23 THE CLOCK TICKED

The stately grandfather clock stood tall in the parlor hallway, its mechanical, muffled heartbeat sounding from deep within its oaken cabinet. It had stood in that same place, ticking in that same manner, ever since Thomas could remember. He'd learned to crawl on the thick Turkish rug under its brass feet when his family came up to Grandmother's for the summer when he was young. Now he sat on the upholstered divan where, years ago, dimly-remembered adult faces had sat watching him struggle with gravity on the floor. Back while Mom was still alive, and when Dad used to pay attention. Now he listened to the regular rhythm of the clock and the distant sounds of his grandmother moving methodically about the kitchen.

It was mid-morning in the rest of California, but one wouldn't know it within Grandmother Whidman's subdued domain of stained oak and gold brocade. Here, in Walnut Creek, within these walls, it was always late afternoon. The only evidence to the contrary was an errant beam of sunlight sneaking in through the thick drapes, turning a narrow column of dust motes into a swirling cascade of amber light.

Although Grandmother's house was an hour's drive from where he lived in Berkeley, it always seemed to Thomas that, from the time he left his apartment to the time she welcomed him in her parlor, he'd been transported from a land of malls and freeways, he had sunk through time and space, to be mysteriously delivered into 1950's southern elegance: to an island of the refined, the understated, the smooth. Somehow the woman even managed to have a stately magnolia thrive in her front yard.

The clock ticked. The motes danced, lazy, turning. Grandmother, distant, took the kettle from the stove top She was always like that with her guests, family or otherwise: first the greeting, then the serving, then the conversation. In that order.

Thomas settled, sinking back into the cushions. Burning questions had been with him for several days now; they could wait a few minutes longer for tea. If anyone would know who Josiah Whidman was, it would be Grandmother. Finding out about this man had become a bit of an obsession, taking priority over getting specific on his Masters' thesis, over spending time with Talia, over bodily hygiene.

This obsession, Thomas realized, was not well-timed. He was supposed to meet with Cavanaugh tomorrow morning, presenting thoughtful specifics regarding a clear thesis topic. And was he in the library, dutifully preparing? No. Instead, he was chasing down some dead guy from Gilman with his same last name.

Grandmother Whidman backed her way deftly through the swinging parlor doors with a fully appointed tea tray. She turned to face Thomas with a warm smile.

"There, dear." She placed the tray down on a low table between two high-backed chairs. "Now we can converse like civilized people. Now tell your Grandmother Whidman all about what's happening at school."

From here the two debarked on small talk, catching up. Thomas enjoyed his grandmother, but she clearly liked hearing more about his accomplishments than his doubts, so the conversation remained light and circular. His relationship with Talia delighted Grandmother immensely, but soon even that was exhausted. The flow of words gradually ceased. Thomas looked across the table to see a pair of wizened eyes looking at him expectantly.

"Grandmother, I didn't just come for a visit today. I wanted to ask you about something."

"I had an inkling you did. I'd thought that it might be about your lady friend, but we've already covered that topic. Talk to me."

"Have you heard of a man named Josiah Adam Whidman?"

The ancient lady's eyes blazed for a brief second. She took a long sip of tea.

"I knew it," Thomas blurted. "Who was he?"

She put her antique china cup back down on its filigreed saucer with an unsteady hand, making a small rattle of porcelain. "I guessed you might find out about Josiah Adam sooner or later. I told him it'd be near impossible to bury a man's whole history, even someone dead for fifty years."

Thomas waited. His question had now become electric.

"How in heaven's name did you find out about him?" she said softly. Her face now bore a smile more curious than knowledgeable. She loved a good mystery. He knew now by the gleam in her eyes that he was going to get the information he wanted.

"Chance." Thomas shrugged. "I was researching the subject of end-times prophecies for a paper I'm working on, and suddenly the computer pulled up the title of a book written by some guy named Josiah Adam Whidman published in Gilman *freaking* Arkansas! The only folks I know who have even *heard* of Gilman are members of our family. What is he, some long-lost relative?"

Grandmother's eyebrows arched. "You're researching end-times prophecy? Man alive, you're going to have a field day with Josiah Adam and the Faithful Remnant!"

Thomas could contain his curiosity no longer. "You still haven't told me who he was!"

Grandmother looked down at the ring of tea stained on her saucer from years of use. "He was your grandfather's uncle. About thirty years older than me. From what I've been told, Josiah Adam baptized your grandpa just a few days after he was born, right in the Buffalo River where it runs through Gilman, when the town was nothing but a few rough houses and a plank church and the printing press."

Thomas sat for a moment in silence, letting it all sink in. "So he was a preacher." His mind reeled. "Why...why haven't I heard of him before?"

His question was answered only by the muffled tick of the stately old clock. Grandmother, her drawn face a blank to him, no longer looked so amused or curious. Suddenly small, the old woman closed her eyes, and let out a great sigh. Holding her cup seemed to take effort. Thomas had never seen her look so frail.

An anger that surprised Thomas rose up within him, and overrode his manners. "Grandmother, why haven't I heard of him before?" He set his cup down and leaned forward. "You've told me all about our family 'til I was sick of hearing about it. You've told me about every Whidman there is. But you never mentioned a Josiah. You told me some of us lived in Gilman. You told me the family ran a publishing house. But you never told me about any Whidman *writing* a book! What are you hiding from me? *Why haven't I heard of him before?"*

Grandmother looked stricken, pale. She was muttering under her breath and wouldn't meet Thomas' eyes. "Oh, Tommy...someone in the family felt it was best to let the dead lie. Keep them dead, without a lot of loose talk and sensationalism. I told him we couldn't hide it forever. Knew it wasn't healthy for the family, keeping secrets. But he insisted. Oh, child. I'm so sorry."

"Uncle Ben," Thomas said grimly.

The old woman suddenly looked at her grandson, her eyes moist. "Thomas, I didn't want to hide anything from you. It's just, well, Josiah Adam was eccentric. He was ...an embarrassment."

With that final word, she buried her face in her sweater, hunched and hiding in the drapes next to her chair. Her frail body shook with restrained sobs. Thomas had never seen his Grandmother like this, never been with her like this. He was torn. He did this, made her cry. But how could she have lied to him all of these years?

He sat in silence for several minutes, paralyzed, shaken. Grandmother remained huddled, sobbing, a creature he'd never known. This wasn't how it was supposed to turn out. Eventually, the situation became too much for him. He stood up, grabbed his jacket. "I need to go."

- - - -

Grandmother came out to the drive and caught him at his car window as he was pulling out of the driveway in his VW. Her eyes were red, but no longer wet. Thomas started sputtering, apologizing and furious all at once, when she cut him off, placing her hand on his shoulder.

"This has been a long time coming, Thomas," she said simply. "You deserve an explanation." Her voice hardened in resolve. "I'll send you some papers within the week."

Artifact # 2: Excerpt from Paul Silas' Thesis,
"The Crisis of Faith of Josiah Adam Whidman"

A resident of the Faithful Remnant Community testified to a journalist in 1921, "If Reverend Whidman would only preach what the people want preached, he could be known as one of the mightiest men anywhere and could command any salary he wanted." But Josiah Whidman believed that his mission to uncover the secrets of Biblical prophecy was divinely appointed; therefore, he had no choice in the content of his sermons. In his own words:

> "Brother, do you not know this is the biggest battle I ever had to fight in my life? I am willing to confess that, as I have traveled over these United States, I have not found other preachers of the Word who are working to reveal the great Seven-Fold system of the Kingdom Prophecy...

> "Now I know that, unless I do the things that the Lord has set down in the message, he cannot accept me. I must fulfill my task. As by the power of the Spirit our Lord God created the stars of the heavens and set them into their constellations long ago when the world was new, so He has also brought on the face of the earth today a small but mighty host of fore-ordained characters, destined before time, each one to take his place in his own community as a herald, announcing God's Coming and the End of the Age. I am one of those heralds. My flock that awaits upon the Lord shall dwell together in harmony and it shall be called the Faithful Remnant community, as in days of old." (from a sermon by J. A. Whidman, recorded by dictaphone, Dec. 15, 1921)

> --Excerpt taken from "The Crisis of Faith of Josiah Adam Whidman," Master of Divinity thesis written by Paul Silas, Bay Area Theological Union, 1985.

24 MEN IN MOTION

"Hello, Whidmans." Joe Whidman's voice came over the line, distracted. He'd been muttering something about men in motion as he moved the phone to his mouth.

"Hey, Dad. It's me."

"Thomas! So good to hear you. Hold just a sec. Chargers are on." The phone clunked on a card table. Thomas heard the sound of papers shuffling. Too late, he remembered it was a Monday evening. Football night. A winter Monday evening twenty years ago meant his father was watching football, sunk into his favorite loveseat in the den of their Orange County tract home. It wasn't any different now, twenty years later.

Joe Whidman was a lover of football. But he was also a scientist. Joe didn't just watch. He researched. Monitored. The television was on, but by no means did that mean that Joe was simply watching a football game. Occasionally he would glance up for confirmation, but most of Joe's attention was fixated upon a card table covered with scrawled legal pads and the Radio Shack AM pocket radio that he held tight to his left ear.

Joe was a fan of football in general, and the San Diego Chargers in particular. Never mind that the Los Angeles Rams, a perennially winning team, was closer to Orange County. Never mind that the Chargers were one of the most unsuccessful teams in the history of the sport. In fact, it was precisely the Charger's famous ability to lose that drew Joe Whidman's attention like a magnet. Joe's personal mission, ever since Thomas' mom died, was to discover the missing ingredient that would bring the Chargers to victory in the Super Bowl. His latest interpretation of the data showed a significant correlation between Charger victories and incidences of abnormally high offensive penalties made by the opponent's wide receivers.

"How's the research going?" Thomas opened casually when his dad picked the phone back up from the card table.

"Still too early to be sure, Tom," his father responded. "Tonight's game should tell me a lot." The announcer from the AM radio was audible. Thomas hoped his dad had bothered to remove the jack from his ear.

"Nice to hear your voice, son. Doing well?"

"Fine, dad, fine." Thomas didn't know how to begin. "The Chargers doing well?"

"Good, real good," said Joe. From far away, Thomas could hear the announcer arguing with the referee's most recent call. "Hey, can I call you back after the game?

"Actually, Dad, I need to ask you one question right now."

"Oh?" Joe Whidman's raised voice conveyed his surprise. "What about?"

"Dad, why didn't you tell me about Josiah Adam?"

"Who?"

"C'mon, dad. Josiah Adam Whidman. Preacher. Author. Gilman, Arkansas. The brother of your grandfather."

"Oh. Him." To the side, Thomas could hear his father flipping pages. "What do you want to know about him?"

"It's not that I want to know about him *now*," said Thomas, exasperated. "Why didn't you tell me about him earlier?" This family conspiracy of silence was really digging at him.

A pause, then his dad cleared his throat. Papers stopped shuffling. "Let me see if I get this straight. You don't want to know anything about Josiah Whidman, but you're angry that I didn't tell you anything about him."

Thomas was so close to crying that he surprised himself. "Dad! Come on! Pastor Josiah Whidman, our ancestor, thought the world was going to end in the 1920's, and he convinced 250 people to create a Christian commune with him in backwoods Arkansas to print a newspaper and wait for God to come on a cloud!"

"Okay," Joe Whidman said. "Yes." There was another pause on the other end of the line. "Sorry, Thomas, but I'm still trying to understand your point. I already know that."

"Why didn't you ever tell me about my own great-grand-uncle!" Thomas yelled.

This time the pause was heavy, pregnant. Thomas suddenly noticed that he could no longer hear the radio on the other end. "Frankly, son, he never really meant that much to me," his dad said in a common-sense tone. Too late, Thomas remembered that Joe Whidman was a man who liked life in concrete packages. He didn't have use for fervent spirituality or eccentric stories about the end of the world.

His father continued. "Josiah Adam Whidman, my grandfather's brother, was a nut whom I never met, a distant relative who hurt a lot of people with his ideas. He was in his prime about seventy years ago in a part of the country I hardly ever go to. He's somebody I never think about except at family reunions. Honestly, it never occurred to me you'd care about him."

At these words, Thomas sighed. *Some family conspiracy*, he thought to himself.

"I'm sorry I let you down, son," Joe Whidman said softly. "I would have talked to you about him when you were younger if I thought you cared. The rest of the family didn't like talking about him. I just went along, I guess."

25 ANOTHER MAN, ANOTHER TIME

"Silas," Dr. Clement J. Fowler repeated in deep, sonorous tones. "Yes, of course. I'll remember the name of Paul Silas for quite some time, I'd imagine."

Thomas sat across a large mahogany desk from the tall, dignified academic, on the third floor of one of the seminary's older brick towers. Today, Professor Fowler wore a tan suit with a blue tie. "Paul Silas was one of the most passionate young men to ever enter the doors of this hallowed institution. And a brilliant mind, I might add, with a superb knack for languages. He carried the Word with him at all times, day or night. 'Thy sword and thy shield, they protect me.'"

Thomas had seen Dr. Fowler around the seminary campus before, but only now, in early November in his third year at seminary, had he ever sat in the dignified man's presence. He was a steel-haired gentleman with a handlebar mustache, and was the first person Thomas had ever seen who actually used a monocle. Thomas had set up the appointment with Dr. Fowler as soon as he'd discovered the professor had been Paul Silas' adviser when Silas wrote his thesis in 1985.

Among the seminary students, Fowler was simply known as "Preacher," due to his evangelical bent, rare for BATU, as well as for the well-crafted sermons he often delivered during special all-school ceremonies. That, and the fact that his gangly frame resembled that of Ichabod Crane.

"You were important to Silas, as a professor and guide. He was often a student of yours, yes?"

"One of my finest. He chose me as his informal mentor early in his second year, and we became very close…until the thesis." Fowler trailed off, shaking his head.

"And you were his thesis adviser also, correct?"

"Quite correct, young man."

"Tell me about it…the thesis, I mean. Do you recall the topic?"

"The topic? Certainly. Silas was an older student, not just a boy fresh from college. In fact, he was almost a peer, as he'd been a lay preacher of the Word for several congregations. A few years before entering seminary, while he was interning at a church in Arkansas, he found out about a Disciples of Christ pastor named Whidman who had prophesied the world would end in the 1920s. As far as Silas knew, no scholar had researched this historical figure before, so when he had to choose a topic for his thesis, he set before himself the task of compiling a spiritual biography, something along the lines of 'The Life and Times of a Misguided Pastor.'" Fowler broke eye contact, gazing out the window, crossing his lanky legs. "And that's when he began to break down."

"Break down?" Thomas perked up. "So he never completed the work?"

"You misunderstand." Fowler said. "Silas certainly did complete it. It began as the most thoroughly researched thesis I've seen emerge from this place in my twenty-seven years of service."

"Then why did you decide not to endorse it?"

"Not endorse it? Hah! That would've been good." He paused, savoring the idea, and smoothed his significant mustache. "No, I endorsed it all right, though I was loathe to do so."

"So it was both endorsed and completed?"

"Yes, of course," said Dr. Fowler, a bit confused. "Why are you asking these questions?"

"Well, sir, because it's missing from the Hanselmann Wing."

"Misplaced, you mean," he said, waving a hand in dismissal. "Lost by a student. Or overdue. Happens all the time."

"No, Professor, I mean missing. Gone."

"Odd." The refined professor looked squarely at Thomas, his monocle searching for clues. "Very odd indeed."

"But back to the thesis, sir," said Thomas. "Why did you not want to endorse it?"

"Yes. Well." The man they called Preacher leaned back, pursed his lips. "From a scholarly standpoint, I could do nothing but give it some of the highest technical marks I've ever given a thesis. The research of primary documents was exhaustive, masterful." He shook his head. "However, the liberties he took in the latter half of the paper were appalling."

"Tell me more."

The professor sighed. "Well, how shall I put it? The work was seemingly written by someone with the dual character of Dr. Jekyll and Mr. Hyde. Severely schizophrenic in style and content. After 77 pages of brilliantly researched historical narrative, the author suddenly launches into a most bizarre postscript. 66 pages of the most bizarre ranting I have ever encountered."

"Ranting?"

"Disturbing texts, full of despair. Twisted nursery rhymes, certain phrases repeated over and over, math problems, biblical quotes, numerology. And all those numbers! Repeated over and over. Nobody writes a thesis like that. Nobody in his right mind, anyway."

"How did the seminary handle that?"

"Our thesis committee was completely unprepared." Fowler tried to explain. "The evaluation process at a liberal institution like this did not have any mechanism to condemn a manuscript for its heretical qualities or its creative license. The committee requested that Silas remove his ending, but he refused. He said the seminary had to "face the cruel truth," whatever that meant, and he would alter none of it. Because the 66-page rant was all postscript—not technically part of the thesis--the committee decided it would not be evaluated, and so the paper stood. It was as if another person inhabited his skin at the end. The postscript showed not one bit of the Paul

Silas I once knew and admired." He paused. "I am aware that the concept of demonic possession is not taken seriously by the majority of Christian academics these days, but I could give it no other name."

What century is this anyway? The thought struck Thomas as he stared into Fowler's animated face, hearing a man with a monocle and a handlebar mustache talk about demon possession in the upper stories of some aging brick tower. For a few moments, Thomas was distracted, and had to work hard to pick up Fowler's current line of thought.

"Others on the committee—those of a more psychological persuasion--were convinced that Silas had suffered a psychotic break," Fowler was saying. "Some thought the fellow was having a life crisis and dropped everything he once believed in: academia, Christianity, divine intervention, God, everything."

What did you just say? Thomas almost blurted aloud. He leaned forward, even more interested than before.

Professor Fowler sank back into his upholstered chair, spent. "I still don't know what to make of it after seven years. During his research, something shattered inside that man. And something dark emerged." Thomas thought the shadows in the corner of the office near the coat rack were growing darker, but he wasn't sure.

"He still haunts me occasionally." Fowler's gaze turned to the window; he was no longer focusing on Thomas, but rather upon another man, another time, another life. Thomas took the respite to scribble down notes from the conversation, but was only halfway done when Fowler spoke again.

"I believe I still recall the final line Silas wrote in that twisted paper. It was a phrase he'd repeated in other parts of the manuscript. It pops up in my thoughts sometimes, even now, seven years later."

"It does? Tell me."

"Give me a moment." The professor rubbed his temples. "Oh yes. 'It is fitting that my faith, too, dies in numbers.'"

"Hmm…weird." Thomas shuddered inwardly at his lack of appropriate words. Whatever one was supposed to say in response to a situation such as this, he was sure it was not such a sage comment as, "Hmm…weird."

Professor Fowler seemed oblivious. "Yes, odd, isn't it? And tragic. Silas had been an extremely passionate minister of the Word, one of my top students. Then, with this thesis, he suddenly dropped out, cut off all ties and vanished just before ordination ceremonies."

Thomas' heart sank. "Vanished?"

"Mmm," Dr. Fowler concurred, nodding. "Since then I've heard from him only once.

"You've heard from him?"

"Yes, strangely. Just last year. Let's see." The silver-haired professor fumbled in an oak desk drawer for a minute, then gave up. "Ah well. It was an odd little postcard. I don't remember much of it, just the tone. It seemed full of emptiness, like he no longer cared about anything. I still don't know why he chose to write me after all these years. Maybe a cry for help. Maybe to mock me."

"What do you mean?"

"The card gave no mention of what he was doing, where he'd been, nothing like that. Just some more cryptic statements. One phrase I remember: he said that sometimes, when something dies, it's reborn; other times, when something dies, it simply dies. Sounded like a lost soul."

"Hmm. Strange." Thomas found himself fascinated by this mysterious Silas. Something about the man drew him like a magnet. Another one of God's broken toys. Like me. He got up from his chair. "Well, thank you, Dr. Fowler, for making time for me."

"My pleasure. Do come again if I can be of any further help."

The two men shook hands, and Thomas turned to leave. At the door, he turned back to the professor. "By the way, you wouldn't remember the postmark on that card Silas sent you, would you?"

"That I do, actually." Fowler gave him a look through his monocle. "Still remember the cactus. South Tucson, Arizona."

Thomas mumbled a second thanks and shut the office door. He walked down the tower stairs, his mind afire. Heresy. Intrigue. Silas over the edge. End of the world. A hidden ancestor. Demonic possession. A missing thesis. Lost souls. South Tucson. He felt like hopping in his car and driving into the desert this very minute. The trail left by Paul Silas was turning into a real mystery, just like in the movies, where clues led macho guys on crazy goose chases. *The only problem*, thought Thomas, *is that this isn't the movies. This is my life.*

26 INTO THE LABYRINTH

The stairs leading down into the Labyrinth were easier for Thomas to navigate this time, partly because this was his second descent, partly because this afternoon there was an eldritch light glowing up the stairway from below. Emanating even stronger than the light, however, was the sound of whirring machinery.

Dr. Moses Chartwood, the King of the Labyrinth, took his volunteer position in the seminary library very seriously. If it wasn't for him, the basement storage vaults in the Hanselmann Wing would be strewn with heaps and mounds, boxes of file folders and damaged books and other unpleasant things placed there by the librarians. Things they weren't ready to keep, but weren't quite ready to throw away, either.

Into this chaos Moses brought order. Not unlike the Creator, every other Thursday Dr. Chartwood could be found here separating light from darkness and giving form to the void. Rain or shine, Moses came to the Hanselmann Wing to organize and to log, to alphabetize and to file, to bind and to shred.

Shredding was a cleansing, a purging. Shredding was something he deeply enjoyed, and shredding was what he was doing now.

In the stairway, Thomas plunged down toward the light and the noise. Through the main door and down the left hallway to the Labyrinth, the noise increased in pitch and decibels until it became painful in its intensity. No other sound was possible. *Since when did the library operate a lumber mill?*

Thomas had to cover his ears with both hands when he made the final turn of the hallway into the Labyrinth's main room. There in front of him lay the source of the infernal racket: the largest, most archaic paper shredder that Thomas had ever seen.

He approached. A massive, slope-shouldered dark-skinned man with a sweating bald dome, oversized headphones, thick black glasses and a long white beard was shredding thousands of pages of dusty student theses. From behind, the figure looked uncannily like a small mountain wearing a Hawaiian print shirt and low-slung Levi's. Thomas watched. The man was in a flow, glancing at the spine of each work and deftly scribbling down each title and author in a logbook before shoving it efficiently into the maw of the shredder. His head was subtly and steadily bobbing to a rhythm, but Thomas guessed it must be internal: no cord or antenna emerged from the massive earphones.

It was several minutes before the enormous man even noticed Thomas standing nearby. The aged volunteer simply nodded a deeper bob of the head in greeting without breaking the flow of his work, shredding the full height of an additional stack before turning off the machine and removing his headphones.

"Making room for newer and, ah, slightly more coherent works," the big man explained in a gentle rumble, wiping his dust-covered glasses on an equally dusty shirt. Thomas nodded. "Doctor Moses Chartwood, former Professor of Moral Philosophy, currently the King of the Labyrinth," the man explained, introducing himself. "What can I do for you, son? You lost?"

"That sounds like a spiritual question," Thomas responded. Moses smiled, waited. "Actually, sir, I'm in search of a hard-to-find thesis. I've been led to believe that it might be filed away down here in the Labyrinth, but I already scoured the shelves by myself and I couldn't find it."

"That's what can happen when a man searches by himself down here...he can get himself lost. 'Course, he might find something else he never knew he'd been looking for." The big man's smile became even wider. "Well, son, I'm sorry you didn't find the work you're looking for. Too bad. I've probably fed it to Dante." He jerked his thumb backward to indicate the behemoth paper shredder that dwarfed even Chartwood's imposing frame. Over the feeder chute where the man dropped in documents, a sign in calligraphy read:

"Despair All Ye Who Enter Here."

Thomas' heart sank.

"Don't give up all hope yet, lad," Moses said kindly, taking Thomas under an arm which closely resembled a sawdust-covered ham roast. "At least look through my logbook to see if it's truly been eaten." He harrumphed, and changed to a scholarly tone. "This logbook contains the title and author of each document shredded by this machine, in chronological order, since it first began operating in 1974."

Thomas couldn't be positive, but it looked as though Moses petted Dante affectionately as he finished speaking.

Professor Chartwood replaced his headphones and switched on the machine. "Break's over. Grab some earmuffs and stay awhile!" he yelled, barely audible over Dante's roar.

Thomas did so. He began with logs from early in 1985, the year Silas wrote his thesis, and examined page after page of scribbled entries until his eyes blurred and a monster headache come on. *Damn fluorescent lights,* Thomas thought. *Damn noise.* The dust made his nose red and his eyes itch. He was deep into the entries when suddenly his heart sank. There it was, what he had hoped not to see: "The Crisis of Faith of Josiah Adam Whidman," by Paul Silas. Shredded on May 19, 1990.

All hope of unlocking the secret of Paul Silas died with those words. All hope of an easy road to Josiah Whidman. Thomas closed the heavy book with a dusty thud.

But wait. Something was strange. Thomas flung open the logbook again.

He returned to May 19, 1990. Silas' thesis was the last entry on that day. Thomas noticed something odd: the entry had been written by the same hand as the others, yet with a different pen.

The logbook stated the thesis was shredded in May 1990, about two and a half years ago. That was four months before Thomas himself had entered this seminary. Why then, of all times? The theses should have been first delivered to the library five years before, in 1985, when Silas wrote it. Why in the stacks for five years, then shredded in 1990?

Thomas couldn't get his head around it. He reviewed what he knew. Professor Fowler had confirmed that the thesis had been completed, and then endorsed by Fowler himself, despite his misgivings. The library had it in their system; at one point, it had been part of the regular collection. Then, five years after it had been written, it was shredded. Had it fallen apart or been damaged? Did someone want to expunge it because of its heretical rantings? Or did it become slated for destruction for some other reason?

Complaints forgotten, Thomas tugged on Moses' giant Hawaiian shirt, and signaled to shut off the machine. Thomas pulled off his ear protection and began talking before Dante had fully quieted down. "Professor Chartwood, do you shred any theses other than those labeled 'Unendorsed or Incomplete?'"

"Nope, I sure don't. Only those with a big identification label saying so."

"I have a rather bizarre question for you, sir," Thomas said. He brought the dusty log close to Chartwood, under the bright cone of light that emanated from the single overhead lamp in the murky basement. "You don't remember anything unusual about the shredding of this particular thesis, do you?" Thomas pointed to the entry in question and crossed his fingers, knowing the chances were absurd. "It would've been two and a half years ago."

The King of the Labyrinth peered at the entry for a painfully long time. His massive frame cast a huge shadow away from the light, his glasses like inscrutable mirrors.

Eventually a long, rumbling, chuckling emerged from the man-mountain.

"Why, yes I do," he said, slow as molasses, rubbing his chin. "A certain professor came down at the end of the day when I was shredding and asked me to add this one to the stack. That's why I wrote it down later. Mighty unusual."

"What was mighty unusual? The request, or the professor?"

"Both."

Thomas thought he was going to beg the wizened volunteer to elaborate when Moses Chartwood began again. "None of the other professors ever come down here. I retired some years ago, and I never came here when I was employed either," he said. "Frankly, this area is not usually part of a professor's awareness. And if a professor ever *does* stumble down here out of curiosity, *none* of them ask me to shred something. That made it unusual enough. But then there was something even more unusual."

In the next long silence, Thomas couldn't wait. "What was it?"

"The professor had a long forked beard and sparkly eyes. Like a magician."

Thomas blanched. His mind reeled. He only knew of one person he'd ever met in his life who had a forked beard. The same person had intense, sparkling eyes, like a magician. Or a demon.

Before the King of the Labyrinth could set the weathered logbook back in its place of honor, Thomas had bounded up the steps three at a time and was pushing through the main exit of the library.

27 A BIRD'S NEST OF CLUES

"Happy Family, please, and General Tso's chicken for him, both to go." Talia told the waiter as Thomas sprinted up to join her at their usual stools on the bar at *Hunan*. The cozy place was an indoor/outdoor sidewalk café just off Clairemont near BATU that churned out authentic Chinese food and made lots of money on pre-paid long-distance telephone cards.

Talia appraised a panting Thomas. "Lather down, stallion," she said, kissing his flushed face. "Get your breathing back. Then tell me the latest." With a foolish grin, Thomas hopped on a bar stool and grabbed the glass before him. "Don't stop your drinking," Talia said as Thomas worked on a long chug of ice water, "but nod if we've found the missing thesis."

"No," he blurted between sips. "But we do know it's not missing. It was shredded without authorization almost three years ago." He wiped his mouth on a sleeve, eyes alight. "And we know who shredded it."

"We do, do we? Well *one* of us is still in the dark. Come on man, spill it!"

Thomas grinned devilishly. "My uncle. Uncle Ben."

"No freaking way."

"Way."

Although Ben had never worked anywhere near BATU, Thomas had known immediately who it was by Chartwood's description. For some unknown reason, his uncle Reverend Benjamin Whidman came to the Labyrinth that day two and a half years ago and sent Paul Silas' thesis to the shredder to disappear forever. First swearing Grandmother to secrecy about their ancestor, and now this. But why? Thomas was not certain, but he sure had some guesses.

- - - - -

During the eight-minute bike ride back to Thomas' apartment, he caught Talia up on the details of his Labyrinth visit, of Dante and Moses Chartwood, of the dusty logbook and Thomas' discovery of the shredded title, and finally Moses' description the mysterious professor who visited his underground kingdom.

"But your uncle doesn't have a forked beard," Talia said as they turned the last street corner toward Thomas' apartment. "At least not in any pictures I've seen."

"You're right," Thomas explained. "He's sporting the goatee action right now."

"But before?"

"The forked beard thing used to be his trademark, bizarre as it sounds, all the years I was growing up. It always creeped me out just a little. Set him apart. Mike and I thought he looked like some dude out of the Old Testament."

They stopped at Thomas' gate. Agnew bounded up to the low chain link fence and slobbered a Great Dane hello. "Ben just shaved it off about a year ago, Mike told me. He said some members of Church of the Harvest had confronted Ben about it. They were upset by...what'd they call it? His 'fearsome aspect,' Mike said. So he finally shaved it down to something socially acceptable. My uncle loved that beard. It made him look serious, powerful." While Talia juggled their Chinese take-out and Agnew's affections, Thomas closed the front gate behind them. "Now, with the little goatee thing, he just looks kind of old and chubby faced."

They hurried up the walk bearing the still-molten food. Sesame oil stains darkened the to-go boxes, and Thomas could hear his own stomach grumbling as the wonderful aromas assaulted him. He burst in the front door of his apartment, keys in mouth, and nearly tripped over a large brown paper bundle that had been dropped through his doggie door by the postman.

The return address was familiar. "The Grandmadre comes through!" Dropping his food to the tile floor, Thomas began to tear at the wrapping until Talia put her foot on the package.

"Simmer down!" she shouted, laughing, as he struggled to get at the box. Agnew's tail whipped back at forth, threatening to knock over several flower pots, as the huge pup joined Thomas tugging at the brown postal paper. "Wipe your paws, Whidman. Let's put our dinner on the table, not the floor." She took the package away while Thomas calmed down enough to take the paper towel she offered, hastily wiping the sesame oil off of his hands. "What's with you tonight?" she said.

"Tal, you know what that is?"

"I know. But remember, you've risen above the beasts." She handed him some scissors. "Opposable thumb. Use it." She returned the package to him. "Be careful. Could be some fragile stuff in there."

Slowly, Thomas clipped the twine and sliced through the copious amounts of fiber tape that held the bundle together. Talia was right. Sesame oil would've been bad. Within was a bird's nests of fragile yellowed newspaper clippings, old photos, wrinkled handwritten missives and frail typed letters, every one of them concerning his grandfather's uncle, the Reverend Josiah Adam Whidman, founder and leader of the Faithful Remnant Christian Community of Gilman, Arkansas.

Artifact # 3: Excerpt from Paul Silas' Thesis,
"The Crisis of Faith of Josiah Adam Whidman"

The Faithful Remnant community was launched in September, 1920, in Gilman, Arkansas, after a preparation which involved a year of scouting and seven preliminary trips to the site (II:3, Mar. 19, 1921). Mr. C.E. Jordan, an oil-rich farmer of Allendale, Illinois, bought the entire Gilman site and divided it into lots of two or three acres, then sold the lots to incoming colonists at his own cost (II:2, Oct.14, 1920). According to the Faithful Remnant's newsletter *The Harbinger,* only seven families composed the first delegation (II:4, Nov. 22, 1920), but by early January, seventy more people had come to the community (II:4, Jan. 18, 1921).

During the *Harbinger's* first year of publication, the movement attracted new followers at a surprising rate. The majority of new members who packed their earthly belongings and came to join the Faithful Remnant were profoundly dissatisfied with their local churches.

The usual source of discontent among these new adherents was the rise of "liberalism" in larger society, especially among formerly rural people who felt ill at ease in city churches. One shocked follower wrote to her friend who was already living with the Faithful Remnant community that "the churches here in Denver have theatre plays...and large suppers in their church buildings most every Wednesday evening. I can't feel that this is right."

For people across the United States who by geography or by belief were cut off or alienated from regular church services, the *Harbinger* newspaper was often their one link with an earnest, life-changing kind of Christianity they were hungry for.

Knowledge of the Faithful Remnant movement spread in curious ways. One minister found a scrap of the community's newspaper on a train and wrote to inquire about the movement, later moving there. Another man found a used copy of the paper in a Chicago public library and made his decision to join the movement and transplant his family to Arkansas. Many friends of the movement traveled from job to job by railway and left copies of the *Harbinger* on the train, thus spreading Faithful Remnant teachings more widely.

Five months after the initial seven families settled, the population of Gilman was over 100 (II:4, June 4, 1921), and by December of the same year the population had more than doubled to 232 souls (III:4, Dec. 24, 1921). They were ready. And they were waiting for God's coming.

--Excerpt taken from "The Crisis of Faith of Josiah Adam Whidman," Master of Divinity thesis written by Paul Silas, Bay Area Theological Union, 1985.

28 WE BEGAN POLITELY ENOUGH

"Why are *you* here?" Thomas' eyes blazed as he stepped out of Cavanaugh's *Faith and Fanaticism* to see an unexpected relative waiting on a nearby bench, pipe smoke drifting into the November air.

"Wow. I'm underwhelmed," Reverend Benjamin Whidman said, his dark, glittering eyes looking up from his Bible. He tapped his pipe. "Hello to you, too."

"Sorry." Thomas forced a smile. "Caught me by surprise. Hi, Uncle. What brings you here?"

"That's slightly better." Ben got up from the bench, set his pipe and Bible on the slatted seat, and buttoned his long black wool coat. Today, his trim goatee looked like it was oiled. "I was in the Bay Area for a speaking engagement, so while in the neighborhood I thought I'd inspect my new billboard in Berkeley. Maybe see my favorite nephew as well."

More by habit than by inclination, Thomas accepted his uncle's expansive embrace. In his uncle's arms he suddenly realized: *for Ben, nothing's changed.*

"How'd you find me?" Thomas wondered, genuinely mystified.

"Registrar's office," his uncle replied. "I asked for your class schedule."

"I thought they weren't supposed to give out that kind of information to just anybody."

"Well, I'm not just anybody, am I, Thomas?" Chuckling, Ben put his arm around the younger man. They walked toward the main quad. "I'm your uncle. Same last name. And besides, I do have a certain measure of influence, my young seminarian, even at an institution as liberal as this."

Oh God, Thomas realized. *He doesn't even know I bagged the M. Div. program.*

"Let me buy you a hot chocolate," Ben said with a broad smile. "We can catch up."

"Can't, Uncle. I have to do some stuff."

Ben's smile tightened. "That's okay. I can be flexible. You don't have another class for a few hours."

"I just can't. Thanks for coming by."

"So it's going to be like that." Ben removed his arm. "Maybe I'll just walk next to you then for a minute or two. Pretend we're still close. While you do your important things." The preacher shoved his hand deep into the pocket of his long coat. "I was really hoping to get closer in Guatemala, Thomas. We were starting to, I thought. But then you took off. Ever since those last days of our trip, I don't understand you."

Thomas barked a laugh. "Been a lot longer than that, Uncle," he said, moving along the walkway at a brisk pace. "I haven't liked hot chocolate since high school."

Ben was taken aback. "What does—well, Thomas, of course you can get any drink you want."

Thomas stopped and turned. "You don't get it, do you?" he muttered. "I'm not in your youth group anymore." Thomas started walking again. "I have to go."

"I know you're not." Ben pulled Thomas' sleeve, forcing him to turn. "You're an adult. That's why I'm here." The older man's eyes gleamed with earnestness. "You've changed. I want to understand you. Again." Together, they moved toward the quad.

"You sure about that?" Thomas' voice was sharp. "My changes haven't been all that pleasant."

"I'm sure."

"Alright. What do you want to know?"

Ben paused. "Well, I guess we're past the place for small talk, eh?" He looked out to the distance, then back to Thomas. "Why'd you leave the group, Tom? You just disappeared into the jungle. For days."

A confrontation with Ben had been long overdue. But Thomas hadn't imagined it like this. He struggled for words. "Ben, the truth wasn't inside the church with your sermon and the food line. The truth was outside, with the peasants. I was following the truth."

"Poetic, is it not?"

"What's poetic?" Thomas frowned, puzzled.

"Look where the Lord has brought us."

Thomas looked up. "The Lord, huh? I thought *you* suggested we walk this way."

There, looming above them, was the larger-than-life image of Reverend Benjamin Whidman, goatee and all, plastered with the message that Thomas had come to despise:

WHERE DO YOU FIND TRUTH: THE BIBLE, OR A BOX OF BONES?

"This is the dilemma that's eating at you, isn't it?" Ben's dark eyes sparkled. "In this complex world, where do you find truth?"

Thomas kept his eyes on the billboard's question. "Why can't it be both? Bible and bones?"

"Both?" Benjamin Whidman scoffed. "The Lord Jesus, having an older brother because some atheist archaeologists say so? Naïve, Thomas, naïve."

He shook his head. "I'm afraid you're much less rooted than I thought. The Truth we need is right here." He patted the large, leather-bound Bible he'd been carrying under his arm. "Everything else is just shifting sand."

"And some truths are so threatening you'd rather leave them buried. Isn't that right, Uncle?"

"The discovery of a box of bones doesn't scare me," Ben scoffed.

"I'm not talking about a box of bones."

Ben gave a strange laugh, confused. "Then what *are* you talking about, nephew?"

"Why'd you make our family keep Josiah Adam Whidman a secret?"

The preacher coughed, his face hidden behind a curl of pipe smoke. "What's that, Tom?"

"You know what I'm talking about. Why are you hiding him from the family? From me?"

Silence. "Now it's you who's caught *me* by surprise, nephew. So that's what's between us."

That, and a few other disturbing questions you'd rather avoid, Thomas thought. *Like what kind of God does nothing when his people are burned alive?* His mind went back to Bailey, ten years ago. *And what kind of religion refuses communion to a man in need?*

"Let's sit down, shall we?" Ben said, motioning to a nearby park bench with a broad view of his billboard. "Let's talk about Josiah Adam Whidman. That is, unless you have too many important things to do."

"They'll wait." Thomas sat down. So did Ben.

"Thomas, the decision to hide our heretical ancestor was not something I did for my own ego."

"Sure it was."

"Tom, hear me out. I did it for us. I did it for God. So we could be the messengers He wants us to be."

"God told you to do it, did He? For us?"

"Of course. You're too young to understand, Tom. You don't have a career in the ministry yet. The Disciples of Christ have a long memory. When I was growing up in the South, any Whidman doing the Lord's work had a long shadow of suspicion cast upon him just because we had the same last name as Josiah Adam. *Heretic!* they'd call him. *Madman!*

"God showed me a long time ago that our family line doesn't need that kind of stain hanging over our lives," he concluded. "So I asked the rest of the family to never say another word about him and his misguided work. They agreed. We wanted to bury his memory like they buried his body, so we could be taken seriously as we spread Christ's message."

"How neat. How tidy," Thomas said. "Did God tell you to shred it?"

Reverend Benjamin Whidman almost choked on his pipe. "Shred?" he said. "I shred many things as a pastor. Old documents, outdated bulletins, that sort of thing."

"How many things did you shred on March 19, 1990 in the basement of this seminary's library?"

The profound silence told Thomas all he needed to know.

"Been doing your homework, have you?" Ben looked keenly at his nephew with his dark, sparkling eyes. With his goatee and long coat, he did look a bit like a magician. In an irrational, primitive part of his brain, Thomas was convinced his uncle was trying to read his mind.

"Like I said, Josiah Adam's reputation left a dark stain," continued Ben. "It's been my job most of my life to clean it up."

Defender of the faith, Thomas thought silently. *Just like I told Paloma.*

"They called Josiah a kook, a nut," Uncle Ben went on. "A stain like that can drag a preacher under, even a prominent one, drag him under like a millstone around his neck. I couldn't let something like that happen to me. Or to you. Or to my ministry. Josiah Whidman and his misguided prophecies are better left buried. I tried to tell that to the man when he first nosed around, before he wrote that thesis."

"Wait—you spoke with the author? Paul Silas?"

"Silas," Ben recalled, "yes, that's the name. How did you discover him?"

"Not important," Thomas mumbled. "You spoke to him, you said?"

"Yes, a few times. Then wrote to him after he wrote to me, asking too many questions. Must've been eight or nine years ago, now."

"Seven, actually," corrected Thomas. "How'd he find you?"

"He was doing his research in Gilman when an old historian there put him in touch with me."

"Gilman—the place where Josiah's community waited for the end of the world?"

"Silas was based there, doing his research. Once he started writing he never stopped pushing." Benjamin Whidman looked away. "I stopped communicating with him when he wouldn't take no for an answer."

"What do you mean?"

Uncle Ben tapped his pipe against the bench. "The communication began politely enough, but when I told him I was done helping him, he seemed obsessed. I told him in no uncertain terms to drop the subject, for the good of everyone concerned. But he kept digging, and wrote the cursed thing anyway. Against my wishes."

"So you knew he finished it in 1985?"

"Of course."

"Why'd you wait?"

"To shred it?" Thomas nodded. "I thought it would be buried in the seminary's archives, lost in obscurity. Thought I'd let dead dogs lie. But then you enrolled *here*, of all places." Ben gazed out into the distance and repacked the bowl of his pipe, shaking his head. "When we awarded you the Promising Young Preacher scholarship ten years ago, Thomas, you were one of us. We never imagined you'd use our money to come *here*. Once my bright young nephew decided to attend the same seminary as Silas did, the risk became too great." He lit the pipe again, and efficiently brought the flame to life. Smoke whorled about his head. "So I did us both a favor and shredded it."

"Erasing inconvenient relatives."

"I can see you don't appreciate the favor, Tom, but you will someday. You're not going to be under the shadow of a religious madman like I've been. I let you start your ministry with a clean slate."

"Did you ever think you might've been shredding a deep truth?"

"Truth?" Ben scoffed. "From that madman? What truth?"

"Josiah expected God to arrive. God didn't show up. What does that tell you?"

"Thomas, our ancestor was a misguided numerologist who--"

"Our ancestor was a true believer who dared to knock. God didn't answer."

Uncle Ben spoke warily, eyeing his nephew. "God doesn't jump to human schedules, Thomas. God's timing is not ours."

"What if God *isn't* home, Ben? What if our ancestor did you the favor of finding that out?"

Ben got up and buttoned his long coat. "Something has hurt you inside, nephew, and you're lashing out." The pastor held his leather-bound Bible close to his body and glanced at his watch. "Time for me to go."

"Now that it's difficult, Uncle?" Thomas inquired, lounging on the bench. "I thought you wanted to see how I've changed."

"I've seen enough," Ben said. "You have become a seriously ungrounded young man, Thomas. Right now I'm not sure how to help." The reverend took a few steps toward Claremont Avenue, and motioned for a cab. "Goodbye, nephew. I'll keep you in my prayers."

"And I'll keep you in mine!" Thomas called as his uncle opened the door of a taxi. "I pray you finally realize God's big message," Thomas cupped his hands and yelled as the taxi pulled away. *"Do not disturb!"*

- - - -

Later that night, as they spooned in the darkness, Thomas told Talia about his uncle's surprise visit. November moonlight poured in through Talia's bedroom window, and the comforter was pulled up to their chins.

"So Ben just took off in a taxi without another word?"

"Yeah," Thomas smirked. "Once I started to tell him how I've changed, he couldn't get out of there fast enough. He couldn't handle the dark questions."

Cradled in Thomas' arms, Talia turned to look into his eyes. "How about you, Thomas?"

"Huh?"

"How are you handling the dark questions?" She looked at him earnestly. "After Guatemala, how are you doing inside?"

Thomas' face darkened. "Now I see fires that never go out."

"I miss the other you," she said, brushing back his curly hair from his forehead. "When I first met you, I thought your religion was old school, but it was sweet. It made *you* sweet. You were in the arms of a caring God and you were crazy in love with Jesus. You were different than anyone else I knew."

"In a good way?"

She nodded. "It made you love people in a way my mom never did. She talks about peace and human rights, but she walks around tight and afraid—afraid she won't have enough, afraid someone will take advantage of her, afraid she'll get hurt. You, you gave everything away. You walked around defenseless, like you had special protection."

"That's 'cause I did." Thomas leaned on his elbow. "Thought so, anyway."

"Do you think that part of you will ever come back?"

Thomas didn't answer. After a moment, Talia gave a soft laugh in the moonlight. "Did you know I made fun of you when we first met?"

"Me?"

"I'd never met any real Christians before I started coming to meditation class at the seminary," Talia said. "I thought you were cute and kind, not like the fake Christians I'd seen in high school. So I told her about you."

"Your mom?" Talia nodded at Thomas' words. "When did you start talking to her about me--before or after you pulled my pants down?"

"After," Talia said, laughing softly. "Right after our first date. I'd never met anyone who loved Jesus like you did." She paused, and spoke in a whisper. "Not all the time, but once in a while when we were together I could tell he was so real to you, it was like he was standing at your shoulder. I told my mom you had an imaginary friend."

"I guess I did," Thomas said, rolling onto his side and staring at the ceiling. "Tal, ever since I was eight I was sure Jesus walked with me. That's why I felt so protected. God had my back."

Talia rested her head on Thomas' chest. He blew out a big, slow lungful of air.

"Tell your mom you guys were right."

"Hmm?" Tal said drowsily.

"I did have an imaginary friend." He rolled over, his face to the bedroom wall. "And once I stopped believing in my make-believe friend, he didn't come back."

29 DARK QUESTIONS AND LOST CAUSES

Ten minutes ago Thomas decided he was a lost cause: his brain was whirling with thoughts that wouldn't float away like a fucking boat on a river. Meditating, his mind kept circling back to images of Ben's visit last week. *You've become a seriously ungrounded young man, Thomas.* Thomas pictured Ben standing under his own massive billboard, stroking his goatee and smoking his pipe. Thomas would try to breathe and relax, but in his mind Ben would hop into a cab and shout: *Madman! Heretic!*

Minutes after the gong sounded and the session ended with the usual clap, Paloma joined Thomas and Talia as they put on their shoes in the foyer. "You seemed distracted today, Thomas," Paloma said, slipping on his clogs. "Mind if I ask what's on your mind?"

"You can ask," Thomas shrugged. "But you don't want to know. Difficult things."

"Try me."

Thomas just shook his head.

Talia looked up from her shoes. "Existential angst," she volunteered on Thomas' behalf. "The problem of suffering. The end of the world. Disturbing family secrets. Bad uncles. Goatees and pipe smoke. That kinda stuff."

"Don't doubt it, with an uncle like yours," commented Paloma. "By the way, what--"

"Ready?" Magda, Paloma's wife, burst in from the student union hallway, dressed for walking. Her scarf was snug around her neck and her sculpted head was covered against the cold. "Oh." She paused, noticing the mood. "Sorry. Did I interrupt something?"

"Heavy things," Talia said, lacing up her green high tops. "For Thomas."

"Seminary can do that," commented Paloma. "If you're doing it right, studying religion brings up more questions than answers."

"My questions are the dark kind," said Thomas, grabbing his fleece jacket. "Not really fit for polite society."

"Politeness has never been my strong suit," commented Paloma.

Thomas laughed. "I've noticed."

"I'll take that as a compliment," Paloma smirked. "Anyway, dark questions don't usually disturb me. Had a few of my own." He turned to Magda and kissed her a greeting. Paloma then slipped out of his scarlet kimono and put on a black leather jacket over a white t-shirt. "Thomas, I don't want to sound like a corny coach on a TV after-school special, but..."

"But what?" The younger man stood up from the bench, impatient to go.

"Do you want to talk about it? You sound like you're in a hard place." Paloma caught Talia's eye while Thomas' back was to him. She nodded encouragement. "Magda and I are going to get a bite at *Tolstoi's Tea House*. You two should join us. My treat."

"That same place where we drenched you?"

Magda nodded. "We can walk and talk," she said. "Been in some dark spots myself."

Thomas looked over at his girlfriend, questioning, and Talia shrugged. "Why not?" she said with a winning smile. "Paloma sounds like he might even act nice today."

"Okay then, you're on," Thomas said. "Hopefully not so rainy this time. I'll bring enough gloom."

- - - - -

They left the brick of the seminary campus and hit the bustling thoroughfare of Claremont Street. Navigating traffic, they began the long walk to the cafe. Paloma and Magda led, while the younger couple trailed behind on the tight, busy sidewalk.

"Your plans the same for Thanksgiving?" Magda said over her shoulder to Talia. "Still going to Portland?

"Yep," the younger woman responded, coming closer. "Pretty excited for Thomas to meet my family for the first time."

"You excited too, Thomas?" Magda inquired.

"Sure, in a nervous way," Thomas said over the street noise. "But I'm more excited to spend some time with Ed and Mike. I'm psyched to take them to the *Sharing the Table* thing you talked about," he said to Magda. "It's really both free *and* gourmet?"

"That's what my friends tell me," responded Magda. "Night before Thanksgiving. I hope you Rubber Biscuits have a good time."

"Life is too short for small talk," Paloma interrupted, looking over his shoulder. "We could get run over at any moment, still chatting about travel plans. Me, I'm ready for some dark questions."

"And you thought he was going to act nice," Magda whispered loudly behind her.

Paloma slowed so he was side-by-side with Thomas, and the women forged ahead through the oncoming pedestrians. "I'm guessing your dark thoughts have to do with what you wrote for my class assignment?"

Thomas nodded grimly, hands deep in his jacket pockets. "Bingo."

"I think you wrote something like 'most of us die believing we're protected by a loving God.'"

"A nice story," Thomas said tersely. "About an imaginary friend who doesn't exist." He shook his head. "I'm surprised it took me so long to figure it out. Guess I'd just never been exposed to real suffering before."

"Before this summer, you mean."

"Yeah. Before Guatemala."

"You've never told me about what you saw, Thomas. Try me. What was different?"

Thomas looked sideways at his teacher, making sure the man wanted to listen. "Paloma, I'd been to other countries and seen real hunger before. Poverty. But this time I met people whose whole families had been burned alive. Their mothers raped and slaughtered. Babies' heads smashed in, right in front of their eyes."

"No." His teacher's eyes narrowed. "No."

"I met people whose brothers were burned alive in a church," Thomas confirmed. "They were screaming, praying to God to help them. And they fried anyway."

Paloma shook his head. "It's hard to believe in a caring God after facing something like that."

"No shit." Thomas looked away. "And to think I almost became a pastor."

They walked. After a while, Paloma spoke. "So you're done with Christianity?"

"Yeah," Thomas responded. He kicked a stone off the sidewalk. "At least I thought so."

"Tell me," Paloma said patiently.

"I want to be done with it," Thomas said, his mouth a tight line. "But it's not done with me."

"Tell me what you mean."

Thomas didn't answer. Talia, listening from ahead, broke in softly. "Thomas just found out he has an ancestor who predicted God would come to end the world in 1923."

"Seriously?" Magda and Paloma said together, looking at him. Thomas nodded. "Do tell."

After Thomas gave silent approval, Talia provided more. "Turns out his great-grand uncle was a preacher who formed a commune in Arkansas. He convinced a bunch of true believers to sell everything they owned and come live there, waiting for God to come."

Paloma arched an eyebrow at Thomas. "You *just* found this out now? Seventy years later?"

"It'd been a family secret until I stumbled upon it by accident a little while ago." Thomas twisted his lips. "Turns out my uncle Ben had convinced the family to bury it."

"Your uncle Ben?" asked Paloma, stopping in the middle of the sidewalk. They had already traveled several blocks from the seminary, but when Paloma pointed to the sky, the others knew he was pointing to the billboard back at campus. "*The* Uncle Ben?"

"Yup. He made everybody else in the family promise to never speak about it."

"This Ben's turning out to be one interesting man," Paloma said with a half smile. "Having an ancestor like that could be... inconvenient for him."

"No shit."

"Didn't you say Ben himself preaches all the time about God coming?"

Thomas nodded. "Yeah, his *Millennial Harvest* gig. He tours up and down the West Coast ranting about Jesus returning. Ben doesn't say *when* the end of the world will happen precisely. It keeps everybody on their toes."

"Smart business move to not set a date," mused Paloma. "Sounds like he's learning from your poor ancestor."

"No doubt." Thomas, a step ahead at this point, suddenly threw out his hands and turned around. "Why does everyone keep thinking God is going to come and rescue his chosen people?" He gave a harsh laugh. "More than that, why is everyone sure that *they're* the chosen ones?"

Talia gently spun him around and pushed him forward. "Food. We're going to get some food."

"Ben would have a lot to lose if people knew he had a crackpot preacher for a relative," observed Paloma. "An ancestor in the 1920's who predicted the end of the world, just like he's doing now? He'd lose a lot of credibility. People might think he had a genetic disorder."

"Maybe he *does* have a disorder," Talia interjected. "Guess what he sent his favorite nephew?"

Thomas rolled his eyes. "Tal, c'mon."

"A personally-signed invitation to attend *Bible Before Bones!*" she crowed.

"How thoughtful," said Magda, eyes amused. "Your own backstage pass. Was he really thinking you might come?"

"He must've sent the invite the day before he met me at the seminary," Thomas said with a bitter smile. "Back when he thought I was still saveable."

"This *Bible Before Bones* thing is like a concert tour, a big ol' West Coast orgy of fundamentalism," Talia added. "They've got dates booked in three cities along the coast." She looked over mischievously. "Thomas, you missed LA, but you can still go to the one in Portland when we're there for Thanksgiving."

"That would be rich," Paloma laughed. He turned abruptly to Thomas. "Actually, you should go. Surprise him!"

"Tempting," said Thomas. "Not."

"Why?" inquired Paloma.

"You serious?" Thomas halted and stared at Paloma. "Joining thousands of fundie-zombies worshipping my uncle up on stage?" He started walking again. "I get a rash just thinking about it."

Magda gave him a sly glance. "If I know Horace Cavanaugh, you *do* have an extreme religious event to attend for your *Faith & Fanaticism* course."

"Oh my God, Thomas, this would be perfect!" Talia said.

"A perfect nightmare," Thomas growled.

"Just imagine the boldness of it," Paloma said. "Go undercover, take notes, surprise your uncle backstage."

"I'm imagining the *creepiness* of it," Thomas muttered. "Who'd be the stalker then?"

"I *dare* you to go backstage." Paloma stopped in the middle of the busy sidewalk and looked right at Thomas. "Interview Ben for your class. Get to see what's behind the man. I guarantee you'll learn something unexpected about extreme Christianity."

"I don't get it!" Thomas blurted. "Why the obsession with my uncle Ben?"

"He fascinates me," Paloma answered, walking again. "Maybe yin and yang, like you said."

"I think you should go," Talia said. "You've been needing a recharge lately. Maybe your soul *does* need a good saving."

"Yeah. Maybe all you need is an altar call to set you on the right track," said Paloma.

"A little conversion experience," offered Magda.

"Fuck you all very much," said Thomas. He snorted. "Maybe you guys are right. My soul does need a little cheering up, that's for sure. I'm just not going to get it from one of his stadium events."

After a few steps he looked at Paloma. "Knowing the truth underneath a happy lie really sucks sometimes. I miss being so sure about everything."

One by one, the four crossed a busy street. As they regrouped on the other side, Magda changed the subject. "So, as we were saying before my husband outlawed small talk, Thanksgiving Break's coming up in what...three days?"

"I'm psyched," said Tal. "We've told you our plans. What are you two up to for Thanksgiving?"

"Nothing much," Magda said, looking at Paloma. "We'll probably stay close to home. Eat some good food and give thanks with some friends at the Catholic Worker house. And you--after Portland, where are you guys traveling? You said you're headed different directions, yes?"

"Yeah," Thomas replied. "Tal's got to get to an Outward Bound climbing trip in Arizona, so she's driving all the way to Prescott," Thomas responded. "Me, I'm flying straight back to the Bay Area to squeeze in a wild goose chase before classes start back up."

"How wild? And what goose?" Paloma asked.

"I have a meeting with Cavanaugh on the first of December when I get back. But right after, I'm taking a three day-blitz to Tucson before classes start back up." Thomas glanced at Paloma. "Want to come on a road trip?"

"What's in Tucson?" his meditation teacher inquired.

"The wild goose. A guy named Paul Silas. He's the only person who ever wrote a paper about my ancestor, and I want to talk to him. You know what's weird? He used to go to BATU."

"Former seminary student?" Paloma inquired.

"Yeah. Turns out my uncle Ben knows him—he kept calling Ben for information when he did his thesis on my ancestor seven years ago. He's my only lead right now, and I think he's in Tucson. I only have a few days to find him, and not a lot to go on, so it's a risk. But it'll be good. I always like road trips in the desert."

Talia waited a minute. "He's not your *only* lead," she reminded her boyfriend. "Remember the box."

"What box?" Paloma asked.

The four came to a plaza were they could walk as a group. Thomas described for Paloma and Magda his initial visit with his Grandmother in Walnut Creek and her promise to deliver more information. "Her package came what, ten days ago, Tal?"

"Yeah, we just about tripped over the package when we came home," Talia remembered, nodding. "The box was a gold mine of papers and correspondence. A bulging butcher-paper wrapped shoebox stuffed with news clippings, photos, articles from magazines, all kinds of stuff."

"Remarkable, really," added Thomas. "My grandmother kept everything she found, even though she had promised Ben she wouldn't talk about it. It was like a jumbled secret scrapbook of all types of things, all detailing the life and thought of Josiah Adam Whidman. In addition to keeping a bunch of Josiah's own writings and evangelical pamphlets, Grandmother also kept a lot of articles about the community itself."

"How did the community begin?" said Paloma. "Tell me a little."

"At first it was pretty cool," Thomas began. They'd walked twelve blocks already, and they were finally in the home stretch to reach *Tolstoi's Tea House*. "Josiah called the community the *Faithful Remnant*. He founded it with his brothers in Gilman, Arkansas right around 1920, and it stayed together four years. It was right on the Buffalo River, and they'd share common meals, take hikes together and help build each other's houses. People seeking something better would give up everything and come join. After a while it grew to 250 people. They'd build handcrafted furniture, sew leather shoes, and run a printing press, praising their God and waiting for the big Second Coming."

"What happened to the community when the prediction didn't happen?"

"That's what I've been trying to find out," Thomas responded. "But no luck so far. I'm guessing people just left, one by one. They probably lost faith and disbanded once God pulled a no-show."

"And Josiah?"

"The news articles say he went nuts. He fell apart when everything else fell apart." He shook his head. "Fascinating."

"Why?"

"Why what?"

"Why's it fascinating to you?" Paloma asked. "Is Josiah's betrayal part of what you're wrestling with?"

Images flashed uninvited in Thomas' mind: Flames, babies broken on the stones, people and horses screaming, a church afire. A man nailed to a cross two thousand years ago, abandoned. Josiah Whidman, alone on a barren hill at his Arkansas commune. All of them crying out to a silent sky: *Why have you forsaken me?*

"Maybe," said Thomas. Suddenly, he stopped in his tracks. Tears were flowing down his face.

Paloma turned on the sidewalk, cars passing in a frantic blur just inches away. "What is it, Thomas? What's wrong?"

"Josiah."

"What about him?"

"He didn't just have a breakdown. I just found out he spent his last thirty years in a fucking mental institution!" Thomas gazed at the frenzied traffic whizzing by, tears in his eyes. "Is that what happens, Paloma? Is that what happens when everything you counted on turns out to be a lie?"

30 JUST THE RIGHT TIME

"Try not to get grease on the car seats, dear."

Wrists, don't fail me now, prayed Thomas as he nudged the huge aluminum roasting pan toward the back of Helen Simmons' station wagon. Splashing gravy around the family car would not be the best "new boyfriend" impression he could make. Neither would revealing how hungover he was. *Eleven is still too early for skilled turkey handling after a night with the Rubber Biscuits.* He and Talia had arrived at Helen Simmons' home yesterday after driving up from the Bay Area, then after a few hours, Thomas excused himself to meet Mike and Ed at McMuddleman's Pub. It had been a late night, and now, balancing a gravy-filled platter under the eyes of his girlfriend's mother, he needed to be at the top of his game.

Together, he and Talia manhandled the turkey out of the car, across the icy downtown sidewalk and toward the entrance to Portland's Catholic Worker Community Center. The heavy institutional door threatened to slam closed in the blustery wind, so Helen Simmons propped it open with a coffee can filled with sand and cigarette butts. In their winter coats and gloves, Thomas and Talia entered with the monstrous, foil-covered turkey balanced between them.

Coming in from the bone-chilling grittiness of downtown in winter, the entry room of the Portland Catholic Worker House was a sanctuary. Its cracked linoleum and plywood walls were an oasis of warmth.

"We were only outside for maybe two minutes, from the car to the door," commented Thomas to Talia, chilled to the core. "How can anyone survive out there overnight?"

"It's not easy," said a throaty, cigarette-damaged voice.

The three newcomers turned to see a stringy, weather-beaten woman sporting an apron and a hairnet. "Bringing a turkey for the food drive, are ya?" she said with a broad smile.

Helen Simmons stepped forward in her Bloomingdale's wool coat. "With oyster stuffing and cranberries, just like ours," she said proudly.

"That's what I'm talking about! No second rate bird here. Somebody's family is gonna be pretty happy," said the aproned kitchen worker, with a wink of her blue mascara. She opened her arms wide.

Thomas panicked for a moment, temporarily unsure if the woman wanted a hug or a turkey with those open arms of hers. He opted for bringing forth the turkey. To his relief, this appeared to be her intention as well. She peeked under the tinfoil, sniffed, and grunted with approval.

"Now that's a bird," she said. Helen Simmons beamed. The kitchen worker tucked the foil back and moved toward some double doors. "Since you young ones are already carryin' it, follow me on back to the cafeteria."

Carrying the turkey pan between them like the ark of the covenant, Thomas and Talia followed the woman down a long corridor, passing several office doors on their way to the kitchen. They were already moving through the kitchen's swinging doors before something they saw back in the hallway hit them both.

"Was that who I think it was?" Talia blurted. "No way."

Sharing a glance, Thomas and Talia deposited the turkey on the nearest kitchen table without a word, and bolted back through the double doors into the hallway.

Thomas and Talia peeked in an open office door they'd passed earlier. Within, a small group of people were holding hands in a circle. A bald, olive-skinned woman in a dark pea-coat stood with her back to them.

The group released their hands and began to break up. A graying, dignified black man in a blazer and scarf spoke. "Let's do it, people. Remember, this is how solidarity happens. And solidarity is the building block for revolution...a revolution of relationship."

The woman in the pea coat turned and reached for her wool cap hung on a nearby chair. She caught Talia and Thomas staring in through the open doorway.

"Magda?" Thomas said in utter disbelief. "You didn't say you were going to be here!"

The woman's face broke into wonder. "Well, I didn't exactly say I wasn't, either!" She approached. "You two have a habit of stumbling into people at just the right time, don't you?" Her open arms enfolded them, and her delighted laugh rang through the hallway. "Clarence, come here!"

The elder African-American man who'd led the small group took off his tortoise-shell spectacles and came over. "Clarence Washington, at your service," he said in a deep baritone with a warm smile. "Who do we have here?"

"Meet Talia and Thomas, our friends from Oakland I told you about. Stephen's their meditation teacher." Thomas exchanged a quick glance with Talia. *She told him about us?* "They're visiting Portland for the Thanksgiving holiday, and I mentioned we might see them at *Sharing the Table* tomorrow night. They're here because..." Magda paused, laughed. "Why *are* you here?"

"Here in Portland?" asked Thomas, confused.

"No. Here. Today. Standing in front of me in the hallway of the Catholic Worker two days before Thanksgiving."

"Turkey," explained Talia. "My mom was supposed to deliver a turkey today for the Thanksgiving food drive. She needed help carrying the thing." She looked back toward the kitchen. "We just walked down this hall with the bird, and saw you in this office. Right now my mom's in the kitchen, probably wondering where we went."

"Funny how the universe brings people together," Magda said with a gleam in her eye. "Didn't think I'd see you guys until *Off The Vine* tomorrow night. But here you are."

By now Thomas had regained his composure. "That explains *us*. But why are *you* here?"

Magda looked at Clarence. "Just brewing up some holy mischief with some old friends."

"You made it sound like you were staying in Oakland over the holiday," said Talia accusingly.

"I said I'd stay close to home, and eat some good food with some of my Catholic Worker friends, remember? This is one of my best." Magda grabbed Clarence's arm. "This is the guy who saved me from the streets."

"And now, you better save *me* from being late," said Clarence, extricating himself. "Excuse me, I have to be at the microphone in about two minutes."

"What's going on?" asked Thomas.

Magda threw a glance at Clarence's back as he walked down the hallway. "Well, now that providence has brought you here, we better run with it," Magda said with a curious smile. She grabbed the hands of the young couple. "This might be a risk, but come on. Let's get your Mom. It's about to start."

31 BLACK COFFEE AND WHITE STYROFOAM

Thomas, Talia and Helen Simmons stood at the back of the crowded cafeteria with Magda. They were shoulder to shoulder with people who looked and smelled like they just came in off the streets. Because they had.

From the back, they watched while Clarence Washington weaved his way underneath long banks of fluorescent lights to the podium set up on the other side of the vast room. Despite the fogged windows and damp warmth of a room filled with a few hundred bodies, Clarence was still bundled up in blazer and scarf, as were most of the ragged individuals gathered. A few had set down bulging backpacks or stuffed shopping bags next to their seats at the long cafeteria tables, while others stood warily at the sides of the room guarding shopping carts filled with their worldly possessions.

Almost everybody was drinking black coffee out of white Styrofoam, the cups cradled tenderly in gloved and cracked hands. The noise of the assembled host was formidable.

"Welcome, my friends," Clarence said loudly from the front podium in an attempt to begin the meeting. The crowd ignored him. He adjusted his glasses, cleared his throat and tried again. "Welcome!"

The few white acoustic tiles that remained in the ceiling of the cavernous space did little good. Clarence tugged on the lapels of his blazer and waited a few seconds for the crowd to settle, but the din continued unabated. He grabbed the microphone and tapped it; the reverberations in the sound system assured him it was working.

"Welcome to the Catholic Worker House of Portland." This time his amplified voice boomed. "I'm Clarence Washington, your neighbor, and a founder of this House." The crowd began to pay attention. "I used to be a professor, but I'll spare you the lecture and get straight to the point: we're here to talk about the event we're doing tomorrow night, *Sharing the Table*." He paused as the crowd quieted, now interested. "Some wealthy people I know said they thought I should schedule this event for another time of the year. They thought nobody would come, it being right before Thanksgiving and all. Rather inconvenient."

He looked around the crowded cafeteria and laughed. "But you all seem to have the time. You're all here today because we promised you free food at a fancy restaurant tomorrow night, ain't that right?"

Shouts of assent issued from the throng, even some clapping. "You got that right, Clarence!" bellowed a heavy-set man standing next to an old shopping cart. "Free meal! Free meal!" someone else yelled from the middle of the cafeteria, laughing, and the chant was picked up briefly. Thomas joined in, but stopped when Talia gave him a warning look. Clarence stood patiently, grinning out at the crowd. As the chant died and the noise began to settle, eager whispers rose from the crowd like steam, like the vapor that hissed from the side wall boiler, struggling to heat the cement-block building on this icy winter afternoon.

"Anything on the menu you want, people!" he said, working the crowd. "*Anything.*"

"Did my sweet little ears hear you right, Clarence?" a tall, gorgeous man with long beaded braids and a puffy pink sweater teased from the back.

"That's right, Rashaun. That's right, brothers and sisters—and not just at any restaurant. It's going to be at *Off the Vine,* one of the finest dining spots in Portland."

Roars emanated from the assembled throng. This time it was Talia who gave a whoop, and Thomas who gave the look.

"It's in your own neighborhood," Clarence Washington continued, "just blocks from here. Tomorrow night, the night before Thanksgiving. You get to order anything on the menu you want."

He waited. Murmurs raced through the crowd. "Our anonymous donor wants you all to have a little taste of heaven." Clarence licked his lips. "New York steak," he whispered sensually into the mike. He moved off the podium and strolled through the eager crowd sitting at packed cafeteria tables, looking a bit to Thomas like an intellectual game show host. "Fresh-caught shrimp with white wine and garlic," Clarence purred. "Velvet Cheesecake. Fettuccine Alfredo. Clams with Pesto." The speaker had them now: all eyes were on him, side conversations stopped. "Anything on the menu you want, all for free," he repeated. "But I have to tell you, there's a catch."

Some grumbling ensued. Glances were exchanged at the long cafeteria tables. Expectancy hung in the air.

"Now most of you know, I'm a religious man."

At this, several amens floated up in the room, but some people looked distinctly uncomfortable. A few got up to leave.

"Now, hold on," Clarence held up his hands. Through sheer force of personality, a dozen people sat back down. "I want to make--"

"You said there wasn't gonna be no convertin'!" an older, sinewy man with bloodshot eyes shouted from the back, furious. Thomas flinched as the man erupted, not ten feet from where he stood. "You all church people is always lyin'! Fuck this!" The old man jumped up, surprisingly spry.

"Please sit down, William," Clarence Washington requested as he strolled back up to the podium. A woman came over to the angry man, who still stood, yes defiant, chest working. "As I promised, there'll be no converting," Clarence continued. "We don't do that here. The catch I was talking about is this: the only way to get a free meal is to tell a stranger who you are."

A bunch of small conversations burst forth at this. Now *other* people looked nervous.

"Anybody ever heard of Martin Luther King, Junior?" Clarence asked the audience. "Anyone heard of Mahatma Gandhi?" A few amens sprung from the crowd. "As I said, I'm a religious man. So were they. Are you going to walk out on them?"

With that, the grumbling quieted a bit. William still stood, the woman hovering beside him, but he stood in one place.

"Martin and Gandhi believed that right relationships could change the world," Clarence continued. "Right relationships—when we turn away from no man or woman, no matter how different they may be. Right relationships—when we treat our neighbors as ourselves." His voice, deep, melodious, washed over the crowd, calming, healing. William eventually sat. Others relaxed back into their seats again.

"This is how we take back our city," Clarence said. "One relationship at a time. The relationships we make tomorrow night at *Off the Vine* might heal a world of division. What might happen if two strangers—two people who come from different worlds--get to know each other tomorrow night?"

"A stalker is born," muttered Helen Simmons to Talia, "that's what. This doesn't sound very safe."

"Maybe it'd stop a mugging!" someone in the back near them shouted.

"Maybe an old lady won't die alone in the cold this winter," an old lady said, voice trembling.

"Maybe a stockbroker won't commit suicide once he sees what real problems are," called out a grizzled Vietnam vet perched against the side wall, leaning heavily on his shopping cart.

"Maybe the park finally gets cleaned up," said a young mom in the front, a hooded baby tucked into her greasy down jacket.

"Maybe I'll get a new boyfriend!" Rashaun crowed, the charms woven into his braids jingling. The gathered crowd laughed.

"Maybe to all of those," Clarence Washington conceded. He pushed his spectacles higher up on his nose. "Miracles can happen, even for you, Rashaun."

The crowd laughed even harder, and some hoots rang out from the back.

"My brothers and sisters, maybe none of these things happen," Clarence continued. "Maybe everyone goes back to life as usual on Thanksgiving. But maybe some will." He paused, and looked straight out at William. "Perhaps, because of this event, this town might gain a little more connection, a little more compassion. Because a few hundred people come to know each other in new ways, maybe a robbery gets stopped, or a junkie gets help, or a kid gets a better education. Maybe some new insulation finally gets put into those row houses on 34th."

At this, a small cheer rose from one table of senior citizens. Clarence gave them a wink. "*Sharing the Table* is about right relationship, my friends. Sure, one meal isn't going to change the world. It might not change America. But it just might change Portland."

32 SCRAPE AWAY THE GOLD & LAQUER

Thomas couldn't stop staring.

"Blessed are the poor in spirit, for theirs is the kingdom of God," the figure seated next to him read from the onion-skin pages in a breathy voice. Absorbed in the text, Rashaun flipped his long ebony braids, the stiletto heel of his right foot dangling unconsciously below crossed legs in fishnets and a mini-skirt. A faux-ermine stole graced his neck above a pink cashmere sweater. Looking up, he smiled coyly behind dark lips when he caught Thomas staring. "That's Matthew 5:3. Did you want me to go farther, Big C?"

"No thanks, Rashaun, that's all just now." Clarence Washington turned his gaze to encompass the group of six others in his tiny office, joining him in a circle of donated chairs. "Most of you know, but that's the first Beatitude, folks. That's the kickoff phrase of Jesus' core teachings, what we call the Sermon on the Mount."

Well, this is a more diverse bible study than I ever had with Uncle Ben, thought Thomas. He looked from side to side. *Caught between cross-dressers and criminals.* Though the people were fascinating, Thomas didn't feel like sitting through a scripture study. *Why won't Christianity leave me alone?* He'd thought this was a planning session, not a come-to-Jesus meeting.

Fifteen minutes ago, when Thomas and Talia were walking out of the big cafeteria gathering, Magda had suggested they stay for a follow-up meeting. She'd said it would be a small group session for some of the organizers of *Sharing the Table.* Thomas and Talia had assumed it was about the nuts and bolts of planning tomorrow night's dinner, which seemed like a cool event, so they decided to stay. They sent Helen Simmons home in the family wagon, saying they'd take the bus later.

But when the Bibles cracked open a few minutes ago, it dawned on Thomas that this was a meeting of an entirely different sort.

In addition to Thomas and Talia, the small group consisted of Clarence and Rashaun, Magda, an older street guy named Charlie and a young Hispanic woman named Maria. Thomas remembered Maria as the mom up front who spoke during the cafeteria meeting, the one with an infant bundled inside her soiled down parka. Now, in the circle, Maria nursed the baby boy and hummed softly, the hood of her jacket covering her dark hair and most of her features.

Thomas caught himself staring again, but not at the nursing mother. He'd never been this close to a transvestite before. Rashaun's enameled fingernails were toying with one of his braids as he continued to read the passage silently to himself.

"You've probably heard the Beatitudes more than a few times in your life," Clarence continued.

"So much that I never thought about it." Charlie, a grizzled man with close-cut white frizzy hair, scratched at a burn scar that drew an angry pink line across the dark skin of his cheek and brow. "S'funny how such a radical phrase can become so familiar."

"Tell us what you mean, Charlie," prompted Clarence.

"'Blessed are the poor in spirit; they've got the kingdom of God.' That's revolutionary. But it's so familiar, it becomes ignored. Like wallpaper. Always there, but you never think about it." His voice grated on Thomas' ear. "All those pompous rich Christian politicians think they got it together, and their own boss is telling them it's the poor in spirit who got it right."

Something must've happened to his larynx, thought Thomas. His voice sounded like his throat had rocks in it.

"You know what's even more shocking, Charlie?" Clarence replied.

"What?"

"Matthew softened the message."

"What d'you mean?" Thomas was surprised to hear the words come out of his own mouth. *Don't want to be here,* he reminded himself. *I'm done with the Bible. Let them have their thing.*

"Matthew made it easier to swallow. Scholars think that Luke's version of the Beatitudes is closer to the real thing." Clarence borrowed Rashaun's Bible and flipped from Matthew to the Gospel of Luke. "See," he said, referencing a line with his finger. "Luke leaves the hard words as Jesus probably spoke them originally: '*How blessed are you who are poor; you have the kingdom of God.*' The text in Luke also says: '*Alas for you who are rich.*'"

"Fuckin' A," responded Charlie. "Luke was a Marxist."

"No, he was a follower of the Jesus Way. Jesus ushered in a new social order he called the kingdom of God. In God's new society, strangers treated each other like family. Shared tables. Shared resources. Shared lives. In this kind of society, capitalism isn't possible and Marxism isn't necessary." Clarence Washington held out his hands. "Luke's message wasn't communist, but something far more empowering: Jesus told the poor they were the privileged ones in God's kingdom, which was already here. He turned the tables."

"Being poor don't feel too privileged to me," said Maria, cradling her baby under her jacket.

"Jesus was speaking to the poor, and they couldn't believe it either," said Clarence. "But he declared it anyway. Notice in both versions he speaks in the present tense: In Luke, he says the poor *have* the kingdom of God already; in Matthew he says the poor in spirit are blessed because the kingdom of God *is already theirs.*" Clarence looked around at his small group. "Present tense. Jesus is saying, 'you are the radically free ones *now.* He's saying the rich—the ones who are worried about protecting, defending, hoarding, advancing, chasing after so many things—they're the trapped ones. Jesus turns the value system of Empire on its head."

Fuzzy-haired Charlie rubbed the scar on his face and flipped to Luke in his own Bible, a dog-eared, black faux-leather affair with lots of highlighting, and started reading to himself. Thomas noted that the words "Portland Correctional Facility" were embossed in gold print down the spine of Charlie's Bible. Bookmarks sprouted randomly out from between its many gold-edged pages like mismatched straws. *This dude probably has some stories to tell,* guessed Thomas.

"Let's contrast his audience with Matthew's," Clarence suggested. "Matthew led a middle-class community--folks who probably had good jobs in the business community and the defense industry."

Charlie laughed. "If he was in *that* kind of community, no wonder he didn't use the word *poor.* His audience would've walked." He smirked. "Matthew wimped out."

"Nah," Clarence disagreed. He pushed his spectacles up to the bridge of his nose. "He just met his audience where they could hear him, Charlie. The truth is still there: to be poor in spirit means to live without the need to be better than others. To not think you deserve more than everyone else."

"That boy knew what he was doing," observed Rashaun.

Clarence nodded. "Matthew knew that if you're truly poor in spirit, it won't be long before you're poor. When you're poor in spirit, you make sure everyone else gets as much as you do, 'cause you're not any better than they are. You know that radical sharing is the only way to live." The retired professor paused. "But I want to get back to something important. Back up a minute, Rashaun, and read us the start of Chapter 5."

Rashaun's long nails traced the sentences back to the beginning of the chapter. "Now when he saw the crowds, he went up on a mountainside and sat down. His disciples came to him, and he began to teach them--"

"Okay," Clarence broke in. "Is this just an introduction to get to the important stuff of the Beatitudes, or does it say something?"

"Says something," Maria said from under her hood. "Says he hiked up away from the crowds."

"And his disciples followed for a teach-in," observed Rashaun. "Private lesson."

"Exactly," Clarence agreed. "This is important. Sometimes we overlook it. Jesus didn't reveal all his teachings to everyone. He shared his core teachings—his harder truths—with only his inner circle."

"Never noticed that before," admitted Charlie.

"Most people aren't ready for hard truths. Jesus only shared his hard truths with people who had already chosen to walk the Way. People who had done deep personal work."

"What kind of personal work?" Talia asked. Thomas was relieved she did, because he'd been wanting to ask the same question. At this point he kind of wanted to stay.

"The Gospels don't dwell a lot on the spiritual formation that people went through to become disciples,"said Clarence, glancing at Magda. "But they clearly underwent radical life-change. Testing, emptying and rebirth as a kingdom person. A first step for any follower of the rabbi Jesus was to walk away from the traps of security, family, and reputation."

"Modern Christianity seems so tame," confessed Talia. "But following Jesus was radical back in the day, wasn't it? For the establishment, following him would've been like cultural suicide."

"Girl, you're right on." Rashaun leaned forward in his pink sweater and put a hand on Talia's knee. "The disciples were Jesus' posse. They had to leave everything behind. Way different than how it is now, honey. Why, these days people think they're following Jesus when they put a fish sticker on their BMW." Rashaun rolled his eyes, disgusted. He sat back and stretched like a panther, his long legs encased in fishnets. "You can't just change your bumper sticker. You have to change your life. Imagine: those boys with Jesus on the mountainside probably came from good families. They left their identities to follow the Man."

"And they left their possessions," grated Charlie. He too now faced Talia, his burn scar blotchy and pink in his animated face. "They were free, man.

Hardcore. They ate whatever the universe gave 'em and slept where a bed was offered. Didn't carry much but a cloak. Homeless, we'd call 'em."

"That's right," Clarence nodded. "They were an affront to everything respectable. The Roman Empire didn't know what to do with them. How could they be controlled? They had nothing to protect. Nothing left to lose. These were the people that Jesus was teaching."

"They were *pobres,*" said Maria, getting it. She smiled. "Poor ones like us. The ones who society says are down and out."

"Exactly, Maria," Clarence said. She beamed. "Let's be clear: if a man is judged by the company he keeps, then Jesus didn't win any homecoming contests. He was spat on by polite society. What else can we say about someone who surrounded himself with scum and criminals?" Clarence smiled at Charlie, who returned a wide grin. Thomas could now see the man had four teeth missing in a row in his left upper jaw. *Don't sign up for Portland Correctional Facility's dental plan,* thought Thomas. Clarence continued: "He didn't just hang out with criminals, but also beggars, prostitutes, and lepers."

"Cross-dressers?" asked Rashaun.

"They would've been welcome," Clarence laughed. "Tax collectors and peasants, the unclean and the demon-possessed. The poor and the landless."

"Worse than that."

All heads looked toward Thomas. Self-conscious, he continued. "When Matthew and Luke report that Jesus said 'Blessed are the *poor,*' they both use the Greek word *ptochoi.* This word didn't just mean poor peasants. It literally meant 'the very empty ones, those who are crouching.' The bent-over beggars."

"Impressive." Clarence was looking at Thomas in a new light. "'Those who are crouching,'" the professor mused, trying on the definition. "With that rendering, I almost *feel* their poverty." He addressed the group. "Whether they were poor or poor in spirit, Jesus hung out with them all. This was a man who knew what it was like to live on the outside: his parents were unwed, his disciples were unschooled, and his authority certainly did not come from the establishment. When we scrape away the gold and lacquer put on him by Christendom," Clarence said, "we're left with a man who dwelt with society's underbelly—the desperate, the despised, the dismissed, the disrespected and the disposable."

"So he never separated himself from others," Maria said. "He saw all those people as family." She adjusted her infant inside her shirt.

"And you know what?" Clarence asked the group. "He embraced them as citizens of the new kingdom. He didn't require them to change before he'd talk with them or eat with them. Messed up as they were, he treated them as sons and daughters of God. And as he did, they changed. They blossomed."

"Can I add something here?" The voice was Magda's, who until now had been silent. "I was disposable once." She looked around the small group. "Like those *ptochoi*. I came here—right here-- twenty years ago as a strung out street kid. The Catholic Workers found me and took me in, no questions asked. More nights than not, I'd sell myself for a chance to get high." She looked at Maria, who was staring at her intently. "Clarence didn't try to change me. He just gave me some food and some safety." She pointed three rooms down the linoleum hallway, toward the kitchen, to a peeling green door. "He gave me a room, right down that hall."

"That's where I live," Maria said in a soft voice.

"I saw the crib through the window," Magda said with a kind smile. "When I arrived, I was one of those 'unworthy poor' that nice church people can't stand. The kind who would rather say 'fuck you' than 'thank you.'" She shook her head. "You weren't going to get me anywhere near a group of sober people, much less anything to do with God."

"Hell yeah," said Charlie, nodding. "Been there. That was me, just two years ago."

"My attitude didn't matter to Clarence and his crew," Magda continued. "Just rolled off their backs. They kept loving me, helping me. Letting me be a wounded wild animal when I needed to be." She shrugged. "And after a while, I didn't need to be a wild animal so much anymore."

"Hear that," said Charlie, nodding. "I healed too. On my own, with God. With Clarence some, too." He looked across the circle at his mentor. "But I healed when it was my time. Nobody told me I had to. God and Clarence just kept waiting, 'til I was ready."

Nobody said anything for a few moments. The circle sat still, digesting Magda's story, Charlie's story. Thinking of their own.

"Amen," said Clarence after a short while. "Thanks for those words, sister," he said to Magda. "Sometimes it's nice to know your life has made a difference for somebody."

"You made a difference for me," Magda replied. "*The* difference." Charlie nodded, too.

"Let's hope tomorrow night we make a difference with *Sharing the Table*," Clarence said, standing up. "Let's give 'em a little bit of an *agape* feast, like the earliest followers of the Way did."

"*Agape?*" Maria questioned, her hidden baby nuzzling her breast, gurgling. "What's that?"

"An *agape* meal means a love feast in Greek," Thomas interjected. "The original body of followers of the Way called themselves an *ekklesia*, which--"

"Like *iglesia* in Spanish?" Maria asked. "Church?"

Thomas realized he was interjecting more than he'd intended. He looked to Clarence to answer.

"Yeah, Maria, I guess it is," Clarence considered. "But not church as building; church as people. *Ekklesia* means the--"

"'The called out ones.'" Thomas bit his lip. "Sorry. I get a little excited about ancient Greek."

Magda made a startled noise. Clarence couldn't hide his surprise either, and looked at Magda. "Thomas, most scholars today translate *ekklesia* as 'the assembled ones.' Why did you say *called out ones?*"

"These earliest groups weren't just about assembling," Thomas explained. "They were also about separating. Jesus called out his disciples from their families, from the Roman empire and the Jewish hierarchy."

"That's right," Clarence confirmed. "Jesus' followers were called out to a new kind of kinship network. They shared everything in common. That's where the *agape* meal comes in: the early followers had love feasts, where everyone in the new family brought things and shared what they had."

"And that's what we're going to do tomorrow night at *Sharing the Table*?" Rashaun wondered, bringing the conversation back to the present.

"In our own way. The food will be provided. We'll share ourselves."

"How many people are planning to come?" asked Charlie.

Clarence looked to Maria for the current total. The young mother reached down to pick up a rumpled piece of lined paper from under her chair. "After today's cafeteria meeting, let's see...." She looked to the bottom of a column of numbers. "348 have reserved seating tickets so far."

"Reserved seating?" said Thomas, startled. "I thought this was a first-come first-serve thing. The flyer said just show up—first five hundred free."

"Last will be first," Clarence said. "Everybody who wants to come will be able to get in. But some of the folks arriving by private car or taxi may have to wait a bit. We're going to honor the street folk who walk up to the door on foot. Don't want 'em to catch cold." He winked. "Don't look so surprised," Clarence said, reading Thomas' face. "Most of these people have never had a reserved seat in their lives. Never been treated special. These are the crouching ones Jesus was talking about."

With those words, Clarence Washington stood up. "Jesus had a vision in which everyone was welcome at the table, my friends. He called this vision the kingdom of God. And on the night before Thanksgiving, we're going to put this vision into practice in Portland, right under the nose of Empire." Everyone else started to stand too, so Thomas followed their example. He was startled, but didn't pull away when Maria and Charlie took his hands. The seven individuals became a closed circle.

"This kind of thing is contagious, folks." Conviction gleamed from Clarence's eyes. "Maybe *Sharing the Table* will be nothing but a big party. That'll be fine enough. Hundreds of people will be fed, kept warm on a freezing night."

"*Gracias a Dios,*" murmured Maria.

Clarence looked around the circle. "But maybe it'll spread like leaven in the loaf, like a torch that gets passed through the streets. Tomorrow night, Portland's going to get a taste of what the kingdom of God is all about."

33 IN THE COMPANY OF OLD FRIENDS

Mike, Ed and Thomas burst into a familiar scene of warmth, noise and good smells when they entered the doors of McMuddleman's pub later that same evening. Like so many other times over the years, it seemed that half of the college population of Portland was here tonight.

At first, no seats were available in the entire place, so the trio stood near the pub's busy entrance. Thomas entertained himself during the wait by scanning the walls. The wood-paneled entryway was plastered with all types of announcements—for massages, concerts, house sitting and book signings—and the counter tops near the front door were filled with stacks of flyers.

A familiar stack of neon orange sheets decorated with green vines caught Thomas' eye. The flyer looked just like the one Magda printed earlier today at the Catholic Worker. He grabbed a sheet and showed it to his friends.

"Hey boyos--we're going to this tomorrow night," Thomas declared decisively. He held the neon announcement aloft and read aloud to the other Rubber Biscuits over the noise of the pub:

Come experience Abundance on November 21st,
the Day before Thanksgiving from 5-10pm:

Sharing the Table

an urban mixer culinary event highlighting the great
new feel of Portland's re-energized downtown
business and residential district.

211

BRING A FRIEND! MEET A FRIEND!

This adventure in fine dining will be held at the five-star Off the Vine restaurant, masterminded by internationally-renowned chefs.

Brought to you by gracious donors and the Catholic Worker House of Portland

"*Que interesante*," commented Ed. "You know I'm a sucker for the finer things in life."

"Sounds pricey," said Mike in contrast. "Why go to that, instead of burgers at McMuddleman's like we always do?"

"Take a walk on the wild side, whitebread," Ed joked. "What, you only wear one pair of underwear, too?"

"This thing is gonna be awesome," Thomas said, slapping the flyer on Mike's head. "Some friends in Berkeley told me about it, and said it's an event we shouldn't miss." Thomas tried to sound casual. "And this is the best part, Mikey: *'free fine dining for the first five hundred participants.'*" Mike pulled the flyer from his forehead, unconvinced.

"Five hundred free diners, Mikey!" Thomas pointed at the line at the bottom of the announcement. "That's a heck of a lot of people who would have to beat us. We'll be eating free, boys!"

"Then I'm in," Mike said, suddenly enthusiastic. Ed nodded his assent.

"It's decided then!" Thomas exclaimed, giving high fives to a grinning Mike and Ed. "The Rubber Biscuits shall descend upon *Off the Vine* to thanksgive before Thanksgiving."

A hostess came over with a smile, and led them through the crowd to a comfortable booth.

Looking up at the chalkboard for the pub's specials, Thomas noticed a turkey Reuben was the sandwich of the day. Suddenly his mind went back to this morning. *Was it only this morning they'd dropped off the turkey? Was it only a few hours ago when he joined in a homeless rally and had studied Scripture with cross-dressers and criminals?* The Catholic Worker House was only three miles away on Burnside, but sitting here in McMuddleman's with his friends, it felt like another world.

"Wait a minute," Ed said, bringing Thomas back to the present. "Rewind. T. Did you really just say *thanksgive* a minute ago?"

"I did," Thomas said with pride. "I predict it'll be next year's big verb. Very 1993."

"Trendsetter," said Mike.

"You are the master of the makeup," Ed marveled. "*Thanksgive.* I'll try that. What about *to halloween?*"

Thomas shook his head. "Sounds painful. Keep trying, Ed. There's an art to making shit up, and I'm the freaking master."

The trio laughed. Mike laughed longest. "The art of making shit up," Mike repeated acidly, drawing on his brew. "You are indeed the master." He wasn't laughing now. "I'm just gonna jump into it, T, since we're back in our old testing grounds. You've been making up your own rules for a while now, and it's time to stop."

"Oooooh," Ed gasped. "It's a Rubber Biscuits smackdown. Mike, in the conservative arena, lays down the gauntlet."

"Come on, Mike," Thomas said, uncertain. "You're rusty. If you're going to lay out a smackdown, you gotta be specific in your challenge."

"You. And Talia. You're sleeping with her, aren't you?"

Thomas wasn't expecting this. "Sure," he said defensively. "I think I love her, Mike."

"So marry her," Mike countered. "I know it's old school, but so are most things that are right."

Thomas gave a nervous laugh. "We're not ready. We've only been together about six months."

"If you're not ready, then stop sleeping with her. It's against God's rules."

"I'm kind of done with rules," Thomas responded.

"Wow." Mike was stunned. "You actually said it." Thomas started to respond, but Mike cut him off. "Here's the truth, Tommy: for a few years you've been changing, and not in good ways. I've tried to bring you back." He took a drink. "Even talked to Ben about it."

Thomas almost choked on his beer. "About what?"

"About you. Told him I was worried about you drifting away. Last year we got the idea of you coming to Guatemala with us. We thought it could be like old times, bring you back."

"Back to what?" Ed snorted, digging with a toothpick at his large toe. "The Dark Space?"

"To the Church. To Jesus."

"To freeze-dried Christianity, you mean." Ed looked up, right at Mike. "Tommy's seen the world, man. He can't go back to high school in Orange County."

"Guatemala changed me, Mike," Thomas admitted. "But not like you hoped for."

Mike looked perplexed. "What do you mean?"

"I've tried to talk to you and Ben about it." He trailed off.

"You mean when you left us? When you went off with those villagers for days?"

"Yeah." With his eyes, Thomas tried to reach past the beer and the bluster and into the heart of his old friend. "Guatemala made me see some things. A lot of what we've been told about God just isn't true, Mike."

"Like what?"

"God doesn't save good people from harm. People die. Shit happens. And Jesus isn't coming back on a cloud to save us from our problems."

Mike shook his head. "What kind of a God *do* you believe in, then?" he said stiffly.

"I don't know. I'm at sea right now. But I'm pretty sure God doesn't rescue. Or even seem to care."

"Wow, you *have* changed. Do you even call yourself a Christian anymore?"

It was a while before Thomas spoke. "Unclear on that one too. I think Jesus himself was filled with God-energy, and tried to bring life-changing love and justice to the world."

"That's a start," snorted Mike.

"So if the justice and love of Jesus are the basis of Christianity, then I'm a Christian. If not, then I guess you can count me out."

Mike took in a breath. "So if a clear command in the Bible is at odds with what you call love or justice, then you'd throw out the Bible rather than alter your judgment?"

"If I was sure, you bet." Thomas didn't hesitate. Not after what he'd seen. As he said the words, though, something inside of him quivered, then broke. He felt freer, bolder. But part of him didn't like the freedom.

"Dangerous ground, Tommy, dangerous ground. You just made yourself God."

"Nah," Ed countered. "He just decided to stop treating the Bible like God."

Mike was about to say something to Ed, then seemed to think better of it. Thomas took advantage of the pause. "I'm not looking outside of myself so much for answers anymore."

"You started talking about this love and justice thing back in college," Mike scowled.

"Senior year in high school, actually," Thomas said. "Letter of James, remember?"

"Whatever, Whid. Some of it made some sense back then. It was biblical. But now you've taken it too far. There's no grounding to it. No authority you respect more than your own opinions." Mike took a drink and wiped his mouth with the back of his hand. "And now, the First United Church of Thomas. Membership: one. Motto: justify whatever you want."

"Mike, I don't want to fight." Thomas' head hurt, and his soul ached, and he just wanted to be real. "Growing up, the church fed us a lot of fear and a lot of lies. I'm trying to find my way out of that, and my relationship with Talia's a big part of finding a better way. I'm just trying to figure out a path that feels life-giving."

"That *feels* life-giving?" Mike mocked. "God didn't say to trust our *feelings*. He said trust His laws. They're called the Commandments. They're pretty clear. Like 'thou shalt not commit adultery."

"I'm done with what humans say are God's rules," Thomas said. "And I'm done with what the church says is right or wrong. Being with Talia feels right, more right than anything I've ever known. I'm going to trust that."

Thomas paused, looked in his drained beer. He felt drained himself. He was mildly surprised when Mike didn't immediately attack. He was even more surprised when Ed said, "You okay, Mike?"

Thomas looked up. Mike was crying. *Crying.* Shoulders shaking, Mike's giant frame hunched over as he cried into his beer. Literally.

Ed and Thomas exchanged glances, at a loss.

Mike finally looked up, eyes red, and wiped his nose with a meaty forearm. "That's what she said. It didn't *feel* full of life anymore." He looked pitiful and ridiculous as he glanced through tears and mucous at both friends.

"Mary?"

Mike nodded. "She's been gone for two weeks. And she took the kids."

34 WHAT WOULD IT LOOK LIKE

"Who else have you talked to about this?" asked Thomas the next evening. Mike, his legs stretched across the back seat of the rental car, seemed not to hear. He was gazing out at the skyline as they crossed the Hawthorne Street Bridge into downtown Portland, towers and high-rises poking into the night sky illuminated with red and green lighting for the holiday season.

Last night after the pub, the trio had returned to their run-down hotel suite at the Days Inn. Mike had stayed up crying for another hour, squatting in his tighty whities on the living room couch. "Said she's lost her sense of self, or something," Mike had snorted. His eyes were red and puffy, his nose dripping. *Never been a good crier,* Thomas thought.

"In my world, people don't just quit when things aren't working perfectly," Mike muttered. "They don't just leave when things get hard." He yawned, bleary-eyed, and scratched himself. "They stay in it, and stick with it. I'm not going to divorce my wife *or* my religion."

Although still not great, Mike looked a lot better now than he had last night on the couch, largely because tonight he was wearing pants. Khakis, even, matched with a dark blazer and dress shoes. The day had passed reasonably well, with only a few crying outbursts, and Mike had surprised the other guys by shaving for the *Sharing the Table* dinner event. Ed, in the passenger seat, sported a linen blazer over a black t-shirt with jeans and checkerboard Vans. Thomas decided on a v-neck brown cashmere sweater and black jeans, mostly because they were the least wrinkled items in his suitcase.

Thomas tried again. "Hey big man!" he said to Mike. "Who else have you talked to about this?"

"No one," Mike mumbled reluctantly. "Just you guys."

Thomas looked into the rear view mirror, shocked. "No one? Why not?"

"Can't tell my friends at home," Mike conceded. In the back seat, he pivoted to hunch close to Thomas and Ed in the front. "They're all...*church* friends."

Ed glanced across at Thomas with a look of confusion. "You talkin' loco, hombre," said Ed, half turning in the passenger's seat. "Don't you have any real friends besides us?"

"All my friends are people from our church," Mike explained. "I can't go anywhere without some sweet Christian mom saying, *'and how's Mary and the kids?'*"

"Well, what do you say back?" Thomas asked.

"Tell 'em the Florida story," Mike sighed. "That Mary's taken the kids for a vacation with Grandma in Boca Raton."

"You *lie?*"

"What am I supposed to say?" Mike countered. "'She's gone, I have no idea why she left me, and I'm all screwed up?'"

"That'd be a good start," commented Ed.

"I think so too," Mike conceded, surprising both Thomas and Ed. His wide face, always a little pasty, was paler than usual in the dim light captured by the rear view mirror. "But you can't say that stuff to church friends," commented Mike. "If I tell them the truth about Mary leaving me, they'll be nice to me, sure. They'll put me on their prayer lists. Bake me casseroles. But I'll suddenly be on the outside. One of *those* people who need our help."

"Ouch," Ed said. "I get it. Feeling broken must be hard in the midst of a bunch of shiny, happy Christians who won't get real." Thomas listened with half of his attention, while the other half scanned the large green freeway signs for the Vine Street off-ramp.

"I know that Christianity has problems, Ed," Mike responded. "But you, you're insane about its failures. It's like the evil empire to you. Why are you so tolerant of everything else, but you can't accept Christianity as it is?"

"Rubber Biscuits smackdown, number two." Thomas grinned as he intoned the ritual. "Mike drops the gauntlet yet again. Ed on the defensive. Ed, your thoughts?"

Ed took the challenge. "I don't have a problem with *Christianity, the original version*," he began. The freeway lamps gave consistent pulses of illumination inside the car, periodically lighting up half of Ed's braided goatee and ponytail as he spoke. "My problem is with *Christianity, the Sequel.* It's how modern Christians *practice* their Christianity that bugs the hell out of me."

"Such as?" Mike asked.

"Such as, did Jesus encourage his followers to judge others?" Ed blurted. "No. Did he tell them to organize special interest groups to persecute people who were different than they were? No siree. He put his body in the line of fire to protect prostitutes. Did he tell his followers to amass personal wealth? Did he tell them to buy a personal mansion and sign their life away in debt? No way."

"Yeah, but—"

"Did he tell them to be all worried about the future, take out large insurance policies, and give their money to their IRAs instead of to the homeless? *Noooo.*"

"You're one of those guys who calls in ranting on talk radio, aren't you?" asked Mike, as Thomas signaled and got into the right lane for the Vine Street off-ramp looming ahead. "I get it. Christianity's pretty imperfect," Mike said from the back seat. "It's been corrupted through most of history. So because of other people's practice of Christianity, you don't want to be associated with it, right?" Unlike some smackdowns, Mike seemed genuinely interested in Ed's perspective.

"Damn straight," Ed replied. "Christianity's got too much of a bad rep. Too many people living poor examples. Don't want to be associated with that kind of crowd."

Coming down the off-ramp, the light ahead turned red, and Thomas slowed the car to a stop. A crowd of pedestrians, dressed for a wintry night out in downtown Portland, braved the intersection in front of them. The light turned green, and Thomas began driving down Vine. They were close, very close.

Mike stuck his head in close to Ed, almost in the front seat. "So you're saying that, if you called yourself a Christian, you'd feel like you were joining the same club as Christopher Columbus, Adolf Hitler, and Jimmy Swaggart?"

"Exactly," responded Ed. "You join a club of crazies when you call yourself Christian."

The deep burgundy neon sign of *Off the Vine* restaurant suddenly emerged out of the darkness on the left side of the street. Despite being early, the trio saw a line of diners already stretching around the block, everyone bundled up against the winter chill. Thomas took the next side street and found a parking place.

Mike continued the conversation as he got out of the car. "But those people aren't good examples of Christianity, Ed. They're people who were living a twisted mockery of what Jesus wanted."

"So are the rest of you!" Ed said. "Don't you get it? There's no actual Christians, just *Christianity, the Sequel.* No examples of the real deal." He got out and talked over the hood to Mike from the other side. "What would authentic Christianity look like, anyway?"

A silence suddenly hung in the chilly air, the quick words bandied about inside the car giving way to quiet thoughts. The trio buttoned up their jackets to traverse the three icy blocks back to the restaurant.

"What would authentic Christianity look like, anyway?" Ed's question made Thomas think of his ancestor, Reverend Josiah Adam Whidman: a relative he hadn't even heard of until a few weeks ago, a man who gathered a group of

true believers to live communally in a utopian rural society founded upon the power of Jesus, living simply and singing hymns and waiting for the appointed day in 1923 when they knew beyond all doubt that their God would come with power.

**Artifact #4: Excerpt from "Fifty Years Ago in America"
column published in *Christianity Today* magazine,
September 1973**

Throughout the centuries of Christian tradition, the prophecies found in the book of
Daniel and the apocalyptic visions contained in Revelation have proved to be
tough nuts to crack. Yet Bible scholars have never hesitated to take a shot at it.
"Numeric" interpreters have abounded, and their efforts – counting the number of
words in certain key passages; counting the number of syllables or letters in
certain key words – have produced some of the most amazing instances of
theological convolution in the history of the planet. Reverend Josiah Adam
Whidman was a pastor and prophet who claimed Biblical prophecy revealed to him
that the end of the world would occur beginning in the year 1923.

It was in 1916 that the Reverend Josiah Adam Whidman "cracked the secrets" of
the Biblical books of Daniel and Revelation. Reverend Whidman, an Arkansas
minister, used numeric techniques based upon the number seven, and determined
that the Second Coming of Christ was imminent. Christ's arrival would happen
sometime in 1923 at the close of a World War between Catholics and Protestants,
and coincide with the destruction of pagan centers and of Roman Catholicism.
According to Whidman's research, these signs were all essential for the Last Days
to commence.

His secret knowledge of impending doom and ultimate salvation caused Reverend
Whidman to found an apocalyptic utopian Christian community called "the Faithful
Remnant" along the banks of the scenic Buffalo River in rural Arkansas in 1921. At
its height in 1922, the Faithful Remnant community boasted over three hundred
residents. They manufactured shoes, built custom furniture, joined together for
housebuildings and barnraisings, milled timber, and grew the majority of their own
food. In addition to meaningful work, they had plenty of time for daily chapel,
chorale singing, hiking, picnics at the river bank and community prayer.

Living a faithful, authentic Christian life was vital to the community; however,
spreading the urgent message of God's coming was even more so. Josiah
Whidman's followers began spreading his theology from their home base at Gilman
through a newspaper called *The Kingdom Harbinger* and by means of
broadcasting his electrifying sermons and radio programs. The message of Josiah
Whidman seemed to reach a significant amount of searching souls throughout the

nation: at its height, 10,000 copies of the *Harbinger* each month were published and distributed, usually via railway. This message seemed to engage readers in a powerful way: in the letters column of the *Harbinger,* enthusiastic missives from more than 400 different subscribers from thirty states were published over a period of four years (1919-23).

– Excerpted from the monthly news column *Fifty Years Ago in America,* written by James L. Swaine, published in <u>Christianity Today</u>, September 1973.

35 THIS WASN'T IN THE FLYER

Once the Rubber Biscuits and a dozen other diners had taken their winter coats to the cloakroom and assembled in *Off the Vine's* front room, the maitre'd began her spiel yet again. The crowded restaurant fairly buzzed with energy, and after twenty minutes of waiting in line, the mouth-watering aromas made it hard for Thomas to concentrate on the woman's words.

"Good evening, and welcome to *Off the Vine,* everyone," the smartly-dressed hostess said gaily, a stack of menus in her arm. "I hope you brought your taste buds and your sense of adventure." She beamed. Thomas started when he realized it was Magda, acting for all the world as if she'd worked the front of the restaurant for years. *When will this woman not surprise me?* She gave him a small wink, and plunged into her talk.

"Tonight we are hosting *Sharing the Table,* an urban mixer celebrating amazing food and the amazing people of Portland. Thanks to a wonderful donor, everything on the menu is free."

"Everything?" said Mike, still unbelieving. Other heads looked around too, unsure of this news that seemed too good to be possible.

"Everything," Magda the hostess confirmed. "You can order anything on our menu and enjoy it absolutely free of charge. Consider it a gift of appreciation from one citizen of the world to another." Astounded, the small crowd murmured with delight as she handed out the menu.

"But there's a catch," Magda said. "This is an urban mixer, and now's the time to mix it up." Faces glanced up from menus, cautious. "Everything

225

about this feast is free," she explained, "as long as you sit only with people you don't know."

The statement caused a stir. Eyes of families and friends darted back and forth, sharing glances. "Portland has a glorious diversity, especially right here in downtown," Magda continued. "Incredible people pass one another everyday on our streets, isolated in their own worlds, not feeling community, not experiencing connection." She paused. "*Sharing the Table* changes this by bringing strangers together over a common meal."

"What? We're supposed to eat with total strangers?" Mike whispered sideways, still processing. Ed nodded. Both glanced at Thomas, who tried to act surprised.

A few other people in the group were having stronger reactions. An older couple stood up, holding their coats close to their chests. Thomas remembered they'd been asked to leave their coats in the cloak room minutes earlier, but had refused. The red faces of both the man and woman bore looks of anxiety and betrayal.

"This wasn't in the flyer!" the woman snapped. "I knew there would be something fishy like this, Harold!"

"Delicious food and interesting people await you," the hostess reassured the elderly couple. "All you have to do is step out of your routine. Eat with some new people. Share your table. Share your self."

"This is preposterous!" the man shouted, his watery eyes fierce. "I'm not sharing my table with anyone but my wife. We're going home, Glenda!" He helped his wife put on her coat.

"You may leave if you wish," Magda said with a gracious smile. She turned to include the whole group. "No one is forcing you to share your table. But make a choice, and decide quickly!" There was a note of challenge in her voice. "Go or stay, but don't be lukewarm. The feast is prepared! The tables are ready, the food is hot. Other hungry people are waiting to join the banquet!"

"You don't have to convince me," said Mike, rising up on his hind legs from

226

his vinyl seat and scratching his stomach like a jolly grizzly bear in a blazer. The prospect of food seemed to make him forget his marital troubles. "I'm ready to share a table and fill my belly. Just point the way." The two other Rubber Biscuits stood next, followed a split second later by everyone else in the group.

"Count me in, darlin'," Ed beamed at Magda the hostess. Happy murmurs from the rest of the group echoed his sentiment. "I'm ready to mix it up. What a deal. Hello, Portland!" Ed boomed. "Let's chow!"

"Our wait staff will bring each of you to a table they select," the hostess informed them. "I have to bring in the next diners, so I'll leave you now. Have a great time sharing the table!"

Ed waved goodbye to her, then continued to wave bemusedly at the small, angry couple as they marched to the exit through the crowded foyer. They looked like undersized trout struggling upstream. The man and woman held on to each other fiercely and fought their way through the oncoming crowd, through the sea of humanity waiting behind the steamed glass of the foyer, people swathed in their winter coats, people yearning to be part of the food and warmth promised inside.

Even though it was five minutes before the official starting time of the event, nearly every table at *Off the Vine* was full. A waiter led Thomas' party deeper into the restaurant. The group stopped at the top of a short flight of stairs leading down to the dining floor. Thomas paused at the landing to survey the scene below.

The museum-like space was alive with candles. In the diffuse warm light, an ocean of white linen tablecloths floated below them like lily pads, long glowing tapers and red napkins dotting the surface of each.

After a minute, Thomas spotted Talia in a blazer and jeans and boots, talking animatedly to a few total strangers. One, wearing a wool beanie and a gigantic Mexican poncho, Thomas recognized from the cafeteria at the Catholic Worker: his friends had called him Munch, the big chunky guy who leaned against his own shopping cart during the whole meeting. No shopping cart was in evidence tonight lurking near Munch's table, although Thomas had seen several outside while he'd waited to get in. The carts had been padlocked to a wrought-iron fence not far from the restaurant entrance, each covered by a weathered plastic tarp that protected the prized contents from prying eyes and threatening elements.

From his vantage point on the landing, Thomas caught Talia's gaze. She flashed a dazzling smile right at her boyfriend before she turned her attention back to Munch and another companion. An unexpected warm feeling spread in Thomas' chest, kindled by seeing Talia's excitement in what she was doing. Not for the first time he thought: *I love seeing her on fire.*

Most tables were already occupied. With quiet efficiency, attentive wait staff led individuals away from the friends with whom they'd entered, threading the newcomer through the maze of tables to arrive at an unoccupied chair somewhere in the gorgeous, cavernous room. With the golden candles, the warm plastered walls, and the huge arched ceiling rising into darkness, Thomas felt transported to another world, perhaps an underground grotto in ancient Italy.

He could tell the others felt it too. Incredible smells of fresh bread, sautéed garlic and sun-dried tomatoes wafted up from the tables below as starters began to be served.

"If this isn't heaven, I don't know what is," croaked a gruff man at Thomas' side wearing a ripped army jacket over a gray hoodie. The man smiled. Half his teeth were gone. With a start, Thomas recognized Charlie, the grizzled guy with the burn scar who had been part of the Catholic Worker's inner circle the other day.

Suddenly Mike poked Thomas in the ribs. "If I'm gonna eat with strangers, I hope I get that stranger," he whispered, pointing. "I might forget about my own sorry state for a few hours if I dined with a fine lady like that."

Mike was pointing to the far side of the dining room, where the low-hanging lamp above a small corner table framed a slinky figure in a pool of light. She sat alone, with seats available. The illumination accented her high cheekbones and well-framed face, and sent blue-black highlights shimmering through her lustrous ebony hair. Trails of smoke lingered around her head as she took long puffs from the cigarette she held in a slim onyx holder. White gloves, a midnight blue silk dress, and skin the color of rich coffee completed the picture: a starlet waiting in the wings of a Bogart movie.

Four waiters in black and white arrived at the top of the stairs, and began leading the members of Thomas' dining group to different tables. Mike was led away first. He glanced back with a smile.

"Try to be back before dawn," chuckled Ed. Then it was his turn. "See you on the other side," he called over his shoulder to Thomas as each was led away by the arm in separate directions.

36 I SEEN YOU BEFORE

"I seen you before."

The words dripped out of the man's mouth like acid as Thomas sat down.
The waiter left, leaving him alone to face this ball of hostility across the table.
Thomas desperately racked his brain to remember where he'd seen this thin,
ragged man. Thomas' dining partner was an elderly figure with night black
skin and twitchy, bloodshot eyes. His mouth was a tight line so pursed and
wrinkled it looked as if it was badly sewn together with stitches.

The man cracked his mouth open again before Thomas could place him.
"You're one o' those rich crackers who was in our assembly the other day,"
he said accusingly. "What're you up to?"

Now Thomas remembered. *William.* That was his name, the cuss who'd stood
up and cursed at Clarence during the big meeting the other day.

"I'm not up to anything," Thomas answered. "Just showed up for some food.
Like you."

"Right," the wrinkled mouth dripped sarcastically. He took a bite of salmon,
ignoring Thomas. It appeared that William had already been here a while,
alone. *First in line,* Thomas guessed. Despite the fact that the event was just
getting started, William's salmon was half-finished and a red residue was all
that remained of his wine.

The old man lapsed into silence, and Thomas picked up his menu, unsure of
how to proceed. In the quiet, a waiter came to offer William more wine, and

Thomas got the man to fill his own glass too. He took a long drink of the house red. *This dinner conversation might need some serious lubrication,* he thought, wiping his lips with the back of his hand.

"You're the third."

The waiter, who had just helped Thomas decide between the eggplant parmigiana and fresh manicotti stuffed with herbed sausage, had already left. It took Thomas a moment to realize the old man had spoken to *him.*

"What's that?" Thomas said, looking up from his menu.

"You're the third."

"Third what?"

"Third rich cracker they put at my table. Other two left."

"Left?"

William shrugged one shoulder. "Guess they didn't like what they found."

"Why's that?"

"Guess your team thought we'd all be grateful, all talkative or something. Instead I told those bitches to get out of my face."

"I'm not on anybody's team," said Thomas. "Just a guy who's hungry for a free meal, like you."

"Hungry. Like me," William repeated with a dismissive chuckle. "Man, we're sitting here at the same table tonight, but we're in two different worlds. Free meal won't change that, motherfucker."

Thomas' eggplant arrived, interrupting the flow of harsh words. As the waiter departed, Clarence Washington came over in a tan linen suit with a rose in the lapel.

"Evening, William," Clarence began, putting a hand on the man's shoulder.

"I just wan –"

"*Don't fuckin' touch me!*" the old man hissed, batting Clarence's hand away. "This isn't some Sunday School potluck where we all hold hands! I said I'd eat at a table with somebody I didn't know so's I could eat. But I never said I'd like it. Never said I'd be nice."

"Thomas, you don't have to stay," Clarence said, looking with concern across the table.

"See, you *are* on the same team!" The old man's bloodshot eyes gleamed with vindication. "Assholes."

"Thanks, Clarence, but I'll stay," Thomas replied. "Those are the rules for tonight. Besides, I love eating with interesting people."

As Clarence Washington walked away, William stood and yelled after him across the restaurant: "I never said I'd kiss your ass and say a prayer, neither!"

Thomas stood up right after and made his own shout across the room: "I love eating with complaining old bastards!"

As he sat down, Thomas was aware that all other conversation had stopped. Out of the corner of his eye, he saw Magda distant on the landing above, silently watching the scene. Next to her stood a bald, refined waiter in a black tuxedo, a small smile playing about his mouth. *Paloma?* The thought vanished as soon as it came, since William's face now loomed inches away, livid.

"What the–why'd you do that, you crazy cracker?" William whispered loudly, nervously looking side to side at the other diners as he sat back down. "You think that just because you're sitting here–"

"Fuck you," said Thomas, cutting the startled man off. "You call me 'cracker.' You call me rich. You say we live in different worlds. You say those white bitches wanted you to be all thankful. It's all true. Congratulations."

William just stared at Thomas, at a loss.

"Congratulations," Thomas plunged on. *What the hell,* he thought, *I'm never going to see this guy again.* "You've named your world, and it's never gonna change. No one's gonna make big bad William do anything." Thomas took a slug of wine, and smacked his lips, staring at the red drips moving in slow motion down the edge of his glass. "Nah, William's gonna always be a pissed off poor old black guy hanging around with other pissed-off people, and everyone else is gonna be a rich cracker or some asshole trying to convert him. Good for you. You've put your whole life in a box that you can't get out of."

When Thomas dared look up across the table in the silence that followed, he saw that William's eyes had turned to steel.

"You don't know me." William was staring at him, biting each word as it came out. "You have no idea what I deal with every day." His right eye twitched.

"No," Thomas said. "I don't. But I do know that you turn your pain into rage and you drive people away before they even have a chance to breathe."

"What, you a fucking psychologist now?" William bristled. His hands gripped the table, a hound dog with his hackles up. "Go back to your heated BMW and warm girlfriend and leave us here on the streets in the real world, motherfucker."

"You know, just a minute ago I said I loved eating with interesting people," Thomas retorted almost lazily, swirling his glass. "But William, I just realized how boring you are. You might've scared off two white ladies, but to me you're not scary at all." He hoped that his calm was not quite the reaction the old man expected. "You're just a broken record, pain hiding under anger and insults. If you want to talk about real pain, real life, then I'm all ears. I have a feeling you've had a lot more than me. But if you say another complaining or insulting thing, I think you're going to bore me to death. Pass the salt."

William's pursed mouth flapped like a fish once, twice. No words emerged. Thomas held out his hand expectantly in the silence. Somehow, almost without permission, William's hand moved to pass the salt.

For the next twenty minutes the old man sat fuming, his face a tight mask of rage, while Thomas slowly ate his eggplant parmigiana and swirled his wine.

233

37 THE REAL DEAL

So much for transforming Portland, thought Thomas as he headed for the restroom. *That whole scene could've gone just a little better.* Despite his cool act, Thomas was jangled. He'd gotten up as soon as he could, leaving William without a glance. He wanted to see how his friends had fared with their dining companions.

The rest of the place was a hubbub. A waiter had come by to explain that, now that dinner had been shared with strangers, it was now okay to roam the restaurant and see familiar faces. Coffee, tea and dessert would be served at whatever table the diner chose. Due to this announcement, hundreds of people were walking, talking, up from their tables and congregating. New friends were being introduced to old. Spontaneous groups were huddling in animated conversations. Thomas looked back over his shoulder. He could see William a football field away sitting alone, staring forward. *Won't leave without a couple free desserts,* Thomas guessed.

Thomas approached Talia's table. From yards away Talia pointed him out to her table mates, and Thomas was a bit startled to be called over by her burly dining companion in the large Mexican poncho. *Munch, that was his name.* The guy was still wearing his wool snowcap.

"Telling your girl here I've got too much stuff," Munch explained hoarsely, "but she don't believe me." They were already deep into their desserts.

Thomas looked questioningly at Talia. "What does that make us?" she asked, shrugging. "He keeps all his possessions in that shopping cart we saw him with the other day," she said. "*One* shopping cart."

"Still, more than I need," Munch replied. "Gotta have a street sale with the extras." Then he reconsidered. "No. Not all the extras. Gotta keep the two coats I leave in the bottom of my cart, 'case I see som'un in need."

"They get used?" asked Thomas, leaning against a chair at their table.

"Hell, yeah, they get used. Lots. I live on the streets, man. I see a lotta some'un's in need."

"I never thought about it that way," Talia said. "If you're on the streets, you see the need. And if you live in the suburbs – "

"You live in a bubble," said Munch. "Mini-vans and manicured lawns."

"I grew up ten miles from here," said Talia, "surrounded by plenty of nice people who never needed anything. Driving around my neighborhood in winter with an extra jacket in our trunk would've been silly. When you're surrounded by stuff, it's hard to give."

"Maybe not so hard to give," suggested Munch. "Maybe hard to see."

"Yeah," Talia said, rethinking. "Hard to see *where* to give."

"When you live in a sububble, you drive in a bubble, you work in a bubble, you play in a bubble." Munch stabbed a creamy strawberry with his fork. "You float right over life in the street."

"Speaking of bubbles, mine's about to burst," said Thomas, excusing himself. "Be back in a minute."

- - - - -

Returning, Thomas took a different route. Seeing Talia with Munch got him curious: how were Ed and Mike faring? Scouting his way through the sea of tables, Thomas heard that same grating voice he'd heard before dinner at the top of the stairs: Charlie. He followed the voice, not unlike following the sound of gravel being rolled in a tumbler, until he located the ex-con with the burn scar. The man was presiding over a small group of fellow diners. A book was open in his hand. Thomas' first surprise was that Ed was one of

235

the listeners. His second surprise: Charlie was reading straight out of his Bible, the gold-edged one embossed with the words "Portland Correctional Facility." And the biggest surprise: Ed was spellbound.

"This guy's a freakin' street prophet!" Ed exulted when he saw Thomas approach. "Look around you, T, and listen to this stuff. This is the real deal." He turned back to Charlie's ravaged face. "Read it again, my man!"

Charlie's gravedigger voice began again. Thomas' gaze took in the vast, motley party populating the cavernous room as Charlie's words drifted out across the tables.

"When you put on a feast," Charlie began, "don't just invite your fuckin' friends and family and fuckin' rich neighbors, the kind of people who will return the favor. Instead, invite some people who never get invited out, the misfits from the other side of the tracks. Invite the poor, the crippled, the blind, the fuckin' desperate. Invite them, and you'll not only give a blessing, you'll experience a blessing. You'll *be* the blessing. The world needs you to be that kinda blessing. The desperate ones won't be able to return the favor, but the favor will be returned—oh, how it will be returned—at the rebirth of the new humanity."

Thomas stared at Charlie. "I added a few bits on the fly," Charlie explained. "For color."

"That's just it," Ed exclaimed. "Jesus was underground like that, man. He was so underground, and Christians today don't even know it! But Charlie knows it. He's reading me messages from the Man that I've never heard before. Not like this." He paused to motion with his extended arm, taking in the whole room. "This is it, Tommy! This is the kingdom he was talking about. The real deal. Genius!" He sighed, and turned back to Charlie. "Who organized this shindig, anyway? The Catholic Workers and a mysterious donor, right?"

Charlie nodded.

"They're startin' something, man," Charlie just smiled. Ed caught Thomas' gaze. "Something badass, T. Can you feel it?"

Thomas *could* feel it. Ed was right. Something incendiary was happening. And

Clarence had been right the other day: revolutionary relationships *were* happening tonight, across tables, across worlds. Portland might not ever be the same. People who normally never met were coming together.

"Hey, strangers," Rashaun called gaily as he approached across the lush carpet, his cigarette holder and his tiny purse dangling from long, manicured fingers. Thomas had to say, he looked ravishing in his black pumps and midnight blue gown. "My new friend says he knows you." Rashaun's other bare arm rested in the crook of Mike Shaw's elbow who, despite a goofy smile and a deep shade of red flushing his face, made no move to break away from the elegant diva.

Mike took a deep breath. He took in the room, the wonderful chaos: homeless meeting hairdresser, bag lady meeting business suit. He took in the group gathered around Charlie, an open Bible resting on his army pants.

"Looks like we're all getting to know people from different walks of life," Mike commented. He looked at Rashaun with a huge smile. "Very different walks of life."

38 A RARE HEAT

Benjamin Whidman's *Bible Before Bones* West Coast tour was in full swing at the Portland Coliseum, and Thomas had yet to flee.

Not that he hadn't thought about it. Sitting with angry William at *Sharing the Table* three days ago had been difficult; braving Thanksgiving Day with Talia's mother had been nerve-wracking; but now, squirming in his seat as Uncle Ben worked the crowd into an evangelical fervor, Thomas realized this was by far the most uncomfortable thing he'd done all week. It brought Thomas back to when he was sixteen, sitting in the front pew at Church of the Harvest in Orange County, entranced by his uncle up in the pulpit. *Back when I was a promising young pastor.*

Difficult as it was, Thomas hadn't bolted for more than a half hour now. Talia's presence helped; he gripped her hand tightly whenever he felt the desire to flee. *Focus on the task,* he said to himself. *Don't get nervous. It's just an assignment.* For the course *Faith and Fanaticism,* Cavanaugh required his students to observe and comment upon an extreme religious event. And that's exactly what he, Thomas Whidman, was going to do. Observe. Comment. He looked once again at the invitation sitting on his lap. *Be careful what you wish for, Uncle. I actually came.*

The praise band finished a rousing number, and now Reverend Ben leaped back into the spotlight. "Thank you Jesus!" the preacher cried. "Let your light shine!" His midnight blue suit gleamed as he moved to the front of the stage. The mood quieted. "God is watching us tonight," Reverend Benjamin Whidman intoned, his voice reverberating. "God wants us to set his example in the world."

"God wants us to get the hell outta this coliseum and get a beer," Thomas whispered.

"You're bad," Talia whispered back. "Keep it together, Whidman. Half an hour more."

Breathe, Thomas told himself. *You can take a shower when it's over, wash it all off. By tomorrow you'll be back in the Bay Area and never see these people again.*

While Ben preached, Thomas did what Cavanaugh asked him to do: observe. He tried to be detached, but Thomas couldn't help but be dismayed – no, *deeply disturbed* – by the amount of glassy eyes and rapturous expressions he saw. He prayed to whatever deity existed that there were no paparazzi prowling the aisles of the Portland Coliseum, taking pictures of *Bible Before Bones* for the local papers. He could just see a photo of himself on tomorrow's front page, staring vacantly, surrounded by the enthralled faces of religious zombies, with a headline reading: "Zealous Christians Rally in Record Numbers; Ignore Facts." That was a moment of fame he'd rather avoid.

"These are times of light and darkness, my friends, light and darkness," Ben Whidman's voice rang through the Portland Coliseum. "Like I said, a box of bones is going to be unveiled in Berkeley, California about six weeks from now, in the middle of January." Hisses and boos resounded through the arena. *Breathe,* Thomas reminded himself. *Associating with these people does not mean that you are one of them. You are merely observing a social phenomenon.*

"Some atheist scientists claim that this box reveals a new truth," Ben continued. "They say this bone crypt contains the bones of Jesus' brother, James. They say this James was older than Jesus."

"They say you should pay attention to something called carbon dating," Talia muttered under her breath as Ben paused for effect.

"Who's being the bad one now?" Thomas responded.

"You know what they're trying to do with this box of bones?" Ben Whidman cried. Inchoate yells of anger floated down from the higher seats. *"They're attacking the Word of God!"* The audience raged. The crowd was seething now, of one

mind. "But we know where truth is found, don't we friends?" Ben continued. "The truth is always found in the Bible. God's word. God said it, and I believe it. *Can I get an amen?*" The coliseum roared. Thomas dug his nails into Talia's arm.

"Brothers and sisters, I've told this story before, but I want to tell it again tonight," the preacher said, quieting down. "I received a message from the Lord when I was a child. 'Defend the faith,' the Lord told me in a dream when I was nine. 'Benjamin Whidman,' He said, 'I place the sword of truth in your mouth. Defend the faith from all who would corrupt and deceive.'" The preacher strode across to the other side of the stage. "Defending the faith has not been easy in this age of darkness," confided Reverend Ben. "Sometimes it's been a hard road, and sometimes I've felt all alone. But recently the Lord has given me a companion in this work." The crowd perked up. "The Lord works in mysterious ways, does he not?" Shouts of affirmation floated down to the stage. "A few months ago, the Lord brought to me a man who— without knowing my story – told me that he too had this same vision as a child. At an early age, he felt the Lord place the sword of truth in his mouth as well. He too has been called by God to be a defender of the faith, a prophet to the nations. And this new friend is bringing an inspired message to us tonight. Brothers and sisters, I give you the Reverend Billy Swanson."

Amidst a large round of applause, an unassuming middle-aged man with buck teeth, thick glasses and bad hair ambled into the Coliseum's spotlight. Dressed in a white dress shirt, suspenders and slacks, he looked more like an accountant than a prophet.

"Is he wearing a toupee?" Talia wondered. Thomas poked her in the ribs.

"I pray I might inspire you tonight," Billy Swanson said humbly. He quietly took the microphone from Reverend Ben. He walked with a noticeable limp, and spoke softly but powerfully, with a slight Southern twang. "But inspiration's up to God. I'm just tryin' to wait upon the Lord, and let the Spirit do its work through me."

"Uh-oh," Thomas muttered to Talia under his breath. "This could be long. People who say they're led by the Spirit usually haven't practiced their speeches."

"You remember what Jesus said was the greatest commandment?" Swanson began. Shouts rang out in the arena. "That's right. He told us to love God with all our heart, all our soul, and all our mind." He looked out into the crowd, his glasses silver mirrors under the harsh lights. "A lot of us Christians today say we do that. But we still make a lot of room to love our houses and cars and ski vacations in Mammoth, don't we?" Knowing laughter rippled through the crowd. "You know, when you really learn to love the Lord, there's no room for anything else—no room for your pride, your reputation, your possessions, your concerns about not looking foolish." Swanson looked down and chuckled. "You may have noticed, I'm wearing a toupee. You might be saying, 'that short guy looks funny up there. He needs some dental work and talks a little funny.'" The preacher's left arm jerked involuntarily. "'His body twitches funny, too. In fact, he looks downright foolish. What's he doin' up there?'"

"Ouch," whispered Thomas into Talia's ear. "I was thinking that very thing."

"You know what?" Billy Swanson looked directly out into the audience again. "I don't care a fig about what you think about me. I don't care if I look foolish. 'Cause it's not about me—I'm a fool for Christ! And I got a message for you: it's not about you either."

"Sounds like a fundie version of Paloma," Talia whispered back.

"How many of you know the Lord's Prayer? C'mon, how many?" Billy Swanson shielded his eyes from the stage lights as thousands of people raised their hands. "Just seein' if y'all were awake." The crowd laughed. "The Lord's Prayer is so familiar that we forget its power sometimes. But I gotta tell you: when you say, "Thy Kingdom Come," you also better be prepared to make the promise, "My Kingdom Go!"

Wow, that actually made sense, Thomas thought to himself.

"To be a follower of the Jesus Way requires *metanoia*—a complete transformation of your mind. Did you know that what Jesus said about loving God is the same thing the prophet Micah said in the Old Testament? 'What the Lord requires of us is this: to love mercy, act justly, and walk humbly with our God.'"

"Tal, I actually kinda like this guy," Thomas confessed in a whisper. He felt himself getting more comfortable in his seat. Something about this preacher's style allowed Thomas to relax. As his muscles loosened, he realized he needed the restroom. "Be right back," he said to Talia, and darted up the Coliseum's cement steps.

- - - - -

By the time Thomas returned to his seat a few minutes later, the Reverend Billy Swanson had worked himself and the Portland crowd into a rare heat. "What'd I miss?"

"Just the best part," commented Talia, eating some ice cream they'd smuggled into the arena. "This guy's electric." Even from a distance, Thomas could feel the raw energy coming from the stage. Steam rose from Billy Swanson's open collar as he engaged the crowd under the Coliseum's harsh tungsten spotlights. The preacher's white dress shirt and suspenders were dark with sweat; his thick glasses gave off flashes of silver as he paced the lit stage. Talia fed Thomas a secret bite of ice cream. "People liked your uncle up there, Thomas, but they are *way* into this guy. He twitches like crazy. Something is going on."

Something *was* going on. Billy Swanson was no longer mild-mannered. He was a man possessed: licks of fire seemed to ripple out from him and into the audience, energizing the crowd. Paroxysms ran through him at random intervals, as if he was channeling more Spirit than his mortal frame could handle.

"The apostle Paul says that God requires *metanoia*," the preacher boomed, a bit of the South coming through in his rough voice. "A complete revolution of your mind and heart." The stadium resounded with approval. Thomas was pleasantly surprised at the Greek. *Metanoia*, Swanson had said, one of Thomas' favorites. *An utter transformation of the mind*, the word meant in ancient Koine. *To go beyond the self you already are.*

"Nothing less is acceptable," Swanson continued. "When Jesus, sweet Jesus enters your heart, there's room for nothing else." The crowd roared its affirmation, urging the preacher on. His apoplectic face and red neck contorted as he prepared for another outburst, like a snake rearing back to

242

strike. "Jesus told us the Kingdom of God is at hand!" He exulted. His voice rolled out over the standing masses and up to the highest decks. "It's right here, waitin' to invade your heart and invade Portland! And when God's kingdom comes, your kingdom has to go!" Applause and amens rocked the Coliseum.

"When God's kingdom comes, you don't *want* there to be room for anythin' else," he half-growled into the microphone. Swanson's frame shook with a spasm that caused him to stagger. "Christ died so that others may live. He is askin' each of you tonight to do the same. Turn your life around, turn away from the powers of this world, and turn your life over to his Kingdom."

Reverend Billy Swanson prowled from center stage to a side wing. "Who's gonna turn it over?" He suddenly swayed as if hit, reeling with the massive, exultant crowd. "*Who's gonna turn it over?*" Thousands of individuals raised their hands as if one body. Many in the multitude were crying, swaying. "Paul wrote in Romans, 'Make your life an offerin' to God.' He didn't say to offer a few bucks on Sunday, did he?"

"*No!*" the crowd shouted.

"No way!" The preacher's toupee and thick glasses shook from side to side, a vigorous negative that sent refracted slivers of light in the front rows. "Paul said to offer your *life*. All of it!" He staggered back toward the middle of the stage again, steam and sweat pouring off his body in the chilly, humid evening. The man seemed powered by another source.

Billy Swanson beamed a pillar at center stage, and motioned with a raised hand for quiet. The crowd hushed, attentive. "The first step, the only step that matters, is surrender." His intense voice, now barely an amplified whisper, drew the crowd like a magnet. The entire arena waited on the words of this one man. "Make your entire *life* an offerin', a gift laid out for God to do as he wills." In the pregnant quiet his soft words carried to the coliseum's ceiling. "That's what the Lord is askin' of you tonight. That's the *metanoia* Paul was talking about." Reverently, Billy Swanson held the mike out to the crowd in an attitude of prayer, and bowed deeply at the waist, reminiscent of a karate student in a dojo. "God bless you, Portland! Be God's blessing to the world!"

Swanson stood upright to a standing ovation of praise. In the tumult,

Reverend Benjamin Whidman came out to join the circuit preacher for a curtain call.

"Praise the Lord, brothers and sisters!" Ben Whidman crowed, exultant in the applause. He attempted to raise Swanson's hand in a gesture of victory, but the fire had left the other preacher. Swanson was suddenly small, just a middle-aged man again. He appeared spent, barely able to stand. Ben didn't seem to mind. He took the energy that Swanson had built and drew it to himself. "Brothers and sisters, I have one last thing to say." The coliseum audience quieted. "Jesus has given me a last message to share with you tonight. Will you hear it?" The crowd roared its assent.

"The Lord wants you to come down to San Francisco next month to defend God's Word," he continued. "I'm going to be sending a big white bus up here to Portland six weeks from now, and God wants you on that bus. In fact, I'll bring as many buses as needed. If you feel led, come on down these aisles tonight to meet with members of our team, who can help make sure you have a space on that bus. We need thousands of good Christians to come down to San Francisco and testify that the Word of God is true above all things. No box of bones is going to win out over the Word of our God. *Can I get an amen?*"

The crowd let out a final massive roar. A giant neon cross behind Ben's head exploded into fireworks, and the praise band started a last number. Reverend Whidman saluted the crowd, took Swanson by the arm and exited stage left to the night's final applause. The stage darkened, the house lights went up and the sound system began to play Christian rock music.

Talia looked across at Thomas. "You made it, Whidman. Congratulations."

"Can't believe it. I really can't." The event was done. He'd stayed for the whole thing. Hordes of people were marching upstairs to the exits, but an equal number were heading down toward the stage, eager to meet with prayer volunteers and bus coordinators.

"Not finished yet for you, though, lover," Talia reminded him. "Time to interview your uncle."

"Sure you don't want to come with me?" Thomas asked. "There could be more preaching."

"Tempting. But no. Gotta make some miles toward Arizona before I fall asleep in the back of the Pathfinder tonight." Talia was scheduled to lead a week-long climbing course for Outward Bound at Jack's Canyon outside of Prescott. It started in a day and a half; more lingering wasn't an option.

After a quiet pause, Thomas took her outstretched hand and heaved himself up out of his seat. "I think your mom likes me."

"You put on an impressive showing," Talia agreed. "That first day when we dropped off the turkey, you didn't spill the gravy in her car, and then on Thanksgiving Day you had thirds of everything she cooked. Like I said, she likes you because I like you. You're part of the family."

Thomas grabbed Talia's waist and nuzzled her from behind, their hands clasped together around Talia's belly. Talia leaned her head back and nibbled Thomas' ear. Then she turned in his embrace, their foreheads touching. "You're starting to grow on me, Mr. Whidman."

"I think we've become grafted, Ms. Simmons. You're hard to leave."

They held each other a while longer before Talia reluctantly broke away with a sigh. "Duty calls for both of us. You take three steps down and I'll take three up." They did, slowly. Backwards, Talia kept moving up the stairs toward the coliseum exit and her road trip. "I'll call you from the road tomorrow," she said softly. "Go get 'em."

Thomas watched her go, then turned. Down. That's where Thomas needed to go, if he was going to fulfill his assignment. He recalled Paloma's strange comment: *I dare you to go backstage, Thomas. Get to see what's behind the man. I guarantee you'll learn something unexpected about extreme Christianity.*

Down he went.

39 YOU'RE THE LAST PERSON I
EXPECTED TO BE HERE

The coliseum was huge. The surging upward momentum of the throng had mellowed, but Thomas still fought a strong current as he descended, looking for his uncle's dressing room backstage. Although Ben's evangelical stadium events were popular, preachers weren't of the obsessive cult status of rock stars or politicians, so security was light. Thomas identified himself as a member of the family, and was led to an open backstage door.

He found the two preachers sitting on a brown couch in a white dressing room. Ben was tying the laces of his wingtips, freshly showered, while Swanson had changed shirts and was carefully parting his bad hair in a mirror with a little black comb, his eyes squinting behind thick lenses. Something about Swanson seemed vaguely familiar, but Thomas couldn't place it.

Reverend Benjamin Whidman looked up from his shoes. "Thomas?" His face was puzzled. "That *is* you." Ben's gaze was a combination of shock, curiosity and undisguised hostility. "All the way from the Bay Area. I know I sent an invitation, but after our last contact, you're the last person I expected to be here. Total surprise."

"Well, Uncle, I sort of surprised myself." *Surprised I would willfully enter the same room with you ever again.* Thomas crossed the dressing room to stand next to the two men and shake his uncle's hand. "I was in Portland visiting my girlfriend over Thanksgiving break when I remembered your invite."

"You haven't been to one of my events in years." Ben combed his slick black hair. He looked at Thomas, thoughtful. "In *years.*"

"Well here I am."

Calculation entered into his uncle's gaze. "The Lord works in mysterious ways, Thomas."

"He certainly does," Thomas said, moving to include the other preacher in his gaze. "You two sure were on fire tonight."

"It was a group effort...me, Billy, and Jesus Christ!" Ben crowed. "Thomas Whidman, my nephew, meet the Reverend Billy Swanson, a new ally. Another true defender of the Word!"

Swanson looked more like an eager accountant again, clean shaven and red-faced. He gave a fleeting smile to Thomas, showing his bad teeth. Thomas tried to smile back, but ended up staring at the man's eyes, distorted and overly large behind his coke-bottle glasses. He was sure he'd seen this man somewhere. Before he could ask, Reverend Swanson whirled to engage his fellow preacher.

"The Holy Spirit came down tonight, Brother Ben, did it not?" His hoarse voice carried a touch of southern twang. "The road crew just told me that nearly three thousand souls came up to the altar afterward to dedicate their lives to the Kingdom. The Spirit surely was moving!"

Just listening to talk like that made Thomas' flesh crawl. Thinking back, though, there was truth in what Swanson said: something powerful *had* happened this evening. Something had drawn a horde of searching people up to the altar, people who were burdened and hurting who wanted a clean start.

"People sure were feeling something," Thomas conceded to the both of them. "But I'm wondering. Do you think a spur-of-the-moment conversion really sticks? Do you think people are changed for the long term?"

Reverend Benjamin Whidman's face darkened. "Did you really come backstage just to argue some more, Thomas?" He stood up. "Billy, you can indulge this troubled young man if you want. I'm going to get my things."

Reverend Whidman stalked out of the room. Billy Swanson looked at Thomas cockeyed. "So you're the troubled young man, are you?"

247

"That's me."

"I don't think you're troubled. I think you're searching." Swanson came to stand right in front of Thomas, his voice raw from preaching. "A spark of the Kingdom was glowing tonight, was it not?"

Thomas thought the question was rhetorical. But the barnstorming preacher remained standing right in front of him, his eyes huge behind thick wire-rimmed glasses. "Was it not?"

"Yeah. Maybe," Thomas acknowledged. *What was it about this man?* "There was some high energy flowing."

"Your soul felt the spark," Billy Swanson said with certainty. "But your intellect is havin' a hard time with it. 'God is dead,' your mind says. 'There is no good news.' But your soul felt the spark of the Spirit spreadin' and risin' tonight, like leaven through a loaf. Thousands of people opened their hearts tonight, gave their whole beings to the Lord. Will it last?"

This time, Swanson wasn't expecting an answer, but as Thomas stared he simply shrugged his shoulders. "How long it lasts will be up to them, and how they choose to live from this moment forth. We might close off from God, but God keeps enterin' wherever we make some room."

Benjamin Whidman began whistling from the other room. Swanson turned to look, and Thomas followed the bespectacled preacher's gaze. His uncle was turned away from them, adjusting his bow tie in a distant mirror. Just the two of them were in the room.

Abruptly, Billy Swanson removed his glasses and stared hard at the young man, faces inches apart. Up close, Thomas saw the preacher as if for the first time, and was shocked how different he looked without the distorting lenses and heavy frames. Those eyes. Thomas was sure he knew those hawk-like eyes. *But from where?* The sweaty preacher pulled a kerchief out of a pocket and wiped his perspiring face. Makeup began to come off, revealing tan skin beneath. "The Spirit is moving among us, Thomas. But sometimes it's in disguise." Swanson then removed a set of false upper teeth, and a Buddha smile now played about his lips. "Sometimes it's hard to believe that God is real, that God's somehow with us even in a world where babies are tortured and men are burned alive."

Thomas stared, speechless.

"Hard to believe, isn't it?" The preacher said. He rolled back his sleeve directly in front of Thomas' face, revealing a graceful tattoo of vines encircling his left wrist. He cocked a familiar eyebrow and, while Thomas gaped, pulled off his toupee to reveal a shaved head. "Are you going to believe again?" the man whispered, and darted out the door.

Ben Whidman called to Thomas from the other room, but Thomas couldn't hear. Blood rushed in his ears. As Swanson dashed through the open exit door, Thomas was having a hard time catching his breath.

"Ran him off, did you?" Ben said in exasperation, hastily pulling on his jacket as he came back into the room. With a scowl he looked after the departing preacher. "You must've – "

But Thomas wasn't listening. Without a word he bolted out the door, leaving his uncle mid-sentence in the dressing room.

- - - - -

"Wait!" Thomas called. He ran madly down an echoing coliseum hallway chasing the retreating preacher. He was gaining on the man and thought he'd catch up, until he turned the next corner and ran smack into the back of a massive crowd loitering near the stage.

"Come back!" Thomas cried. He battled along the right edge of the crowd, finally breaking free of the horde and gaining the bottom of a flight of wide stairs leading up to the parking level. Two levels up, he saw a bald head bobbing among the sea of people exiting the arena. *Was that him?* Having no better lead, Thomas raced upward. He summitted the steps in leaps and bounds and snaked through the coliseum's crowded corridors. Finally reaching the nearest stadium exit, Thomas raced through the final concrete arch and ran right into a milling, faceless mass of people loitering outside the coliseum after the event. *Where'd he go?* Frantically, Thomas scanned the mass of humanity. *Was that him at the curb?* A bald figure in a blazer was getting into a yellow cab fifty yards away. Thomas tore through the maddening crowd, ran, stumbled, apologized, called out, picked himself up and ran again.

"Wait!" he screamed as the distant cab moved into the flow. *"Paloma, we need to talk!"*

Twenty yards too short, Thomas watched the taxi's red taillights pull out from the curb and disappear into an endless stream of cars bound for the freeway on-ramp.

40 BUT HERE I AM

Bachelors are dangerous creatures, Thomas thought as he moved two pizza boxes from the kitchen counter to the overflowing recycling container in his garage. *When is a pizza box too cheesy to get put in the recycling shredder?* He mused, smashing the new boxes down on top of the old. *Does a particularly bad box gum up the machine?* Considering it his civic duty, Thomas began peeling old cheese bits off the top box, nibbling them as he returned to his kitchen of despair.

Bachelors writing theses are especially dangerous, he sighed to himself as he reshelved an open box of cereal. *Pizza and Trix four meals in a row can't be good.* He'd flown home yesterday morning with his mind whirling from the events at the Portland Coliseum Saturday night, and then he'd spent all day and night Sunday trying to get his head in thesis mode, and prepare for today's meeting with Professor Cavanaugh.

Thomas looked at his kitchen table with loathing. The surface had become command central for his thesis, a repository for all things Josiah Adam Whidman. Bookmarked texts sat haphazardly in towering piles. His grandmother's collection of stapled xeroxed copies from magazines and yellowed newspaper articles, in an orderly box just a day ago, had gotten loose under the table sometime during the night. The mass of spilled papers looked like prime bedding for any vermin who might come along, hoping for a snack of pizza and Trix.

Overall, the paperwork chaos in the kitchen gave the whole apartment a charming "spilled filing cabinet" motif. *At least Talia's not here to see this,* Thomas thought as he tried to bring order to the table top. Then he cursed

251

aloud. *Bachelors with highlighters are especially dangerous creatures.*

Peeling back layers, Thomas discovered an unholy neon yellow saturating the tablecloth.

I'm just not into this, Thomas thought, dropping into his chair and rubbing his tired, dry eyes. His watch read 11:20am, Monday, November 28th. Forty minutes until his meeting with Cavanaugh, and Thomas felt at sea without a raft. He'd been skimming and highlighting all night and he still couldn't write with authority about the soul journey of Josiah Adam Whidman. He didn't have a center for his thesis, and he knew it. He'd taken a lot of notes, summarized loads of articles. Lots of pieces but no puzzle.

And the other puzzle that swirled in his mind he couldn't do anything about.

Paloma is Swanson? Swanson is Paloma? Impossible! But there it was. That tattoo. His words. Those eyes. That smile. The bald head. The two had to be the same. Didn't they? Thomas was sure what he saw. *But why would Paloma pose as a revivalist preacher? And what does he want with my uncle?*

Thomas' mind reeled. Documents dealing with Josiah Adam Whidman lay open, ignored. His thoughts returned yet again to what he'd seen backstage at the Portland Coliseum. *Either I'm losing it big time or Paloma is playing a serious fucking mind game with me.* Images of Billy Swanson, the bespectacled fundamentalist preacher with a bad toupee, intermingled with the visage of Paloma, serene and cool with his dark, magnetic gaze and his carefully shorn head. *'There may come a time I need him to think we're on the same side,'* Paloma had said about Uncle Ben as they stood gawking at the billboard months ago. *What was Paloma up to?*

Over and over, Thomas' thoughts circled like hawks around an ungraspable prey.

Under the kitchen's overhead light, Thomas' body mechanically leafed through a stapled Xeroxed document about apocalyptic Christian groups of the 1900s that contained a few references to the Faithful Remnant community. His hands successfully found the yellow highlighter and he even bolded a few key sentences. But images of Paloma and Swanson still haunted his thoughts.

He realized for perhaps the eighteenth time this morning that he had no way of contacting either of them. Paloma, Swanson, even Magda—all oddly uncontactable. He thought again of Magda playing the hostess at *Sharing the Table,* and now this undercover role by Paloma. *What are they, secret agents? If so, for what?*

A few hours ago Thomas had become keenly aware of how little he knew about his meditation teacher. He had always just shown up to class, and Paloma was always there. Whenever Thomas was on break from seminary, Paloma's class was on break, too. Thomas had never needed to know more.

Until now.

In the phone book this morning, he'd found no listing for a Stephen or a Magda Paloma in the larger Bay Area. Reverend Billy Swanson had a downtown Oakland number, but hadn't returned any messages. When Thomas finally gathered up the courage to call his uncle an hour ago, Ben had been terse and to the point: He only had the same phone number for Swanson that Thomas had. He confirmed the man was a traveling preacher not affiliated with a particular church. As far as Ben knew, Swanson only had a post office box for an address. Before he hung up on Thomas' insistent questions, Uncle Ben made it clear he'd never heard of a Stephen or Magda Paloma, either.

And when Thomas called the Bay Area Catholic Worker, the voice on the other end confirmed that, yes, Magda Paloma had been involved for many years with the organization, but she was gone on vacation for a week or two and left no way to get a hold of her during her time away. No, her phone number was not available to the public, but yes, Thomas could come by any time.

Thomas became even more imbalanced when he found out that his meditation teacher was not contactable through the Bay Area Theological Union administration, either. Paloma was certainly not on the seminary faculty. The meditation class was part of the authorized "Campus Clubs and Extracurricular Activities" list that Thomas located in his student handbook, but enrollment went through the registrar. No contact information was listed.

A half an hour ago Thomas finally struck gold: Gladys, the clerical staffer at the student union who had *'[Meditation / S. Paloma: Room 121B]'* scrawled regularly every Tuesday on her "Year-At-A-Glance" wall calendar actually produced a phone number. But when he called it, Thomas was dumbfounded: it was the number for *Tolstoi's Tea House*, not a number for Paloma. Fool's gold, after all.

In the last twenty-four hours Thomas also learned he was incapable of saying anything coherent about his suspicions to Talia. She'd called last night from a pay phone in remote Arizona canyon country to tell him she'd made it safely to her course site, and after hearing the weather forecast she expected it to be an excellent week of rock climbing. The static-filled phone call got cut off when Talia ran out of change; during the short conversation, Thomas hadn't been able to convey his certainty that Paloma and Swanson were one and the same. Even if the conversation had continued, Thomas doubted if he would have said something believable.

Thomas got up from his kitchen table and walked to the bathroom mirror to practice.

"Hi Tal," he said to his reflection in the glass. "I got something to tell you. You know the sweaty fundamentalist preacher we saw in Portland? Well he's really our meditation teacher in disguise. Paloma was wearing a wig and fake teeth and funny glasses and he's working undercover with my uncle." No matter how he explained it, it sounded so improbable that Thomas began to doubt his certainty. And his sanity.

Even more than the faces that floated through his thoughts, it was the floating question that haunted him: *"Are you going to believe again?"*

"In what?" he yelled at the mirror. Even as he shouted, Thomas realized something: if he needed to ask, he already knew the answer.

- - - - -

Thirty minutes until Cavanaugh. Thomas wandered back to the kitchen but continued to avoid his thesis. He put away a few semi-washed glasses, pacing. Paloma's mystery was driving him crazy. *But soon,* thought Thomas, *all will be revealed.* Paloma's class resumed again tomorrow evening. He'd find out everything in about thirty hours.

But I'm here now, Thomas reflected, once again coming back to his chair of pain. *Chained to pursuing questions about a crazy ancestor, when all I want to do is race after a mystery meditation teacher. Chained by my own mind that wants to be somewhere else.*

Breathe, Thomas reminded himself, looking at Einstein sticking out his tongue on the kitchen calendar. Somehow the man's untamed hair calmed him. *Breathe the wild hair. This isn't a prison. I chose this. I'll see Paloma tomorrow. I'll see Talia next week. Right now I'm seeing Cavanaugh. That's right. Meet with him. Show him my progress. He'll advise me. That's his job. Show me where to go next. Thesis. For now, it's all about the thesis.*

"Shit," Thomas muttered aloud as he loaded his grandmother's documents into his bookbag and grabbed his bike helmet. "It's all about the thesis."

41 DEMON WITH SPURS ON

"I think it goes without saying, Mr. Whidman, that for you, this upcoming month is all about the thesis." Professor Horace Cavanaugh leaned back in his large office chair, and swiveled. The seat was upholstered in some kind of animal hide—*deer? horse?* – but Thomas dared not ask. "If you're not living it, eating it, breathing it, you're not doing enough."

"Yes, sir, I know." *All too well.*

"Getting this done in the time you've allowed is going to be a big challenge for you. Big challenge." Looking over his bifocals, Cavanaugh set down Thomas' thesis proposal on his desk next to his ten-gallon hat. "This task timeline is adequate in scope, but painfully compressed." He shook his large head. "Six weeks."

"I think I can accomplish it, sir."

The burly professor picked up Thomas' paperwork again. "You just came up with your thesis topic a few weeks ago."

"After our great meeting last month, sir, it took a while for a topic to crystallize. I really wanted something specific, like you said." Thomas didn't want to admit that-- after stumbling upon his apocalyptic ancestor--he'd grabbed onto Josiah Adam Whidman like a lottery ticket.

"Most prudent scholars would ask for an extension." Cavanaugh let his words hang in the air. "Say perhaps until the end of Spring semester."

"Thank you, Professor, but I intend to complete my thesis before next semester begins. Before classes start up again in mid-January."

Cavanaugh pursed his lips. "Your mind's made up, then?" Thomas nodded from across the broad desk.

"You really want to get out of here, don't you?"

Exposed, Thomas nodded again.

"And you truly think you know what you're in for?"

Almost against his own will, Thomas found himself nodding a third time.

"Well, alright. I've done what I can do to advise you differently, Mr. Whidman." Dr. Horace Cavanaugh picked up his ten-gallon hat, twirled it, and placed it on his head. "Now I'm going to ride you like a demon with spurs on."

Thomas blanched. *Disturbing image.* The professor got up from behind his desk. *Oh my God, is he really going to –*

Cavanaugh reached his arms in the air and arched his back. A cracking sound came from a few places along his spine, and he growled like a bear. His pot belly strained mightily at the stitching of his white Wrangler shirt, but somehow the pearled buttons refused to burst open wide and reveal the morass of body hair that must surely lurk beneath. To Thomas' great relief, Cavanaugh sat back down.

"Let's get down to brass tacks, then." He flipped through Thomas' papers, all business. "As I'm sure you are acutely aware, you currently lack a summary of your primary sources."

"But – "

"On page two you mention a packet of personal correspondence and newspaper articles," the professor cut in, waving his hand, "but a shoebox of news clippings does not a thesis make."

Thomas decided silence was his best strategy.

"You're at the beginning of writing your thesis, so your lack of organized notes can be excused," judged his adviser. "For about a day. However, considering your timeline, you cannot afford to remain in this preparatory phase any longer."

Thomas nodded dutifully, and made a show of writing down notes. He jotted: Devil with spurs on, devil with spurs.

"You also seem to lack a review of the current research," Cavanaugh continued. He rifled through the last few pages of Thomas' modest thesis proposal and then looked up. "That, son, cannot be excused. We need a synopsis of previous research to determine if your topic is one worth pursuing. I see you've narrowed to a specific population—let's see, "the *Faithful Remnant Community* in Gilman, Arkansas"—but it still sounds too much like a junior high book report. What *about* this Faithful Remnant Community?"

Thomas was actually ready with a response. "I really want to focus on what happened in the mind and soul of their leader when his prediction of the end of the world didn't come true."

"Now *that* sounds more interesting. Go with it," Cavanaugh said, providing a glimmer of hope to Thomas for the first time. "Take a minute, son, and phrase a specific question about his psychological evolution. A question you can pursue through research." The professor paused to take a bright white Chiclet out of a round green Skoal can on his desk and pop it in his wide mouth. "Better for the gums," he remarked.

Thomas took the moment to frame a well-formed question, and then launched: "How did the personal world of millennialist preacher and community leader Josiah Adam Whidman change when the world did not end in 1923 as he had prophesied?"

"Not bad," said Cavanaugh, leaning back and putting his boots up on his desk. "Wordy. But you're starting to get specific. Has this subject been researched by any other parties, to your knowledge?"

"Yeah, kind of. The Arkansas Historical Society published a chapter about the history of the Gilman apocalyptic community, but that's just – "

"An overview," the professor finished his sentence. "A book report on the community. What about research on the man himself?"

"Only one person's tried that I know of. A former seminarian here at BATU by the name of Paul Silas. He wrote his M. Div. thesis seven years ago on the preacher's crisis of faith. His work is listed in my summary of the current research, on page six."

"On page six? I must've missed it," the professor commented, going back through pages. He turned his head to cough and adjusted his bifocals. The side view was just long enough for Thomas to see three monumental hairs of white on the ridge of his adviser's nose, silhouetted against the window behind.

Cavanaugh found the citation and frowned. "No wonder I missed it," he fumed. "A title and author is not a research summary!"

"Let me explain," said Thomas hastily. Dr. Cavanaugh was getting his dander up again, and Thomas dared not risk the man rising to be backlit once more.

"Where's your synopsis?" Cavanaugh roared.

"Our seminary doesn't have the paper!" Thomas squeaked, worried that Cavanaugh might throw something. "It's gone. Honest!" He thought quickly. "I'm getting it through interlibrary loan," Thomas lied. "It should be here any day. I requested the work over two weeks ago."

"Interlibrary loan, interlibrary loan," the professor muttered. Cavanaugh peered over his spectacles, his amazingly bushy eyebrows now capturing all of Thomas' attention. "Glad you're already two weeks into that process," said the professor testily. "Interlibrary loan takes time. And time, my young man, is something you simply do not have."

The professor glanced at his desk calendar. "Speaking of, our time is done for today. We'll see each other in a week."

"Maybe two weeks might be better because – "

"One week from today," Cavanaugh cut in. "Same time, same place."

"Yes, sir," Thomas mumbled.

"At that meeting you will have three things." The professor held up three long fingers, one adorned with a thick silver and turquoise band. "First, a full set of note cards outlining the organized contents of your box of news clippings. Second, a full synopsis of any research published about this man and his community. And third, you'll have this Silas thesis from interlibrary loan for me to examine."

"Sounds good." Thomas nodded with a confidence he didn't have. *Crap, the Silas thesis in a week. He better be in Tucson still or I'm a dead man.* "See you next meeting, sir." He headed for the door.

"Thomas." He turned to see Professor Cavanaugh peering over his lenses. "You do realize it's unwise to make false promises to your adviser, don't you?" The man's smile was not pleasant.

Thomas was a nodding machine.

"Have those three things to show me in a week, son, or don't show up."

42 ABSOLUTELY KNOWN

Paloma was nowhere to be seen the next evening when Thomas arrived at the meditation room a few minutes before class. He came in alone, and felt the pang of Talia's absence as he began the sit. He imagined her lean body in the Arizona winter light, reaching out to gain another handhold on a sun-warmed granite wall at Jack's Canyon. Behind his closed eyes he smiled, knowing she was doing that which gave her life.

The pleasant vision quickly lost out to fidgeting. He'd skipped last week's sit for Thanksgiving week in Portland, and his body felt out of practice. More so, his *mind* felt out of practice. Thomas could barely contain himself, waiting to see Paloma. He tried to center.

Meditation hadn't officially started yet, so Thomas popped his eyes back open. Several cushions were now occupied by other figures, none of them Paloma. *"Where's our instructor?"* he wanted to scream. He felt like shaking the other students until he got an answer. Instead, with great effort, he tried to silence himself. Calmed his rapid breathing. Adjusted his ankles. Even recited Greek.

Despite his efforts, Thomas couldn't focus. Instead of going deep, his eyes darted up at the slightest noise. Muffled footsteps from the busy hallway outside the dojo had gone unnoticed during other classes; today, the sounds drove Thomas crazy. Three other figures, none of them Paloma, tardily entered the room. He finally gave up, and counted to five hundred with his eyes closed, trying to concentrate his unhinged thoughts.

When he opened his eyes Paloma was among them.

Stoic, regal, the meditation teacher sat serenely as if he'd been there for hours. An inscrutable smile played across his lips and his closed eyes were at peace. After fifteen minutes of agonizing silence, Thomas opened his eyes at the sound of the gong, signifying the end of the sit.

Joints cracked as bodies slowly emerged from lotus positions. Eventually, all participants had returned to the room. All eyes rested on Paloma. "Apologies for my lateness, friends." He clapped once. "There will be no dharma today."

After a brief moment to make sure that class was really over, students began leaving one by one, making the traditional bow to the center of the room as they exited.

Soon only Thomas and his teacher were left. Neither moved.

The two men remained sitting, facing one another across the still space. A myriad of questions tumbled in Thomas' brain. But it was Paloma who spoke first.

"Thomas, are you going to believe again?"

That question. Thomas' answer was the first thing that came to his lips. "I'd like to."

"But."

"But so much of Christianity doesn't work for me anymore."

Paloma nodded. "Like why would an all-powerful God let his people burn alive in a Guatemalan church?"

"Yeah, like that." Thomas looked up, eyes burning. "That's a fuckin' good start."

"Like why would a God of love set up a world in which, by default, all of his children are destined for eternal torment? That the only way to escape the fires of hell is to proclaim that Jesus is the one and only Son of God?"

"Exactly. Those concepts are just so..."

"Silly," Paloma concluded his sentence.

"I was going to say bullshit."

His teacher smiled. "They're sad. Narrow traps for fearful children."

"Then how can you ask me if – "

"If you want to believe again?" Paloma waved a hand in dismissal. "I stopped believing in that kind of God a long time ago."

"Well then, what are you talking about?"

"The question is not, 'Do you believe that Jesus is the one and only Son of God'?"

"Well then what – "

"It's not even, 'Do you believe Christianity is the only ticket to the afterlife?'"

This time, Thomas exercised his right to remain silent. And listened.

Paloma shook his head, smiling. He gazed at Thomas across the carpet. "Of course God is much bigger than these questions."

Something hard melted inside of Thomas. "But that's what they always said."

"God's love is too great to allow eternal damnation. God's presence is far too grand to be captured in just one religion." Flexing, he cracked his finger joints. "Narrow traps for fearful children."

Thomas waited. When nothing came, he blurted: "Then tell me what you're talking about!"

"This is the question I ask of you, Thomas, when I ask if you want to believe," Paloma said slowly. "It's the same one that Jesus asked." He pointed directly at Thomas' eyes. "Do you dare believe that the kingdom of heaven is already here?"

For Thomas, the room closed in. There was just one voice. One candle. One flame.

"Do you dare believe that Jesus was ushering in a new humanity, right here, right now?" Paloma asked.

"Are you sure that he was?"

"This is the good news that Christendom has been hiding for two thousand years, Thomas. Jesus declared that all of us are children of God. That the kingdom is already among us, if we realize it. Do you dare grasp what Jesus meant when he said 'you will do greater things than I?'"

"That line never made sense to me," Thomas confessed. "I mean, I know those words are in the Bible. But how can that be true?" His eyes were wet. "Jesus is supposed to be totally different from us."

Paloma gave a knowing smile. "Totally different," he concurred. "Utterly above us."

"Yeah, like God. God's only Son, the Bible says. It says he's supposed to come again on clouds with angels and save us all at the end of the world."

Paloma uncrossed his legs from the lotus position. "Like your ancestor Josiah, you've believed in a God that rescues, protects us from harm, provides miracles. But this God has fallen silent, or abandoned ship, or maybe never existed at all. That kind of God doesn't exist. And because of this, you say Christianity is dead. Yet there's a hole inside of you. Am I right?"

Thomas nodded. Paloma rose, and took three strides across the room to crouch directly in front of the younger man. Candles illuminated the dark pools of his eyes. "At your core you are paralyzed, because the religion that once was your rock has turned out to be a bedtime story for children."

Paloma reached out, and placed his hands on Thomas' shoulders. "You ache for a God that still provides hope in this crazy, broken world. This isn't a selfish desire for your personal soul. No, you ache to be used for a mighty purpose."

Thomas felt known. Absolutely known.

"The deepest part of you aches to serve completely. To surrender yourself to a Way worth following. To a God worth following."

Thomas couldn't speak. Mute, he just looked into Paloma's eyes and nodded. Eventually, he whispered, "I would die for a God like that."

"Good." Paloma smiled and stood. "That's exactly what you'll have to do."

43 A DIFFERENT GOAL ENTIRELY

"Man, I haven't done a road trip like this in years," Mike said, slurping his Mega Gulp Mountain Dew. The massive cup was sweating. Beads of condensation dripped onto his pink Izod and madras shorts as he drove. With one hand on the wheel, he leaned out his open window to take a deep breath. They sped through the dry black night, full of stars. "That's desert, man."

A mumble emerged from the passenger seat.

"Tucson in December's going to be awesome," Mike continued. "Not like Cali's really cold or anything, but it's gray right now. Gray for me. Full of fake holiday glitz. The Christmas stuff was out way before Thanksgiving was even gone. Man, I need some wide open space to clear my head. My best friend, some cactus, a tan, and some space. I can use all of that right now. *Right now.*"

The passenger gave no response.

"I know it's selfish, but I'm kinda glad Talia couldn't come. Just time for old buds."

He looked over at Thomas, who was doing a strikingly real imitation of a man trying unsuccessfully to sleep in the passenger seat of a 1979 Jeep with bad shocks traveling at 80 mph on a highway in the middle of the night, somewhere outside of Needles, CA. "Thanks for coming with me, bra."

"I'm not a bra," growled Thomas from under the jacket he'd thrown over his head. The coffee and the handful of chocolate-covered espresso beans he'd downed earlier while driving were still coursing through his veins. And Mike didn't appear to be having quiet time anytime soon.

"It's just a figure of speech, dude. Like 'man' or 'brother' or something," responded Mike. "Don't get your undies in a bundle."

"Yeah, it's a figure of speech. A *stupid* figure of speech." The caffeine was making Thomas twitchy. "What is it with people from Lower California?"

"*You're* from Lower California."

"Yeah, but I don't talk like a surfer. You don't even like the beach. You're the financial officer for a church. So stop calling me bra. That's like me saying, 'Thanks for joining me on this road trip, panties.'"

Mike was silent. He stared at the double yellow line emerging out of the darkness. "Sorry, dude," he said softly. "Just trying to say thanks for your company."

"Got it," Thomas grimaced. "Sorry for being a dickwad just now." Silence hung in the air. He threw off the jacket and punched a startled Mike in the arm. "Forget it. Call me bra all you want. Panties."

Mike howled, but his smile quickly faded. His need to talk was bleeding out all over the car.

"What are you thinking about right now?" Thomas prompted. "Mary?"

"I guess I should be. But no. I'm thinking about the kids."

"Must be tough this time of year, Christmas coming and all."

"I keep wondering how they're dealing with things. What are they thinking about me? Is Mary telling them I'm a bad guy? She says she doesn't know when she's coming back. Does that mean they'll have Christmas without me?" Mike shook his head. "My mom raised me and my brothers by herself, and I swore that if I ever had kids, I'd never leave them. Now my kids left *me*, and I can't do anything about it."

"Relationships are hard enough by themselves, just between two adults. I can't imagine trying to raise kids in the middle of all that. To know what's best for them."

"What do you mean?" asked Mike. "It's hard to raise kids, sure, but knowing what's best for them isn't the hard part. Getting them to *do* it is the hard part."

"Really? Parenting isn't confusing?" Thomas asked.

"Sometimes, sure. But I've raised my kids in a Christian household. I give them lots of love and teach them what's right and wrong. That's what's best for them. The hard part's getting them to obey. To not do the wrong things."

"To not do the wrong things," mused Thomas. "Have you ever heard of Saint Clement?"

"I'm assuming this has something to do with child-raising."

"He was a saint in the Middle Ages. You know the main reason why he was sainted?"

"Do tell."

"Because he never dared look at a woman. How holy is that? Maybe if I ignore half of the world's population, I could be a saint too."

"C'mon, Tom, that's twisted. I'm not talking about raising my kids like that."

"I know, but Clement's an example. So many kids grow up thinking that being good means simply avoiding the bad. I know we were. Remember? In youth group, Ben tried to make us like Clement: no sex, no drugs, no foul language. Like avoiding all the bad stuff and following the rules was our highest goal. But life doesn't have a rulebook."

"Sure it does. It's called the Bible."

"You still think the Bible's a rulebook?"

"Sure it is. Everything we need to know is in there, if only we know where to look. Why are you so resistant to what's right in front of your face?"

"Wait a minute," Thomas grumbled. "We were just talking about raising kids. Why is it that we always end up arguing about religion when we get together?"

"Because you're like a pissed-off teenager these days. You're always struggling and fighting and questioning," said Mike. "Thomas, Christianity doesn't need to be a wrestling match. God's made it clear for us. He's given us the Bible. You don't have to doubt it. You don't have to cook up conspiracy theories about power-hungry priests and co-opted gospel writers."

"A bunch of very imperfect human beings have – "

"I know you've gone through a lot of stuff in the last few years, Tommy, but you need to learn to trust the Bible again. Trust God again. Don't you think God wants to help us get to heaven?"

"Sometimes I wonder."

"Think about it. If a father wanted his child to meet him in a faraway, unknown place, wouldn't he leave a map for every step of the journey?"

Thomas was quiet for a minute as they cruised into the night. "Only if the father's intention was to get his child safely from point A to point B," he mused.

"What else would he want to do?" Mike stared at his passenger.

"What if the father wanted the child to grow on the journey?" Thomas wondered. "The destination's important, but what if the true goal of the journey was for the child to become like the parent?"

"To become like..."

"The journey would have to be a little risky, wouldn't it?"

"Yeah, I guess," consented Mike.

"If *growing* was the goal, the journey couldn't be too clear. No huge billboards, only clues. Stories. The kid would have to become resourceful. Find her own way when the going was tough."

"I get what you're saying," said Mike. "But there'd be maps, too. Like the Bible. I said it was a rulebook. But I don't mean it's always easy to follow."

"But don't you see? If you call the Bible a specific rulebook, you make the journey of life so small for the traveler. Options become limited. If the child is always told what to do, or is always rescued from dangerous consequences, then how could the kid ever grow into the person the parent wants her to become? What if instead the Bible is a collection of powerful stories to draw from when the going gets tough?"

"The Bible's still my rulebook," said Mike grudgingly. "It's a lot more than stories for me. But I do like the idea that the journey is meant to change the traveler." He rolled his shoulders and cracked his neck behind the wheel. "Speaking of changing, I've got to pull over soon or I'm gonna have to change my shorts."

Mike found a spot to pull over and the pair unfolded their bodies from the car. Outside, under the stars, Thomas thought back to last night in the seminary's student union, sitting across from Paloma in the candle-lit dojo.

'*Do you dare believe Jesus was ushering in a new humanity right now?*' Paloma had asked. Thomas didn't quite know what to make of this new Paloma, this bizarre Budeo-Christian, but he wanted to know more. In fact, Thomas wished his teacher was here right now, having this conversation. He'd like to hear what the mysterious bald man would say about God's desires for humans to change and grow. He'd tried to get Paloma to talk more last night, to explain his secret identity, but in this the man was immutable: he would not reveal anything more until Talia returned next week and the two of them joined Magda and Paloma for dinner.

Paloma was holding a fascinating secret behind a curtain, and Thomas was about to burst with curiosity. He knew he'd go crazy hanging around the Bay Area waiting for Talia to return next week, and he knew Cavanaugh needed to see Silas' real thesis when they next met, so Thomas came up with a perfect activity: a Tucson road trip for a few days with his oldest, most available friend.

"Mike, I didn't come on this road trip just to help you, you know," Thomas said as he and Mike hopped back in the car and drove farther into the night. "I want you to help me, too."

"Oh?" The big man brought the Jeep back up to cruising speed.

Thomas hesitated. "I want you to help me meet someone."

"But I thought that you and Talia were—"

"No, not like that. I need to find this guy."

"Whoa there, cowboy, I'm not really into—"

"Shaddup. Not like that either. It's for my thesis. I don't want to *meet* a guy. I want to *find* a guy, for my thesis. As in locate. Track down. And I want your help. I didn't want to tell you about this before we left Orange County because you might've refused to come on a harebrained man hunt."

Mike laughed. "But now that it's 2:00 AM and we're at the Arizona border, I pretty much have no choice, right?

"Exactly."

"So does this guy have a name?"

"Silas. Paul Silas."

"So what does this have to do with your thesis? Why do you want me to help you hunt down Mr. Paul Silas of Tucson?"

"Not hunt down, exactly. Just find. Seven years ago Silas wrote a research paper about my ancestor Josiah Adam Whidman, a relative I never knew existed until a few months ago. Turns out Josiah was a preacher who convinced himself that God was coming to end the world in 1923. He convinced about 250 other folks, too, and they formed a commune in Arkansas to wait for the Apocalypse."

"Wow. That helps to explain your own religious instability," observed Mike. "You want to talk to this guy in person so you can find out more?"

"Yeah. I've decided to make my ancestor the centerpiece of my own thesis. I think this Silas guy can link me to some important sources."

"Don't you have any records in your family? Can't Ben help you?"

"Funny you should ask," Thomas said bitterly. "Uncle Ben thinks our nutty ancestor's an embarrassment. He's been trying to keep him a secret since before I was born. But once I found out about Josiah back in September, I asked my grandmother about him. She sent me a whole box of stuff—news stories, sermons, letters. They're good, but I still need Silas."

"What's he got that she didn't?"

"I want to know what happened *after* 1923. What happened inside of Josiah when God didn't come to end the world like he'd predicted."

"When God didn't come." Mike faltered. "Wow. How'd he deal with that?"

"That's just it. I don't know, but I want to. I need to see if there's original research still to be done about Josiah Whidman. Finding Silas is one way to find out."

"You can't tell just by reading his thesis?"

"That's the weird thing. Paul Silas wrote his paper seven years ago when he was a grad student at my own seminary, but I've never seen it. I can't find a copy of it anywhere. The copy at the BATU library vanished." *Interlibrary loan my ass,* Thomas thought.

"Vanished as in lost, or vanished as in stolen?"

"Vanished as in shredded, I think. By Uncle Ben."

"What?" Mike exclaimed. "Sure, he might be embarrassed, but you really think Ben would do that?"

"I know so."

Mike stared across the Jeep's cab at Thomas. "Do you mind me telling you this is becoming a bit bizarre? And what does any of this have to do with Tucson? You sure Silas lives there now?"

"I think so. He wrote a postcard to a former professor that was sent from Tucson. A year ago."

"That's your evidence? We don't happen to have a phone number, do we? "

"No phone number. There's no listing for a Paul Silas, at least in Tucson or in Pima County."

"Well, have you written him, or are we just showing up at his doorstep?"

"Umm," Thomas paused. "Haven't written. And I don't know exactly where his doorstep is. Or if he has a doorstep."

"What are you getting at?"

"I don't have his address."

"I thought you saw a letter of his!" Mike retorted.

"I did. But it had no return address. I guess he didn't want anyone to write back. It just had a South Tucson postmark."

"Hoo, this trail of clues is steaming hot," said Mike. "Sizzling, even. This is going to be a cakewalk, my man. No address, no phone number. Do we have any proof that he was in the city any longer than it takes to drop a letter in the mail?"

"Erm. No." Thomas went on to explain the detective work he'd done over the phone before the road trip. He'd called information, and found no listing for either a Paul Silas or a Silas Paul. Because Silas had been a seminary student, Thomas then took some time to call the forty-eight Christian churches in the larger Tucson area. None of the pastors, priests or office personnel handling Thomas' calls knew anyone by that name.

On his eighteenth church—a Methodist church by the name of St. Mark's on the Mesa—the answering pastor surprised Thomas. "Is this some kind of crank call?" the man asked.

"No, not at all, sir, " Thomas sputtered. "I'm just trying to track down the author of a thesis written some years ago. Why do you ask?"

"The names, that's all," replied the reverend. "Paul and Silas. The two most influential apostles of the early church. Silas was the behind-the-scenes guy and Paul did most of the talking. They did some serious jail time, too. When you started asking about a guy named Paul Silas, I couldn't help but think you were setting me up for some joke. You sure this is the author's real name?"

Hearing this as they entered the outskirts of Yuma, Mike narrowed his eyes. "This is whacked!" he exclaimed. "We got no address, no phone, no proof that he lives there, now we're not even sure we have a real name. You expect to drive into a large urban city and find this guy? What do you want to do— conduct a house-by-house search asking for fingerprints? We're dealing with over half a million people, bra."

"No we're not, panties. The letter didn't come from Tucson. It came from *South* Tucson."

"Tucson, South Tucson, what's the difference?" Mike retorted. "A quarter million people instead of half a million?"

"Not even close, woman's underwear. Do you mind if I call you woman's underwear? It's more formal than panties."

Mike, one hand on the wheel, took a wild swing at his passenger, but Thomas dodged the blow. "Honest, *South* Tucson is much different than Tucson. It's the *city* of South Tucson."

Thomas grabbed his backpack from behind his seat and pulled out some statistics he'd gathered at the library. "The City of South Tucson is its own incorporated entity within the larger metropolis of Tucson, which is in Pima County. The whole city of South Tucson is about one square mile in dimension. Only 1,810 homes and apartments, to be exact. So South Tucson is like a little yolk, sitting in the middle of a big egg, which is Tucson. Then the egg is in the middle of a huge-ass frying pan, which is Pima County."

"That's poetry," deadpanned Mike, shaking his head. "Especially the 'huge-ass' part. And what makes you think that Paul Silas wasn't just a tourist driving through your little yolk of a city the day he mailed your letter?"

"South Tucson isn't a place an Anglo gets to by accident." Thomas had done his homework. "You have to *want* to get there." He took a crumpled post-it note out of his pocket. Using the sporadic light from the ghostly freeway lamps set at intervals along Interstate 8, he peered at some notes he'd scribbled earlier that day, preparing for the trip. "South Tucson. No freeway exits, no car dealerships, no malls. 95% Latino immigrant and Yaqui Indian, according to the last census. 82% of the households speak Spanish as the main language at home. 38% unemployment rate. Median income of $12,800 for a family of four. One city park, one baseball field, two schools, a few playgrounds. Everything else looks like asphalt and buildings on the map."

"Okay, so our chances are looking up. Now we're trying to find a white fleck in a dark yolk in a big egg in a huge-ass frying pan."

"Exactly," said Thomas.

"Impressive work, Kojak. But before you get too excited, how do you know the fleck in the yolk is white?"

"Huh?" said Thomas. The metaphors were confusing him, even though he started it.

"How do we know Silas is white? Maybe he's a black guy named Paul Silas. Did you dig up his picture in a school annual or something?"

That would've been easy enough, thought Thomas. "No." He sunk down into his seat.

"So we don't even know what he looks like? Height? Age? Skin color? Anything?" Thomas just shook his head. Mike continued: "And even if we do find this guy, what makes you think that he has a fresh copy of his old thesis in his shirt pocket ready to give to you?"

Thomas' lack of a response was the only answer Mike would get. They drove in silence for a while, both heads full of thoughts. Then Mike spoke. "It *was* my idea for us to take a spontaneous road trip to Tucson, wasn't it, Tommy boy?"

"Of course, panties," said Thomas, grinning hugely, and threw the jacket back on top of his head as they sped into the desert night. "Of course."

44 PADRE

"Cálmate, amigo," the gaunt man said quietly as he stepped among the many bodies sleeping on the carpeted floor. *"Es nada. Duérmense."* With these words and a reassuring touch on the shoulder, the tall figure calmed the anxious dark head which had jerked upward at the unexpected noise outside. The head relaxed back onto its pillow, joining the rest. All was tranquil again.

The man reached out a weathered hand and peered through the battered venetian blinds into the graying light of the early Tucson morning, even though he knew exactly what he would find. Every Thursday the trash collector always came at an ungodly hour, and each Thursday a fresh one would jump at the noise.

As the first dirty streaks of dawn appeared, the mass of figures that minutes before had been asleep on the floor began to rise and disappear, one by one and in bunches, slipping silently out the back door like brown ghosts. Soon there was no evidence that anyone but the watchman had been there overnight.

It was unspoken Southside protocol that the last refugee would be gone by no later than 6:30 AM. With that in place, and the first office workers arriving no earlier than 7:15 each morning, it would be easy enough to establish reasonable doubt in a court of law. Any prosecutor would have a difficult time proving that the daytime staff of Southside Social Services of Tucson had any direct knowledge of its controversial nocturnal operations. The day staff made it a habit never to visit the office after hours.

That left all the responsibility for harboring undocumented refugees squarely on the night watchman's shoulders. But he didn't mind. He had nothing more to lose: no family to feed, no bright future to ruin. No beloved ones to care for. No one after Lisette, not after what happened in Gilman. In an ironic way he considered himself lucky: he was truly free, one of those rare people who could act as his conscience dictated. And, in a very different way, this job allowed him to be a shepherd again, and to use some of the skills he had gained during those lean years when he wandered in the Sonoran hardscrabble: watching, listening, enduring, tending his flock.

About twenty minutes after the trash truck, he heard a familiar jingle of keys and the sound of the deadbolt moving in the front door. Before he saw the newcomer he knew it would be David Chavez, routinely the first social worker to arrive. The young man came through the door and flicked on the lights.

"Morning, Padre," Chavez said as he did every day, making a beeline to the coffee machine. In turn the night watchman looked him kindly in the eyes and nodded his silent greeting from his wooden chair near the entryway. Clockwork. The scene was a comfort to him, a ritual of greeting that would be repeated with each of the office workers as they passed his chair on the way to their cubicles.

But this time Chavez surprised him with something new. Returning with his coffee, the social worker stopped at the grimy front window. His eyes scanned the desert horizon in the breaking light. "Just met two gringos walking the barrio looking for you, Padre." Chavez blew steam off his coffee and stirred the Styrofoam cup with a plastic straw. He looked into the older man's face. "Can't figure them out. They stopped me on the sidewalk as I was coming over this morning. Funny looking. Like tourists, but not." The watchman nodded, taking it in.

The entire cast of Southside Social Services had assembled by 7:45 this morning and gathered in a side room to start their day with shared prayer. The man they called Padre joined them today as he always did, sitting in their small circle as if he was one of them. He took the silver cross from around his neck and held the heavy chain like a rosary, although he was no longer religious. He'd given that up seven years ago in Gilman, the day he lost Lisette. The day he started the numbers.

The man they called Padre enjoyed attending the prayer circle because he valued being part of a compassionate, focused group. Somebody had to do God's job, after all. There was strong energy here, united in mind and purpose. He appreciated it, and deeply. Maybe he appreciated it so because he knew it was all too transient: someday they'd be caught, and their fragile community would scatter like the dust that never stopped blowing across the desolate playground outside.

45 TOO TIGHTLY OVER THE BONE

Mariscos. That was the name of the restaurant, and it made Thomas nervous. They'd driven past it a few times during the long sweaty morning of door-to-door searching, and the place seemed lively enough with customers. But any restaurant in Arizona specializing in seafood gave Thomas pause, and a seafood restaurant in an inner-city low-income neighborhood in the heart of South Tucson seemed downright dubious.

Thomas thought himself as open-minded as the next person, but long before he and Mike entered, he'd decided on the *chile rellenos.*

"No lo conozco," had been the most common response as they'd walked the neighborhoods, that is, if you don't count a closed door as an answer. Several residents assumed the pair were Mormons, and kept their iron screen doors shut. No one seemed to know – or have even heard of – a man named Paul Silas.

One woman actually greeted the pair and let them in. But when she asked for a description, suddenly Thomas knew Mike had been right: Thomas was an unprepared idiot. He had no idea what Paul Silas looked like. Everything was up for grabs – his height, weight, ethnicity, hair color – everything. Thomas *guessed* that Silas was Anglo, and somewhere between forty and sixty years old, but he wasn't sure, and he had no idea whether the man was fat or thin. This lack of descriptive information ended the living room conversation pretty quickly. The woman ushered them back out to the street. "There are some older Anglo guys who drive by our street," she said as she closed her screen. "Usually at night, looking at the *chicas*. I can't tell them apart. *Buena suerte.* "

Good luck, Thomas translated as they walked away from the woman's house. *Yeah, I wish. What was I thinking?* It was this kind of luck all morning – closed doors and dead-end leads – that brought the defeated duo to lunchtime at *Mariscos.* It seemed the only place open, anyway.

Thomas took a moment to let his eyes adjust to the restaurant interior as they came in from the noonday sun. Looking around at the clientele, he recognized a few from their morning of fruitless door-to-door seaching. Mike said hi to some folks, but his efforts were met by avoiding eyes and the occasional curt nod. Mostly, the residents of South Tucson found the two gringos about as interesting as peeling wallpaper.

"Real gregarious bunch," Mike said, slumping into the red vinyl booth. Gaudy murals of seascapes and fishermen with nets were painted at random on the restaurant's plastered walls. In a Corona mirror hanging opposite where he sat, Thomas could see that he was being bodily threatened by a gaggle of lobsters looming mere inches above his left ear. Mike, meanwhile, was seated out of mortal danger, surrounded by a peaceful blue ocean. Small fishing boats bobbed gently around his head.

"Any luck?" The two friends looked up, startled. Their waitress was familiar. *Angela,* Thomas recalled with effort, a young woman who'd actually spoke to them earlier at her door when they inquired about Silas. Didn't let them in, he remembered, but did speak to them.

"Luck? Not any of the good kind." Thomas shook his head with a beaten smile. Angela flipped them two menus. Without looking at his, Mike ordered a cheeseburger, medium rare, and a Coke. Thomas pretended to study the menu, asked her questions about the seafood specials, and then agonizingly decided upon the *rellenos.* Angela left with the orders and returned with some ice waters while Mike and Thomas began sticking to their vinyl seats. In Tucson, even the first of December was hot. The restaurant was cooler than outside, but not by much.

Mike took dead aim at Thomas' forehead with the paper cloaking his straw and scored a direct hit. "What was it like when Jeanne left you, Thomas?"

Thomas looked up, surprised. Mike had dredged up Thomas' only serious girlfriend before Talia. He and Jeanne had been together for three years after college, and at one point Thomas had told Mike he was sure they'd get married.

"She didn't exactly leave me," Thomas remembered, fumbling for words. "Not like Mary did. We'd been growing apart for a long time. We left each other, I guess."

"Yeah, but what'd it feel like?"

"The hard part happened months before we broke up," Thomas confided. "That was when I began to realize Jeanne didn't understand me. Those were some painful days. Even more painful nights." He took a sip. "As for when we actually split, by then it was just mechanics. I didn't really feel anything at all."

"Wow," said Mike. There was no mirth in his face when he laughed. "That sure isn't me." He made his laughing noise again, a harsh and strange sound. His hand began tearing fragments from the edge of his water-stained paper placemat. "I'm falling apart here, Tommy. It's like half of me is ripped out. When she left it was like a car hit me out of nowhere. I just came home one day and – *wham!* – my entire family was gone."

Thomas had been dreading this moment ever since he concocted his plan for the road trip. Dreading it, but hoping for it, too. Back in Portland, Thomas had listened to Mike's pain; now it was Thomas' turn to talk.

"Mikey." Thomas' friend peered at him red-eyed over the top of his upturned glass. "I just – "

Angela the waitress caused Thomas to halt when she arrived with food on big white ceramic plates. Mike began chomping into his burger with gusto, grief obviously not affecting his appetite. *Funny,* thought Thomas. Mike always used to do a little silent prayer, even at restaurants.

"Mike, look," Thomas started again. "I've known you since we were freshmen in high school. You've been with Mary almost that whole time – what, thirteen years?"

"Thirteen and a half," corrected Mike.

"Right. Now, you and I, we used to be best friends. We grew up together—in Ben's youth group, same schools for seven years, playing basketball together all the time. Then we went to the same college and roomed together. We were like Siamese twins. But let's face it. We're not so tight anymore."

Mike opened his mouth, but Thomas cut him off. "It's okay. That's just the way it happened. It's the way life happens. We changed over the last ten years, Mike. People change, even best friends. I think you two have been changing. Mary changed."

"Yeah, she's changed," the big man's mouth was a tight line. "I've changed. But *love* isn't supposed to change. Commitment isn't supposed to change." Mike looked into the bottom of his glass, now a barren pile of ice. "Now I'm not even sure if she still loves me. Or if she ever did."

"What do you know of love?"

The unexpected voice was hoarse but it carried clearly across the noisy space. From a booth of old men across the restaurant, a solitary figure rose. The afternoon sun shining through a window backlit the man, silhouetting the body and making features indistinct.

"You say love isn't supposed to change," the man's voice continued, reaching across the room. All other conversations stopped. The figure approached the *gringos'* table, closing the distance across the restaurant. "I say love is a drug that keeps you happy as long as you get your next fix." To Thomas the voice sounded harsh, ill-used over long years.

"You say commitment isn't supposed to change." The stranger advanced like a predator. "Commitment 'til death do us part, right?" His grin was not particularly pleasant as he stepped out of the light and into Thomas' view. "Death may do you part tomorrow, *hombre*. Maybe you walk off the curb at the wrong time. Maybe your love dies by a bee sting."

The man was just a few feet away now, bony hands on his hips, head cocked, listening to the ceiling. "Yes, Lisette, I know," he muttered quietly. "I know. The numbers." Thomas and Mike just stared. The man refocused his smoldering gaze upon them. Now that he stood close enough to observe, there was a quality about the man that Thomas could only describe as early homeless. Dark circles under his eyes flowed into the equally dark stubble of an unshaven, mottled face.

"Your wife left you, eh? Took your kids? Nothing left to lose." He crouched down at the table and stared into Mike's red eyes. "Don't cry, amigo. Blessed are you, for you've seen the truth: it's all empty." He stood up, and laughed, bitingly. "The truth has set you free, whether you wanted it to or not! Now you know that happy endings are fairy tales. Welcome to the club." The man stopped talking a moment and turned slightly. He seemed to be listening to the ceiling again. Thomas took the moment to regroup his thoughts: yes, he remembered, he'd seen the man at a far table when they first came in. With his dark complexion Thomas had assumed the guy was a Hispanic *viejo* like the rest of the oldsters at his table. But now that the figure was up close, Thomas wasn't so sure. Brittle and unruly hair – gray with white streaks – was untidily bound into a short ponytail that splayed down the collar of a dusty, stained black coat. The skin of his face seemed to be stretched too tightly over the bone beneath, worn thin like parchment.

"So your love left you," the stranger resumed. He now towered directly in front of their table and pointed a long skeletal finger at Mike. "But when she was there, did you ever really love her?"

"Sure I did." Mike somehow responded to the stranger, despite the fact that the big man looked like he was going to cry. "We've been together for half my life."

"But did you truly love her?" The man leaned down just inches from Mike, who squirmed back a few inches into his vinyl seat. "Or did you just love yourself being loved?"

Intense, beady eyes stared at Mike from deep within the man's leathered face. A large silver cross hung on a heavy chain around his neck, flashing from within the folds of his cloak. Though tall, the man's thin body seemed lost inside his oversized coat and baggy pants. "Were you really loving her, or just intoxicated with someone else paying attention to you?"

Thomas couldn't help but wonder who was the intoxicated one in this scenario.

"Have you been listening to what she needs?" Impossibly, the man leaned even closer into Mike's fleshy face, his sour breath hot. "Or has your wife been crying out to deaf ears while you prayed to your God for her happiness?"

Suddenly the strange man slumped into the booth next to Mike, his bizarre tirade spent. "I know, Lisette, I know," he muttered softly, looking up. "I'll stop now."

Mike began to breathe again.

"Love. Permanency. God," the ragged man whispered to Mike and Thomas. "Comforting ideas. Shared lies."

Mike still looked like a deer caught in the headlights of oncoming traffic when Angela the waitress came over with the bill and two mints. "Gentlemen, I see you've met Paul Silas."

46 LOST

Thomas sat in stunned silence. Mike was sputtering. *They'd actually found him.* Unbelievable. They'd found Paul Silas. Correction: Silas had found *them*.

"Now, why have you two *extranjeros* been knocking on every door in South Tucson, looking for me?" Silas spoke calmly, almost chatty, as if nothing weird had transpired in the past several minutes. "Have my *enemigos* from Immigration finally discovered me?"

The pair's blank stares caught Silas a bit by surprise. "You *are* from the border patrol, *no?*"

Mike shook his head before Thomas could even think of something to say. Silas look relieved, but not as relieved as Thomas would've expected from a man who thought he was being hunted by a branch of the Federal government. In fact, Silas looked more amused than relieved.

"Well, you don't seem to be from the FBI, or even the police. You're not Boy Scouts, are you?"

"Nah." Thomas inwardly grinned at this bizarre man's humor, and decided to play. "We're something much worse. Bounty hunters." Mike looked as surprised as Silas did. "Mr. Silas, you're on the San Francisco Bay Area's *Most Wanted List.* Library misdemeanors. Hombre."

Before a startled Silas could respond, Thomas pulled out a pocket notepad and started reading from imaginary notes. "Bay Area Theological Union. Early 1985. A library book you checked out at that time is now overdue by, let me see…seven years, eight months, and thirteen days. Your fine is currently $4,736.84, payable in cash to me. Either that, or it's six months of hard labor at the library's return desk without parole."

Silas just stared. He glanced between the grave face of Thomas and that of Mike, who was now nodding and repeating, "payable in cash."

Silas was sputtering when Thomas finally cracked, unable to remain serious.

"Paul Silas," Thomas said, extending his hand. "I've driven a thousand miles to find you." The confused older man shook hands, not knowing quite what to do, while Thomas continued. "My name is Thomas Whidman, and I'm a graduate student at the seminary you once attended. I believe you know more about my ancestor Josiah Adam Whidman than anyone else on the planet." He looked Silas in the eye. "I want to know what happened after 1923."

- - - - -

Thomas paid the bill, and the strange man named Paul Silas joined the pair of visitors as they emerged from *Mariscos* into the late afternoon desert light.

Though December, South Tucson had grown warm enough by afternoon that the asphalt grew soft and seemed to breathe. The trio walked the cracked sidewalks of the *barrio*, walked and talked, past the cactus and gravel gardens, running children and angry pit bulls behind chain-link fences. Soon Mike and Thomas were down to t-shirts, but the leathered older man seemed oblivious to the heat, even in his heavy black coat.

Everywhere they went, whether they encountered *viejos* sitting on their porches or groups of teenage boys in hairnets tricking out their Honda Civics, Silas was greeted with a friendly nod and greeting.

These are the same people who had never heard of Paul Silas this morning, Thomas mused with pissed-off admiration. He returned the wave of a smiling old woman on a nearby porch who had only hours ago refused to open her screen door to him.

Silas was talking about the ancestry of the people of South Tucson when Thomas found his opportunity to direct the conversation. "I want to find out more about my ancestry, too, Mr. Silas. One ancestor in particular: Josiah Adam Whidman. He wrote a book that was supposed to be in the seminary library, but it's been missing for years. Ever since you checked it out."

"Oh, I burned that book long ago."

"What?"

"Three other copies from other libraries, too," he added, oblivious to the horror on Thomas' face. "If there are any remaining copies still on this planet, they're probably gathering dust in people's attics in Gilman."

"But that was my great-grandunc – "

"Good riddance," Silas retorted, his face graven in stone. "That book's full of spiritual arrogance and broken promises. He came to know that, too late."

"Who?"

"Josiah. In the book he writes of a God who saves, a God who listens. Who performs miracles for his people."

"Who rescues," added Thomas. "Sounds like the Bible. Like Christianity."

Silas nodded. "Your ancestor wrote an inspiring fairy tale that a lot of people believed, including my family." The old man picked up an aluminum can from the gutter and dropped it with a clatter into a pocket of his voluminous black coat. "Seven years ago I did the world a favor and burned all the copies I could find."

"Well, that's pretty decisive," said Mike. "So much for part one of our quest."

"Part one?" Silas queried.

Thomas knew this was no time to be timid. "We also came for your thesis."

Silas chuckled. "You're the first person who's ever asked for it." He looked out in the distance with bloodshot eyes. "I might even still have a copy."

47 YOU SHOULD BE MORE
WORRIED ABOUT THEM

The earliest of morning light had painted the world a faint gray when Thomas awoke in the Jeep, his body smashed into the vinyl seat for the second morning in a row. At least this time when he arose, they hadn't been driving across the desert all night.

Why is my life suddenly all about vinyl? he thought groggily. Their vehicle had been parked all night at the curb of Southside Social Services, and the car radio clock read 5:15 AM. His head hurt. The inadequate blanket he had draped across the two of them last night did little to ward off the desert morning chill, and Mike, snoring like a bear in the passenger seat of the Jeep, had managed to hoard most of it for his beefy frame. Scrubbing his tongue around his parched and dusty morning mouth, Thomas noticed his teeth were each wearing wool sweaters of *chile relleno* from yesterday.

Half asleep, he was just turning over to find a better sleeping position on the bucket seat when he saw a dark figure steal silently out of the door of the office building right in front of him. Then another figure, holding a bag. Then a third.

Thieves? He was wide awake. In the pre-dawn light, Thomas now saw an entire family scurry out the back door of the brick building, hurrying in silence right by his car window. As they passed the Jeep, the tiniest of the three small children locked eyes with Thomas lurking in the vehicle just a few feet away. The little girl yelped in fear. The father and mother looked back and blanched, their brown faces suddenly ashen. Thomas guessed an Anglo face spying at them from the other side of a tinted window in the early morning was not a breakfast surprise they wanted to see. The immigrant couple scooped up their little ones and darted down a side alley. As they disappeared from his view, the last thing Thomas saw was the father's swollen duffel bag banging against his legs.

Thomas withdrew a respectful distance from the window and pretended he was asleep from then on. Doing so, he could be a fly on the wall, surreptitiously watching the procession of figures silently slip out of Southside Social Services. The flow was slow, but steady. Some were carrying nothing but Ziploc bags stuffed with toiletries. *These folks aren't thieves,* Thomas realized. *They're undocumented.*

By the end of twenty-five minutes, Thomas had witnessed forty-two individuals depart on different routes from the building's many doors. And it wasn't even six in the morning.

- - - - -

He must've dozed off again. Slowly waking up in the Jeep in the half-light before dawn, Thomas remembered yesterday's remarkable encounter at *Mariscos*. He reached in the back seat to grab the manila envelope Silas had given him last night, make sure it was still there. Opening it, he stared at the cover page to reassure himself. *He really had it.*

Although he'd struck out on finding the library book, he still couldn't believe his success. Here it was, the morning of December 4th in Arizona, and if everything went as planned, about thirty hours from now he was going to walk into Professor Cavanaugh's office back at Bay Area Theological Union with Silas' entire thesis in hand.

All would be good as long as he got the rest of the thesis like Silas promised.

Thomas looked at the clock again in the half-light of early morning. Before Guatemala he used to start every morning with prayer, but not these days. He had a lot of driving ahead of him to get back to the coast, but before that he and Mike needed to fulfill some mysterious deal for Paul Silas.

After a few more minutes, sunlight burst over the Santa Catalinas and brought the full stark beauty of a morning in the desert. The low angling sun sharply glinted off of the metal playground equipment and reflected off of the rear-view mirror right into Thomas' eyes. He looked at his watch again and wondered what was taking Silas. 7:20 AM. He said he'd be off shift by about now. No refugees had come out of Southside Social Services for more than an hour.

It was 7:24 AM when Silas emerged from behind the tinted glass doors of the building. He stood there, a scruffy statue, looking straight at the Jeep. *Is he looking through me?* wondered Thomas, unnerved. Then he heard the footsteps, and realized Silas was watching someone approach. The old night watchman's grizzled face broke into a gentle grin, greeting a young Hispanic man in a suit coat and bolo who was coming from directly behind Thomas' vehicle. While the man approached, Thomas elbowed Mike who was trying to stay asleep in the passenger seat.

"*Buen dia, David,*" On the sidewalk, Silas greeted the man with a familiar handshake.

"Morning, Padre," the man replied. "*Como le va?*"

"Just the usual," Paul Silas replied. "*No te preocupes.* Coffee's on for you."

"Not joining us for morning circle, Padre?" the young man inquired. "Need some shut-eye?"

"In a little while," Silas said, patting David on the shoulder and moving toward the Jeep at the curb. "Right now I've got some visitors."

David raised his eyebrows. "Visitors? You?" Silas walked over to the rear of the Jeep. "Those two guys from yesterday?" Chavez said. Silas nodded and opened the back door, getting in. The young man came closer and eyed Thomas and Mike behind the tinted windows. Mike waved sleepily.

"Padre, are you going to be alright?" David said, leaning in from the curb.

"Me?" Silas cackled. "You should be more worried about them."

Artifact # 5: Excerpt from Paul Silas' Thesis, "The Crisis of Faith of Josiah Adam Whidman"

No, the members of the *Faithful Remant* were not greatly disturbed when the world-wide Armageddon expected in 1923 didn't come according to schedule. As Bartholomew Whidman, brother to Josiah and the preeminent scholar of the movement, wrote in the Spring 1924 edition of *The Kingdom Harbinger:*

> "If the End of Days is coming, but we have mistaken the
> Divine's time limits and are a few years too early, have we done
> ourselves an injury? Have we done wrong by segregating from
> this pleasure-mad society and establishing godly communities
> in the mountains? No, we are not hurt, by no means. With
> houses built on rock we are establishing a society of like-
> minded individuals. We have the opportunity to rear our young
> people under Christian influences, teaching them the evil of the
> excessive Babylonian life around us, and shielding them from
> it..." (III:2, March 1924).

When half of 1924 had come and gone without the expected world war, Josiah Whidman remained noticeably silent. We can only surmise what was churning in his mind and soul when his specific prophecy did not materialize on time. Josiah's brother Bartholomew, however, continued to take a long view of the subject, writing: "The important emphasis is not a date, but a lifestyle that emphasizes a joyful obedience and readiness toward God." As examples of right living, he pointed out the level of care and compassion that community members exhibited to one another, their devotion to song and prayer and worship, and the community's ability to grow an abundant harvest and share with one another throughout the winters. However, this Eden was not without its snakes: Bartholomew also denounced those in the extended *Faithful Remnant* community who had incurred significant debt in the past few years, expecting that it would never be collected (IV:4, August 1924).

--Excerpt taken from "The Crisis of Faith of Josiah Adam Whidman,"
Master of Divinity thesis written by Paul Silas, Bay Area Theological
Union, 1985.

48 TRUE BELIEVERS

"Not so bad of a deal now, was it?"

Thomas and Mike glanced up from their work to see Silas giving them a wry grin across the plank table. Thomas grudgingly nodded. He didn't like making deals, especially with people who might be crazy, but he had to admit this wasn't so bad. He was just glad the man had actually given him the thesis he'd been seeking. Most of it, anyway. For some reason, yesterday the eccentric old man kept some of the last pages back, saving it for a "later deal," whatever that meant. Now Thomas knew.

"So this is the end of the job, right?" Mike said hopefully. "Deal's a deal?"

"Oh, about another half hour," Silas replied slowly, glancing at his watch.

"But when we finish the last of these bags, then you give us the rest of the thesis, and we're outta here, correctamundo?"

"Correcto," corrected Silas.

"Great," said Mike, zipping closed yet another plastic pouch. Cardboard boxes of the survival bags sat on the hardwood floor all around the trio, surrounding them like circled wagons on the prairie suspecting an attack. The three men sat around a simple pine table in the main room of Silas' tiny bare apartment, a steam humidifier in the corner keeping the temperature uncomfortably high. The worn hardwood floors and sparse furniture giving the place all the coziness of a monastic cell. Thomas and Silas had the luxury of chairs. Mike improvised with a milk crate.

Thomas wasn't sure, but he thought that the large Ziploc in his hands was the 308th immigrant pack he had prepared this morning. That's what Silas called them, anyway: immigrant survival packages. The bulky Ziplocs were what they had seen in the hands of the refugees yesterday morning as they left Southside. To Thomas, the items seemed like what anyone might take on a weekend trip – toiletries, first aid supplies, some snacks--except for the sobering phone list of an underground railroad network of local churches, hospitals, civil lawyers, soup kitchens, Guatemalan restaurants, social workers, and emergency shelters.

It was an odd deal from an odd man. But in its own way it made sense. In exchange for most of his thesis duplicated last night at Kinko's, Silas had required a few favors: first, chauffeur service in the Jeep all around town to buy supplies for the survival kits, and then three hours of labor from each of them to help put the hundreds of kits together. To fulfill the deal, Silas let the two visitors into his apartment, part of a low cinderblock housing unit just a few blocks away from Southside Social Services.

Looking around the spartan room, Thomas didn't feel too resentful about not being able to spend last night under the roof of Silas' apartment. *The Jeep was probably more comfortable, anyway.* Thomas was swigging water out of the big recycled mayonnaise jar that Silas had provided for a drinking glass when Mike broke the productive silence with a question.

"Excuse me, Paul, I hope you don't mind me asking, but why do they call you *padre?* Are you some kind of a priest?"

Silas smiled a tired smile. "I gave up on religion a long time ago. Right about when I wrote that thesis."

Thomas entered the conversation. "Is that when you gave up believing in God too?"

Silas looked at Thomas. "I didn't give up on God. God gave up on me. Showed me who and what he really is. *Nada.*" He paused. "A big zero. Pass the Ziplocs."

Shit, that's what I told Paloma two weeks ago, Thomas thought to himself. *Is this me twenty years from now?* Thomas dropped the line of conversation. Mike, however, moved right in, ever subtle. "Well, Paul, if you think there's no God and you're not a priest, then why do you wear the black frock thing and a cross around your neck?"

Silas' gnarled hand went to the heavy silver cross on his chest, and his shoulder lifted in a sighing half shrug. "I could give you lots of answers, *niño*, but I'll give you two. First, it reminds scared immigrants of something they're familiar with, and it helps them trust me. Second, it reminds me of something I'm familiar with. The cross is an old symbol, not just Christian. The crossed bars remind me that it's human nature to be pulled in different directions. Part angel. Part beast."

"It just doesn't seem...right." Mike said, troubled. "Assuming a role that's not yours."

Silas snorted and glared at Mike. "Am I milking your sacred cows?" He nodded to himself. "I'll wear it if it gives others comfort and security in something familiar. Especially refugees who risk their lives to come to foreign land."

"Why *do* you do this work?" asked Mike, picking up three bags he just filled and putting them in the wagon circle of boxes around them.

Silas shrugged again. "Somebody has to do God's job."

Mike started, disbelievingly. "You think God doesn't help us? Who causes us to live and move and have our being?"

The older man gave a tight smile, but remained silent as his fingers continued working.

"I think something painful happened to you, Paul, something that drove you away from God," Mike ventured. Thomas, intrigued, just listened as Mike plowed boldly on. "Ask Jesus into your heart again, Paul, and he will come to you. We cry out, and he listens to our prayers. In fact, I prayed the other day that we might somehow find you, and look where we are!"

"You're a true believer, aren't you?" Silas broke in, caustically. "You're as zealous as Josiah Adam before his crisis."

"What do you mean?" Mike asked.

"You're talking just like him. Just like I used to." Silas abruptly turned his penetrating gaze to Thomas. "How much do you actually know about what happened to your great-grand uncle?"

"Me?" Thomas blurted, unexpectedly now in the conversation. "Not much, really. My family's kept him a secret until just a few months ago."

"A secret," Silas echoed, muttering. "I can see why." Suddenly, Thomas saw a new awareness in the man's eyes. Silas chuckled darkly. "You don't even know the real reason why the Gilman community broke up, do you?"

"Well, sure. Because their leader was wrong. The world didn't end in 1923."

Silas' eyes gleamed like wet black stones. "Really." His words came slowly, biting. "Then why was the community still thriving in 1925?"

Thomas opened his mouth, then closed it. "I assumed they just trickled off once the date turned out to be wrong."

"And where did Josiah go?" Silas queried. "What happened to him?"

"I only know he ended up in a sanitarium. I don't have any other details. That's why I want the rest of your thesis."

Silas calculated something in his mind, eyes distant, then brought his attention back to his guests. "Deal's changed," he said suddenly, eyes on Thomas. "Not giving you the rest until you do something else."

"Wait!" Thomas protested. "You said – "

"I know what I said. But you'll get the last part of my thesis when you make a trip to Gilman."

"Arkansas?" Thomas said, disbelieving. "Where they established the community?"

Silas nodded. "There's still a long-buried secret you need to uncover there."

"But you just can't..." Thomas' words trailed off, caught flat-footed by the other man's rapid change of direction. He wanted to yell, to negotiate, to think of *anything* that would get this crazy coot to give him the rest of the thesis right now. But before he could say another word, Silas had already returned to the conversation.

"No, the Faithful Remnant community stayed solid for two years after 1923 had come and gone. People were happy and living good lives. But then in 1925 something else occurred." The older man looked directly at Thomas once again. "Something far more traumatic." His mirthless smile was painful to behold. "You really don't know, do you?"

Thomas shook his head.

Silas drew both young men in with his small, dangerous eyes. "True believer Josiah Whidman tried to raise a man from the dead." He smiled. "You've got some digging to do in Gilman."

49 RAMBLING

As they drove back to California through the warm desert night, Thomas used his headlamp, his headphones and a clipboard to create a private study chamber in the passenger seat. Smarmy Christian rock blared and Mike pounded the steering wheel to the beat, singing at the top of his lungs out into the starlit sky. Thomas didn't care what Mike did, as long as he kept driving and allowed Thomas to read his newfound treasure in peace.

Thomas flipped through Silas' rambling thesis. He was confronted yet again by the odd litany of numbers. Professor Fowler wasn't kidding when he'd described Silas' thesis as the work of a disturbed mind. Numbers repeated like a mantra throughout the latter half of the text, erratically placed. Sometimes they interrupted otherwise cogent material in neat typewritten lines, sometimes they stood alone on a page in bold black marker, sometimes they crowded the margins in hasty penciled longhand:

$$480,000 \quad 210,000 \quad 42{:}1\text{-}3,9 \quad 1923. \quad 74.$$
$$3{:}12 \quad 42\% \quad 64 \quad 162,238 \quad 84.88$$

What do these numbers mean? thought Thomas, not for the first time. He recalled the chilling line Fowler had cited: 'It is fitting that my faith, too, dies in numbers.' He rubbed his face in bewilderment, wondering yet again what had happened to Silas. The fact that Josiah tried to resurrect a man in 1925 was new, fascinating, disturbing. But equally so was the bizarre enigma of Paul Silas: *What had happened in 1985 to turn an earnest seminarian into the black-coated wraith we met in Tucson?*

Shaking his head, Thomas turned back to the more rational parts of the Silas document. As Fowler had noted, much of the thesis was brilliantly written—absorbing, well-organized and meticulously footnoted. But Thomas' attention did not linger long in the body of the text, because right now he was pursuing a much more selfish purpose: he wanted Silas' sources, the names of real people in Gilman who could serve as Thomas' key sources too. As he reviewed the thesis under headlamp, an elderly Gilman resident named Bert Wood kept resurfacing as a source from whom Silas gained first-hand information. *Well, Mister Bert Wood, I sure hope you're still alive when I come visiting, seven years later.* Wood's name would be important when he made a trip to Arkansas some time in the future, but right now the name served a more immediate need: it was one of a growing list of sources he needed to show Cavanaugh tomorrow back at BATU.

Wow, Thomas suddenly realized. *Tomorrow.* Monday. He looked up and out into the night, and thought about what was waiting for him back in Berkeley. He lit up. He was looking forward to seeing Talia again after so long, that's for sure; she should be returning from her Arizona climbing trip sometime tomorrow afternoon. But if he was honest, he was burning even more for dinner tomorrow night with Paloma and Magda, and the mysteries his teacher had promised to reveal once the four of them were together again.

50 YOU'RE THE SMART GUY

"I have the three items you asked of me, sir."

Thomas found it a little comical that he was sitting calmly across from Professor Cavanaugh within the ivy and stone walls of the Bay Area Theological Union. To the outside world he probably appeared to be a diligent graduate student who'd been toiling in the library all week.

He'd arrived in the parking lot from Tucson twenty minutes ago. With a clean shirt on, an organized file box under his arm holding the best of his Grandmother's artifacts, and a briefcase stuffed with an inspiring volume of index cards and a copy of Silas' thesis—at least a majority of it – Thomas couldn't help but be impressed with himself. The bags under his eyes from the road trip and the stubble that climbed his cheeks above his beard only added to the look of a serious grad student.

"Let's get to it," Professor Cavanaugh drawled, poring over his notes inside a manila file labeled "Whidman, Thomas." Today, the professor was wearing his ten-gallon hat and a turquoise bolo, which somehow went well with his dark blazer, denim shirt and Levi's. *He has got this gentlemen cowboy thing down,* Thomas mused.

"'Proposed thesis topic,'" the professor quoted from his notes: "'How did the personal world of millennialist preacher and community leader Josiah Adam Whidman change when the world did not end in 1923 as he had prophesied?' Interesting angle."

As he continued to review his notes from last week's meeting, Cavanaugh's fingers fished in his top drawer for an elegant cigar box, from which he produced a handful of toothpicks. A thick silver and turquoise watch adorned his right wrist.

"Toothpick?" he queried, looking up. Thomas politely declined. "Better for the lungs than my previous habit," Cavanaugh explained, shutting the cigar box lid and turning his attention back to his scribbles. "So, Mr. Whidman, I assume you've been busy. You look more organized, anyway. You say you have the three items I asked for? Let's see 'em."

First, Thomas laid the file box on top of Cavanaugh's desk. After showing the organization of the filing system and some sample primary sources, Thomas explained the main subject headings he had established—headings such as *Initial Plans for the Gilman Community; Millennial Movements in 1900s America; Biblical Foundations for 1923 Prophecy; J.A. Whidman Personal Correspondence;* and *J. A. Whidman Biographical Notes.* Thomas had fourteen other subject headings, and each file was moderately thick with notes and copies.

Cavanaugh nodded. "This is more like it." He tipped back his hat, and glanced at his ornate wristwatch. "Little more than five more weeks, Mr. Whidman. You might have a chance. Might."

Thomas smiled at the rough compliment. He had worked hard to create order from the chaos of Grandmother Whidman's package. It had been a mother lode of information, rich and dense with primary source material. Over the day prior to the Tucson trip, Thomas had carefully read and copied each personal letter, each newspaper clipping, each evangelical tract, each photo, and then filed and cross-referenced each item under his list of headings. He had been ready for this meeting with Cavanaugh, and his work had paid off.

Although he was still smiling, up bubbled a troubling question: *Why was Silas the first to tell me about Josiah's resurrection attempt?* Why hadn't it been included in the information he got from his grandmother? His eyes narrowed. Someone in the family was still hiding information.

Thomas' mood darkened, but Cavanaugh was oblivious, thumbing through Thomas' files with his large, calloused hands. After another minute

Cavanaugh set down the file box and stared at Thomas in the face. "Next item, son. Let me take a look at that Silas thesis."

"Yes, sir," Thomas muttered. Thomas reached into his briefcase and presented the thick sheaf of copied pages for the professor's inspection.

"Interlibrary loan came through, eh?" Cavanaugh perused the document, tilting back in his rawhide office chair.

"Yeah, finally," Thomas mumbled.

Cavanaugh snorted knowingly. "Sometimes it takes so long, you'd be faster just driving across the country to get the damn thing yourself."

Thomas stared at Cavanaugh. *Is he playing with me?* Luckily, the professor's attention was turned toward the pages. *Shit, here comes the moment.* Thomas prayed the professor wouldn't be attentive enough to see that the thesis in his hands was missing an ending. *It's thick enough to appear complete,* Thomas reminded himself.

In addition to Silas withholding several pages for his own mysterious reasons, Thomas had removed all the pages where the author repeated his bizarre litany of numbers. Between the two men's edits, Thomas guessed that at least sixty pages of the original thesis were currently in his adviser's hands. *C'mon baby.* He crossed his fingers. *It's gotta work.*

Cavanaugh glanced at the title page. "'The Crisis of Faith of Josiah Adam Whidman,' eh?" he mused while flipping. Thomas began to sweat. "His commune in Arkansas was called… the Faithful Remnant Community, is that it?" The older man set the manuscript down on his desk and sucked on his toothpick. "Okay, item three." He held out a big, hairy hand. "Your summary of the Silas manuscript."

Thomas let out a deep breath, and handed over the index cards and many handwritten pages torn from a yellow legal pad bound by a paperclip. He had scribbled the summary on a notepad cradled between his knees while he and Mike sped back from Tucson in the Jeep, finishing only an hour ago. He had barely skimmed Silas' manuscript to jot down important points, and had stopped taking notes before the thesis got weird. There was no need to reveal to Cavanaugh that Silas was disturbed unless he had to.

"Unusual," said Cavanaugh slowly, at a loss for words, flipping through the yellow pages. "But seemingly not for you." His tone was icy as he glared over his bifocals. "Customarily, Mr. Whidman, research summaries requested by one's thesis adviser are not submitted in Bic pen."

"I know, sir," said Thomas hastily in a rush of words, "but the computer I was working on crashed and I had to do it all over and – "

Cavanaugh held up his hand. "Give it a rest, son." He pursed his lips and templed his fingers together. "I told you it was unwise to anger your thesis adviser. Especially one with spurs."

He leaned back in his chair. Thomas didn't breathe. "At least the rest of your stuff looks good," the professor conceded. "But no more excuses. Fix your computer problems and drop a proper summary by my office by five o' clock this evening. Slip it under my door."

"But – "

With one withering glance, Cavanaugh silenced all protest.

"Yes, sir." Thomas groaned inside.

Satisfied, Cavanaugh glanced down at his own notes. "Now, where were we? You've got your thesis topic," he said, tapping his pad. "You've got your primary sources"—he pointed, indicating the file box—"you've got the previous research on the subject"—at this point he pushed Silas' manuscript across the desk back at Thomas—"and you've got your summary. Such as it is." With that he tossed the paper-clipped yellow pages and the box of index cards back in Thomas' general direction. "It seems that you have the basic building blocks for a research paper."

"Yes, definitely," Thomas agreed, fastening his briefcase and rising.

"One more thing."

"Sir?" said Thomas, freezing in mid-flight.

"I've been thinking. Your topic is about what happened to Pastor Whidman's world *after* his prophecy failed, is it not?"

"Correct, sir." Thomas paled. *That's the piece Silas is still withholding.*

"I didn't see a lot of sources about that time in his life."

"Working on that, sir," Thomas said. "There aren't a lot of sources readily available about the man's later life or about post-1923 Gilman. That's why this thesis is worth doing. I'll be digging into unresearched territory." Thomas thought fast, remembering Silas' demand. "I've scheduled a trip to Gilman, Arkansas to collect primary sources from the site of the Faithful Remnant community. Face-to-face interviews with folks who were alive at the time, things like that." He thought of Silas and his strange bargain. "Certain sources have guaranteed me information about his later life when I visit Gilman."

"Well, why didn't you say so, son?" The professor growled, leaning forward in his chair. "Could be an interesting trip." His tongue rolled a helpless toothpick around in his mouth. "By the way, I've been meaning to ask you. This Josiah Adam Whidman. A relation of yours?"

"My great-granduncle sir," Thomas responded. "I found out only recently. He's been somewhat of a family secret up until now."

Cavanaugh nodded again, and glanced at his ornate watch for the date. "Mr. Whidman, I said I'd ride you with spurs on to finish this thesis, and it's time to get riding." Thomas paled at his professor's words. "Drop off that summary by tonight. We'll meet again two weeks from now."

"But I – "

"Love your enthusiasm," said Cavanaugh drily. "Okay, I'll make it December 22nd, last day before winter break. That will give you a chance to make this trip of yours to Gilman. This *essential* trip."

"Thank you sir. I know how important this trip is."

"I don't have the faintest idea how you're going to do it and still pass your classes, including mine, but that's your business," the professor drawled. "All I care about is what you bring to our next meeting. You'll bring me a complete first draft of your introduction, an extensive bibliography, summaries of new primary sources you find in Gilman, transcripts of your interviews, and your chapter outlines. Typed. No excuses. No Bic pen."

"Can't I – "

"You're the smart guy who made the timeline," Cavanaugh shrugged. "After that meeting, you'll have—what? – twenty four days over winter break to turn in a completed thesis before next semester's classes start January 16th."

The professor leaned back in his hide chair and put his boots up on his desk. Thomas couldn't help but notice that today the heels bore ornamental silver spurs, small but wicked. Cavanaugh grinned, reached for the Skoal can in his top drawer, and plucked out a small white square object.

"Chiclet?"

51 FISHING FROM TWO DIFFERENT STREAMS

"So how can you be a meditation master *and* a revivalist preacher?" Talia challenged Paloma as the subway rumbled away from the Claremont station bound for the East Bay. She'd returned from her climbing trip earlier today, and she and Thomas had done nothing but unpack and catch up for the last few hours—that, and take a long shower. Now Talia, Paloma and Thomas were taking the BART to meet Magda at the older couple's home for a much-anticipated dinner. Although she was snuggling up against him on the long orange subway seat, Thomas knew Tal's attention was all on the magnetic bald man standing next to her. But that was okay. So was his.

"Thomas explained a lot to me," Talia continued, "but I still can't wrap my head around your double identity."

"I know it's a stretch," Paloma conceded, leaning on one of the train's metal poles. The subway car was packed as usual this evening, but Thomas and Talia had found a single seat together while Paloma stood a foot away. "I am fishing from two very different streams, at least on the surface. But if you sink deep enough, you see that the streams connect."

"Not for me they don't," Thomas interjected. The vulnerability Thomas shared with Paloma after meditation class a week ago was gone. Now what he mostly felt was tricked. Manipulated. "Just when I thought I understood what you meant about crushing the ego, yours is toying with mine."

Paloma held out his hands. "What did I do that was so wrong?"

"What did – ?" Thomas exclaimed. "You're my meditation teacher. You can't go all born again on me!"

"But we are born again. Every day."

"Stop with the cheesy wisdom sayings," said Thomas. "Just when I thought I could trust you."

"Why would you trust me less?" Paloma inquired with a smile. "You're just pissed off because you had no idea your meditation teacher was so multifaceted."

"I'm pissed off because I had no idea my meditation teacher was an undercover Christian!" Thomas barked. "Or is it the other way around? Maybe you're a televangelist who's an undercover Zen teacher."

"You're bent out of shape because your little boxes are getting rattled," Paloma said to Thomas. "Like I said, let go of the boxes. What, are you suddenly worried that I'm a Buddhist who thinks you're going to hell?"

"No," Thomas said, a grudging smile coming to his lips.

"Okay then. What?"

Thomas just shook his head, so Talia tried. "I think it's like this. He thought you were helping him escape the chains of messed-up Christianity. Now it feels like you're dragging him back in. Like you're working for the enemy."

"Enemy! Hah! What did I say or do as Billy Swanson that unnerved you?"

"Well, it's..." Thomas halted. "I'm just not sure what to make of you anymore."

"I get it. Fishing from the two different streams is not usual, I know. But sit with it a while. See if the streams connect for you. True Buddhism and true Christianity are both about ego death, surrender and transformation. For both traditions, the small self is the obstacle." He glanced up. "By the way, make sure to get your small selves out the door at the next stop."

Thomas was still uneasy, but some of the eagerness he'd felt the other night returned. Paloma had hinted at a Way worth following, something utterly different than what passed for Christianity these days. Now that Talia had returned from her trip, Paloma and Magda were finally hosting them for the dinner they'd been promised. Thomas was hoping for a lot more than a meal.

The three of them sat with the rest of the subway crowd in a lull of silence as the BART lurched along, finally in downtown Oakland. The stop was announced and the train came to a stop, its wide doors sliding open with a hiss. The trio exited with the throng. Talia stood one step above Paloma on the escalator as they rose to street level, and as they ascended Thomas saw her looking closely at Paloma's shorn head.

"If I squint I can almost see the resemblance in the nose and jaw," she said, pinching up her eyes. "But Swanson's bad hair made you look totally different up on stage, compared to your usual chrome dome. He was meaty, too. Pudgy, even."

"I wear four wet undershirts when I'm Swanson," Paloma explained. "Helps me look thick and perspiring." They exited the terminal and began to walk east, following their teacher.

"And the big ol' glasses threw me off," marveled Talia. She shook her head. "Thomas saw you take off your disguise backstage, but not me. It's still hard for me to believe it was you up there."

"I actually didn't plan on it, you know."

"Plan what?" Talia asked.

"Being a revivalist preacher," Paloma confessed as they headed down the windy sidewalk. "Not in my wildest dreams. Now I kind of like it—I get to act like a wild man."

"A yang to your usual yin."

Paloma actually snorted at that one. "A new side, that's for sure. I only started doing it a few months ago, to get into Ben's inner circle."

"So you *are* a spy!" Thomas insisted.

"More of a tool for a greater purpose." Thomas wanted Paloma to expound on that comment, but instead he continued with the story. "After one of his Millennial Harvest events, I met Reverend Whidman backstage. Posed as an evangelical circuit preacher looking for a team to join." He looked at the younger man. "Because of your tip, Thomas, I got in."

"What tip?"

"I told him I'd had a vision as a child where Jesus put the sword of truth in my mouth, telling me to defend the faith."

"But wait—that's what *he* said."

"*Exactamente.*" Paloma grinned. "You should have seen him. He was dumbstruck: he'd found his spiritual twin. It took all of two minutes to earn his confidence."

"I don't get you." Feelings of mistrust rose up again. "Why'd you need to get cozy with my uncle in the first place?"

"I need to be part of his *Bible Before Bones* event happening in Berkeley next month. It's going to be on national television."

"You?" Talia cackled. "Wanting to be famous?"

"Wanting to stir up a little holy mischief." Paloma's face was inscrutable. "Defend the faith in my own way."

"Wait a minute." Thomas demanded. "First Magda invites us to this crazy homeless socialist dinner in Portland. Then we find out our meditation teacher goes undercover as a fundamentalist preacher. Now you're plotting some subversive guerrilla action on live TV to monkeywrench my uncle's big campaign. What are you guys up to, anyway?"

"Perfect timing." Paloma smiled as they turned the corner to see the Bay Area Catholic Worker House half a block down the street. "I think Magda has some lasagna coming out of the oven just about now."

52 SOMETHING BIGGER AND OLDER

This time, when Thomas entered the Bay Area Catholic Worker, he came in with new eyes. Last time, he'd been part of a class of gawkers that Professor Cavanaugh herded like sheep in search of religious extremists; this time, he was being invited by Paloma and Magda into their home.

Passing by the front entrance that fed into a large and crowded community center, Paloma led his guests around the side of the main building to a small door. It was painted a cheery sky blue; a small mailbox and a doormat emblazoned with a smiley face completed the strangely domestic scene. "There's a time for public, and a time for private," Paloma said as he found his keys. "This is a time for private." He grinned. "Come on in."

The older man opened the door wide, and the smells of warm lasagna and fresh-baked bread wafted out to greet them. As he stepped through the portal, Thomas noticed above his head the same painted words he had seen gracing the main entryway: 'Christ has no hands but yours.'

The door opened to a small tiled landing that stepped down to an open floor plan. From the foyer, Thomas could view the totality of the apartment: bathroom and bedroom off to the right, wood-burning stove, couch, dining table and kitchen to the left. Two beautiful loaves of fresh bread rested on the stove top, and Magda was craning over the oven, removing a large pan of lasagna. She turned in an apron and red quilted mitts, looking like a cheery lobster.

"Welcome!" she called, coming forward from the kitchen to give the newcomers huge hugs. "Our house is your house, so get comfortable. Coats can go on the hooks, shoes can stay on or off, and wine can go into your glass as often as you want." The pair followed their teacher down the steps to the dining table, where a Merlot was already open. While Paloma poured the glasses, Thomas gravitated over to the fresh baked Italian loaves warming on the wood-burning stove. "Fresh bread and wine," he said admiringly toward Magda in the kitchen. "Now that's communion." He wandered over to smell the bubbling, cheesy pan that just came out of the oven. "Throw in some of that lasagna and I'm in heaven."

"Nice to know you're easy to please," Magda came forward to join the others at the couch. "How about you, Talia? A glass of wine, perhaps?"

"That would be delightful," Talia responded, accepting a glass from Magda. She looked around the apartment, charmed. "I love the size of your place. It's like an island of coziness. I didn't expect such a treasure to be hidden in the back of the Catholic Worker."

"A time for public, and a time for private," Paloma repeated. "That's our philosophy, anyway."

"If the workers here didn't have private spaces, we would've burned out a long time ago. Three other Catholic Worker families live in little apartments like this, right next to us," Magda explained, pointing though the walls. "We deal with the poor and destitute every day, either in the health clinic or in the big kitchen or out on the streets of Oakland. It can get pretty exhausting. Sometimes you need your own space."

"I can only imagine," Talia marveled. "And I thought working with teenagers was hard."

"In the front of the building we have a great common room where the community hangs out or eats together. We usually do. Some days, though, I'd go insane without this apartment." Magda kicked off her shoes and drew her feet up under her as she sat on the couch. "It's small, but it's our refuge."

"We don't need a mansion," noted Paloma. "Just a little place where we can turn off the world for a while and recharge." He stood up. "But as you might have guessed, we didn't invite you here to discuss community planning."

The room became electric. Thomas and Talia exchanged glances. This is why they had come.

"Why we're here is to eat lasagna." Paloma smiled broadly. "Come, it's chow time."

He held a chair for Talia while Magda did the same for Thomas, and, after a fresh pour of wine, they all settled in. The four faced one another, beaming, around the simple pine table laden with steaming lasagna, a warm loaf and a fresh green salad.

Without a word Magda and Paloma gently reached for the hands of their guests between them. Thomas instinctively began to bow his head. No words came. He glanced back up to meet the gaze of the other three, who were smiling and looking directly into one another's eyes. The silent connection of energy around the table was only broken when Paloma, almost regretfully, released his grasp on the hand of Thomas to his right and Talia to his left. "Thanks for sharing our table, friends."

Slowly, the quiet that had briefly occupied Thomas' mind receded, and the questions flooded back in. Before he could pose a query, Paloma spoke.

"First, a bit of stage-setting," he said. "I've shared with Magda what I know of the two of you from meditation class. And she's told me about your experience at *Off The Vine* in Portland." He began serving steaming portions of lasagna onto plates, while Magda across the table began breaking large hunks of the warm, crusty bread. Thomas started eating with gusto, the flavors of the lasagna and Merlot mixing wonderfully on his tongue.

"And Talia, it was just today that Thomas told you I moonlight as a revival preacher, yes?"

"He was telling me about it before I even got out of the truck," she said. "It sounded so far-fetched, it was quite a while before I was willing to believe him." She ate a cheesy bite and sent a smiling glance at a shrugging Thomas. "Like I said, this whole secret identity thing is a little hard to swallow."

"It's all true," Paloma admitted, dipping his bread in garlic olive oil.

"And what about you, Magda?" Talia turned to her other side. "First, you make it sound like you were staying home for Thanksgiving, then we see you in Portland as the maitre'd for the *Sharing the Table* thing? Another secret identity. Very sneaky. What are you guys up to?"

"My question exactly," said Thomas. "No more stalling. Here we are. We have the lasagna and the wine. We want answers."

"Persistent. I like that," said Paloma, wiping his mouth. "You're right. You deserve some answers. Here they come." Their meditation teacher took a long, thoughtful draught of his Merlot, rolled the vintage across his gums, and gave a satisfied swallow. "You really don't know much about Magda and I. Think I'll start with us."

"Good choice," the striking bald woman commented from across the table, her ear bands flashing silver.

"Magda's my partner in many ways. She's been my wife for seventeen years. Even more, however, she's my spiritual partner, one of my true companions." From her seat, Magda raised her glass in a silent toast.

"Excuse me, but companion in what?" Thomas was burning. "The Catholic Worker movement?"

"Something much bigger. And older."

"An underground group?"

Paloma smiled. "Definitely."

"Spill it, man."

"Be patient, grasshopper," Paloma smiled. "A little more stage setting." He turned to his other student. "We invited you here too, Talia, because no man is an island. We all exist within webs of relationships. I've been watching Thomas for a while, and after our walk the other day when he poured out his struggles, I thought he might be ripe for what we had to offer. So on a hunch I revealed to him parts of my life that very few people know."

"You mean like sticking your wrist tattoo in front of his face backstage in Portland?" Talia asked.

Paloma nodded. "Yes, like that. Thomas needs to integrate some very different streams in his life." He paused. "Is this what you're seeking, too?" He took a bite of lasagna. "From class, I sense you're a woman of strength, humor and integrity. And I see the growth of a strong, abiding relationship between the two of you." He paused for another bite and looked across the table at his wife.

Magda now entered the conversation. "The two of you seem good for each other, Talia. But what Thomas is searching for right now and what you need in your life may be two different things."

"Different people, different paths," Talia suggested. "Different passions."

"That's it, yes," said Magda. "We don't know if any of this will grab you, but we invited you here tonight because you're so much a part of Thomas and you've seen much of what we do already. You saw what we organized in Portland."

"Who's the *we* you're talking about?" interrupted Talia. Thomas couldn't have agreed more.

"That's what we're about to tell you," Paloma said. "It may change Thomas' life, and it's only fair that you know where it came from." He wiped his hands on his napkin, and withdrew a small black leather book from his chest pocket. "We call this *The Commentaries*." It looked like a personal journal, slim and black and unadorned, with no visible title. "Sometimes, it's good to begin at the beginning. Why don't you read the first page."

Section One, The Theologos Commentaries: Preface

Dear fellow traveler,

If you are reading this, it means three things:

1. My work is actually completed. The *kairos* moment has come and these Commentaries have been published.
2. The Council of Twelve was right—Christendom is indeed cracking open again. The wild spirit of an undomesticated God is once again bubbling like yeast through the halls of Empire. Kingdom is spreading.
3. You, dear reader, are surely one of the new generation of initiates to whom the Society of Leaven has been revealed. Welcome, with all of my heart.

Behold, I am doing a new thing! Now it springs forth; do you not see it?"
– Isaiah 43:19

Something is breaking open. Something is bursting forth. God is doing a new thing. We in Leaven have discerned that after nearly two thousand years, the Empire of Christendom—that unholy alliance of state power and religious ideology—is beginning to crack. Soon there may be enough space for something new to emerge...or re-emerge. There may be enough cracks in Empire's armor for the Society of Leaven to rise into the public eye for the first time in hundreds of years. Perhaps we've caught your attention.

That's our hope, anyway. After so many generations of comfortable corruption and tasteless religion, the Way is nearly invisible within dominant culture. Western society seems bent on destroying itself, and few alternatives are in sight. The Council of Twelve has discerned that a massive body of disillusioned seekers exists in modern society, people who yearn to follow the authentic Way of the Master, but need the guidance and wisdom that the Society of Leaven offers. These hungry souls ache to encounter real Called Out Ones, spirit-possessed men and women who are boldly embodying the kingdom of God right under the nose of Empire.

Are you one of these seekers? Have you encountered a member of Leaven who exploded your reality, then showed you this dangerous little book?

If so, congratulations. Welcome to the Way. It's not always pleasant, but it's certainly not boring.

Be clear right now: you can still turn back if you want. Just close the book and go back to your well-tended life. But if you're tired of being ruled by fear and selfishness and want to try God-sized living, keep reading.

What you have in your hands is a modern English version of a book we call *The Commentaries.* The Society of Leaven has commissioned me, Pater Theologos of Mount Athos, to revise and update it. This book is to serve as a *didache,* a teaching instructing those who seek the authentic Way of the Master. Trust us: you need to be instructed. After nearly two millennia of repackaging by Christendom, the Way has become massively distorted; a new initiate might have a hard time finding the authentic path laid out by Jesus. These Commentaries are meant to assist an initiate under the guidance of a mentor—in ancient Christian language, a *catachumen* being guided by a *catechist* – as he or she begins walking in the path of Leaven.

Blessings on the journey –

Pater Theologos, Mount Athos, 1965

53 LEAVEN RISING

"Oh my God," Talia said, looking up from the first page of the slim volume. "This is for real?"

Thomas echoed her thoughts. "You're part of some secret brotherhood?"

"Sisterhood too." Paloma looked to his partner.

"Sounds all mysterious, but it's true," said Magda. "And it has to stay secret."

"But why – "

Paloma's raised hand caused Thomas to pause in mid-sentence. "We'll get there in just a minute, Thomas. But first, Magda and I need to be sure of something: no one else can hear a word of what is shared tonight."

"Fair enough," said Thomas. "I've already been keeping your double identity a secret."

Talia nodded. "You can count on me. If you bribe me with more lasagna."

Paloma grinned and served another ample portion. "Well then, I'll dive in." He stood up with his wine glass. "Magda and I are part of what is called the Society of Leaven. For almost two thousand years this organization has existed in one form or another. Although members come from all walks of life and have lived in all parts of the world, we are dedicated to the same path, the same cause. We are all followers of the Way."

"That's what the book said," Talia commented. "But what Way are you talking about?"

The older couple exchanged glances. Smiling, Paloma said, "Actually, we are not going to talk much about the Way. Talking about the Way at this stage often leads to trouble; it is to be lived."

"Stephen's right," Magda said. "As our brother Francis of Assisi said, 'preach the Gospel at all times. If necessary, use words.'"

"Saint Francis was – " Talia began.

"So you're Catholic," Thomas blurted at the same time.

"Only catholic with a small 'c,' Magda replied, smiling at the burst of comments. "Originally, *catholic* meant universal. But no, we're not an organization within the Catholic Church. Although some of us, like Francis and Dorothy Day, were members of that Church also."

"And as for your question," Paloma looked at Talia, "yes, Francis of Assisi was part of Leaven. One of our brightest."

"But he was a monk. He started the Franciscans!" said Thomas, unbelieving.

"No he didn't," Paloma responded. "Others created an organization after he died." He held out his hands. "Francis himself – he lived his life dedicated to the Master. He just followed the Way, and in so doing, reshaped the world."

"So the Way's a form of Christianity," Thomas pressed.

"This is where labels can be confusing." Paloma paused. "Yes, the Way's a form of Christianity, but it's rarely seen in churches. It is not part of Christendom. It's the life force within Christianity, the blood that pumps within the body."

"What do you mean exactly, 'Christendom?'" asked Talia.

"Stephen might give you a more nuanced definition," Magda said. "I call it what it is: the hijacking of Jesus."

Section Two, The Theologos Commentaries:
The Rise of Christendom and the Fall of the Way

We in Leaven can point to the mid-fourth century as the time when the Way began to be methodically marginalized. This was when the Roman emperor Constantine adopted the Christian faith and declared Christianity to be the imperial state religion. He invited the *ekklesia*—a word typically translated as "church," but originally meaning the "Called Out Ones" – to come in from the edge of respectable society, where it had been existing for hundreds of years, and join him in Christianizing the world. I cannot emphasize enough what a radical change this was—in short, it could be compared to a political dissident suddenly becoming an adviser to the President. Not only did the institutional Church rapidly acquire lands and resources as a partner of imperialism, but also it became the authority of spiritual well-being and the judge of moral values throughout the massive Roman Empire.

By initiating this partnership of church control and imperial will, Constantine set in motion a process that would last for hundreds of years and eventually bring all Europe under a vastly powerful machine known as 'Christendom.'

We of Leaven are convinced that, whatever its many benefits, Christendom twisted Christianity into a mockery of itself. In particular, we are convinced that the church left the Way of Jesus behind as it traveled from a place of non-cooperation with Empire to a place of government popularity and privilege. The institutional church stopped giving allegiance to the upside-down Kingdom of God as it took an honored place in the Kingdom of Caesar.

Following Jesus, no longer a part of Christendom? There is plenty of evidence for this. Contrast the sermons preached at the end of the third century with those preached at the end of the fourth, and ask where the teaching of Jesus has gone. Compare pre-Christendom artwork with Christendom depictions of Jesus and note how the good shepherd has been replaced by a remote, imperial figure (not unlike Constantine, in fact). Consider the creeds produced by the institutional Church in the early Christendom period, which move straight from Jesus' birth to his death ('born of the Virgin Mary, suffered under Pontius Pilate'), with no reference to his life or teachings.

Before Christendom, entry into Christian community was granted to a new initiate only after a careful formation process (a process known as 'catechesis'), in which the life and teachings of Jesus figured strongly. This process of initiation and formation was powerfully counter-cultural, and lasted up to three years, strengthening the new convert to "be in the world but not of it." However, by the end of the fourth century, this lengthy training had to be modified to serve the crowds flooding into the churches now that Christianity enjoyed imperial favor. Much less time was devoted to the teaching of Jesus. The church's teaching of new converts emphasized doctrinal belief and avoiding heresy, rather than a lifestyle of counter-cultural discipleship and non-cooperation with Empire. Newly-established creeds were crucially important to this process, but it seems the life and teachings of Jesus were not.

There were understandable reasons why the imperial church marginalized Jesus as fourth-century Christians struggled to adapt to a new social and political context. His teaching, which had been challenging enough for a powerless, marginal community, seemed utterly unrealistic and inapplicable for Christians who were in charge of an empire. What did it mean to 'love your enemies' (Mt 5:44) or 'not worry about tomorrow' (Mt 6:34) when one was in charge of defending the self-interests of a nation? How could such instructions be translated into foreign or economic policies against hostile neighbors? Jesus seems not to have anticipated this development or given any counsel to those with an imperial administration to manage. Church leaders turned instead to the Old Testament for guidance: after all, ancient Israel had an economy to run, borders to defend, resources to protect, and a social system to organize.

54 UNDERGROUND FOR CENTURIES

"Christendom's a concept with a lot of baggage," Paloma explained. "It's a word often used by academics, but rarely understood. Christendom began to take over Christianity almost seventeen hundred years ago, when the Roman emperor Constantine made Christianity the religion of the empire."

"You're saying that's when Jesus got jacked?" Talia asked.

"His Way certainly did. What now was called Christianity became a power structure aligned with military rulers that controlled state religion throughout Western civilization. It managed doctrine and salvation and became *the* moral authority on earth, acting as God's judgment."

"Ugh," said Talia. "Sounds like the military-industrial complex, but with the fate of your soul thrown in."

"Christendom became the gatekeeper to heaven, handing out tickets to the afterlife based upon conformity, financial contributions and correct belief."

"The religio-economic henchman of the state?" Thomas suggested.

"In bed with empire," Paloma concurred as he swirled his wine. "So far from what the Master wanted."

"The Way was almost strangled out of existence, and went underground," Magda explained as Paloma lapsed into a rare, brooding silence. "Literally underground, in caves outside of Jerusalem. Near a place called Suba. That's where some followers of the Way first began to call themselves the Society of

Leaven. The Way's been underground for centuries upon centuries, so these days it's a life path that has very little in common with the habits and practices of most people who call themselves Christian. But that's where it should be, I guess. Underground. Percolating."

"The Master said it like this," Paloma added. "'The Way is like leaven mixed into a large amount of dough. Invisible, tiny, it spreads and does its work unnoticed, transforming the whole until it's all leavened.'"

"No, he didn't," Thomas responded. "He said the *kingdom of heaven* is like leaven mixed into a large amount of dough. Not the Way."

Magda only shrugged. Paloma gave that smile of his. He drank the last of his wineglass and set it on the table. "Before we get ahead of ourselves, we need to discuss the early Jesus movement."

"Weren't we just doing that?" asked Talia with a raised eyebrow.

"I guess you could say that," Paloma considered. "But now I'm taking us three hundred years earlier. The *really* early Jesus movement. The earliest people who'd walked with Jesus simply called themselves 'followers of the Way.' The term Christian wouldn't be invented for another hundred years."

"That's hilarious!" Talia blurted, cracking up. Thomas stared at his girlfriend.

Paloma smiled. "I didn't realize I was being funny. What did I say?"

"Jesus wasn't a Christian!" Talia crowed.

"True," Thomas laughed. "Wonder what Uncle Ben would say to that?" A new gleam entered Thomas' eyes. "I wonder if the bible-thumpers in Ben's church realize that the early Jesus movement didn't *have* any Bibles?"

Talia looked momentarily confused.

"Jesus, and those who followed him, were all Jews," Paloma explained. "They had the Jewish scriptures – the Torah, the Tanakh, and the Prophets—but the books that eventually became the Christian Bible didn't exist yet."

"And those books came from a lot of people?" Talia inquired.

"Not as many as you might think," said Paloma. "Most of the New Testament is from the perspective of one man who never knew Jesus in the flesh: Paul, a man who spent his earlier life murdering the original followers of Jesus."

"Poetic, isn't it?" Magda said. "The man who tried to wipe out the early followers of Jesus was the one who almost single-handedly spread the dominant version of Christianity into the world."

"I don't quite get it," interjected Talia. "Did Paul kill the Way but spread Christendom in its place?"

"It's much more complex than that," said Paloma. "Paul was an absolutely God-possessed human being. We all have perspectives, and Paul's was unique. There's no evidence he ever met the flesh-and-blood Jesus, but his life was turned upside down when he had an encounter with the risen Christ on the road to Damascus. It utterly transformed everything about him, and he couldn't stop talking about it. Paul's take on Jesus caught on wherever he traveled. It spread like wildfire throughout the Roman Empire at a key moment in history. He fostered groups of worshippers all around the Greek-speaking Mediterranean. Paul's followers practiced parts of the Way, but it seems that they focused less on following the *example* of Jesus and more on worshipping the risen Christ. Paul himself encouraged the imitation of Christ in this life, but those who came after him focused much of their energy upon saving souls for the afterlife. Paul's letters to these groups, written about thirty to fifty years after Jesus died, make up much of the New Testament."

"And the Gospel accounts of Matthew, Mark, Luke and John were written decades after Jesus died, too," Thomas added. "Probably penned by scribes who were the foreign students of the first followers, written in a foreign language far removed from Jesus' native tongue."

Paloma noticed Thomas' pained face after he spoke. "What is it?" he asked.

"A year ago I had a tough conversation with my uncle Ben about this," Thomas explained. "We both love Koine Greek, and he'd taught me nuances of the language since I was eight. He also raised me to believe that the Bible is the inerrant Word of God. So in my first year of seminary, when I learned that the New Testament wasn't written in Jesus' language, I was pretty troubled. Ben and I had already parted ways, but I didn't have anyone else to go to, so I came to him to talk about it. Or tried to." The young man shook his head. "One part of Ben knew the undisputed facts, but another part of him didn't want to deal with the ramifications that all of the New Testament—the Scripture that Christians regard as bible truth – was written decades after Jesus died in a language that was foreign to him."

"All but four pages."

Thomas started. "What, you mean the *Letter of James?*"

Paloma nodded.

Thomas raised his eyebrows. "You're saying *James* was first written in Aramaic?"

"I most certainly am," Paloma responded. "Our favorite Budeo-Christian."

"The guy in the bone crypt?" asked Talia. She looked at Thomas. He just stared, mouth open.

Paloma nodded. "James the Just. The older brother of Jesus. Leaven's spiritual father." He looked at Thomas. "The man who took the Way underground."

Section Three, The Theologos Commentaries:
The Earliest Followers of the Way

Christendom has long claimed that Peter was the rock upon which Jesus built his church. A closer reading of history makes it clear that Jesus' brother James (known as "the Just") was actually the first among leaders after the Master died. Passages in the book of Acts show Peter (called Cephas), John, and the other disciples—all known as "Pillars" because they'd actually been in Jesus' inner circle – all deferring to James' wisdom and leadership. When the itinerant apostle Paul comes to Jerusalem, it is James the Just he comes to visit. It was James who was the original leader of the disciples gathered in Jerusalem, the earliest group of people who had known and followed Jesus. It is James, listed first along with Peter and John, who gives Paul his blessing in Galatians as the missionary prepares for his journey, asking Paul to make sure to remember the poor.

Who were the earliest Christians before Christianity existed? By what names and actions were they known? James' community simply called each other "followers of the Way." They were, by all accounts, both poor and poor in spirit, for they had given up the self-seeking values of Empire long ago, and placed little emphasis upon the self. Seeing their ragged appearance, their surrender of personal property, their solidarity with the lowest classes and radical humility of heart, Romans and Jews alike called them *Evionim* – in Greek *Ebionites,* a derogatory term meaning "the Poor Ones." These Ebionites, led by James the Just, are the forefathers of Leaven, and followed the Jesus Way long before anyone ever heard the term Christian.

Just before Rome destroyed Jerusalem in AD 70, these early Ebionites fled the violent atmosphere present in the Holy City and settled in nearby caves, near present-day Suba. Their isolated, primitive community stood in stark contrast to the Roman Empire and Jewish Temple worship. Caring for outcasts and treating others compassionately were not just aspirations or noble deeds for these earliest followers of the Way—they were the basic tenets of authentic religion. For those of us raised in modern Christendom, the previous statement seems preposterous, even heretical--until we understand the message comes to us straight from the original Jesus community, through the Aramaic writings of his brother, James the Just.

55 A SLIM THING, OFTEN IGNORED

Growing up in his uncle's church, Thomas had been trained to view the *Letter of James* with suspicion. "Too Jewish," Pastor Benjamin Whidman had commented during a Bible study in Thomas' freshman year in high school, a lifetime ago. "Too much about works. No emphasis on being saved by the risen Christ." Uncle Ben was proud to say his opinion was the same as that of Martin Luther himself, who in the 16th century had dismissed James' letter as "an epistle of straw." Luther suggested *James* should be thrown out of the New Testament because of its emphasis upon correct action—doing the right thing—rather than focusing primarily upon the power of divine grace. When Thomas lingered in *James* as he and Mike read through the Bible as Promising Young Pastors, Ben had scoffed. When Thomas had latched onto the tiny book and refused to move on to Revelation, Ben had been horrified.

Now, dinner was over, and Paloma had brought the young couple out to the back porch of the Catholic Worker while Magda prepared dessert. Under the light of a table candle, he opened a Bible to the *Letter of James*. Looking over Talia's shoulder at the scripture, Thomas reeled, mystified that such a slim thing, the letter that pulled at his heart a decade ago, might be the most direct link that the Bible had to the first followers of Jesus. Ben had wanted to discount it entirely, but here was Paloma asserting it was the only text in the entire New Testament written in Jesus' native language. How did Paloma know this? Thomas had never heard this claim before, not in seminary and not in any book. Thomas had always assumed the ancient Greek version he read in his uncle's study was the original.

But Paloma seemed to have a special knowledge of *James*. He even asserted the Aramaic was written by Jesus' brother himself in his own hand, scribed well before he was thrown to his death from the High Temple in 62 AD. Paloma's claim would make *James* the oldest book in the New Testament—

before Paul, before the Gospels, before everything. It caused Thomas to examine James' words in a brand new light.

"Here it is, the line you preached at *Peace Surplus*," Talia said to Thomas as she nuzzled close, sitting on the back porch. "*'Pure religion is this: to look after orphans and widows in their distress.'*

Paloma had gone inside to help with dessert, and left the two of them alone. Talia had never seen the *Letter of James* before, and was devouring it. Through her eyes, Thomas did too. Her finger moved through the verses as she murmured aloud. "*If you truly love your neighbor as yourself, you are doing right.'*" She tapped the page. "Now I see what Paloma means about James sounding Budeo-Christian. This line sounds like it's from the Dalai Lama."

Seconds later she found another passage that stopped her. "Check this out! *'Suppose a brother or sister is without clothes and daily food. If one of you says to him, 'Go, I wish you well; keep warm and well fed,' but does nothing about his physical needs, what good is it? In the same way, faith by itself, if it is not accompanied by action, is dead.'*" She looked up to Thomas' face, inches away. "Now I see why this rocked your world."

She read on silently, and so did Thomas, absorbed in a two-thousand year old message that went straight to their hearts. But only a few minutes after they'd started, Talia looked up, disappointed. "That's it?" She checked the back of the fourth page to make sure it was done.

"Well, it's not a book. It's really just a letter."

"Barely." She laughed. "More like 'A Sticky Note from James.' Or maybe 'James' Quick Tips.'"

"He didn't mess around," Thomas agreed. The words were so different from the miraculous stories and flowery theology he found in so many other places in the Bible. Practical, immediate, wise. Transformational.

"Dessert is served," Paloma called from inside the kitchen. "Magda says come and get it."

"You go in, I'll join you in a minute," Talia said, pulling the candle closer. "I want to read this again."

Thomas had taken but two steps toward the kitchen when Talia's voice stopped him. "Thomas, you wrestle with stuff inside of you that I'll never really understand."

He stopped and turned. "You don't wrestle inside?"

"I wrestle inside. But not with the things you wrestle with." She turned a little more to look directly at him. "I wrestle with relationships. I wrestle with broken humans and the terrible things we do to each other. I wrestle with the war and those bastards who send young kids to go kill for oil in Iraq. You, you wrestle with those things, but you keep going. You wrestle with God."

"Yeah," he said darkly, "I can't seem to stop." He turned to go.

"Hey."

He turned once more to her voice. She looked at him with kind gray eyes. "Your wrestling makes you stronger," she said quietly. "Stronger, and more messed up." He made a face, and she smiled. "The hard stuff you're wrestling with right now is going to make you a better person for the world. I know it." She turned back to her reading.

"How'm I'm doing?"

"What?" she laughed, startled. "Wrestling with God?"

"Yeah."

Talia got up and came over to wrap her arms around Thomas' neck. "He's got you in a freaking half-nelson, chump. Now go eat your dessert."

56 A JOB AHEAD OF US

"Where's Magda? Turned in early?" Thomas said as he returned to the kitchen, picking up a stack of used plates from the table as he came. After they'd all had dessert he'd excused himself to the bathroom, and came back to find Paloma alone at the sink.

"The women had some sort of huddle a few moments ago," Paloma commented. "I think they're both out on the back porch watching the stars. They seem to have concocted a plan to leave us alone. To talk. With the dishes."

Paloma handed Thomas a dishtowel. The sleeves of his dark denim shirt were rolled up, hands deep in steaming soapy water. Surveying the scene of dishes covered in lasagna sauce, Thomas sighed. "Got a bit of a job ahead of us," he stated, drying the wine glasses.

Paloma looked directly at Thomas and stopped, as if he just said something significant. "Yes. Yes, we do."

"You Zen masters really like cryptic sayings like that, don't you?"

Paloma laughed out loud. "Yes. Yes, we do."

Alongside his teacher at the sink, Thomas saw something on Paloma's exposed left wrist he'd been wondering about. "So now that we've shared a meal and you've revealed that you're a closet revival preacher working for a two-thousand year old secret bread-making brotherhood, do I get to know about your matching tattoos?"

Paloma held up his left hand in the light: a slim, dark braided design encircled his wrist like a bracelet. "Not yet," said the older man, gazing for a moment as the suds dripped down past the tattoo. "But there may soon come a time."

"Tell me about something else then," said Thomas. "I know you said you shouldn't talk about it much, but I'd like to know more about the Way."

"*The Commentaries* got you a little curious, did they?"

"Curious, and conflicted," Thomas admitted, shaking his head. "Talia just named my condition perfectly." Paloma gave an inquiring look, and Thomas went on. "On your porch just now, she told me that I'm always wrestling with God. And right now she says He's got me in a freaking headlock."

At that image, his teacher laughed out loud. "Sounds pretty dead on."

"I know. It's funny." His smile faded. "And not funny at all. I'm messed up, Paloma," Thomas confessed.

"How so?"

"What I experienced in Guatemala showed me there's no loving God out there caring for us." Thomas paused, and glanced over at his teacher. "But I don't want to live in a world without one."

"That's a hard place to be," Paloma said. "Trust me, I know. For the first half of my life, despair was a much closer friend than hope. Life wasn't very pretty for me." He scrubbed at a crusted lasagna pan. "I tried to kill myself twice."

"Ouch. That makes my crisis seem pretty silly."

Paloma looked kindly at his student. "Maybe. We all come to this point in different ways, but at the end it's the same: we all want a life that's more than just randomness and cruelty. We all ache for a God that's present, a God worth believing in and a Way worth following. Those things can be hard to find in today's world." He arched an eyebrow. "Isn't that why you're here tonight?"

Thomas examined his motives. He remembered the words he spoke to Paloma in the candle-lit dojo: *I'd die for a God like that.* "Yeah, it is. I guess I'm came hoping you and Magda can help me find those things."

Paloma dried his hands on the dishtowel and crossed to the living room. Picking up *The Commentaries*, he grabbed Thomas' hand and placed the slim black volume onto the younger man's palm.

"Read a few more pages and see what you think. It's a good introduction to Leaven and Christendom, and it should give you a strong sense of what Leaven is like. Be careful, though. The book can be dangerous."

"Dangerous?" Thomas smirked. "Isn't it just a bunch of words? Words can be ignored any time you want."

"Words can be traps," said Paloma. "Information without action is one of the great failings of modern society. Reading *about* something often tempts us to imagine we actually *know* something.

"I get it. *Knowing about* the Way is a very different thing than actually *knowing* the Way."

"Very good," replied Paloma. "To actually know the Way requires practicing the Way. So I encourage you to read *The Commentaries* with that warning in mind. Even though it is merely words, it *is* a good place to begin. It helped me when I was a *catachumen.*"

"You read this during your training?"

Paloma looked down to Thomas' outstretched hand. "That very copy. My mentor was the author, a Greek monk named Pater Theologos."

Thomas opened the thin book to its title page. A thought struck him. "Hey, I have a question that's been bugging me. Why did Leaven write a book to train apprentices for their secret society two thousand years *after* it began? Isn't that a little late?"

Paloma laughed. "One of many, Thomas. This is the seventh version ever written in English, I believe. I have an old copy in Spanish, too. There have been many other versions, other languages. Many other *kairos* moments across the centuries. This one was written about thirty years ago, when a *kairos* moment was identified in the English-speaking West."

Kairos, Thomas thought. The right or opportune moment. It was one of his favorite words in Koine, one that could convey so much more than it's counterpart in English. The ancient Greeks had two words for time: *chronos*, meaning sequential time, and *kairos*. *Kairos* was a time when something special could happen, an opportunity in line with the will of the gods.

"In the late 1950s, some of our wisest leaders sensed a *kairos* moment coming," Paloma continued. "They began to sense a new spirit moving in America, as well as a massive cultural shift beginning to happen in the Western world. God's ancient dreams were becoming real--captives were being liberated, justice was rolling down like waters, outcasts were receiving dignity. Some folks in Leaven were pretty involved during that time in the struggles for civil rights in America and social justice worldwide. They – "

"You're not trying to say that Martin Luther King was part of Leaven, are you?"

A smile played across Paloma's lips. "What do you think?"

Before Thomas could voice a response, Paloma continued. "Like I said, Leaven sensed the possibility of a massive shift happening in the English-speaking world. We were in pretty deep. Have you heard of Vatican II?"

"Sure. It shook up the Catholic world."

"Yes, a lot of fresh air blew into Christendom then. We had more than a little to do with that."

"Wasn't that the biggest reform in modern history?"

"Yeah. The Church opened its windows for the first time in ages. People were hungry to live the Way again, and a new spirit was moving across the land. Leaven sensed the *kairos*, and bubbled up into the loaf of dominant society once more to feed that hunger. In order to do that well, the Council of Leaven asked Pater Theologos in the early 1960's to write a modern version of *The Commentaries* to serve as a kind of teaching manual. Its purpose is to help prepare apprentices who are ready to be God's hands and feet in the world."

"And you're giving this book to me? To be the hands and feet of God?" Thomas let go of *The Commentaries,* leaving the book hanging in the grasp of the older man. "I'm not sure I'm ready for that."

"Hacemos el camino al andar."

"What?" The Spanish phrase took Thomas a moment. "You said that to me before I went to Guatemala." Thomas' eyes flashed. "What if I don't want to make the road by walking? What if I don't want to be the hands and feet of God?"

Paloma held his gaze. "What are you afraid of, Thomas?"

"You. Leaven. God. Getting crucified."

Paloma laughed, full of warmth. "I get it. You're right to be afraid. I think you realize—better than I did as a young man—that once you come to know Leaven, your life will never be the same." Hawk eyes glinting, Paloma stretched out his arm, presenting the book. "There comes a point when you need to make a choice, Thomas Whidman. There comes a point when you need to jump out and trust. Despite your doubts, despite your fear. Do you want to walk the Way?"

Chills went down Thomas' spine. "Six months ago I would've scoffed at that question, because I was sure I was already on it, like the rest of Christianity. Then two months ago, I was so done with God I would've laughed in your face. But now..." He looked directly at Paloma. "Now I say yes." He took the outstretched book., then chuckled to himself and shook his head. "Meeting the two of you has messed everything up. Again."

"Messy things are usually more interesting."

"Finding out that you're a Zen Buddhist *and* a circuit preacher....being part of that *Sharing the Table* thing in Portland...Coming here tonight to your house...." Thomas halted and looked down at the book in his hands. "My boxes are breaking wide open. I better go before I change my mind."

"Don't worry," Paloma said. "We've entrusted you with a lot of secrets just now, but we're not holding you to anything. If you don't like what you read in *The Commentaries*, give it back and pretend you never came to our house tonight." He walked toward the coat rack in the foyer and found Thomas' jacket. "Go now," Paloma said. "Take the book, go find Talia and take a walk in the moonlight. Sleep on all we've shared tonight. I'll be at the tea house tomorrow for lunch. Read a few pages between now and then, and find me there if you want to start the journey."

Section Four, The Theologos Commentaries:
Worshipping Without Following

The Master's teaching wasn't the only problem for Christendom as it began to grow through Western Europe under Constantine and those after him. More troublesome was Jesus' lifestyle. What was the institutional church to do with a Lord who was homeless and shared food with outcasts? How could Christendom erase his thirst for justice, his care for the downtrodden, and his confrontations with wealth and power—the very things the church was now coveting? As the church gained more power, the upside-down, last-will-be-first values Jesus taught and practiced were fast becoming alarming and impractical.

Even more vexing was the embarrassing reality that Jesus had been crucified by the same Roman Empire that now claimed him as its Lord. Many in Christendom sought to blame the Jews as the 'Christ killers,' but in truth there was no escaping the role of Rome. To their credit, the early framers of the creeds of Christendom still named Roman governor Pontius Pilate as the man responsible for the death of Jesus. To the earliest followers of the Way, the cross had been a powerful symbol of triumph of love over hatred and forgiveness over vengeance. Not only was the cross a visceral reminder that the Jesus Way was to lay down one's life rather than take the life of another, but to the earliest Christians it also was a stark reminder of how brutally the Roman Empire treated anyone who opposed it, including Jesus.

What could the imperial church do with a revolutionary Jesus and a troublesome cross? Now that Christendom was in league with Empire, both had to be radically reinterpreted. Obviously, Jesus himself could not be entirely whitewashed out of the story. But his teachings, lifestyle and message could be redesigned and domesticated.

The handling of the Sermon on the Mount is a classic example of how Christendom repackaged Jesus. The church found several ingenious ways to evade its challenge. Some theologians decided its life-changing value system was mandatory for the clergy but beyond the reach of most Christians. Others said its socially explosive message was not for the present age, but rather must be describing life in the coming kingdom of God. Still others affirmed that Jesus' instructions applied only to interior attitudes, not to outward behavior, so that agents of Empire could still love enemies into whom they were thrusting swords.

This recasting of Christianity's founder ensured that Jesus could be simultaneously honored and ignored. By reframing him as a remote, imperial figure and emphasizing his divinity much more than his humanity, the church of Empire could worship and honor Jesus without needing to take his teachings seriously. Since this repackaging more than 1600 years ago, the juggernaut of Christendom has given to the world a form of Christianity that spiritualizes and dehumanizes Jesus while domesticating and devaluing his transformative Way. This kind of Jesus should be worshipped as a romanticized personal savior, but by no means is he to be followed. It is safe to say that, under Christendom's ancient and immense shadow, most of the modern world has heard only whispers of anything else.

Yet the Society of Leaven embodies a very different kind of Christianity. We try, anyway. It is the whole life of our Lord, rather than just his death, that remains at the center of our tradition. We have stayed true to the way of life-change in the desert and the Way of Jesus as passed down through his brother, James the Just. Like a number of other resistance movements throughout history, we strive to resist the temptations of Empire. We know with certainty the existence of a Spirit-filled alternative kingdom, one that rejects Caesar and uplifts the downtrodden. This is the true good news.

We of Leaven are broken people, imperfect as anyone, yet we have something to offer this world. New winds of change are blowing. Empires and institutions are becoming brittle and being dismantled. Christendom is cracking. There are signs that the Master and his teachings might be making something of a comeback in modern society – not so much as an object of belief but as an example to be followed. A movement is awakening, and it seems that the Jesus of the Way, rather than the Christ of the creeds, is the one who attracts seekers today.

A new spirit is rising in the loaf of society. Are you ready to play your part?

57 AN UTTERLY INSANE CULT

"Read any good books lately?" Paloma inquired with a wink the next day at noon.

"'Til about two in the morning," Thomas replied as he crossed the little cafe. He'd come in from the December cold into the steamy warmth of Tolstoi's Tea House, and now his nose was dripping. He took off his jacket and book bag, and flopped into the booth. "*The Commentaries* are mind blowing, Paloma. I can't read too much without my mind spinning."

"It's rich," Paloma acknowledged. "Take it slowly and take time to digest it."

"It's hard to believe you guys are for real," Thomas admitted. "Two thousand years in hiding? For all I know, you and Magda made up this Theologos character and are part of an utterly insane cult."

"Fair enough," Paloma laughed. "Many people today would say we are. The Way we follow is absolutely contrary to the logic of Empire."

"No kidding. Take your first step: *metanoia*. Line up, everybody, to commit social suicide."

"I told you that you might have to die to join a Way worth following," Paloma said with a wry look. "Romans 12:2." Without another word, Paloma stood up from his side of the booth and loomed tall over the table, placing his body right under the restaurant's overhead lamp. "Do not conform, Thomas, to the values of this world," Paloma said in the deep Southern tones of Billy Swanson, "but rather be transformed by a complete revolution of your mind." Seeing the man's bald head lit up and gleaming under the lights,

Thomas flashed to an image of the same man lurking behind a bad toupee and glasses, sweating and pulsating under the harsh lights of Portland Coliseum.

When Paloma sat back down Billy Swanson was gone, and the Zen teacher had returned. "As you know, many Christians give lip service to this kind of transformation, but they aren't willing to do the work. They don't realize the degree of emptying that needs to happen in order to be filled by the Spirit. The surrendering is our work; the filling is God's."

"Kenosis," Thomas murmured. "That's the Greek word for the radical emptying you're talking about."

Paloma nodded, impressed. "It's the absolute surrender of the self needed to live the Christ, be the Christ."

"Like Paul wrote, 'It is no longer I who live; rather, it is Christ who lives in me.'"

"The transformed man himself," Paloma concurred. "A lot of progressives today say that Paul had it all wrong. But he had a lot more right than wrong. He knew exactly what it was like to be stripped of everything and be born into a totally new life." Paloma paused. "In the Gospels, you remember how Jesus attracted his first followers?"

"The disciples? He found them fishing at the Sea of Galilee."

"That's right. There's an urgency in those meetings. He challenges them to turn away from everything familiar if they want to walk the Way. When he says, 'Drop your things and follow me,' he's calling for *metanoia*. So later, when he says things like, 'I am the Way, the truth and the life,' when he says, 'There is no other way to the Father but through me,' he's not talking about belief. He's not saying, 'you must worship me.'"

"It's more like he's saying 'experience me.'"

"Exactly!" Paloma said, looking right at Thomas. "He's saying 'Experience me! Trust my Way!' Drop everything, and be filled. 'I am the vine and you are the branches.' Eat of my body, drink of my blood. Think about what communion really means, Thomas. Take part in my body, he's saying. Be me."

"Like the words over your door," Thomas remembered. "Christ has no hands or feet but yours.'"

"This is the way of Leaven, Thomas. God needs a body in this world." Paloma looked up, an unspoken question in the air.

"You make it sound so clear." Thomas drank his last sip of chai, his lips pursed. "I want to believe in a God-filled world. But I'm not seeing it."

"What aren't you seeing?"

"God. I'm not seeing a loving God hovering around, just waiting to fill us up." He paused. "Leaven reminds me of a football team waiting for a pass. Everybody's blocking, the receivers are running deep, the running back is fanning out for a short dish, they're all looking for the ball...but when it comes down to it, there's no pass. Everyone's playing their heart out, and the quarterback's not even on the field." He shrugged and reached for his backpack. "I better get back to campus. Cavanaugh's really breathing down my neck about my thesis."

"I can see you're busy," Paloma said, looking down into his cup. "We'll just see each other at meditation from now on."

"No." Thomas' answer came to his lips at a speed that surprised him. "I didn't mean that." He slipped back into the booth. "You and Magda blew my mind the other night. What you shared with me..." He paused, searching for words. "God, I want to believe it's real. I never even imagined something like Leaven existed."

Paloma looked kindly into his student's hesitant face. "But."

"But until I see the quarterback, I'm not ready to join the team." Thomas looked up at Paloma, eyes full of a fragile hope. "Do I have to decide now?"

Paloma shook his head kindly. "You've got *The Commentaries* on a long-term loan, Thomas. Let's see what happens."

"I'm sorry I'm so confused," the younger man said. "If God would just knock me flat on my back like Paul, it'd be easy." He laughed at himself as he got out of the booth again. "Thanks for being patient. I'll keep reading, and I'm sure I'll have a lot to talk with you about before class tomorrow night. See you then."

- - - - -

As his student walked through the tiny cafe to the front entrance, Stephen Paloma turned around in his booth and spoke to a beaded curtain blocking off an arched hallway. "He's gone."

The immense bearded head of the old monk Pater Theologos popped through the beaded opening like a giant puppet, his aviator glasses merging with his fuzzy gray cheeks. "That little *puer!*" he chuckled. "Did that little pup really suggest that I was a figment of your imagination?" With one elegant swish of a black-robed arm, the old monk drew back the full curtain to let Paloma pass within.

"He sure did," laughed Paloma, ducking under Theologos' arm. In a few steps he reached a small side room at the back of the restaurant, and sat down at a table with a few familiar faces. "He called Magda and I insane, and that's before meeting our leader."

"Insanity's all a matter of perspective. I'll take it as a compliment." Sofia Kazantzakis, the woman called the Shepherd of Leaven, was not the largest person at the table, but her presence ruled. Her weathered face was alive below her wild mass of snow-white hair. Paloma knew the Judean desert dweller had dressed up for the trip to a modern American city because she was wearing her least-stained leather jacket over a simple muslin dress. "The more we diverge from Empire," she noted, "the crazier we seem to those shackled to it."

"That makes us a bunch of deviants," chuckled Clarence Washington, the ex-professor who headed the Portland Catholic Worker. Paloma looked around the small table and knew Clarence was right. They *were* a bunch of deviants, round pegs refusing to fit into the world's square holes. They were all members of Leaven, and they'd stopped obeying Empire a long time ago. This group hadn't been together since they'd met at the Cave of the Baptist in the desert at Suba five months ago, and the Ossuary of James had exploded into the public eye.

Now that they were together again, Paloma's heart swelled. His eyes grew moist, and the love he felt for his comrades washed over him. There was Clarence himself, sporting his unchanging uniform of blazer and black t-shirt; alongside the dignified ex-professor sat Sofia, the vibrant white-haired woman who'd taken the mantle of Shepherd thirty years ago. Next to them lounged his own wife Magda, her dark eyes and European features alive with the daring disturbance they were plotting. This group of beloved deviants, along with the lanky prankster Theologos, was about to dive into holy mischief of the highest order in front of national TV. To succeed, Paloma knew they would need precise planning. They would need a hint of divine madness. And they would need Thomas Whidman.

Now that Paloma had joined them, the group entered into silence. Eventually, the Shepherd looked up. "Well, my friends, we're together once more," she said, taking in the whole group. "First point of business: what do you think of the young man? Shall we start with you, Stephen?"

"I know what I think," Paloma responded. "I'll go last. You all heard the conversation. What are your thoughts?"

"Well, Thomas has never stood a Trial in the desert," Magda offered. "That's obvious. He has a lot of potential, but he hasn't been emptied. He's a good kid, but he's soft. Will he crumble when the going gets tough?"

"I wish he could go through the desert, too," said Theologos, his elongated, black-clad body leaning against the wall near the beaded curtain. "But for a different reason than Magda: it's clear he hasn't met the Spirit face-to-face." He spread his arms in a compassionate gesture. "His head and his heart are not one. A man who doesn't even see the quarterback can only help this team so much."

Listening, Paloma knew the old Preparer was right. Those who'd passed through the Trial had a certain look – he'd seen it in Ryan and Angela when they returned from the desert this past summer—that said they had seen God and lived. They glowed. Thomas didn't have it. Not yet.

"What are y'all wishing for?" chided Clarence. "The kid has promise. It's not his fault he's still a first-born. I've seen him in a Bible study sandwiched between cross-dressers and criminals, and I've seen him have dinner with one of the meanest bastards in Portland without losing his cool. And his Greek!" Clarence turned to the monk. "Theologos, he understands nuances in Koine that are impressive. He didn't just translate *ptchoi* as 'the poor,' like I've always done. He went a step further, and translated the term as the completely destitute, 'the crouching-over ones' who wait at Jerusalem's Temple Gate." He's going to be a fine successor for you someday, if only he joins us."

"Clarence, your hopes for what he might be in the future are important, yes," said Magda. "But we're talking about your take on him now."

"I have no worries about the young man," Clarence responded. "Sure, he's first-born, and sure, he's conflicted, but he has promise. He'll do his part."

"That's where I come down, too," remarked Paloma. "He's not perfect, but as we know all too well, when has God ever used anything but broken tools?"

The five around the table were fully aware of their own flaws. "Alright then," the Shepherd said after a moment. "Unless anyone has a strong objection, we're going to move forward with the plan Stephen and Magda have proposed. Anyone?" After a moment of silence, the Shepherd continued. "Okay. The Ossuary's scheduled to be unveiled next month just a few miles from here, at Berkeley's Museum of Man. Stephen, remind us of the date of the opening?"

"January 15th, Shepherd." He looked at Magda. "Forty days from now, the exhibit opens here in Berkeley, whether we've done our preparations or not."

"Forty days," grinned Theologos through his bushy mass of gray and white. "Fitting. The ancient Hebrew period of completeness. We've always loved that timeframe."

"And you're positive this pastor Benjamin Whidman is staging a nationally-televised protest that day?" The Shepherd looked at the Zen teacher.

"He's been planning this event ever since the discovery of the Ossuary hit the papers back in July," Paloma responded. "He's planned his protest to coincide with the opening day of the Ossuary exhibit. Reverend Whidman's an expert at rallying huge crowds. Thousands of people are being bussed in to gather at a massive outdoor plaza just outside the museum's entrance. Because scientists are saying James is Jesus' older brother by Mary, it's causing quite a stir in certain Christian circles. Reverend Whidman is framing the event as a spiritual showdown, a battle for the soul of America. '*Bible Before Bones*,' he's calling it, a shout out to true believers everywhere to defend the faith. In the chaos of the gathering crowd, we should be able to set up without a lot of trouble, and let Billy Swanson do his thing."

"It's a fairly incomplete plan, but it's the one we have." The Shepherd rose. "Any better ideas?" Silence. "Let's set it in motion, then." The rest stood up as well. "Clarence, take Stephen and Magda with you tonight back up to Portland. Rally your people, and come back down to the Bay Area when you can. Stephen, you outline Thomas on his role when the time is right. I'll be thinking of you from Suba."

"And I'll be thinking of you from Athos," the old monk Theologos added.

As the five closed the gathering with a silent prayer, Stephen Paloma held the Shepherd's calloused hand. He could feel her pulse racing, see her jugular standing out subtly at the base of her weathered neck. Elevated respiration, too. He tried to breathe with her in the silence.

By the time they unclasped hands a few minutes later, the Shepherd had regained a sense of calm. Her chest rose and fell easier. Before the circle broke, Paloma touched the Shepherd on the sleeve.

"Something still bothering you, Sofia?" he asked quietly.

The leader of Leaven turned to him. "You always know, don't you?" She sighed. "So much hinges upon this, Stephen. After the event, our secret society will be out in the open, for better or worse. I trust you and Magda and Clarence implicitly, you know that." Sofia's brow knit with worry. "I just don't like that we have to use this untested young man as part of our plan."

Paloma nodded. "I worry about that too. It's not a big part of our plan, but it's risky. I think Thomas has the courage to do it. I have to believe in him." Paloma sighed. "We can only play this one with the resources we have. The tools God has given us are unconventional. Yet something tells me that both of these Whidmans have some key roles to play in the days ahead."

"And you're sure Reverend Whidman won't change his plans?"

"He's locked in, Shepherd." Theologos was waiting at the doorway, and fell in beside the pair as Paloma continued. "He's got confirmations from all the major networks, as well as Associated Press. He's pinned far too much on this date to change it. He wants to send a clear message to Christians all across the nation."

"That's convenient," Theologos chortled. "So do we."

Section Five, The Theologos Commentaries:
The Lord's Prayer

Christendom teaches that, when Jesus taught his disciples to pray, he instructed them to pray these words:

Our Father who art in heaven,

hallowed be thy name.

Thy kingdom come,

thy will be done, on earth as it is in heaven.

Give us this day our daily bread, and forgive us our debts as we forgive our debtors.

Lead us not into temptation, but deliver us from evil.

For thine is the kingdom, the power and the glory forever. Amen.

Christendom has come to call this the Lord's Prayer. For more than a thousand years, millions upon millions of Christians worldwide have recited this prayer—or something very similar—every week. It is, by far, the prayer most spoken in the entire Western world.

So why is it so confusing?

For example, let us examine the prayer's purpose. Why did Jesus teach his followers this particular prayer? Was it meant to lead his disciples to do anything, be anything? Or was it meant to simply be comforting?

The phrasing of the Lord's Prayer makes things a bit unclear. For example, when Jesus says "thy kingdom come," is he saying that the kingdom *has* come already, that it *will* come sometime in the future, that he *wishes* it to come, or that it's coming *right now*? When he says, "thy will be done," is he commanding God to get busy, or is he reminding those in his circle that they should be doing God's will?

And why all the requests? In Matthew, in the sentences before launching into the Lord's Prayer, Jesus tells his disciples that "your Father knows what you need before you ask him." If God knows what we need, then why do we ask God for bread, forgiveness, protection and deliverance? Is this prayer meant to remind God about *our* needs, or remind *us* about what God provides?

Millions of churchgoers recite this prayer every day, but rarely does reciting lead to changed behavior. God's will still too often takes a back seat to individual will— usually focused on personal advancement, entertainment, and security. Debts too often still stand and grudges too often still remain, even though we ask God to forgive us just as we forgive. For most of Christendom, the prayer has become rote. Comforting, but not transforming.

Was that Jesus' intent in teaching this prayer—to conform, but not transform? Hardly.

Read now Jesus' prayer we in Leaven have caretaken through the centuries, passed down in Aramaic from James the Just:

> *Father of Everything,*
>
> *Your presence fills all of Creation.*
>
> *Again today, your kingdom has come.*
>
> *Again today, I join my will with your will to make earth as heaven.*
>
> *Again today, you'll give us the bread we need for your daily work,*
>
> *and you'll show mercy to us just as much as we show mercy to others.*
>
> *Again today, as we face temptation, you'll be with us in our trials.*

For the Master and his earliest followers, this prayer was a daily revolution. For them, it was not rote, nor passive, nor confusing. It was immediate and transformational. It was meant to be said daily by Jesus' followers in order to enlarge their hearts, direct their actions and alter the very way they saw reality.

Seen in this light, is it likely that Jesus taught this prayer to his disciples just once, making sure they were taking notes to write it down later? Unlikely.

More likely, the prayer was part of the disciples' daily rhythms as they walked through life with the Master. Remember, the earliest Called Out Ones traveled as a migratory band. They didn't write, and they didn't carry burdensome scrolls; they were talking, listening, doing, walking. This prayer would have been said hundreds of mornings as the group rose to greet the sun and break their fast; it would have been said regularly around coastal campfires as the hungry group roasted fish and baked loaves in the coals.

Jesus taught this prayer to remind his disciples of the bountiful, unbelievable partnership they had with their abundant God. James the Just, sharing it with his Aramaic-speaking community after Jesus died, called it the Hesed Prayer. *Hesed* is best translated as "covenanted loving-kindness." Our Leaven tradition teaches that through the *Hesed* Prayer, Jesus reminds followers of the Way of their cooperative two-way relationship with their God. It is a daily contract, a renewable covenant, between partners, echoing back to the promise made in the Old Testament, "I shall be your God and you shall be my people."

How can a modern seeker raised in Christendom discern between competing truths? We'd all like to believe that we have access to the original words of Jesus, yet many versions of the Lord's Prayer exist in Christendom. The versions found in Matthew and Luke have substantial differences in wording. All have passed down the centuries through many languages--from Aramaic to Greek to Latin to English, at least--and words have changed across cultures and regimes. Layers of additions over time have turned the basic prayer of Jesus into something more elaborate and inscrutable.

Our Hesed Prayer, too, has likely suffered many changes from the original words of the Master. Even though Leaven has preserved it in the original Aramaic, the first followers of Jesus would have spoken the Hesed Prayer countless times at daybreak or campfire before it was ever written down by the community of James, twenty years after the death of their Master. Oral tradition invites embellishment. Over thousands of prayers spoken by hundreds of people, no doubt words were altered and patterns changed.

Yet the intent of the mutual covenant--the daily promise to embody God's will, trusting in turn that God will provide for the day--shines forth as the authentic message of the Master we follow. Its bold promise of partnership fits the one who dared to proclaim, "Seek ye first the kingdom of God and God's justice, and then all these things shall be added unto you."

58 PEOPLE HAVE LIVES

Due to Unexpected Events –

Meditation class

POSTPONED

until further notice.

Please take this opportunity to deepen
your own practice at home. Check with
Gladys at the student union reception
office for further updates.

–Stephen Paloma

December 6, 1992

Thomas felt like he'd been punched in the stomach. The simple hand-written sign posted by Paloma felt like an ambush. *Didn't we just have tea yesterday?* He tried the meditation room door and peered through the tiny opaque glass window that gave the only view to the room's dark interior. Nothing.

Thomas slumped, reeling. Two nights ago he and Talia had come back on the BART after the lasagna dinner, and he'd been slowly absorbing *The Commentaries* pretty much ever since. Yesterday he'd ignored his thesis work and skipped Cavanaugh's *Faith and Fanaticism* in favor of meeting with Paloma, to try to wrap his mind around the existence of an ancient society. What the book proposed blew his mind: that Christianity had been kidnapped and co-opted by Empire a long time ago, and only a few hardcore resisters in the desert had any real connection to the authentic Way of Jesus. His own hesitation yesterday during his meeting with Paloma left him vaguely ashamed. He'd come to meditation early this evening so he could talk with his meditation teacher before class about some new pages he'd devoured in *The Commentaries.*

Then he saw the note.

Thomas felt adrift, a Boy Scout without map or compass.

"Hey, squid," a quiet voice came from down the hall.

Talia, her lithe form dressed in faded jeans and a vest, crossed the corridor in her river sandals to give Thomas a huge hug. Agnew was right behind, slobbering all over Thomas' lower body parts in greeting. "Missed you in bed last night."

"Look, Talia!" blurted Thomas, pointing at the closed door and the sign. "He's gone!"

"I know," Talia shrugged. "I passed by the door a few minutes ago on my way to change for class, and I saw the sign. So how was your day? Did you get some reading done?"

"Yeah. It was great. It's just that I can't figure out why Paloma would– "

"People have *lives,* sporto. Things happen. Maybe he's doing the undercover Billy Swanson thing at some other big arena. Don't worry, your precious master will be back in his own good time. In the meantime, let's do something better than stand in front of a locked door." She turned, Agnew already straining on the leash. "I'm starving!"

As she started to leave, two other meditation students arrived at the door, and then three more, each expecting class to be starting. Despite Talia's urgings to go, Thomas had to quiz each of the newcomers exhaustively. They had no more information than he did.

Thomas stood at that door for the next twelve minutes, interviewing everyone who arrived, before it finally sunk in that his teacher was gone, and that no one knew when he was coming back.

- - - - -

Talia was out the student union and halfway down the three blocks to *Hunan* before Thomas caught up with her, panting. Agnew seemed not to remember seeing Thomas just minutes ago, so another frenzied round of licking ensued.

"Hey, Tal, wait up," he said, breaking away from the Great Dane's affections and falling in stride. He put her hand in his, but she took it out. "Sorry about that. I just…..Hey, why are you crying? What's wrong?"

Talia kept her eyes fixed forward and shook her head. Kept walking. *"You're* what's wrong. Your head's on wrong."

"But I was trying – "

"You you you. Do you have any room in your life for anything but *your* needs?" she said, her face hard now. "*Your* trip. *Your* thesis. *Your* need to find Paloma. I just thought we might have a little time together after a day apart, catch up, you know, but instead you're obsessed about your missing spiritual teacher."

"Hey, he's your spiritual teacher, too."

"No, he's not!" Talia whipped her head to face him. "He leads my meditation class. We had dinner once. He has some cool perspectives. That's it. He doesn't give me books to read and I don't call him up at home and we don't have daily tea confessions!"

"Whoa." Thomas stopped her as they approached the front patio of *Hunan*. He grabbed Talia's hand and sat them both down at an outside table right near the sidewalk, oblivious of the crowds that passed inches from them. At a command to stay, Agnew became a furry blockade that gave them a modicum of space from the press of passers-by.

"Listen, Tal," Thomas said. "I blew it back there. Paloma's not my girlfriend. *You* are. Besides, I only have sex with him once or twice a week." Talia punched him hard in the arm, not quite smiling yet. "Speaking of, why don't we order Szechuan to go, grab a six-pack, go home and get naked? I promise to take care of your needs before mine."

Tears came to Talia's eyes again, even as a half-smile came to her lips. "No, Thomas, it's just that—"

"What, not romantic enough for you?" Thomas inquired. "I got it," he said, nodding to himself. "I can be a big spender. I'll throw in a video and—"

"Stop it! *Just stop it!*" The streaming sea of people temporarily made space around the arguing couple, then rushed back in as the moment passed. Talia was quiet now. "Just stop joking."

Thomas was completely confused by now, and peered into Talia's face for answers. "What is it, Tal? What'd I do wrong? I know I was preoccupied earlier. I'm really sorry."

No response. "Wait. I did something bad, didn't I?" Thomas continued, panic rising. She looked away, shaking her head, her lips a tight line.

"Oh my God." Thomas' eyes grew narrow and hard. "Are you seeing someone else? Did you want to take me out to eat so you could – "

Before he could get his words out, Talia jumped up from her chair and grasped both sides of his face with her capable hands, squishing his cheeks like a fish. Passersby on the sidewalk swerved.

"Shut up before you hurt someone," she said, her words finally strong and her eyes dry. "I love you, you idiot." She stopped, still holding his startled face in her hands. "And I'm pregnant."

59 A CONNECTED MASS

Red and white to-go boxes holding the last soggy remains of *Hunan's* cashew chicken stood on the coffee table, occasionally lit up by the changing scenes on the television screen. Inches from the food boxes on the low table lay the intertwined feet of Thomas and Talia, who cuddled in a connected mass on the futon couch that dominated Talia's apartment. Agnew lay contented on his own rug nearby. Earlier at the video store they'd tiptoed around Talia's big news and settled on a light comedy. It had proved a good choice. Thomas was freaking out, and needed nothing more than to hold Talia and laugh about someone else's problems for a few hours.

"Listen to this," Talia said as the video credits rolled, chomping on her cookie from *Hunan* and unwrinkling her fortune. *'Your future appears unexpectedly blessed.'* " She looked meaningfully at him.

"Between the sheets," said Thomas, grinning mischievously.

"What?"

"*Between the sheets,*" repeated Thomas, looking up. "When we were in college Ed always used to add that to any fortune cookie we read. 'Your future appears unexpectedly blessed *between the sheets.*' Like that."

"Sounds like an Ed thing."

"Where have you been? Everybody does it."

"Everybody *stupid* does it," Talia said, tossing him the other fortune cookie. "What's yours say?"

Thomas broke it open, unrolled his scroll, and read: "You are about to embark on a life-changing journey."

"Between the sheets," added Talia.

"You said it," said Thomas, rolling over on top of Talia on the futon couch with a sly grin. "So it must be."

"I think I could arrange that," said Talia, laughing and wriggling back on top. She rested her chin on his chest. "Hey, those fortunes got me thinking. A blessed future. A life-changing journey."

"Dish time!" Thomas jumped up. He rolled his shoulders, stretched to the ceiling, and began clearing the dinner mess from the low coffee table. Before he moved too far, however, Talia gently grabbed his leg.

"Come back here," she said softly from the couch, drawing him in. "We need to talk." He sat back down, unsure.

"I'm scared," she began. "But I think I want us to have this baby. Together."

Thomas, on the edge of the couch, felt the walls close in. With a tight stomach he took her hand in his. "That's great, Tal." He lay down next to her and cuddled into her back, reaching around to feel her belly. "Me too. We'll do this together."

"Good." She grabbed the blanket from the back of the couch and threw it over the two of them as they spooned. "Partners."

- - - - -

A few hours later, sometime in the wee hours past midnight, Thomas whispered goodnight. Talia kissed him and drifted back off to sleep as he wormed out from under the covers. He had a lot to prepare before his next meeting with Cavanaugh, and he wanted to get back to his place so he could get an early start. Stealthy as a thief, Thomas slipped on his shoes and out the apartment door, not even disturbing Agnew on his rug.

He coasted home in a semi-torpor, half-lidded, wishing the several blocks between their places would magically transform into several feet. He turned the last corner, locked the bike and came through the gate, yawning, dreaming of his pillow.

He suddenly stopped in his tracks, wide awake.

Thomas moved like a panther up the walkway toward his front door to make sure he wasn't seeing things. "Damn!" he cursed under his breath.

It was almost 2:00 A.M., he'd been gone all day, and his front door was slightly ajar.

His sleepy feeling was replaced by raw nerves. Somebody had broken in, and wasn't trying to keep it a secret. All was dark. *They must've come and gone,* thought Thomas. Long gone. *My stereo system takes two hands.* The vandals probably didn't want to waste time closing the door. When did the break-in happen? A day ago? Hours? Seconds?

In the darkness, Thomas slid through the open door and silently grabbed the baseball bat he kept in the entryway. Flicking on the lights ready for anything, bat raised, he screamed like a banshee when he saw a large body snoring away on his couch.

THE SECRETS OF LEAVEN

60 I KNEW YOU'D UNDERSTAND

"I'd left three messages," Mike Shaw said by way of explanation, yawning and rubbing his eyes. "I thought you got them." He looked sheepishly at the insistent blinking red light on the answering machine. "Guess you haven't been home, huh?"

"Not much." Thomas perched on the couch like a sullen raptor, a steaming mug of tea between his hands. He stared in disbelief at the bloated form of his friend in tighty-whiteys, wrapped in a blanket on his sofa in the middle of the night.

"I knew you'd understand," grinned Mike, laying back down and pulling the blanket up to his chin. "After our road trip, I really felt like we bonded again. I knew I could count on you for anything. Just like old times." He snuggled deeper into the couch. "Wow, T, did you really drop me off in Orange County just three days ago?"

"I really did." Thomas looked at his watch. *Nearly 3:00 AM.* "I dropped you off at your place seventy-one hours ago, to be exact. Technically, we've been apart less than two days. Now here you are in Oakland. On my couch." Thomas' brain was having trouble grasping the fact. "Why'd you come here, exactly?"

"After you left, I started driving up and down the 101 because I didn't want to go home. Thinking about my empty house just got me more and more depressed. But I kept thinking about what you said at that restaurant."

Thomas didn't want to ask, but he had to. "And what *did* I say?"

"Well, that maybe Mary'd been changing, that she needed some space, some time to work things out."

Thomas, perched on the couch, was having a hard time keeping his eyes open. "That doesn't tell me why you came to visit me."

"Well I started thinking, maybe *I* need some space, too. And all that's waiting for me in Southern Cal is a big empty house filled with memories of Mary and the kids. I don't need that. I need some space to sort some stuff out."

"Good thinking. But California has lots of beaches this time of year that aren't crowded."

"So then I thought to myself: where could I go to get some space?" Mike continued, tucked in under the blanket like a giant baby. "Who'd understand what I'm going through?" He looked up at his friend, beaming. "The answer was easy." With that, Mike curled up on his side under the blanket and closed his eyes. "You're a good friend, Tommy my boy. Thanks for letting me stay. G'night."

Thomas stayed perched on the couch a moment longer, his emotions sloshing like the tea he swirled in the bottom of his cup. The words of James suddenly came to mind. *Pure religion is this: to take care of widows and orphans in their distress.*

"You're a good friend, too, bra," he said to the lump under the blanket. "Stay as long as you need."

61 TOTALLY DIFFERENT PEOPLE

After the fourth ring, Thomas knew he'd have to leave a message. Doing so always gave him mild stage fright, because you were supposed to be clear and concise. And often he was neither of those.

"Greetings, fellow human, you've reached Ed's phone. I'm not here right now, but please leave a message and I'll get back to you. If you are calling about the drumming group, we're now jamming on Wednesdays at 7 P.M. at the Taos Free Space. Bueno, bye."

"Hello, Ed. This is David Byrne from the Talking Heads. I saw you doing Tai Chi on the quad at Bay Area Theological Union last summer, and I want you in my next video. Shirtless. If you could stay in that pose, a heron seeking a frog, while I bike around you in a really big suit, I think we would capture--"

"Thomas? Is that you, my man?" Ed's live voice broke in on the other side of the line.

"Hey Ed. What's hangin'?" Thomas laughed.

"You always get me with that shit," Ed chuckled.

"Somebody's gotta keep you on your toes," said Thomas.

Ed laughed. "What's up, holmes?"

"Let's see." Thomas had known how the phone call would go up to this point. Now, all wit and pretense failed. "Mike's been sleeping on my couch for five days. Talia's pregnant. I'm living in the seminary library."

Silence on the other side of the line. "Umm, are these related?"

"No. Yes. Well, yes for me. Not for him. Or her."

"Take a deep breath, Tom. Start from the beginning. Talia's pregnant. By you?"

"Yeah. At least, I assume so. She's not sleeping with anyone else."

"So it's either you or the immaculate conception. Let's assume you're the dad."

"Right." Just hearing Ed say *you're the dad* made Thomas blanch. "And she wants to keep it."

"Got it. How far along is she?"

"Six weeks or so."

"That's good. Keeps your options open. And Mike's sleeping on your couch because…?"

"Because his house is full of memories. After our trip to Tucson he thinks I'm a great friend to lean on."

"And are you being a great friend to lean on?"

"Whaddaya mean? He's sleeping on my couch!"

"And you've moved into the library. So are you being a good friend to him in his time of need?"

"Well, kind of. I mean, I'm letting him hang out and all. He has a free place to stay."

"Uh huh. Go on."

"It's just that, whenever he starts talking to me about his situation, I keep thinking of my own."

"We humans tend to do that, don't we?"

"I don't want to be like him, damn it!" Thomas said. "We both know he and Mary got hitched in a rush because they were going to have a kid."

"I remember. Shotgun, baby. That was a fast one."

"Exactly. Then three more kids came along—*boom, boom, boom!* – and ten years later, Mike's on my couch, dumped by a wife who once loved him. With four kids damaged in the process."

"So Mike squatting on your couch right now sort of wigs you out."

"Damn right it wigs me out!"

"And that's why you're living in the library."

"Exactly!" Thomas began to breathe a little slower. Ed's patient manner was making the conversation easier than it could have been. "That, and my thesis. I'm buried in it."

"About your boy who thought the world was gonna end in the 1920s, right?"

"Yeah. He's pretty fascinating."

"You've got some crazy relatives, hombre. Is your research paying off?"

"Yeah, but it's taking me some unexpected places."

"Like where?"

"I just spent last week in Tucson digging up some information about my ancestor. And pretty soon I'm going to Arkansas to talk to people who actually knew him in the flesh."

"Busy man."

"Yeah. It's amazing how busy I can be when I'm avoiding my life."

"I hear that, brother. Avoiding can be very motivational."

"Seriously," Thomas laughed. "That's why I spend so much time in the stacks. Some nights I work until I can't keep my eyes open and then I just sleep for a few hours on the desk in the back. When I'm researching, I don't have to think about anything else—no serious talks with Tal, no couch sessions with Mike. Shit, Ed, that could be me, eight or ten years from now."

"You mean Mike, camping on your couch?"

"Yeah. I don't want to get married to Talia just because we have a kid on the way. I want to marry her when it feels right. Right now all I feel is pressure. Sometimes I can't even breathe."

"Hey, peace, Thomas," counseled Ed. "Be at peace. I know you're in a tough space right now, but remember what I told you last summer?"

"What?" Thomas said, panic tinging his voice. "Drink the poison?"

"Not that," Ed chuckled. "I said Talia's good for you, man. Remember that. She's good for you."

"I know," Thomas acknowledged. "I mean, I think I actually love Talia. I've never felt so right about a person. Our relationship is the most beautiful thing I've ever had. I don't want to ruin it."

"And having a child sounds heavy, doesn't it?"

"Like a brick on my chest, man. Just thinking about it makes me feel sick. Like a steel collar just got locked around my neck."

"I hear you," his friend said simply.

Thomas suddenly found he didn't have anything else to say, so he just clung to the phone.

Ed sighed. "That's no atmosphere for a child to grow up in, with a dad who feels imprisoned by his kid. Trust me, that's how I grew up. If you're gonna be a dad, choose it. Choose it out of joy."

Thomas was surprised, how good it felt to hear those words. He almost cried with relief. "You're right, Ed. I want to choose it. But I can't right now, not with joy. I'm just not ready. We're not ready. Maybe some day. Not now."

"You both have a lot of growing still to do," Ed continued. "Right now it sounds like you and Talia can either deliver a relationship *or* deliver a child. But probably not both."

Thomas just nodded on the phone. He felt drained. Good, but drained.

"Hey man, I was thinking," Ed said. "Is Mike with you right now for a reason? Do you think the universe might be trying to tell you something?"

"What, to take a vow of celibacy?"

"May be," Ed laughed softly. "Let him stay as long as he needs, Tom. I know it's hard when you're freaking out about your own issues, but try to be a good friend. Listen to him. You may just learn something."

"I have already," Thomas reflected. "You know, Ed, Mike loves his kids. I mean he *loves* his kids. Here he is, in the midst of one of the toughest times of his life, when he should be worrying about himself, and he's worrying about how *they're* feeling, how *they're* coping. He's a bigger man than I."

"Being a parent transforms you, I think," Ed ventured. "Makes you bigger."

"That's just it, Ed. In order to be parents who are happy together, Talia and I would have to be totally different people. *I'd* have to be a totally different person. I'd have to be selfless, working to support a family, cleaning up after poop and vomit. And Ed, I don't *want* to be that person right now. I'd be suffocated. Talia and I are both loving just where we are. Something cool is just beginning to grow into something strong and solid. I don't want to sacrifice that to bring a new kid in the world."

"Then don't, man. Sounds like you just figured some things out. Now all you have to do is tell Talia."

62 TATTOO ARTISTS

ENTER.

Last week's sign on the dojo door was gone, replaced by this simple note.

Thomas hadn't realized until now how one word could restore so much. Candlelight emanated through the small window in the meditation room door. Thomas hurriedly pulled it open.

"Where have you been?" he blurted in a whisper to the motionless figure sitting on the floor.

Four startled students looked up from the semi-circle they'd formed around their teacher. They'd been quietly chatting before class, but they weren't now. Paloma looked up slowly from his characteristic lotus position, assessing his agitated student. "Perhaps I should ask, where have *you* been?" A curious smile touched his lips. His observant eyes roamed from Thomas' head to his toes, taking in the young man's unshaven face and rumpled clothes. "Staging a hygiene protest?"

For all intents and purposes, Paloma looked like he'd been meditating in that spot all week, while Thomas looked like the one who'd dropped off the face of the earth without explanation. Two other students in their *gis* entered the room behind Thomas, bowed to the center of the room, and sat. Before Thomas could say anything more, Paloma glanced at his watch and quietly murmured, "Let's talk after class, Thomas." Then he rang the bell of mindfulness to begin the session.

"It has been a little while since we last met," Paloma said in a clear voice, addressing the whole *sangha*. "Something came up for me last week, and I had to travel and cancel class. I hope you have continued practice on your own." Several students nodded. "Let us prepare ourselves, and enter into stillness." With that, Paloma closed his eyes and entered into deep meditation.

For the next hour, Thomas was useless and miserable, an ignored bottle desperate to be uncorked.

- - - - -

"Don't try to read your tea bag. That only works with leaves, not Celestial Seasonings."

Without realizing it, Thomas had been staring into his mug for an unknown amount of time. He looked up at a smiling Paloma, who slipped into their usual booth at *Tolstoi's Tea House*.

Thomas rubbed his eyes and refocused. "Hey there," he said softly. "Good to see you, Paloma."

"Good to be seen," the older man said, doffing his hat and coat and draping them over the back of the booth. "What's been happening in the world of Thomas?"

It had been only a week since Thomas had talked with Paloma in this same tea house booth, about *The Commentaries*. But in that week Thomas' world had changed. Again. As Paloma waited for his order, Thomas related all the surprises of the last few days: Talia's pregnancy, the midnight arrival of Mike the couch guest, the wisdom and peace gained in his phone call with Ed.

"And you?" Thomas tried to be casual. "Did you do some secret undercover stuff for Leaven during your mystery absence?"

Paloma blew steam from his teacup. "Actually, yes. Had to meet with some of my friends in Leaven to organize an upcoming event. I'd like to tell you more," he said, "but you haven't joined the team yet. Any decision?"

Thomas balked. Eight days since Paloma had invited Thomas to walk the

Way of Leaven, and Thomas still didn't know what he wanted. Take that back: he *did* know what he wanted. Thomas didn't feel ready to give his life to a God he didn't see, but he sure had become thirsty for time with Paloma.

"Still looking for the quarterback," Thomas replied. "Still seeking information." He wanted to know everything he could about his mysterious teacher, and the certain trust he had in a God worth serving. When Paloma served himself a steaming refill, Thomas saw an opportunity. The man's left cuff lifted as he poured, revealing a black leather watchband that covered the detailed design Thomas knew lay underneath.

Thomas took a chance. "Maybe learning more about Leaven will give me the push I need. Will you let me in on your tattoo?"

Paloma looked up with mild surprise, then down at his covered arms. "Which one?"

Which one? Now it was Thomas' turn to be surprised. "Um, the one on your wrist," he said, pointing. "Unless you have more interesting ones." He gulped. At times he felt close to Paloma, like a trusted friend, at other times he felt like a complete stranger. This time was one of the latter. "I hope it's okay that I'm being nosy."

"It's okay. Nose away," Paloma said, looking kindly into Thomas' eyes. Familiarity washed back into him. "I normally wear something to cover it when I'm in public," Paloma continued, "but I'm glad you saw it the other night." The meditation teacher pulled back his sleeve and unclasped the watch to reveal the thin, complex design wrapping his wrist like a bracelet of skin.

The low-hanging lamp over the table projected a comforting cone of illumination, shutting out the rest of the world. In the soft light, Thomas examined the weaving pattern. The design, slightly faded from time, was one of intertwined leafy vegetation ending in some kind of flowers or seedpods. Thomas said as much to Paloma.

"Not bad," commented Paloma. "Pretty accurate, actually. The pattern shows vines and branches merging into wheat."

Thomas nodded. "When did you have this done?" More nosiness at this point seemed okay.

"Ten years ago, in 1982. After my Trial. Have you read about our initiation?"

"The Trial in the desert?"

Paloma nodded. "*Kenosis,* like we talked about last time. Once I did my emptying, then the Spirit got busy and made me part of the *bar enasha.* After I returned to the group, I-- "

"Wait. What's *bar enasha?*" Thomas was unfamiliar with the term, but he knew it wasn't Koine.

"Got ahead of myself," Paloma confessed. "No need to talk about that yet. Let's just say I acquired this tattoo when I entered into full membership in Leaven," he said. "After the Trial, there's a ceremony involved and you're branded with the Mark. We call it the second baptism. Before that, you're a once-born."

"So what happens exactly in these Trials of yours?"

At this question, the older man's flow of words stopped.

Thomas' nervousness came back. "Can't tell me any more about it?"

"Not until an initiate commits to *catechesis,* our training period. It's a formal apprenticeship." Paloma looked thoughtfully at Thomas across the top of his steaming mug.

The younger man avoided the unspoken invitation. "I want to know about the tattoo. You called it the Mark." He pointed to the design on Paloma's wrist. "So everyone in Leaven has one?"

"Yes, although they can be in different places. Men usually have them done on their arms, while women sometimes choose the ankle. Magda went for the wrist." Paloma shrugged. "She said it was the best place, considering the rest of her body art."

"So the Mark represents some kind of an achievement badge? Like a mark of honor?"

"Hardly," Paloma said, amused. "There's no self-pride when one emerges from a Trial, Thomas. In fact, it's the opposite. It's more like a submission. A brand of ownership."

"I don't understand."

"Whenever I start feeling proud of myself, the Mark helps me remember *who* I really am and *whose* I really am." Paloma sipped his tea. "It also serves as identification."

"In what way?"

"Sometimes we in Leaven aren't what we appear. As you've already seen." Paloma stood up in the tea house booth, and his face gleamed under the cone lamp like Billy Swanson's did in the Portland Coliseum. His smile was slightly wicked. "Often too, we've been persecuted by those in power and have needed to seek refuge in foreign lands. The Mark allows those of us in Leaven to identify each other across cultures, languages. Even centuries."

"The design's stayed the same over all that time?"

"We think so," responded Paloma. "The symbols are archetypal for followers of the Jesus Way."

"What do they mean, exactly?" Thomas wondered. "I mean, '*I am the vine, you are the branches,*' that part's obvious. But why wheat?"

"Leaven—or yeast – is pretty impossible to draw on paper, much less with a needle on someone's skin," Paloma explained. "Wheat's a little easier. The original designer may have taken some artistic liberty."

"The original designer," Thomas mused. "Hmm. Never thought about it, but there had to be a first one, didn't there?" He played with his cup. "So when does Leaven think this tattoo ritual began?"

"Lost to history," said Paloma, lifting his hands. "Could've been very early.

Jesus himself described the kingdom of heaven as leaven in the loaf of society. He saw the kingdom spreading through Empire like yeast bubbling through bread. We took that metaphor of leaven as our own. But when this design started, we don't know. Did some Greek-speaking scribe start marking his fellow members of Leaven with this tattoo as a secret symbol, hundreds of years after Jesus?" Paloma raised one of his dark eyebrows. "Or did the Master and his community, from the very beginning, use the symbol of yeast in visual images?"

"What d'you mean," Thomas laughed, startled. "Are you saying that Jesus might've been a tattoo artist? That he and his boys inked this tag onto each other's arms?"

"Interesting to imagine, isn't it?" Paloma made a quirky smile, and held up his wrist. "They had the technology. Slaves were marked with ink. Women tattoed themselves for beauty. As a sign of pledging allegiance to a new kind of family, did Jesus mark his followers with a design like this?" Paloma sipped his tea. "Could be."

As they'd been talking, Thomas had been doodling a drawing of vines and wheat that climbed along the edge of his paper placemat. He was just having the head and tail meet when Paloma softly spoke. "James did."

Thomas' pen stopped in mid-stroke. "What'd you say?"

"James did."

"Get out."

Paloma nodded. "James the brother of Jesus was a tattoo artist. Or someone in his immediate community."

Thomas' world narrowed to a single focus. "Where do you get all this knowledge about James?"

Paloma reached down to his bookbag sitting next to him in the booth, and produced a slim, black book, the leather binding soft and creased with use. Nondescript, dog-eared, unassuming. *Must be Paloma's personal copy*, Thomas thought.

"It's in *The Commentaries?*" Thomas inquired. "I've only read through Section Six. Guess it's still to come."

"This isn't *The Commentaries.*" Eyes alight, Paloma laid the simple volume down on the table. "It's time I showed you a second book."

63 THE CROWN OF LIFE

Paloma flipped through the pages, hunting for something. "No evidence that James and his Ebionites tattooed each other with the wheat-and-vine symbol. But we have evidence of another mark." The book wasn't particularly thick; from his side of the table, Thomas guessed it contained less than a hundred pages. Perhaps a slight bit thinner than *The Commentaries*, but almost indistinguishable in size and shape.

"Not normally one who pulls sacred scripture out at coffee houses," Paloma said under his breath, skimming with his finger. He found what he wanted and looked up to Thomas, turning the book around and pushing it across the table's surface to his companion. "Check out Chapter 1, verse 12."

The book was open to the *Letter of James*. But not.

"What is this book, exactly?"

"That comes later, my non-apprentice," Paloma responded. "Just read it for now."

Thomas read. It was *James*, yes, but a different version than Paloma had shared on his porch the other night. And although this book seemed to be a collection of ancient scripture, this thin volume was certainly not a New Testament. Not a whole one anyway.

To Thomas, the most striking thing about the work was evident on the pages open before him: English words filled the right column of each page, but where Koine Greek typically stood on the left in Uncle Ben's texts, in this book stood a different language altogether. *Hebrew? Aramaic?* Thomas couldn't be sure.

"James 1:12." Thomas found the passage and read aloud: "'A Blessed One perseveres under the Trial, because when he has withstood the Test, he will receive the Crown of Life that the Most High has promised to those who have devoted themselves to Him.'"

Paloma rose abruptly from the other side of the table. A startled Thomas was barely able to scoot over in time as his teacher mashed into the booth next to him. "Paloma, what the – "

"Look at the base of my neck," the bald man commanded, turning his back to Thomas.

Intrigued, Thomas pulled at the bald man's collar.

"Remember when I asked you which tattoo you wanted to see?"

There, at the base of Paloma's neck, was a second design in ink: a bold crown motif of thorns and leaves, perhaps two inches wide.

"Behold, the Crown of Life," Paloma intoned. "Received by those who have withstood the Trial and devoted themselves to the Most High."

Thomas grabbed Paloma's shoulders and jerked the older man around to face him. *"What is this book?"* He held the small black volume between their faces, close.

Paloma smiled, eyes bright. "Why, Thomas, it's the real deal. Written before the Gospels by James and the Ebionites, two thousand years ago. It's the Book of Leaven."

Section Six, The Theologos Commentaries:
The Called Out Ones

As a group, the community of James identified themselves as *ekklesia*. Although later Greek scribes took the term to mean "the assembled," and by the era of Constantine's Christendom the word simply meant "the church," in the beginning the word meant something much more radical: *ekklesia* meant "the Called-Out Ones." Called out from what? Called out from Babylon, from Rome, from the mindset of Empire that rules any age. To be a Follower of the Way meant to be called out from the dominant culture of greed, violence and fear. Called out to the desert, to join the new body of Christ, citizens of a very different Kingdom.

The Called Out Ones were first called to conversion, but not to a conversion that most Christians today would recognize. Conversion--*shub* in Hebrew, *metanoein* and *epistrephein* in Greek--means to turn, return, restore. It means to stop everything and head in a completely different direction. Conversion can also be translated as "a change of lords," and this is exactly what the early Called Out Ones underwent. By changing lords, they now followed the directives of a different ruler. Judaic law and Caesar's dictates no longer held sway.

Claiming Jesus as Lord while under the rule of Caesar was an economic and political act of defiance. The implications were tremendous. Since the Lord of Love was now their king and not the Emperor, these early predecessors of Leaven pledged allegiance to no earthly state or nation. Since they were now all brothers and sisters in Christ, they shared all their resources. Called Ebionites (Poor Ones) by outsiders, they hoarded nothing for themselves but rather pooled their private economies in a common purse, giving to each as was needed. No wonder they were ridiculed as scandalous ragamuffins! They refused to participate in almost every aspect of respectable society. No tribalism or nationalism, no accumulation of personal wealth, no seeking of individual status, no vengeance toward others— these were basic tenets for all Called Out Ones who followed the Way and embodied the kingdom of God that their Lord envisioned. Ebionites saw Christ in the poorest of the poor, and turned Empire values upside down by honoring the destitute and welcoming the unclean to their daily table feast. And as if that wasn't enough, early followers of the Way refused to fight wars for any reason. Their master, the Prince of Peace, taught his followers that violence was not the way to solve any problem, even death. In the face of being beaten, they literally presented the other cheek, even though it was as foolhardy back then as it is now – more so, since personal combat was a daily possibility. Nonetheless, they went weaponless.

Because the Ebionites fled to the Cave of the Baptist before the time of Jerusalem's destruction, our ancient traditions have been preserved with some degree of fidelity. For example, we in Leaven know the earliest Jesus community practiced a *catechesis* initiation process that lasted up to three years, and concluded with a solitary desert Trial similar to Jesus' own testing in the wilderness. Upon completion of the Trial, a new Called Out One would receive a mark on the skin known as the Crown of Life, symbolizing full membership in the community. This brand also indicated bold allegiance to Christ as Lord; it was a direct and defiant response to the mark of allegiance required by Caesar to enter the marketplaces of the Roman Empire, referred to by Called Out Ones as "the mark of the beast."

Lastly, we know the Called Out Ones had their own Gospel, writings that proclaimed the "good news" of the Master. Today, it is part of a group of texts we call the Book of Leaven. The Jewish historian Josephus referred to it as "the Gospel of the Ebionites." It was the earliest text ever written for followers of the Jesus Way, crafted within the community of James just ten years after the death of Jesus. Yet, because our spiritual ancestors went underground with the text during the destruction of Jerusalem in 70 C.E., the "Gospel of the Ebionites" is completely unknown in the world of Christendom. We in Leaven know it to be the common original source—sometimes called "Q" by modern scholars – that informed the writings of Mark, Matthew and Luke. We are not aware of any copies that exist outside of those few published within our society. Over the centuries, the members of Leaven have guarded this text jealously to prevent corruption by Christendom; as far as we know, this Gospel has remained in its original Aramaic and has therefore retained much of its unembellished, primitive nature. Ironically, this has been its best defense: for why would anyone pay attention to such a sparse, unadorned document when there are so many other miraculous and well-written accounts to choose from?

64 A SAD STROKE OF MARKETING GENIUS

"You really think James' people received a crown on their neck after they completed a Trial?" Thomas was poring over the verse that Paloma had just read in his mysterious black book. *"That's* what receiving the Crown of Life means?"

Paloma shrugged, now back in his own seat across from Thomas. "You have a better idea?"

"Couldn't it just be an idiom? Like winning a race and tasting the sweetness of victory?"

"Of course it could," conceded Paloma. "Millions of people throughout Christendom have been trained to think so. But our texts – and our traditions – go straight back to James."

"So when someone undergoes a desert Trial these days," Thomas began, "and you mark him with a crown on his neck to symbolize his allegiance to a different kingdom..."

"...We think they did something similar back in Jesus' day." Paloma finished the young man's thought.

"So the crown imagery might've been around since the earliest followers of Jesus. But what about the wheat and vine symbol?" Thomas motioned to Paloma's wrist. "When do you think it started?"

"Like I said, we don't have any real clues," his teacher responded. "Wheat and vine images abound in the Bible, certainly, but when they became a mark of Leaven, no one knows." Paloma held up his hands. "Maybe when Christianity was kidnapped by the Roman Empire."

"In the fourth century?"

Paloma nodded. "While the Ebionites practiced the Way in desert caves, the successors of Paul had spread a different version of Christianity throughout the vast but crumbling Roman world. In the fourth century, Emperor Constantine decided to hitch his fragile kingdom onto this fast growing phenomenon. When that happened, people who followed the Way had to reinvent themselves."

"I still don't get that."

"You've read *The Commentaries* about the rise of Christendom?"

"The Great Division, yeah," Thomas answered. "Constantine's mad genius, to take this dangerous new counter-cultural Jesus movement and tame it to become the state religion of Empire. But why did the Ebionites have to reinvent themselves?"

"It was a huge change, Thomas," Paloma explained. "When Roman Christendom hijacked early Christianity, creeds took priority over deeds. Everything shifted."

"It became all about dogma."

"Not only that. In a sad stroke of brilliant marketing, Constantine's state religion of Christendom took the name of the Prince of Peace as its rallying cry for war, and took the symbol of the suffering cross and painted it on their shields as a symbol of violent triumph. They twisted everything."

"So in the face of that kind of co-opting, followers of the Way had to go underground, reclaim their own identity."

"Now you see it," Paloma said. "The Society of Leaven was born by those who still sought to follow the Jesus Way seriously. They had to rename themselves, find their own symbols."

"Like wheat and vines," Thomas said, pointing back to Paloma's exposed wrist. "Ways they could secretly identify themselves under the watchful eyes of a violent Empire." Paloma gazed for a moment at the patterns encircling the flesh of his wrist. Then he discreetly replaced his watchband and pulled his cuff back into place.

"I guess this is why I am so wary of words, Thomas," the older man concluded. His tone had turned icy. "Intellectual knowledge and passionate slogans often replace real transformation."

"Calling Jesus Lord is very different than following Jesus."

"Constantine claimed that Christ was his Lord." Even if Thomas had been blind, he could've sensed Paloma's anguish. "He called Jesus his Lord as he was slaughtering his enemies and piling up treasure. Good Christians have been doing it ever since." Paloma drained his cup. "Lesson over." With a sigh, the man got up to go.

"I want to stay here and drink tea forever," Thomas said weakly. "Legends about two-thousand year old tattoo artists are much more appealing than my life right now. As soon as I get up I'll start thinking about my thesis. And about Talia."

"I think you already are," Paloma observed. He rubbed the sleeves of his black turtleneck, preparing for the chill outside, and put on his coat. "But worry not. Way will open."

"What's that supposed to mean?"

"It's a Quaker saying. New opportunities emerge. Stay awake and open, and you'll figure it out."

Thomas didn't like Paloma's patronizing tone. "Enough advice," he said. "Being around you always makes me feel like being an ordinary human isn't good enough."

"Is it?" Paloma's eyes flashed a challenge as he reached for his furry hat. "Maybe, to get this thesis done and do right by Talia, you'll have to become extraordinary."

"That's not what I want to hear," groaned Thomas. "Finishing this Master's degree is supposed to be the easy way out, so I can finish seminary and be done with it all."

"And then you can...?" Paloma let the sentence hang as he headed to the door.

"Then I can get on with my life!" Thomas glared.

Paloma stopped and turned to face him. "And where would you be going with this life of yours?"

"Stop it with the Kung Fu master crap," said Thomas angrily. "Just stop it."

Paloma darted back down into the booth and grabbed Thomas' arm. "This isn't Kung Fu crap!" He hissed into Thomas' surprised face. "And life isn't some fantasy game about what might happen someday. This is real. Now. Real life, real choices."

Paloma released Thomas and slid back into the booth. "It sounds as if you intend to have an abortion," he said matter-of-factly. His eyes confronted Thomas with an unblinking gaze.

Hearing the actual statement come so bluntly from Paloma's mouth, Thomas didn't feel nearly as certain as he had a few days ago. "How does Talia feel?" Paloma continued. "Does she want an abortion also?"

"Well, we're still talking about it," Thomas backpedaled. It was funny: while Paloma'd been gone yesterday, Thomas had been dying to talk to him about the pregnancy; but now that the conversation was actually happening, Thomas just wanted to flee. Truth was, Thomas had spoken openly about it with Talia only once since he had called Ed last week. She'd been moody, distant.

"Has this pregnancy driven you apart a bit?"

"No, not really," Thomas lied. *Damn Paloma.* "I've just been really busy with my thesis, and Mike visiting and all."

"Mmm," Paloma mused. "Too bad Talia wasn't at class today. Didn't see her the week before I left, either, now that I think about it. Meditation is good for pregnant women. Please tell her I'm back, won't you, and invite her to return?"

"I will. She might come next time. But I'll be going on a road trip for awhile. Starting this evening."

"Oh?" Paloma raised an eyebrow. "Another one?"

"Like I said, as soon as I leave this booth I gotta get busy with my thesis. I'm driving to Arkansas starting tonight."

"More research?"

"Yeah, I'm going to conduct my own. Interview people in Gilman for my thesis. There's a local historian named Bert Wood who may be able to help me find people. Most are dead or gone, but when I went to Tucson, Paul Silas told me there's a few older people still around who knew my ancestor seventy years ago."

"Sounds important," commented Paloma, sipping. "Sure this is a good time?"

"First Tal, and now you." Thomas wrapped the string around his dead tea bag, choking it. "Like I told her, I don't know if it's a good time. But it's the *only* time. Cavanaugh's going to kill me if I don't get some primary sources by next week. And Silas won't give me the rest of his thesis unless I visit Gilman. So yeah, I'm crunched. I've got no choice."

"Real life. Real choices." Paloma drained the last of his tea. "Are you sure the thesis is why you want to leave right now?"

"I'm so fucking tired of this!" Thomas shot up from the booth. "After your little mystery trip, you don't get to talk to *me* about leaving when I need to." He zipped up his jacket. "Keep the change," he said as he laid three bucks down on the table. Then he tossed *The Commentaries* at his teacher. "And keep all your little secrets, too. Give 'em to a true believer."

65 TWO CHOICES I DON'T LIKE

"Hello?" answered a sleepy voice on the fifth ring.

"Sorry I've been such a dick lately."

As soon as he'd crossed the Arkansas state line and the sun emerged from the low morning clouds, Thomas had stopped his VW bus at a gas station pay phone and grabbed a bunch of quarters from under the cracked vinyl driver's seat. After so many hours he needed to pee, but that would wait.

"Been thinking again while driving, have you?" Talia said fuzzily, leaning up on an elbow on her futon in the darkness of her Berkeley apartment. "Dangerous habit." He heard her fumble for a glass of water and take a sip. "What time is it, anyway? Wow. 4:30 in the morning. You better be calling me to tell me how much you love me."

"That's all I'm doing. I love you more than anything." Since he'd stormed out on Paloma at the tea house, Thomas had been driving for two days straight, and most of the time he'd been thinking about her. He twisted the curled cord of the pay phone between his fingers. "But I'm scared, Tal, of losing *us.*" In the lush green stillness of the early Arkansas morning, tiny birds hopped among the puddles on the dark pavement of the gas station lot, made by last night's rains. "Real scared."

"Me too, Thomas." She sounded more awake now. "Thanks for telling me the truth. We need to be honest like that if we're going to get through this. Whatever way we go."

"I know. You're the best thing that's ever happened to me, Tal, and I've been pushing you away. Why? Because I don't want to lose you. Is that a dick move, or what?"

"Dickish," she said on the other end of the line. "Very dickish. But I've been a dick too. If that's possible for a girl."

"What d'you mean?" Thomas laughed. "You haven't been a dick." Some of the lightness that he loved so much with Talia returned for the first time since she broke the news.

"Yes, I have." She sat up. "I told you right away I wanted the baby, and put you in a spot. It wasn't easy for you to be honest after that. No wonder you've been feeling scared. You feel trapped. I've been feeling trapped too."

"You have?" Thomas said, amazed.

"Yeah. Part of what I love about being with you is feeling free, like we can do anything. Now I feel like I'm stuck between two choices I don't want."

"Wow," said Thomas, stunned. "That's what *I* wanted to say."

"So listen here," Talia said. Thomas listened. "We need to promise that whatever happens to us in these upcoming months, we're going to be honest. Even if it's not nice. We have to be real about our fears. Leave if you need to, but tell me to my face."

"Got it."

Thomas heard Talia stretch on the other end of the line, and take another sip of water. "So, is going to Arkansas just a short-term thing, or is our Junior going to have a single momma in the Bay Area and a daddy who lives in the South?"

"Tal, honest, after I do my interviews in Gilman, I'm driving nonstop so I can flop into that bed next to you and stay there for the rest of my life. You'll have to kick me out."

"Don't do that," Talia said. "Don't think it's going to be all happy in the future just because it feels good this minute. We both are going to freak out again. Lots. Promise me: we're going to be honest even when it's a lot easier to be polite."

"I'll do my best, Tal. I promise."

"Good. The last thing I want is for us to get hitched and have a baby, and then politely push each other away for the rest of our lives. I couldn't handle that. I'd die inside."

"Me too."

"I've learned a few things about myself while you've been a dick these past two weeks," she said. "I've learned that I'm scared, but I want to have a baby with you anyway, Thomas Whidman. But only if you want it, too. You've got to want it with your whole heart."

Something warm glowed inside Thomas' chest as he stood at that gas station pay phone on that cloudy Arkansas morning. Mist rose from the blacktop as the sun began to creep over the land.

"I love you, Talia Simmons!" he shouted into the phone, causing the sparrows in an asphalt puddle nearby to take flight. "I'm scared shitless but I love you more than anything in the entire world. Junior's gonna have a daddy."

66 DRESSED IN CORDUROYS

"Hello, Mr. Wood? Mr. Bert Wood?"

The worn screen door opened infinitely slowly, not out of suspicion, but out of sheer limited ability of the opener. Mr. Wood, dressed in corduroys and a cardigan to ward off the chill, was already doing his best to manage the coordinated movements of his own frail body, his walker, and his oxygen tank. Adding the porch screen to the list was considerably more complex.

"Why hello, young man," Mr. Wood wheezed eventually, the gleam in his ancient eyes belying his decomposing physical state. He looked Thomas up and down, a curious stranger standing on his peeling front porch. "What brings you to my front door?"

"Well, sir, people tell me you're the unofficial Mayor of Gilman."

"That I am, that I am," the octogenarian chucked. "That and a few hundred other things." The screen door was almost open now, and the elderly man gave the handle to Thomas to hold ajar as he slowly began to shuffle his walker back into the shag-carpeted entryway. "Come on in. What can I do ya for?"

"Well, sir, I've come to learn some of the history of this place."

At that the old man gave a merry cackle. He slowly led the way into the house. "You want the history of Gilman! Lord, don't get me started. You're goin' to have to go buy us some more lemonade mix if you want Gilman's history. I only have a few days' worth." He cackled again, amusing himself heartily.

"That's sounds fine to me, Mr. Wood. I have the time."

"That's rare in young people these days. You on break from the university, son?"

"Actually, sir, I'm out here all the way from California. My name's Thomas Whidman, and my relatives—"

"Wait at the door, there, would you, Tom?" interrupted Mr. Wood. "I have to get a certain something. I'll be back in just a minute."

"Sure, Mr. Wood," said Thomas, slightly baffled. "Do you need any help?"

"Oh no, I can get it myself," came the man's voice, already down the hall a bit. He seemed to be moving a little quicker.

Thomas smiled to himself. He realized that he'd taken a liking to Bert Wood right away. Old codger, hobbling around with his oxygen and walker and cardigan, the self-appointed Mayor of Gilman, drinking his lemonade mix on the porch of his low-slung house with a twinkle in his eye, spinning old stories about this place to anybody who'd listen. Paul Silas had made him out to be a treasure trove of information. *Wonder what he's getting right now?* Thomas thought. *A folder of old news clippings? Yellowed photo albums?*

Thomas waited. From the entryway, he could hear Mr. Wood shuffling about in the back rooms of the small house. Finally, the elderly man appeared around the hallway corner, inching forward across the thick green shag on his walker, loaded down with his oxygen as well as with some sort of small black canister under his arm.

"Looks important," observed Thomas as Mr. Wood approached methodically. "What is it, WD-40? Here, let me help—"

Wood raised the canister, joviality gone. "Get out!" he bellowed. He sprayed unerringly, unleashing the contents full into Thomas' shocked face. "I'm not giving you Whidmans any of it!"

Pepper spray shot up Thomas' nose, burned into his eyes, ripped down his throat. Screaming and blind, the young man reeled backward, crashing through the old screen door and stumbling backwards down the porch steps, smashing his head on the sidewalk below.

Two minutes later, he still had not gotten up from the Mayor of Gilman's front walkway. The local policeman summoned to the scene found him sprawled on the ground, tears uncontrollably pouring from welted, burning eyes and discolored mucus matting his beard.

67 IMMINENTLY AVAILABLE

"*Hola, Padre?* He's on the line again. *Un momentito.*"

"*Gracias, David. Estoy listo.*"

Through a bit of phone static, Thomas could hear the muffled voices of the social worker and the night watchman Paul Silas at Southside Social Services of Tucson. He hoped this was a good time. He looked at his watch. Nearly 7:25AM in Arizona. From the night he spent in the Jeep in Tucson a few weeks ago, Thomas knew the sun would already be hot on the blacktop outside Silas' workplace, and he should be off-shift. The refugees would all be gone by now, and Silas would be thinking of bed.

"Is that you, Thomas?" he heard on the other end of the line.

"Paul?" Thomas said into the phone. "Glad I caught you a second time. The police here in Gilman must've felt sorry for me when they found me sprawled on the pavement outside of Bert Wood's place. They gave me three calls instead of just one."

"You any worse for wear?" Silas gave one of his half-laughs. "That old man can be a tough customer."

"My eyes still sting, but the cops say it'll wear off in a day or so," said Thomas. "Anyway, they may not give me much time, so I'll get down to business. I've called my girlfriend, Talia Simmons, and I can't believe it, but she said she'll be able to leave the Bay Area by lunchtime, pick you up in Tucson tonight and bring you all the way here. If you still think you can come. Sorry for this being so sudden."

"No worry, Thomas. I can come," said Silas. "I just needed a few minutes to think it over. I can be ready by this evening, after I sleep for a few hours." He chuckled dryly. "When you have no salary, no debt and no family, you are imminently available. Just needed to have someone cover my watch for a few days."

"Thanks a million, Mr. Silas. It's weird, but Bert will only let me in his house if you come. You're the only one who can help me out."

"That makes it twice. I find it strangely amusing that I have done all I can to be unlocatable, and yet your need to find me has been even greater. Not once, but twice."

To Thomas, Paul Silas didn't *sound* strangely amused. Not amused at all. Just strange. Even though Thomas had grown to like the former seminarian, he hadn't quite gotten used to him. The desperate phone call he had to make out of the blue this morning from an Arkansas police station did nothing to put either man at ease.

"Will your lovelorn cheeseburger-eating friend be joining us this time?" Silas ventured.

"Who, Mike?" Thomas laughed, real laughter. He had forgotten how Silas had first found them in the Tucson restaurant. "No, just Talia and our dog Agnew. Actually, right now as we speak, Mike's driving from the Bay Area to Southern California to try to make it work with his wife and kids. Seems like he's finally realized what love is. I guess you left quite an impression on him at *Mariscos*."

Thomas thought this would elicit a comment from Silas. A chuckle. An observation. When he remained silent on the other end of the line, Thomas moved on. "So, anyway, Talia should be meeting you at Southside Social Services sometime on your shift late tonight. You can just toss your bag in the back and keep driving through the night until you get to Gilman."

More silence. "Mr. Silas, are you there?"

"Oh yes. I'm here. Just listening, that's all." More silence. "You said Mike has finally realized what love is. Has your friend Talia figured out what love is?"

This time it was Thomas' turn to be quiet. "Yes," said Thomas gradually. "Yes, I believe she has. Maybe I have too." Another awkward pause hung in the air when Thomas finished. *Why am I discussing my love life with this odd stranger?*

"Anyway, you don't know how much this means to me," continued Thomas. "When I told Mr. Wood that I knew you, he finally started talking to me. But he still won't let me in his house. In order for me to see his library—he calls it the Vault – he said that you had to come in person. Guess you know each other pretty well from your time researching your thesis?"

"I know him well. And the Vault."

"Well, that's great for me, 'cause you're my only ticket. You're the one who made me come, and now you're the only way he'll let me in. He still doesn't believe that I'm here just to look at stuff without swiping it."

"This wouldn't have to do with a certain zealous uncle of yours, would it?" Thomas could hear the smile in Silas' voice.

"Yeah, it does," said Thomas, amazed. "You know about that?"

"Bert's told me about a few of your uncle's more colorful attempts. He and I talk every now and then. Usually about old times." *What are they, buddies?* thought Thomas. *When is this guy not a mystery?* "I know first hand your uncle's zeal to keep the Whidman name untarnished," Silas continued. "He's tried to destroy Bert Wood's library more than once. You're lucky the Mayor didn't come at you with a shotgun when you introduced yourself as a Whidman at his front door."

"Well, I just found out about all this myself. Mr. Wood tells me my Uncle Ben's journeyed out here several times over the last decade, trying to get rid of all traces of our wacky ancestor. Ben first came as himself ten years ago, and when Wood refused to part with his collection, he tried again in disguise a few years later."

385

"Insurance salesman," Silas chuckled. "I was there. He said he needed to view important historical information for a settlement. He was in the Vault with a bunch of documents stashed in his briefcase when we realized he was a fraud."

"Serious?" Thomas was floored. "You were there?"

"No lie," Silas responded. "We had to bind him with duct tape and drive him to the police station. What's Bert said that he's done since then?"

"Nothing that obvious," Thomas said. "He thinks Ben tried to burn his house down three years ago when he was away on a trip. He also says the Arkansas Historical Society has offered to buy his collection, and he thinks Ben is behind it. I don't know how much of this is just an old guy's lonely imagination, but I wouldn't put it past my uncle. He's dedicated."

"Your uncle is not well," Silas concurred.

That's funny, coming from you, Thomas wanted to shout into the phone.

"Well, Paul, you'll need to get your sleep, so I'll let you go. Talia should be there in about eighteen hours. You're the one who made me come here to get the rest of your thesis, so I figured I could call you for assistance if I needed some aid. But this—this is huge. Thanks again."

"You are most welcome," said Silas. "But I must say that my reasons for coming are not all about your little quest."

"Huh?" grunted a surprised Thomas, stopping himself in mid hang-up.

"I have some spirits to visit."

68 HERE BEFORE AND LONG AFTER

Mr. Wood was waiting in his paneled Plymouth station wagon outside of the Gilman police station when Thomas finished his phone calls. Together they drove the eight hundred yards to the community cemetery—Thomas, Mr. Wood, and the man's large oxygen tank on wheels.

It took Bert five minutes to pack the car, five minutes to unpack the car, and thirty seconds to make the drive. Thomas offered to assist during the packing process to speed things up, but the Mayor of Gilman would have none of it. Ever since Thomas had identified himself as a Whidman, Bert Wood had refused to let Thomas touch anything.

Mr. Wood parked the car and opened his glove compartment. Slowly, the old man shuffled through a dozen laminated placards. Eventually, he selected one reading *"Caretaker, Gilman Cemetery"* and placed it on his dashboard. "Lets me park in the handicapped space," he commented as he began the painstaking job of getting his walker and oxygen out of the car.

"But…can't you park in the handicapped space anyway?" said a puzzled Thomas, trying to assist with the machinery. "You have a walker."

Mr. Wood stopped and turned to Thomas, looking a little miffed. "Well, yes, but it's not the same. I'm on cemetery caretaker business."

"Of course," replied Thomas, looking around at the utterly empty lot.

Together, the pair strolled through the cemetery. It was an informative but stiff tour, with Bert Wood acting as guide, pointing out the graves and naming the occupations of some of the key players of the Faithful Remnant community that bloomed in the 1920s.

He still doesn't trust me, Thomas observed. *Why should he? He still thinks I might be doing dirty work for my uncle, weaving a tall tale about Silas. Until Talia and that crazy bastard arrive, I'm a huge question mark.*

Bert Wood, Caretaker, straightened things up in the cemetery as they walked. Soon Thomas found himself joining in: repositioning tipped candles near gravestones, rearranging plastic flowers, picking up litter.

As Thomas was tidying up a family plot, he noticed Mr. Wood pull a single red rose from his jacket and place it in a shallow stone bowl on a modest headstone nearby. Approaching, Thomas noticed the bowl was filled with dried petals of varying ages from roses past. The headstone read *"Lisette Magnon, 3:12."*

Bert Wood moved ahead without so much as a glance back at Thomas. The younger man kept his questions to himself.

- - - - -

"And, here we are—the printing press and the chapel," Bert Wood rumbled several minutes later. They'd just moved past the last of the grassy headstones along the graveled walkway, and were now approaching two gray stone buildings made of river cobbles. The smaller was squat and serious-looking, while the larger boasted a soaring steeple and a tall bell tower. "The heart of the Faithful Remnant community," Bert announced. "Here the message was made – " the octogenarian pointed to the church—"and here it was spread," he concluded, indicating the low building alongside.

"Bartholomew Whidman—he'd be your other great-grand uncle, I guess— managed the printing press and distribution, while Josiah came up with the divine inspiration," Mr. Wood reported. He selected a single key from a jingling, bulging ring that boasted no less than forty. *This man has made himself indispensable,* Thomas marveled.

The Mayor of Gilman unlocked the metal door and entered the small, serious building. Two large printing presses silently dominated the single room. Huge metal rollers gleamed dully under a thin layer of dust. Everything about the interior spoke of purpose.

"In its heyday, the Faithful Remnant community produced a few thousand newsletters a week. *The Harbinger,* that's what they called it," explained Wood. "It proclaimed the coming end of the world, and how folks needed to turn away from all the corruption and sin and money of the big cities and turn back to a purer life in God." The old man wheeled his oxygen and walker into the center of the room and spoke to the younger man with the voice of a tour guide. "Now this was just after the first World War, a time of massive change, urban dislocation, poverty and mechanization. In the early 1920s, those newsletters would travel on the trains bound to Santa Fe and Denver and to Boston, get passed all along the tracks like wildfire. People responded to the message and moved here in droves."

Thomas found it hard to imagine: so much activity and influence emanating from such a small, still room. Dust motes floated in the air above the hardwood floor, illuminated by soft light streaming in through small windows placed high in the cobblestone walls.

Mr. Wood stood a moment viewing the presses, remembering another time. "Damn things sure were hard to repair," he said as he turned to go.

They were out of the building and already approaching the large church doors across the way by the time Thomas recognized the import of what he just heard.

"You...worked in there? For the *Harbinger?*"

Bert looked up quizzically from the keyhole as he opened the doors of the musty chapel. "Of course. Thought you knew that, though of course you wouldn't have," he said. "That was my first job," jerking his thumb back over his shoulder at the printing house, "greasing and maintaining those beasts for Bartholomew Whidman and his newsletters. I was all of thirteen, maybe fourteen years old. Best job I could get at that age, by far."

The old man noted Thomas' befuddled expression. "I've lived in this town all my life, son," Mr. Wood explained, fiddling with the locks on the church doors. "Born in 1909, just a few houses away from here, back when Gilman was just fourteen families living by the railroad, in plank houses by the river."

"Before the Faithful Remnant moved in?"

"My family's been here before they came and been here long after they left," Bert chuckled as he pushed open the double doors. The pair of men strolled down the broad center aisle of the plank floor, passing row after row of high-backed wooden pews. As they approached the altar and pulpit, they crossed through alternating pools of sunlight, beams like spotlights shining in from the small windows spaced high along both side walls of the stone church.

"Your great-grand uncle used to preach from right up there," Bert said, motioning to the elevated platform. "Nobody's preached from that pulpit since the community broke up almost seventy years ago." At an approving nod from the caretaker, Thomas went to stand behind the pine-wood podium of Josiah Adam Whidman.

It wasn't hard for Thomas to imagine the space crowded, pews filled with righteous men and women thirsty for the word of the Lord, fans waving in the heat, tanned and calloused hands upraised and praising their Almighty God. It wasn't hard to imagine men and women, confused and despairing by the hardness and temptations of this life, listening to the magnetic words of his powerful and passionate ancestor, a herald to whom God had whispered a secret plan regarding the end of the world.

"I hadn't really noticed before, but standing up there, you look a lot like he did."

"You…knew him, then?"

"You don't catch on real fast, do you, Tom?" Bert Wood said, cocking his head. "'Course I knew him. You may look like him but you don't seem to have inherited his smarts," he said, though not unkindly. "I first saw him when I was just a kid, and he was about your age. Early thirties, maybe."

"Did you and your family ever get caught up in the whole thing?"

"My family never caught the fever," Bert remembered. "Like I said, we were here before he and his kind arrived. But there wasn't a whole lot else to do around here on Sundays for a young man back then. Now, I didn't come every Sunday, mind you…I was just a townie, not a member of the community. But church was usually pretty good entertainment. Especially this church, with their whole 'end-of-the-world' hysteria. It's funny," the old man reflected. "The end of *their* world happened right around the time Josiah Adam said it would, but not for the reason he predicted."

"I know…the resurrection attempt."

"Not just that," Bert Wood responded. "A highly-publicized resurrection attempt, sure. But also lots of other juicy stuff: insanity, suicide, abandonment, mental breakdowns, and smuggling Josiah away under the cover of night to an asylum."

"That's the reason I'm here, Mr. Wood," Thomas said, bounding off the raised dais and coming close to the elder man. "Paul Silas said you and your Vault are a treasure trove of information, and said I needed to come to Gilman to find out about this part myself. I want to know what happened to Josiah's personal world when the world didn't end in 1923. What happened in his soul?"

Bert Wood's face was hard to read in the dim light inside the chapel. Thomas pushed on. "And I want to learn more about Josiah's attempt to raise a man from the dead. What happened to his faith and his mind when it failed? When his God was silent for a second time?"

Wood remained a sphinx with an oxygen tube. Thomas continued, talking to the walls now, not really caring if the man answered him or not. "I didn't even find out about the resurrection attempt until recently." Wandering through the church, Thomas ran his hand along the natural grain of the pews. "My uncle Ben destroyed the news clippings my grandmother had kept about it."

"You didn't know that your ancestor tried to raise the dead?" Bert Wood said skeptically.

Thomas turned to the old man. "Silas mentioned it to me for the first time only two weeks ago, but never showed me that part of his thesis. He said I had to come here to Gilman to get the whole of his thesis, and to help uncover a long-buried secret."

"He said those words?" The old man became animated. "He told you to come here *to help uncover a long-buried secret?*"

"Yeah," replied Thomas, startled. "Something like that."

"Why didn't you say so before?"

Thomas was floored. All suspicion had left the old man. With clear intent, Bert began wheeling his tank to the door. He impatiently motioned with a bony finger to Thomas. "Come, lad. Let me introduce you to the Vault."

Artifact # 6: Excerpt from Paul Silas' Thesis,
"The Crisis of Faith of Josiah Adam Whidman"

1924 proved to be another blissful year of kingdom living for the Faithful Remnant community in Gilman without apocalypse, sensationalism or miracle. In early 1925, two years after the predicted Second Coming, the Gilman colony disintegrated: not because the prophecy of Armageddon failed to come true, but because the community's magnetic leader, Reverend Josiah Whidman, suffered a complete breakdown.

Despite the failed prophecy of 1923, the colonists at Gilman had remained steadfast as the following months turned into two years. As Bartholomew Whidman wrote in 1924, "The Lord's timing is not our timing, but our time remains the Lord's." The colonists seemed to be in agreement: whether waiting upon tomorrow or upon a more distant day, establishing a Christian outpost based upon kingdom values of community, praise and charity was a life mission to which they could be faithful.

What did eventually shatter the colony were the actions taken by their leader during the month of February, 1925. In early February, a community member fell gravely ill. On February 9th, Pastor Josiah Whidman gathered the Faithful Remnant congregation to attempt a prayer healing. When the sick man did not miraculously improve, Whidman blamed the failure on "those in the community who lacked faith." The man's condition declined rapidly over the next two days. During this time Pastor Whidman pored over scripture, and became certain that God would show His saving power by restoring the man to full health.

The critically ill man died early on Thursday, February 11. When the Gilman community gathered for morning prayer, Josiah Whidman startled the congregation by attempting to resurrect the man, who'd been laid out upon the church altar. After the initial attempt failed, Whidman shocked the community further by stating his attempt to resurrect the man had been slightly premature; rather, God would raise the body in three days, on the morning of Saint Valentine's Day, Sunday, February 14 (Arkansas Democrat, LIV: 1, Feb 16, 1925).

The news quickly spread throughout the state and the region. The next seventy-two hours launched a media circus. Accordingly, three days later, on the appointed Sunday, the usually quiet town of Gilman "was a scene of excitement as the hour of church service approached, during which the miracle was to be witnessed (54:5, Feb 17, 1925)."

Reporters and photographers hailing from newspapers as distant as the St. Louis Dispatch joined a sizable crowd of the faithful and the curious to witness the resurrection attempt. Scores of Gilman community members prayed steadfastly on the steps of the church, expecting a miracle. As first-hand witness and Gilman resident Bert Wood describes, the day fairly crackled with anticipation: excited neighbors came by wagonload, city folk came by train, and a few inspired souls even traveled down the Buffalo River by canoe to the tiny community of Gilman, motivated by the prospect of seeing a man raised from the dead.

But community leader and prophet Josiah Whidman never showed. The appointed time came and went, and by evening, the vast majority of the crowd had dispersed. Photographers had a field day, but reporters had little luck finding colonists who were willing to be interviewed.

Confusion and disappointment ruled. The community's leaders were nowhere to be seen. The brothers Whidman, Josiah and Bartholomew, had abandoned the flock. Without the guidance and leadership of the visionary brothers who had held Gilman together during previous hardships, the community disbanded. Most colonists left for good within the next two days.

What had happened? The personal journal of Bartholomew Whidman reveals that his brother Josiah Adam had sought refuge at his house the night before, in a state of mute and feverish collapse. At wit's end, Bartholomew Whidman decided to leave Gilman in the dark of night, transporting his distraught brother all the way to a mental hospital in upstate New York. At intake, doctors diagnosed that Josiah Whidman had suffered a stroke precipitated by a psychotic break.

Though he would live on for more than three decades, Josiah Adam Whidman never returned in body to Gilman again. However, it is certain that the traumatic events at Gilman left Josiah Whidman a wrecked man. Hospital records indicate he remained a patient at Shady Brook Sanitarium for thirty-two more years, bitter and rarely speaking, until his death in 1957.

--Excerpt taken from "The Crisis of Faith of Josiah Adam Whidman," Master of Divinity thesis written by Paul Silas, Bay Area Theological Union, 1985.

69 HELLO, OLD FRIEND

"That was the most awkward eighteen hours I have *ever* spent with someone in a car," Talia whispered as words of greeting in Thomas' ear, hugging him as she stepped out of her red Pathfinder.

Her presence felt so right, Thomas glowed. Who would've guessed that Talia would be here in Gilman, or that he would've pleaded for her to drive across the country, or that she would've said yes? Just a few days ago back in Oakland everything had been so tense. After he'd walked away in anger from Paloma at *Tolstoi's Tea House*, he'd left a note for Talia at her apartment and took off without seeing her. He'd figured the goodbye would be better that way; things had been so strained with the pregnancy, he wouldn't have known what to say if he'd seen her face-to-face.

But the phone call had changed all that. Having her here at Bert Wood's front drive, warm and beautiful and coming all this way just to help him, made him laugh with delight. She felt so good against him, he wanted to melt into her. He wanted to shout out her name again like he did two days ago at the Arkansas state line. *Why had he been so threatened?*

"The first eighteen hours I drove just to pick him up probably didn't help a lot, either," she continued in his ear as they reluctantly broke their embrace. "Eighteen plus eighteen. You owe me *big time*. What's that make? About thirty-six hours of favors, I figure," she said with a malicious smile.

At the passenger side, old Bert Wood had shuffled his walker and oxygen close in order to pump Paul Silas' hand enthusiastically and then embrace him in an awkward, fragile manner. It looked like two mummies hugging.

Thomas had never seen two bonier people.

"Hello, old friend," wheezed Bert Wood softly as he released from the rickety embrace. "I've been taking care of her," he said, tapping a rose in his lapel. With that, he looked across the car and adjusted his oxygen septum plug. "And hello there, my dear! Talia, is it? Bert Wood at your service."

She separated herself from Thomas and the old man gave a little bow, wheezing. "Welcome to our humble town, and to the Wood Wallow Bed & Breakfast, open to all Gilman historians and canoeing enthusiasts."

"I'm more the latter than the former," Talia responded, smiling, taken by the ancient man's charm. "Thanks for having us, Mr. Wood. I know how much this means to Thomas." As she opened the back hatch to get her duffel bag, she spoke out of the side of her mouth in a whisper. "*This* is the nine-foot tall devil who blasted you with pepper spray?"

"The very one," commented Thomas dryly. "Watch what you say about knowing Uncle Ben. He's the antichrist around here."

Bert Wood had already turned his attention back to Silas, and spoke softly.

"Welcome back, Paul. It's really good to see you. Especially with him." His eyes darted to Thomas. "I filled out the form and submitted it to the town authorities yesterday. Everything's set for day after tomorrow. All we need is his signature."

Wood slowly moved to the front of the vehicle to join Talia at the steps leading up to his front porch. "I'd offer to take your luggage, but that wouldn't do either of us any good now, would it?" The old man chuckled, surmounting the first rise with his walker.

"Things haven't changed in seven years," noted Silas as he stood in the entryway, admiring the wooden interior. He walked to the kitchen table. "Lemonade from a box, anyone?" he announced with ceremony, holding up the perspiring pitcher of icy lemonade and glasses. "It's all he serves around here, summer or winter, so you better like it."

70 3:12

"Gonna take Agnew for a stretch," Talia said, ambling down the porch steps a few minutes later with the Great Dane. "I'm so wound up from driving, I might need it more than he does. I'm all jangly." She shook out her arms and legs. "Caffeine and sleep are battling for supremacy right now. Either could win. If I'm not back in an hour, look for me snoring by the river."

Talia hadn't brought in her bags, so Thomas did while she took her walk. He was just returning to the house from the Pathfinder with her luggage when he heard the two older men conversing quietly down the main hallway. He stopped.

"Do you want to stay in your old room?" inquired the voice of the aged caretaker. "Or do you want one with less…memories?"

"My old room will be just fine, my friend."

The two men stopped conversing when they noticed Thomas in the foyer. Bert became a model of efficiency, handing out keys to Thomas and providing directions as to where to put luggage, where to find the thermostat, and where to find clean towels.

Housekeeping details finished, the elderly host returned with Thomas to Silas. "Well, my friends, now that I have a full house, I have some grocery shopping to do. The young lady seems perfectly content with a walk followed by a long nap. As for the two of you…Paul, do you want to take young Thomas on a walk? We can dig into the Vault a bit later this afternoon."

"Never even took my jacket off," responded Silas. "Let's go, Thomas. I'll introduce you to the neighborhood."

The pair walked out into the inn's grassy front yard and then took a circuitous loop around downtown Gilman, stopping at many of the historical houses and buildings of the Faithful Remnant that Thomas had seen yesterday with Bert Wood.

Feels like a living museum, thought Thomas. Gilman would be a ghost town except for about a dozen residents attempting to turn the place into a nostalgic tourist attraction of yesteryear. A general store, a candy factory, an old-fashioned post office and a tack supply constituted the living elements of downtown. The rest of the buildings were uninhabited relics of another age, marked with faded signs identifying a cobbler's shop, a stationery store and a furniture workshop from days bygone.

From the banks of the Buffalo River, Silas and Thomas traversed the four blocks to the cemetery in the central park of Gilman. Here, Talia was resting under a tree with Agnew, and stood up to join them as they walked. In the midday sunshine the graveyard was no longer cool, but Silas still seemed grateful for his long overcoat.

They wandered the cemetery. Tombstones stuck out of the ground in orderly rows like the perfectly spaced teeth of a sleeping giant. Among the grave markers, Silas suddenly turned to face his walking companions. "Will you bury me here in Gilman when I die, Thomas?"

"Me?" Thomas croaked. "Are you joking?" He exchanged a quick glance with Talia, who seemed equally caught off-guard by the mercurial nature of the man. "Paul, I barely even know you." *Or like you,* Thomas wanted to say.

"You know me more than practically anyone alive," said Silas bluntly, his dark eyes flashing. "All of my family is here," he said, waving his arms out theatrically.

"You've been drinking." Thomas' words came out as a statement more than a question.

"Yes I have," the old man said flatly, patting one of the bottomless pockets in his large overcoat. He twirled with hands raised, coat flying. "But that means nothing when I'm with friends." With that he sank to his knees, collapsing and wrapping his bony arms around the nearest tombstone. Gravely, the old man kissed the inscribed face of the carved marble.

Thomas looked to Talia, who shrugged in confusion. He was about to grab the sad, drunken figure by the arm and take him back to the inn when something made him stop in his tracks. He looked at the headstone.

"Lisette Magnon 3:12," he read. "Wait. Old Mr. Wood put that here yesterday," Thomas said, pointing to a single stem rose resting in a shallow bowl full of petals.

"I know," responded Silas, fingering the stem. "I asked him to."

"3:12. What's that?" Talia prompted. Both Talia and Thomas were struggling to gain some comprehension of the mysterious situation and this equally mysterious man. "A date? Time of day?"

Silas sat mute, staring at the inscription.

"Maybe a Bible verse?" guessed Thomas. "But what book is it…wait a minute. That's one of the numbers you kept repeating in your thesis. *'3:12. It is fitting that my faith, too, dies in numbers. 3:12.'*" Thomas took a sudden step back and stood upright. "This is beyond weird. Paul. What's this all about?"

"It's like it says. 3:12."

"I know it's about 3:12." Thomas tried to look Silas in the eye. "You wrote those numbers repeatedly all through your thesis, sometimes typed, sometimes hand-written in the margin."

Talia drew nearer, enthralled. "Paul, who is Lisette Magnon?"

"I told you I had spirits to visit." The man continued to caress the stone. Silas' face bore the strangest mix of longing and sadness and peace that Thomas had ever seen. "I'm here, Lisette."

Even though the hair on his neck stood on end out of sheer unease, Thomas stayed next to the man. Talia was rooted, too. They were on the edge of a discovery, and understanding this man's twisted mind was the prize.

"So what's 3:12...Scripture? Maybe Romans?" Thomas guessed.

Silas shook his head. "Three minutes, twelve seconds. That's the amount of time I was apart from her without her epinephrine," Silas said flatly. He drew back to look at the headstone. "Lisette Magnon," the gaunt man read its surface. "My fiancée."

Talia started to say something, but Silas kept going. "That was all the time it took for her to choke and writhe and die." He looked up and away, to the opposite end of the fenced enclosure. "I was right over there."

"Your fiancée died...here?" Talia said in disbelief. "Right here in this graveyard...and she's buried...here?"

Thomas didn't think the hairs on the back of his neck could stand any straighter, but they did. Talia's eyes were welling up, wanting to deny the tale.

"Yeah, right about here," Silas said in a detached and distant voice. He stood up and looked at the ground as if he was gazing at a body, his eyes blurred and unfocused. The older man suddenly collapsed against Thomas' side and clutched at the younger man's leg. Talia tried to help Silas, but he wasn't interested in getting up.

"Bury me here when I die, Thomas." He was pleading this time. "Promise me!" Silas' eyes were yellowed and bloodshot, but his visage was fierce and his gaze clear. "Promise me, damn it!"

Thomas beheld in Silas' face the pain he'd seen in Juanita and her villagers, those whose loved ones had burned alive in Guatemala. Frantically, he looked at Talia for guidance. She nodded silently from behind the prone man. Thomas took a deep breath.

"I'll bury you here, Paul. I promise," he said, slowly helping the wracked man to his feet. "Right next to Lisette."

Talia added, "C'mon, Paul, let's go home now." Silas rose, weak in the knees, his energy spent. Leaning on the shoulders of the two others, his frail body seemed to be made of fallen leaves.

"Bert took me home last time, just like you are now," Silas muttered softly as they walked him away from the cemetery. "After Lisette died. He found me a few hours afterward, in the chapel. I was a wreck, and out of my mind. Couldn't even walk by myself."

He coughed uncontrollably, rough and ugly. Talia waited for the spasm to die, and then took the man by the arm again, supporting him like a toddler. After a few more steps, Silas spoke again. "Lisette accompanied me when I came to Gilman to work on my thesis, seven years ago. I'd been in telephone contact with Bert—back then he was simply a voice on the other end of the telephone, a Mr. Bert Wood, the town historian – who assured me that he had the most thorough trove of information in existence regarding Josiah Adam Whidman and the Faithful Remnant community."

He coughed again, a wet sound, and regained his breath. "So my Lisette and I journeyed down here with my Smith-Corona and my files to spend some time as I finished my research. We were going to be together in Gilman for the whole month of March and then return to the Bay Area for me to graduate. We were to get married in June. Yes, she wanted a June wedding."

Silas, lost in memories, stopped walking. Thomas turned to give him extra support, and Silas'legs moved once more. "We'd been here only sixteen days when, while strolling the graveyard, she was stung by a bee. She had an anaphylactic reaction and died three minutes later. Just like that."

Across Silas' shoulders Talia's eyes told Thomas to keep quiet. Let the man talk.

"I'd left her reading by a tree while I went to inspect a gravestone," Paul Silas continued. "A certain gravestone..." He looked back over his shoulder at the cemetery for a moment, perhaps looking for a marker. "I came back to her three minutes and twelve seconds later, and found her on her face. Puffed up and swollen. Red at first, but quickly getting blue. Not breathing. No pulse. She hadn't even cried out. I ran to a phone and called emergency services. Twelve minutes later an ambulance arrived, and in twenty two and a half minutes they had taken her body away and declared her dead."

"Oh, Paul." Talia could no longer be quiet. "I am so sorry."

"Asphyxiation, leading to oxygen deprivation of the brain." Silas was so detached it sounded like he was reading a newspaper. He fell silent as the Wood Wallow Bed & Breakfast came into sight across an expanse of grass.

"I'm not sure what happened after that," he continued eventually. "I started screaming and couldn't stop. I must have lost all rational thought, because the next thing I remember it was sundown, hours later. I was in front of the Gilman chapel. My clothes were all full of thistles and rips and mud, my flesh scratched and bloody, not sure how. I felt like something was torn inside. I dragged my body into the chapel and crawled beneath the altar like a baby, just to get somewhere safe. I was shaking and crying so badly I just kept pressing my face against the cool stone floor, trying to push myself into the ground. Then I...remembered something else...and went out of my mind again." Thomas wanted to ask for details, but refrained.

"Sometime late in the night, I came to," Silas concluded as they reached the porch steps. "I remember seeing a flashlight and hearing shouts of men. Bert Wood found me, helpless as a newborn babe mewling under the altar, and brought me back here."

71 THE NINTH HOUR

Thomas wasn't exactly sure when Talia finally kicked him out of bed, but it was definitely after 2:00 A.M. He'd been tossing and turning, unable to find a comfortable spot, unable to exorcise the images haunting his sleep. He kept seeing himself at that pine pulpit in the chapel, preaching until he was hoarse. A young Josiah Adam Whidman with slicked-back hair and dark eyes sat alone in the front pew, staring, while a grown Paul Silas screamed hysterically under the altar, curled in a fetal position. Peaceful sleep was elusive, no matter what he tried. Finally, at Talia's pleading, Thomas got up and found himself alone, roaming Bert Wood's hallway at some ungodly hour of the morning.

He wanted to be mad at Talia, but he couldn't blame her. After all, she needed sleep. His mind was on overdrive. He needed to talk to somebody, take a walk, something. Thomas padded down the hardwood hallway and passed Silas' room. The man's door was ajar, and the room was empty.

Silas' trademark overcoat was gone. *Looks like I'm not the only night owl around here.* After checking that Bert was contentedly wheezing on his oxygen machine in the master bedroom, Thomas silently put on some sweatpants, creaked open the front door and slipped out into the misty Arkansas night.

Ten minutes later he spotted Silas in the graveyard, tottering around like a drunken acrobat. The man seemed alone in the shadowy minefield of his mind, the cemetery etched in black and white. Thomas approached silently to a respectful distance. Then he concealed himself behind a sycamore tree to watch.

The cloaked man suddenly jumped and perched on top of a tombstone, swaying with arms outstretched. To Thomas, the silhouetted Silas in his long overcoat looked like a vagabond scarecrow brought to unnatural life. Thomas crept closer to get a better vantage point.

"And they crucified him." In a hoarse and gravelly voice from the top of the headstone, Paul Silas was reciting scripture from memory. "And at the ninth hour Jesus cried out in a loud voice, '*Eloi, Eloi, lama sabachthani!*'" Silas hopped down, stumbling. He had thrust a rough circlet of thorny vines down around his head. In places his scalp was bleeding freely, matting his hair and mixing with his sweat.

Leaning against a large tombstone, the skeletal man outstretched his arms again and cried out, this time high and wild: *"Eloi, Eloi, lama sabachthani!"* With that, he hurled a bottle at a nearby grave marker, shattering glass everywhere. Silas collapsed and wiped his mouth on the back of his hand. His next words were so low Thomas could barely hear: "And then Jesus breathed his last. That's how it goes, chump."

The ensuing silence in the darkened graveyard was broken by a single set of hands clapping, loudly, slowly, mockingly. Silas jerked his head around, looking. So did Thomas. *Who else is out here in the middle of the damn night?*

"Nice performance," came Talia's' voice through the darkness. "Poor Paul Silas. Did your parents leave you behind a dumpster or something?"

Thomas' jaw dropped. He tried to melt into the shadowy, spindly trees. *Had he been seen?* Silas had heard Talia, Thomas was sure. But the man's head hung low, and he appeared unresponsive. From Thomas' vantage point, he could see the moping silence from the older man twisted Talia's face into a dark scowl.

"You're full of shit, you know that?" Her harsh voice cut through the air with a bite. "Both of you," she said, exposing Thomas lurking in the trees. It wasn't clear which of the two men was more shocked by the sudden appearance of the young woman and her verbal onslaught. Silas looked as guilty as Thomas felt.

"What are you two doing out here?" Talia shouted as she approached across the graveyard grass. "Wrestling with your demons in the middle of the night? You both put on this act like you're big strong men who no longer believe in

God. But you both still think there's a big daddy up in the sky, and you're as mad as hell that he lets his children suffer."

Neither man answered the allegations. Silas, unmoving, appeared as though he might have fallen asleep. Thomas, completely stunned, stood rooted. "You're both addicted to feeling betrayed," she continued, coming nearer to Silas slumped against the headstone. "All you guys do is moan about how God's abandoned you. You need a support group, boys. *Anonymous Dumpster Children,* or something. You guys both need an intervention, and I'm here to give it."

Thomas approached. She'd told him about this side of her, but until now he hadn't seen it, not like this. A part of him was drawn to the truth pouring out of her. Another part wanted to flee.

Talia continued unbidden across the night grass, intoxicated in her own way. She was now close enough to touch Silas. "What happened to you when Lisette died, Paul?" No response. At her feet, Silas appeared dead. "You said your faith died, too." Gripping the unresponsive man, she lifted his head manually and held it in both of her hands, forcing him to look her in the face. Thomas came over and kneeled behind Silas, supporting the older man's body. Without meaning to, his gaze locked with hers. Talia blazed, and it wasn't clear which man she was confronting. "Time to stop this wrestling in the middle of the night. You said you no longer believe in God. But that's a cheap lie. You believe in God, all right, you're just pissed off! Face it--you just can't accept a universe where God lets terrible things happen to good people."

Thomas started shaking now, tears streaming down his face. In the dark of this night, Talia had become a prophet of fire. She was speaking to Silas, to Thomas, to Josiah, to the stones themselves. To the entire graveyard of Gilman souls who'd died abandoned by their God.

"Listen to me, damn it!" Talia grabbed Silas roughly by the collar and shook him. "Your life's in shambles, because all you can imagine is that God's either dead or an uncaring bastard. *Is that all there is?*"

Silas finally looked up into her face. His eyes were red, but focused. "What else is there?" he whispered, his gaze pleading. *"What else is there?"*

Talia, spent, knelt down next to the broken old man and held him. Thomas, too, felt a wave pass through him. His body gave in to the shaking, and he fell against the crooked headstone next to Silas, a crumbling cement crucifix sticking up out of the earth. Even the ground no longer felt solid. He clung to the grave marker like a life raft.

None of the three said anything. Silas' question hung in the night air: *What else is there?*

"How about a helpless God?" Thomas' voice was quiet, but clear. He raised himself to his knees in front of the leaning cement cross. "How about a God who suffers in the streets with the winos and the whores? A God who weeps over all the countless fucking cruelties we do to one another, and he roars, he rages like a gored lion, he screams at them to stop, he screams for a thousand years, knowing he can't do a damn thing to help his children 'cause he nailed his own hands to the fucking wall!"

72 A PUZZLE SUDDENLY FELL INTO PLACE

"I must say, I've never had lunch in a graveyard before," Talia said in the bright afternoon sun of the following day.

"Me neither," said Thomas, throat still scratchy from the night before.

They both looked at Silas with the unspoken question. "Three or four times a week," he admitted, "after Lisette died. Tuna sandwiches and apples. Right here." He shrugged. "I didn't have anyone else to have lunch with, besides Bert."

Talia's attempt at light conversation did little to break the self-conscious mood. Last night's events in this very place seemed like something out of a dream. Silas had woken up this morning at Bert's house chatty and clear-eyed. He seemed lighter.

Birdsong and chewing were the only sounds for several minutes. After taking second helpings, Talia broke the silence. "I have to say, it's a little weird being surrounded by graves of people who aren't just strangers. I mean, your fiancée, Paul, and Thomas, your great-grand uncle and other relatives. Do you think they know we're here?" She took a bite. "Are their spirits wanting to tell us something?"

Silas nodded. "Lisette knows I'm here," he said. "I've talked to her enough, she better be." He wiped his mouth. "And after our antics last night, all the other restless souls are wide awake too." Silas smiled at Talia, a genuine smile. Strange, Thomas thought, but Talia's confrontation with the old man in the graveyard last night really seemed to crack open Paul Silas. Maybe it was the push he'd needed to be human again. He remembered the push he'd needed to talk about Guatemala. She was good at that.

"If any spirit is still hanging around seventy years later," Thomas suggested, "it's Josiah. He still has secrets to tell. I can feel it."

"Like what?" Talia asked. Silas lifted his head in interest.

"I'm not sure." Thomas looked at Talia. "After everything fell apart for him here in Gilman, he spent the next thirty years of his life locked away in a mental hospital. Did he just die a miserable wretch? Or did he ever find anything else?"

"You're thinking he might have discovered something after all that despair," Talia said. "Some kind of hope?"

"I guess." Thomas wiped his mouth. "Hope from beyond the grave. I could use some of that."

"Good luck," Silas said. "Maybe you'll find something." He scratched on the ground with a stick. "I haven't."

Talia turned to the gaunt older man. "But something keeps drawing you back, Paul. You were here seven years ago, and here you are again. You might know the mind of Thomas' ancestor better than anyone alive. What do you think Josiah was feeling when he failed to resurrect that man seventy years ago?"

"Easy," said Silas. "Same thing he was feeling for the next thirty two years. Abandonment. *'Eloi, Eloi, lama sabachthani.'* Just like it says on his headstone."

This statement took Talia a second to absorb. "Wait a minute," she said. "He's buried here?"

"Claro," responded Silas. "Where else?" With a jerk Silas pointed his thumb at a gravestone about ten yards away.

Talia got to her feet and approached the simple marker. "I can't believe we haven't seen this yet," she said, crouching to inspect. "After two days already!" She beckoned to Thomas. "Look, the man himself." Thomas approached and looked over her shoulder.

"Josiah Adam Whidman," she read. *"1886-1957. Eloi, Eloi, Lama Sabachthani."* She looked over at Silas still under the tree. "That's what you were rambling about last night, wasn't it?"

Silas didn't get up, but spoke across the distance. "It's Aramaic. *'My God, my God, why have you forsaken me?'"*

'It's what Jesus said on the cross," Thomas explained. "Just before he died."

"He said that—really? Then he died?"

Silas nodded. Thomas nodded too. "That's what it says in the Book of Mark."

"While he's hanging on the cross," Talia wondered, "letting himself be tortured and killed for the world? Jesus says *'My God, why have you forsaken me?"*

Silas nodded again.

"More abandonment." She slumped down on the ground against the stone. "More tragedy." She looked over at Paul Silas, a new thought in her eyes. "If my fiancée got stung by a bee and died, Paul, it would rip my world apart. It would be a tragedy I couldn't imagine. But tragedies like that happen, Paul. Bad stuff happens to good people. It's part of the world, and we have to learn how to deal with it. You haven't been abandoned more than anyone else."

Silas waited for a long time before he spoke. "Ms. Simmons, I'm sure you're excellent in your line of work, challenging kids and counseling battered women. With your clinical training, you probably think you've got me figured out. That all I need is to push through my despair, and I'll feel good about life again." He looked into the distance. "Do you know who my father was?"

Talia looked toward Thomas, uncertain about this change in conversation.

"No," she said. "Should I?"

Without replying, Silas abruptly turned his back and walked away.

Talia jumped up to follow. "Look, Paul, I'm sorry, I didn't mean to push it too far, it's just that— "

"No," he said, stopping abruptly. "It's not what you think." Thomas got up and joined them. The new look on Silas' face, humor mixed with frustration, made Thomas even more uncertain of the man. "I wasn't walking away from you," the older man said. Silas saw the confusion spreading across Talia's face as she took in a breath to respond. Suddenly his leathered hand darted out, completely covering the young woman's mouth. He stared intently into Talia's surprised eyes. "Look," Silas said forcefully, finally dropping his hand. "Both of you. *Just look.*"

Talia and Thomas followed his gaze to the ground. There, right in front of them, was an unweeded gravestone:

Jacob Timothy Conroy, 1898-1925
"Father, Into Your Hands I Commend
My Spirit"

"That…was your father?" Thomas inquired, shocked.

The grizzled man nodded.

Then Thomas understood. Understood everything. Pieces of a puzzle fell into place: Silas' bizarre obsession with the legacy of Josiah Adam Whidman. His unbalanced anger. His intense bitterness toward Christianity. His overblown sense of abandonment. That suddenly wasn't so overblown.

"Paul, I am so—" Thomas began.

"Jacob Timothy Conroy," interrupted the older man tersely, emotional as a stone. "Died at age 27. Sudden onset of tuberculosis that killed him in a matter of weeks."

Thomas threw a look at Talia. He could see that the pieces were fitting together for her as well.

"Conroy was the man Josiah Adam tried to raise from the dead seventy years ago," she said. Silas barely nodded. "He'd just been married, hadn't he?" she asked. Silas nodded again.

She turned to Thomas. "I just read about this in the Vault this morning with Bert. His wife's name was something like Annabelle – "

"Abigail," Silas corrected. "My mother."

Talia blanched. "Oh my God. Paul, I'm so sorry," she murmured, seeing Silas in a new light. "Abigail Conroy. Your mom. The newspaper article said she never moved from the altar, but instead just prayed over her new husband's decomposing body for three days." She stared at the headstone below her, comprehending. "Your dad." She looked sideways to Silas for confirmation. "She just prayed there. No eating. No sleeping."

Silas nodded. "Standing vigil for the miracle Josiah Whidman promised would come."

"And then, after three days of waiting, Reverend Whidman never showed." Talia painted the scene with her words. "Abigail didn't know it, but he'd had a breakdown the night before. Strangers would've been staring at her. Gawking. Taking pictures. The St. Louis newspaper said she went mad with grief. Found a rope from the barn and hung herself."

"Yep," Silas said flatly. "You got it all right, miss, just like the article said. But you missed one thing. When she died, she left behind a two year-old little boy."

Talia let it sink in. "A little boy named Paul. Listen, I didn't mean to--"

"Paul Josiah Conroy," the older man cut in. "A two-year old orphan with no family, in a community that was breaking apart in craziness and pain. Abandoned." His piercing gaze looked right through Talia. "A dumpster child, you might say."

73 INTO THE VAULT

The trio returned after their picnic to the Wood Wallow Bed & Breakfast to find Bert waiting in a rattan chair on his long front porch, sipping a sweating glass of lemonade. "The perfect beverage when researching the finer details of Gilman history, don't you agree?" inquired Bert with a raised eyebrow, allowing no other answer but the affirmative. They moved as a group inside from the veranda. Bert Wood rubbed his hands together and said, "Let's get down to it, shall we?"

"Of course, *mi amigo,*" Silas nodded, his normal gaunt, gravelly self. As if at lunch he hadn't just divulged his own personal horror story.

Thomas was surprised when even Talia seemed interested in further research. Not so surprising, actually: after hearing about Paul's childhood, the tragic history of Gilman had become personal.

Bert took Talia by the arm as they moved down the hall, and then used an archaic long key to open the door to the basement stairs. A weak overhead bulb illuminated the landing. Wooden steps descended into darkness.

"Into the Vault we go!" Bert said enthusiastically, clanking down the steps one by one with his oxygen cart. They descended into a musty, windowless room enclosed by cinderblock walls. "There are clues to dig into, mysteries to be unearthed, revelations to be excavated!" He winked at Silas. "Bring the pitcher, my friend."

- - - - -

Hours passed as the researchers plunged into the complex archive. Thomas, absorbed in a yellowed 1923 *Kingdom Harbinger* newsletter, yelped when Bert Wood unexpectedly tapped him on the shoulder. The senior citizen and his oxygen cart boxed Thomas into one dank corner of the Vault. The old man's eyes were shining mischievously.

"What do you want?" Thomas asked warily, remembering the pepper spray. He was both intrigued and a little uneasy when his host presented to him a thick, padded mailing envelope.

"The real reason why I allowed you down here," Bert said simply. He drew the envelope back into his own possession. "A secret message."

Hearing these words, Talia came over from some sepia photographs she'd been viewing. From the other side of the cinderblock room, Silas migrated toward the old man as well, but kept his distance.

"Six years before Josiah died—back in 1951, I believe—a reporter from Saint Louis contacted me about a magazine article he wanted to write," Bert began. "He wanted to focus on the people who'd been involved in the Faithful Remnant Community, back in the 1920s." Mr. Wood held the envelope aloft now, taunting his listeners. "The 'Gilman Experiment,' the reporter called it. Kind of a '*Where are they now?*' sort of piece, it seemed. He came to me looking for contacts. He seemed respectful enough, so I helped him with some addresses of folks I still kept in contact with. I gave him Bartholomew Whidman's whereabouts, but never told the reporter about Josiah Whidman being in a mental asylum. Bartholomew could tell the newspaper about his brother's breakdown if he wished, I figured. Not my job."

Bert lowered the thick envelope and held it gingerly in both hands. "I don't even know if his article ever got published, but that reporter's angle got me to thinking: after Josiah's prediction fell apart, what happened inside Reverend Whidman? After twenty-five years in an asylum, did Josiah have faith in anything anymore?"

"That's what I want to know!" blurted Thomas.

"I know, lad," Bert said, patting Thomas' arm. "I know. But let me finish my story. Now, you have to realize that, back in 1951, I didn't even know if

Josiah was still alive."

"You hadn't kept in contact at all?" Talia asked.

"Not in the slightest," Bert explained. "I'd never concerned myself with religious things when I was younger, and what happened to a mixed-up preacher was of no interest to me." The old man cradled the large envelope and looked around at his rapt audience. "Remember, I was just a teenage townie growing up next door to a wacky religious community. Growing up with their fervor all around me, I guess I'd avoided those issues entirely. But later in my life, long after the community disbanded, I began to think about life's larger questions. And by the time the reporter started asking his questions, what happened to the faith of Josiah Whidman was a mystery that had gotten under my skin. So a few months later, I wrote a letter to your great grand-uncle."

"You wrote Josiah?" asked Talia, shocked. She and Thomas exchanged glances. "You had his address all that time?"

Bert Wood shook his head. "Nope." He paused to take a long sip of his lemonade and smacked his lips, clearly enjoying his moment in the spotlight. "All I knew was that his brother had taken him to a place called Shady Brook twenty-five years earlier, somewhere in upstate New York. I had to get the mailing address from Bartholomew. When I finally wrote Josiah, I reminded him that I'd been the printing press boy when I was a kid. I told him I'd become the town historian—which was true even then, 'cause only a dozen families had stayed. I was forty then, with kids of my own, and in my letter I told Josiah that I wanted to complete the history of the Faithful Remnant community by recording any changes in his philosophy now that time had passed. I asked him to share his spiritual journey, if he was willing." Mr. Wood paused for a dramatic moment, looking down at the envelope in his hand. Thomas restrained his urge to grab the document. Silas remained a few rows away, but stood as rapt as the others.

"After several months, I gave up hoping he would write back," continued Bert. "But then this came." The old man looked up at his audience with a gleam in his eye, and removed a small envelope taped to the outside of the larger mailing envelope. He handed it carefully to Thomas. "This is his reply, in 1952."

Thomas opened the small envelope and slid an index card on the table. In careful script, the following text was written in the hand of Josiah Whidman:

My tears have been my food day and night, while people say to me continually, "Where is your God?"

I say to God, my rock, "Why have you forgotten me?"

"Psalm 42," Bert Wood reported. "I looked it up."

"Wow," Talia muttered. "Twenty five years later, and still feeling such abandonment. A betrayal that never changed."

"I wouldn't be so sure about never." Silas' voice cut into the conversation. He came closer, staring right at the old man under the weak light of the overhead bulb. "Something changed. Enough theatrics, Bert. Open it."

"I'm getting there," Mr. Wood retorted. His smile remained, but his expression tightened. "Don't go stealing an old man's thunder."

"Open it already!" Silas demanded.

At that, a look of wonder washed across the features of the aged historian. He stared at Silas. "Why, Paul, I do believe you care!"

"Me?" Silas' face turned red. "Bah! No, I just – "

"You're more curious than any of us!" Bert crowed.

"Just get on with it," Silas growled.

With a satisfied grin, Bert turned back to Thomas and Talia. "Psalm 42 would've been the expected end of the story," he resumed. "A bitter man in a bitter place, his hopes crushed." He took a final long drink of his lemonade, draining it dry.

"But?" Talia asked curiously.

"But." Bert's eyes gleamed under the bare bulb. "Six years later, I received this package out of the blue." Reverentially, the old man placed the bulky mailing envelope into Thomas' hands. "He sent it to me. But it's really for you."

Astounded, Thomas opened the mailing envelope. He glimpsed a book, but as he withdrew it Bert's liver-spotted hands darted back to the package, covering it. Thomas stopped, eyes shooting up to meet those of the old man.

"Before you look inside," said Bert, "examine the outside for something very interesting."

Talia popped her head on her boyfriend's shoulder to get a better look. Together they scoured the envelope's surface. It was addressed to *Mr. Bert Wood, Historian of Gilman, Gilman, Arkansas*. Nothing mysterious there, as the town was small enough to not need box numbers or street addresses. The return address was of Rev. Josiah A. Whidman, Shady Brook Sanitarium in Palma, New York. That didn't raise any eyebrows either. But the package was postmarked April 23, 1957.

"April 23rd," muttered Thomas, staring at the package. "This came to you from Josiah himself?" Thomas noted the addresses were written in his ancestor's hand. "But that's, what…more than two weeks after the date of his death." He stared at Mr. Wood as it registered. *"This package was prepared for you by Josiah right before he died!"*

74 THIRTY FIVE YEARS IN THE MAKING

"A message from beyond the grave," Talia said, staring at the package in Thomas' hands.

Bert nodded, his eyes lit up. "And just wait 'til you see what's inside!" The old man released and stepped back. "Addressed to me. By his hand. Mailed two weeks after his death. Six years after I first wrote him." He chuckled. "*This* is why I let you come down here."

Thomas opened it. Inside was a King James Bible, dog-eared and wrinkled. The inner cover bore an inscription of the initials *'J. A. W, 1913.'* "He probably received it when he graduated high school," guessed Wood.

The Bible's onion-skin pages crinkled as Thomas opened to its single bookmark. "Ezekiel."

"One of his three favorite books," the historian replied, "along with Daniel and Revelation. Bizarre prophecy, all. But look at the bookmark itself." It was the size of an index card, wide and fat. On the bookmark were scrawled a few lines in now-familiar handwriting:

Now, I see through a glass darkly; then, we shall see face-to-face.

I have been deluded most of my life. So much pain, so much despair. Should I cry or laugh? God works in mysterious ways. Only near my death do I now perceive the truth, and it has finally set me free.

Prophesy, bar enasha, to these dry bones. Can these bones live?

For those who know my troubled journey, and have felt the same pain of abandonment as I, know this: for thirty years I wandered without hope through this valley of death. Yet flesh has returned to these dry bones even now. Who would have thought a foul-mouthed rabbi would unlock Christ's real teachings for me? God has allowed me to see a great light.

my treasure is buried with me – J. A. W.

"This is incredible!" Thomas looked up at Bert Wood, slack-jawed. "What treasure is he talking about? What rabbi?"

"I tried to contact Shady Brook about that. They had a file on Josiah, but they would only release information to next-of-kin. Maybe you can do better. But before you do," Wood said gleefully, "there's more I need to show you." The senior citizen reached deeper into the mailing envelope to reveal a few handwritten pages in the same shaky script. "In the same envelope, I also got this." He handed the young man the pages of stationery. "Turns out Josiah Whidman wrote this personal letter to me just days before he died."

"Why you?" Thomas blurted. "No offense, but you didn't mean a lot to him, did you?"

"That's just it," the historian of Gilman replied. "His false promises had betrayed everyone who'd been close to him. He thought I might be the only one left who'd listen."

Thomas glanced at the letter. "Who else knows about this?"

"Just this old coot," Bert said, looking over at Silas, who bowed his head and then met Thomas' astonished gaze. "I showed this package to him when he came to Gilman seven years ago, researching your ancestor back when he was in seminary."

Bert put the mailing envelope back in Thomas' hands, then put his frail arms around Thomas' and Talia's shoulders like a kind father. "Now that you two are here, Josiah's deathbed audience doubles to four. Read this well, Thomas and Talia. He wrote it to me, but only to pass on to people like you." Bert clucked. "I told you we had some mysteries to unearth."

"And I said I had a few spirits to visit," added Silas. "Lisette. My parents. Now Josiah. But this time, face to face."

"What do you mean, face to face? "

"The exhumation is scheduled for tomorrow tonight," Bert said matter-of-factly. "But it can only occur if a member of the deceased's family signs the proper paperwork." The old man looked to Silas. "Paul, I wonder where we could find such a family member?" Eyes shining, laughter cackling, lungs wheezing, the aged historian held the exhumation papers aloft, looking around the room in vain for a relative of the deceased to sign them.

"He is really enjoying himself," Talia whispered into Thomas' ear.

"Gimme those," Thomas growled with a smile, grabbing the papers and signing them, authorizing *Permission for Exhumation of a Family Member for Archaeological or Medical Purposes.* "Is this even legal?"

"Good point," the aged historian frowned. "It'll have to be approved by the town's cemetery administrator, which seems near impossible." He slumped his shoulders, despondent. Then he lifted his head. "Oh wait—I *am* the cemetery administrator!" he crowed.

"He is *really really* enjoying himself," Thomas whispered back to Talia, shaking his head in wonderment. "I feel like a tool in some twisted genius' master plot."

He looked over to Bert Wood again. "With this plan more than thirty five years in the making, you're lucky you didn't accidentally kill me with the pepper spray that first day." With that, Thomas grabbed his girlfriend's hand and turned toward the stairway. "C'mon Tal," he said, his ancestor's large mailing envelope and handwritten pages burning in his hand. "Let's find some better light. We've got some reading to do."

Artifact #7: From The Vault, Personal
Correspondence of Bert Wood

Dear Mr. Wood,

We have not seen each other for more than thirty years, since you were just a boy running the press in Gilman. Yet I write because you may be the only soul alive who still has ears to hear my message. I am not long for this world, Mr. Wood, and I pray that, after my death, the asylum will grant a dying man's request and send you this package. I can only hope.

Why do I send this to you of all people, Mr. Wood? Why only you? Lord knows I've tried others. But to the world, I am a laughingstock. To myself, I am a living irony: I am Sibyl of ancient days, the oracle gifted with true knowledge, yet under a curse from the gods causing no one to believe her.

But to you, Mr. Wood, I might be a prophet yet.

Six years ago you wrote a letter to me. Do you remember? You asked how my mind and soul have changed since those days in Gilman, so long ago. Six years ago I wrote you a note of despair, for my dry bones had nothing to say to you. After my failures at Gilman, God was dead to me. I was dead to me. Yet I could not bring myself to commit suicide.

For three decades I've been a half-paralyzed mockery of life trapped in this asylum, bitterness and abandonment riding a wheelchair. For thirty years I've spent my days waiting to die.

But then a few months ago the rabbi came.

God works in mysterious ways. When I was young and had the wrong message, I spoke to thousands. Now that a genuine revelation has been given to me, I am locked away and reviled. Divine truth is hard to hear when passed through the slurred speech and embarrassing spittle of a cripple.

Mr. Wood, I still have your letter from six years ago, asking if I've changed. On this request I pin my fragile hope that I might share a priceless insight, something that might save Christianity from itself. I can only trust God's plan is bigger than me, and that this truth somehow finds its way to the millions needing the real good news that Jesus brought. In my old age, I find myself to be the man in the Scriptures who found a great treasure in a field and then again buried it.

If this buried treasure intrigues you, Mr. Wood, you must pursue it. Know that it awaits.

   Josiah Adam Whidman

   Shady Brook Sanitarium, 4 April 1957

75 FEELING EVERYTHING

"It seems I'm calling and apologizing to a number of people these days," Thomas confessed to the receiver in Bert's downstairs sitting room. It was four o' clock in Arkansas, but still early afternoon in the Bay Area.

"A perfectly natural state of being," Paloma responded from his small apartment in the back of the Bay Area Catholic Worker. "After being an insensitive jerk."

Thomas winced. "That bad, huh?"

"To Talia, yes. To me, you were only mildly rude. 'Keep the change, and keep all your little secrets, too?' What was that, some corny line from a movie?"

"Hate to say it," Thomas grimaced. "But that gem was all mine."

"At least you paid for my tea before storming out," Paloma responded. "And gave the book back. Frankly, I was thinking I'd never hear from you again. I thought you might've been running away, like I tried to do in the seventh grade."

Thomas chuckled. "I guess I was."

"From Talia and the pregnancy?"

"Yeah, that too. But really, I was running away from you."

"From me?"

"It took me bawling in a Gilman graveyard last night with Talia and Paul Silas to realize why I was running away from you, from Leaven, from all you were offering me."

"Wait a minute," backtracked Paloma. "Talia? I thought you left her in a lurch back here in Oakland. And you told me Silas was the guy you hunted down in Tucson, not somebody in Arkansas. What do I have wrong?"

"No, you're exactly right. But for reasons I'll explain later, once I arrived in Gilman a few days ago I needed them both to come join me. And they came. I knew they'd be necessary for my research. But they're turning out to be valuable in other ways, too."

"Like helping you be less of a jerk, so you can make this phone call," Paloma surmised.

"Yeah. Ever since I first met Silas in Tucson, I've been haunted by how broken he was, how mad he was at God. But when the three of us had a bizarre kind of showdown last night in the graveyard, Talia helped me realize something: it's not Silas' anger I'm haunted by. It's mine. I've been really angry. At God."

"Ever since Guatemala?"

Thomas nodded on the phone. "Before that, too, but that was the last straw. Ever since those peasants showed me their photos, the only God that fits with reality is one that lets his children be massacred."

"That's a hard truth to accept. Like I said, not an easy God to follow."

"Exactly," Thomas said. "I'd rather believe in no God than follow a torturer."

"Remember when I saw you at the bike rack, first day back from summer?" Paloma recalled.

"Yeah," said Thomas, sighing. "You knew I'd changed before I did. So angry. For months I've wanted to scream at God, *'Why aren't you doing your job?'* But now..."

"But now what?"

"Not screaming anymore," Thomas shrugged. "Stopped being angry. In the cemetery last night, Silas was all sloppy drunk. I was trying to hold him up against this stone crucifix when it hit me: God's still being crucified."

Paloma waited. "Tell me what you mean."

"I mean, maybe God's job isn't about *fixing* everything for us, maybe it's about *feeling* everything with us," tried Thomas. "That's what compassion literally means, right? *Feeling with.* I wonder: has God been hanging on a cross ever since humanity began, suffering as his own children keep nailing his hands to the wall, generation after generation?"

"A God who suffers with his children. Like the Hebrew *Emmanu-El,* 'God-with-us.'"

"Yeah. Instead of blaming God, I suddenly imagined him weeping, watching his *own children* burn alive in that church. Watching his own children rape each other. I mean, what if God's been in agony for thousands of years, feeling all the pain that his children feel?"

"Feeling, but not helping in any way? A helpless God?"

"Haven't got that far," Thomas confessed. "This all just came to me yesterday."

"Maybe we can talk about it more over a cup of tea when you get back," Paloma ventured. "A God who feels everything but doesn't rescue us. A God who's with us in our pain," he mused. "Not a real optimistic theology, but at least it helps explain suffering. Have to say, though, for a broken world it doesn't offer a whole lot of good news."

"That's part of why I wanted to call," Thomas said, a new note in his voice. "My ancestor Josiah, the one who went crazy when God remained silent? In the last year of his life it seems he discovered some radically good news."

"What'd you find out?"

"Nothing yet. But I just read some letters he wrote to Bert Wood right before he died, in 1957. They hint at some new secret that gave him wild hope."

"Wild hope, eh? I like the sound of that."

Me too," replied Thomas. "Josiah said he carried his good news to the grave. And guess what? Silas and Mr. Wood think he meant that literally. We're scheduled to excavate the coffin tomorrow night."

"That's certainly exciting." Paloma collected his thoughts for a moment. "Don't mean to be a skeptic, Thomas, but your ancestor exhibits the mood swings of a manic-depressive."

"I thought that, too. But something about his letters seemed real. Like you said, my theology could use some wild hope about now. I want to read these letters to you. See what you think."

"Shoot."

Thomas began with the small note that his ancestor had written on the bookmark found stuck in the onion-skin pages of Ezekiel. When he finished, Paloma asked Thomas to read it again.

"He sounds painfully aware of how his friends and family viewed him," noted Paloma. "To polite Christianity, he was an embarrassment that had to be locked away. To the world, he was a heretic best avoided. Do you know if he shared his secret wild hope with anyone but Bert Wood?"

"I think he tried, but nobody listened. Like Josiah said, Bert might've been the only one left with ears to hear. Remember, my ancestor not only made a failed prediction that God would end the world. He also promised he'd raise a man from the dead."

"Not the easiest person to believe," mused Paloma.

"And that's not the end of it. The file at Shady Brook stated that Josiah suffered an ischemic stroke and a psychotic break just before he was admitted, the night before the resurrection attempt was supposed to happen in Gilman. The stroke left him a mess, unable to move the right side of his face and mouth."

"Ouch."

"Yeah. So not only was he religious nut, but also a drooling fool, locked away in an asylum."

"Hmm. Hard place from which to share a new priceless insight from God. By the way, in his first note you're sure he wrote *bar enasha* when he was quoting from Ezekiel? Those specific words?"

The younger man spelled it out on the phone. There was no doubt.

"Fascinating," Paloma said. "Do you know that term, Thomas?"

"Not familiar with it," Thomas answered. "Wait, I've heard it once. *You* mentioned it."

"I did?"

"When you were telling me about your Trial in the desert, and when you got your tattoo. You said you were getting ahead of yourself. What is it, some code word?"

"It's Aramaic, from Jesus' day. Interesting that Josiah discovered the term in the last days of his life. Very interesting." There was silence on the line for a moment. "Thomas, what do you think Josiah meant when he said a foul-mouthed old rabbi unlocked Christ's real teachings for him?"

"I don't know exactly," Thomas said, "but I have a clue. Earlier, Bert Wood suggested I call Shady Brook, the sanitarium in New York where Josiah lived for the last thirty-two years of his life. They call themselves a residential mental health facility now, but they still have records from back in the day when they were proudly known as a nuthouse. After going through a lot of security clearances and red tape, I was able to get someone to locate my ancestor's file, and give me some pretty intriguing information."

"Oh?"

"Turns out they have records of a particular rabbi who's arrival at Shady Brook changed Josiah's life. In the file, a case worker noted that my ancestor began talking again once this rabbi came to the asylum, after—get this – *being silent for more than thirty years*. Josiah gets admitted in 1925, and doesn't talk until the rabbi shows up in 1957. Whatever wild hope the rabbi brought, it gave Josiah a reason to talk after three decades."

"Were you able to learn anything about this rabbi?"

"He was a middle eastern linguistics scholar. The guy had been somewhat famous, but in his old age had to be institutionalized for seizures and hallucinations after some kind of head trauma. The case worker hinted he might have had Tourette's – I guess that's what Josiah meant about the rabbi having a foul mouth."

"Did you get his name?'

"Levi something." Thomas flipped through his notes. "Shoot. They told me once, but I wasn't focusing on that, so I don't think I wrote it down. But it was Levi something."

"Levi? You sure?"

"Yeah, like the jeans." Thomas was struck by the energy in his teacher's question. "Why? Why does the name of the rabbi matter to you?"

"Might be nothing. Good luck with your dig tomorrow night. I'm going to check on a hunch."

76 IT'S JUST GETTING JUICY

"Here it is."

Talia brought the file over to where Bert and Thomas were standing in the dim light made by the single bulb of the Vault. After Thomas' phone call with Paloma this afternoon, and then supper, it was now dark outside. Unearthing Josiah Whidman's coffin was all they could think about, but that was still twenty-four hours away. So they distracted themselves with another subject of interest.

Together, the three had returned to the basement after doing the dinner dishes, while Silas retired to his room to get some extra sleep. They'd been plowing though files for two hours now. Thomas was just contemplating bed himself, when Talia's urgent words caused him to perk up.

"This is what I was talking about earlier," she said.

"Ah yes," Bert sighed, carefully taking a folder out of Talia's hand and turning to Thomas. "Talia saw some of this yesterday, and I wanted you to see it too."

Thomas craned his neck over the elderly man's shoulder to view the documents.

"Out of anyone, Paul Silas has a right to feel abandoned, by God and man." Bert fingered through the papers in the file. "You know some of his story already, but you'll really see what he's been through after hearing these reports." He pulled a faded magazine article out of the manila file. "Here's an article on the Faithful Remnant commune from the Fall 1965 edition of the *Ozark Historical Review*. What was that, twenty five years ago already?" Bert reflected. "A graduate student compiled some case studies of specific members of the Community. I helped her with a few, including this one."

He began reading in a raspy voice: *"The community did not collapse right away after the prediction of apocalypse did not come to pass; rather, it fell apart two years later due to the disturbing events that transpired in spring 1925. A member of the community, Jacob Timothy Conroy, age 27, fell severely ill with tuberculosis. Instead of sending for a doctor, Pastor Josiah Adam Whidman attempted an immediate faith healing that had no effect. Soon after, the man died. At this point Pastor Whidman did a highly unusual thing: he asserted he would raise the man from the dead in three days.*

Crazy with grief, the dead man's 23-year old wife Abigail Conroy stayed with the decaying body hour after hour. Utterly inconsolable, eating nothing, ignoring the cries of her two year old baby, Abigail lived in the chapel during those three days, holding on to nothing but one desperate hope: her pastor had promised he would soon resurrect her husband. These three days were to be a test of her faith, she decided, and in her grief Abigail became certain that her pastor Josiah Adam Whidman would raise her husband from death.

When Pastor Whidman had a nervous breakdown and never showed, he disappointed the newspapermen who had come all the way from St. Louis, drawn by rumors of a predicted resurrection attempt. Looking for another story to sensationalize – '"

Bert Wood suddenly faltered in mid-sentence, and stared nervously behind Thomas and Talia. "Paul, I was just – "

"Don't let me stop you," Silas said from a few feet behind Thomas at the bottom of the steps. His voice was frighteningly absent of emotion. "We were talking about my happy upbringing earlier today. Please, continue."

"Paul, hear me out, I – "

"Continue!" Silas commanded.

Pale, Bert Wood looked down at the paper in his shaking hands and tried to comply. "Where...ah..yes." He cleared his throat and began once more: *"Looking for another story to sensationalize, the journalists strolled into the chapel and found Abigail Conroy perched on top of her decomposing husband on the altar, shrieking like a wounded animal. She was out of her mind, screaming for the pastor who never came. After taking photos they left…"*

Bert trailed off. "Paul, I think – "

"Don't stop now," Silas urged. "It's just getting juicy." The Mayor of Gilman tried to meet Silas' gaze with a smile, but couldn't. Taking a shaky breath, he started again.

"After taking photos the newspapermen left." Bert Wood looked up, pained. "Paul, this isn't – "

"No, I insist." Silas' tone left no room for argument, stepping further into the room. "Let's finish what you started. It'll be fun."

Bert faltered, then read on. *"Hours later, during an inspection of the site mandated by the governor, social workers found a malnourished two year-old boy curled in a fetal position on the floor of the chapel. In its fragmented state, the Faithful Remnant community was unable to offer the child a support network, and so the baby was taken to – "*

"To the Arkansas Child Protection Services as a ward of the state," spoke Silas over the frail voice of the old man. "The two year-old was then processed and admitted to the institution that would be his cozy new home for the next sixteen years until he reached the age of majority. *The Little Rock Christian Home for Boys.*"

Silas strode from the bottom of the steps into the room now, walking between Thomas and Talia to stand directly in front of a shaken Bert Wood. He took the article and the rest of the thick file folder from the older man's hands. "My old files," he said woodenly, rifling through. "Let's see. My orphanage papers. My birth certificate. Parents' wedding certificate. Ah, my case file. Good work," he said to Bert. "Thanks for keeping it all together for me, trusted friend."

In a clinical voice, Silas read from his case file compiled by the Arkansas Child Protection Services office in Little Rock. *"Case of Ward # AR-33678 B, formerly known as Paul Josiah Conroy…ward of the state…no extended family of record. The child had been born to Mr. and Mrs. Conroy, a young couple residing in Gilman,*

Arkansas." Under the dim light of the Vault, the man now known as Paul Silas drew out more excerpts from the report. *"Admission paperwork stated that both of the child's parents had died suddenly within days of each other just a week earlier, in April 1925....Arkansas Death Certificate indicates that the father died from complications resulting from tuberculosis, also known as consumption. The mother died from asphyxiation four days later."*

The gravel voice of Paul Silas was the only sound that broke the entombing silence of the Vault other than Bert's wheezing, which was more exaggerated than normal.

Silas' clipped, clinical tone was far more frightening than if he was yelling. "Now we're getting to the really good part," he said without mirth. "Here it is. The social worker's summary: *'At time of intake, the orphaned child refused solid food and did not respond appropriately to stimuli. All initial attempts at interaction could not engage the child, who appeared clinically withdrawn.'*

"I like that term," Silas said, looking up. "Don't you, Talia? You're the social worker. *'Clinically withdrawn.'* It covers so much, doesn't it?" Talia stood, frozen. He went back to reading. *"The initial report noted that the Conroys had left no property, no money and few privately held material goods to their orphaned son, as the family had lived in a 'common purse' Christian commune in which all homes and most significant possessions were owned collectively. When the community abruptly disbanded, there was no supporting family structure in which to reintegrate the child...."* He paused. "Let's see...it gets a little boring here," Silas said, skimming the page.

"This is sick, Paul," said Talia, shaking herself from her shock. "Stop it."

"Not quite done," Silas went on, brushing her off. "Ah. Here we are. *'At intake, the social worker also included the Conroy's marriage license in the child's file. The parents had been married in Gilman, AR in early 1922 by Reverend Josiah Adam Whidman, and had declared Reverend Whidman to be the boy's godparent should something tragic befall them."*

Silas looked up at his audience, reading glasses flashing under the single bulb. "Lucky boy, to have such a reliable and caring godparent to lean on after the tragic loss of his parents."

"Paul, enough," Thomas blurted.

"No, not enough," Silas barked. "But don't worry. The story's almost done, kids. '*Upon entering the orphanage, Paul Josiah Conroy's name was legally changed to Paul Silas by the nuns at the Christian Boys Home of Little Rock.*" Silas slapped the file shut. "And I know this last part by heart: '*The nuns hoped to spare the child from the pain and chaos of the failed apocalyptic community, so the child grew up with no knowledge of his parents or the experiences of Gilman.*'"

He handed the file to Mr. Wood. "I'm impressed. You kept my personal documents in order, Bert, just where I left them. Always the diligent librarian." He began to walk very slowly between the Vault's rows of stacked boxes and file cabinets, away from the others.

"Since I left here seven years ago in an ambulance, a raving man in a straightjacket, I never expected to see any of this again." He tapped a tall file cabinet near the back of the room. "But now I'm part of the tapestry, aren't I, Bert? Just another eccentric piece of Gilman history." Silas spun to face the old man. "Since you've told them everything so far, Mr. Historian, finish the case study. Tell them how you found me after Lisette died."

Bert was welling up with tears, his voice high and wheedling. "Paul, I don't want to."

"*Tell them, damn it!*" Silas' voice was terrible to hear.

Bert was pleading now. Talia stepped forward and put her arm around the elderly man. "Paul, don't. Just don't."

"It's not Bert's fault," Thomas said, coming to life. "*We* asked to look at your file."

"Fine." Silas abruptly turned back to the stairs. "You're right. I'll let Bert off the hook. I'll save this story for myself." He slowly ascended the steps, but stopped midway. His shadow loomed down into the basement.

"I know what we'll do, kids." He clapped his hands together, once. "We'll have marshmallows around a campfire, and ol' Uncle Silas will tell the end of this little drama: how he went completely loony and tried to kill himself."

77 THE BROKEN SHEPHERD

Night was finally coming to Gilman. For Thomas, it wasn't a moment too soon. In just another few hours, they were actually going to dig up the body of his great grand-uncle Josiah Adam Whidman.

That is, if Silas hadn't done something desperate. Since the unpleasant scene at the Vault last night, Silas' whereabouts had been unknown to the young couple, and they were both worried. He'd been absent all day. Bert assured them he was okay, and that Paul was doing a solitary job at the graveyard that would take most of the day. Thomas hoped the old man was right.

After sleeping in until about eleven, Thomas and Talia had spent the afternoon gathering together digging tools, a kerosene lantern, dust brushes and other excavation supplies. Bert was taking this night escapade very seriously, checking and re-checking his cameras, batteries, lighting and videotapes.

Evening was now falling along the Buffalo River. The three finished their dinner, and the younger pair cleared the table while Bert prepared to wash the dishes. Silas' chair had been noticeably empty. At the sink together, Thomas and Bert looked out the window into the dark night, a thin slice of moon present just above the silver sycamores. Thomas was reminded suddenly of Paloma, and the lasagna dishes they did together at the Catholic Worker just two weeks ago. His last words face-to-face with Paloma had been full of anger and defiance, throwing *The Commentaries* down on the table. He wondered if he'd ever get the book back. He wondered if he'd ever get his *mentor* back. At least the phone call had helped.

"Perfect," Bert said, looking out at the moon, bringing Thomas back to the present. "Time for the two of you to go find Silas in the graveyard. I asked him to do a deep watering of the grass at the cemetery this afternoon, so a certain grave site would be nice and soft for tonight's work."

Bert accepted a small stack of plates from Talia. "You two go on now," the old man said, ushering them out the door with their pack of digging supplies. "After I'm done with the dishes, I'll come over in the car. Remember, I'll be standing watch at the cemetery gate, looking for any midnight meddlers while you three dig." Thomas nodded, and they were off. "Call me when you're close, kids, and I'll come in with my camera gear."

- - - -

Silas was drinking among the headstones when Thomas and Talia found him. The single rose that once anointed Lisette's grave was now pinned through the lapel of Silas' overcoat, a weary, macabre boutonniere.

Without speaking, the older man took the extra pick from Thomas' hand and led the way to the softened earth at the gravesite of Josiah Adam Whidman. Silas had outlined their digging dimensions with chalk, and they began to work. Large chunks of wet sod came away fast as the trio got into a rhythm. In the humid cool of the misty evening, moisture hung in the air and clung to metal, grass and limbs. Soon all three diggers were sopping with perspiration. Silas looked particularly haggard. His sweat reeked of alcohol.

Thomas took a break to mop his brow after fifteen minutes of quiet digging. Unexpectedly, Silas broke the silence.

"The other day I told you about Lisette's death. But I didn't tell you about what happened next."

Talia shot Thomas a look of concern. "Paul, you don't have to – "

"Yes, I do, Talia my dear." His voice brooked no discontent. "The other night in the graveyard you said I shouldn't feel so personally betrayed, that I hadn't been abandoned any more than anyone else."

"Paul, I'm so sorry for saying that. I had no idea about your parents at that

435

time. But now you've shared your story, and I see how unfair it's been."

"Oh, my story's not over yet," he said with a tight smile. "I still have some goodies to tell. Ready for those marshmallows by the campfire?"

How do I deal with this guy? thought Thomas. He had no idea what to say to this damaged man.

Talia, however, tried something new. "Paul, I know your life has been incredibly painful," she started, slowly. "I can't even begin to imagine what armor I'd need to deal with so much suffering." She stopped digging and looked right at him. "But right now you're hiding. Can you share your pain without masking it?"

Silas' pick continued to bite the clay soil, but he himself remained quiet. An awkward silence grew. Thomas was about to say something when the older man stopped and rested his chin on his pick handle. "Sorry," he said softly. "I guess I've been an emotional recluse for so long I don't know how to be real with anyone anymore."

"Paul!" Talia gasped at the man's openness. Thomas spontaneously reached out a hand in sympathy. Silas quickly batted it away with a grunt. "Don't get ahead of yourself, Whidman," he said, though not too roughly. "Remember, I'm still a basket case. Clinically withdrawn and all." He resumed his digging. "It's just that I finally realized the two of you are good people."

"You've been telling us about your life like it's a news report, Paul," Talia commented. "Like it happened to someone else. In my work, I see lot of people do that who have survived intense trauma. It's a way to distance from the pain. Does that make sense to you?"

"Maybe," Silas considered.

"It doesn't have to be that way," Talia said, resuming her digging at his side. "If you want to, you can tell us how you feel, Paul. About what happened to you. Even the scary stuff."

After a few long minutes of no sound but shovels and picks on earth, Silas started up again. "I'd blocked it out for sixty years," he began without preamble. "Remember when Lisette died, I kind of went out of my mind and ended up in front of the Gilman church?"

"Clothes all full of thistles," Talia prompted. "You said you stumbled into the chapel." The trio kept digging, finding a collective motion.

"Yeah. I ran in and laid there under the altar. Crying, crazy with grief," Silas continued, "Well, as my face was pressed against the floor, something about the experience—the place and what I was doing—suddenly felt very strange. Like I'd done it before."

"Deja vu," suggested Thomas.

"Yeah. Being there felt oddly familiar. But I'd never been there before in my life."

"Were you recalling something?" asked Talia.

Silas nodded. "In the middle of my tears, I raised my head from the floor an inch or two. I saw something beneath me: a broken tile of a shepherd set into the floor below the altar." He paused, and the pair looked up, stopping their work. "I *remembered* it." The weather-beaten old man licked his parchment lips and leaned on his pick once more. "Right then, something clicked in my mind," he said. "The cool floor against my wet cheek. The smells. Pine. Earth. Decay. The overwhelming sense of loss. I suddenly knew I'd cried on that broken shepherd before."

He stopped again, and this time, when Talia rested her hand on his arm in support, he faltered, then plunged on. "My mind went wild. Couldn't think straight, I was so scared. Instinctively, I looked up over my right shoulder—I don't know what prompted me—and...I saw her. In her calico dress. Right over the altar, just like she'd been sixty years before. Swinging there in the air above me like when I was just a two-year old."

"Those images...came back to you?"

"Yeah," Silas grunted. "Some wall broke open in my mind. Something that had been protecting me for a long time."

"Oh, Paul," Talia couldn't help saying, grabbing his hand. "I'm so sorry."

"Me too," Silas simply said. "Here I was, a middle-aged man, and all I'd ever known about my birth mother was what Child Protection Services had told me: that she had died from asphyxiation. Nobody'd ever told me the details." He took a deep, ragged breath. "But that shepherd tile sure did." He slowly let go of Talia's hand and started digging once more. His pick resounded in the deep earth.

"What happened after that?" asked Talia gently.

"Those memories were too much. I cracked. Went somewhere very dark inside of myself. Don't know how long, maybe a few hours. Next thing I remember is hearing Bert's voice. He found me lying there in the chapel, and he brought me back to a bed in his house."

Silas suddenly looked around, coming back to the present. "Hup. Better stop talking so we can get this work done."

"No, Paul, don't stop," Talia said.

"Yeah, keep telling us the story," Thomas added. "It helps us get to know you. We'll dig while we listen."

"Well, alright." The trio fell back into a shoveling rhythm. Silas continued. "For the rest of that year, Bert's house became my world. I never left, other than to have my tuna sandwiches at Lisette's grave or the chapel. Spent every day in the Vault. I found an old article about my mother's death and memorized it, slept with it. Sometimes I spent nights in the chapel with it, lying on that broken tile, looking up at my hanging mother."

That's fucked up, Thomas nearly blurted. He looked at Talia, who looked like she was thinking the same thing. Just a little nicer.

Silas continued talking and working, as if what he'd just said was normal. "Most of the time, though, I just stayed in my room to do my job. Bert's books became my library, his newspapers became my laboratory, his phone became my line to the rest of humanity."

"What do you mean, to do your job?" Thomas asked after a minute. "Finishing your thesis?"

"Yeah, my thesis," Silas conceded. " But my real job was collecting the numbers."

"The numbers?" Thomas repeated. *I think we've just veered into loco land again.*

"They're in the thesis," Silas responded matter-of-factly, as if that explained something. "For three months all I did was eat and sleep in my room, collecting and verifying the numbers."

"Those numbers you scribbled in your thesis—you mean they're data?"

"I didn't scribble them," Silas defended. "I *wrote* them. And typed them."

Wrote, typed, whatever, Thomas wanted to say. Silas' correction seemed absurd, considering the situation, but Thomas didn't bring it up. He just waited until Silas continued.

"Of course they're data. Proof there's no God."

"Proof?" said a startled Thomas.

"Yeah. Your ancestor lost his faith through numbers, and so did I. Fascinating," Silas mused. "I finished my job at Christmas. Then I mailed in my thesis to Professor Fowler and hung myself."

"You what?" Talia blurted.

"In the chapel," the older man said, far too calmly. "Right where my mother did. Once the job was done and mailed I had no other reason to live. I thought it would be a poetic end." Thomas kept on digging like normal, but his eyes screamed with the silent crazy message he sent to Talia over their shovels.

After another moment Talia gently prompted the older man. "What happened next, Paul? Somehow I don't think the story ends with you suspended by a noose. I know it's scary, but try not to separate yourself from

439

your feelings."

"Old Bert found me yet again," Silas said quietly. "Thought I was worth saving a second time, I guess. He must've been following me, because he cut me down from the rafter before I was a goner. Physically, I was still functioning. My brain was even okay, despite the blood loss. But nothing was left inside."

"That's what my ancestor Josiah wrote in his first letter to Bert," Thomas remembered from yesterday in the Vault. "Even twenty-five years after leaving Gilman, he felt dead inside. Abandoned."

"Yeah, I think that's why I've been so interested in Josiah," Silas said. "A lost soul. Lied to by God. Anyway, after I hung myself I didn't care if I lived or died." He coughed into the wet night. "So I just started walking."

"Walking?" Talia said, puzzled. "Where?"

"Anywhere." Silas shrugged between blows with the pick. "Don't really know, to tell you the truth. Didn't take anything with me, and I don't remember much of those first days. Thought I'd walk 'til I couldn't any more, and then I'd die. Most nights, I'd just lie down at the side of a road in the bushes. Just lie there and listen to my heart beat slower and slower, thinking it might stop one day. If I found food or scraps left on the side of the road, I'd eat them. Otherwise, I'd just walk.

"After maybe a month of walking I realized I hadn't died yet." He laughed. "I got kinda mad." At that Thomas' eyes threw another urgent glance at Talia, who put a finger to her lips while Silas kept going. "So I got off the highway and started looking for the emptiest country I could find. After days and days of walking dirt and canyons like a zombie, I found myself at a gas station in Sonora, Mexico." Their picks and shovel were now encountering hard earth, untouched by the surface watering. Work was getting hard. The gaunt man stood erect to mop his brow. "I haven't told anyone about any of this, ever. Until now."

With these words, Silas seemed spent, his need to unburden quenched. Thomas wondered how much more revelation he could expect from this strange and fascinating man on one night. But he had something else he

440

needed to ask. "Paul, may I ask you something that might trouble you?"

At that, Silas burst out laughing, startling the other two. "Sorry, but that sounded funny, considering," Silas said. "Go ahead, Thomas. Trouble me."

"Tell me more about your numbers."

Paul Silas gave a defensive look. "Why?"

"People at the seminary say you went completely loony," Thomas explained honestly, "writing crazy numbers on your thesis like a madman writes on his cell walls." Thomas withered in front of Silas' furious scowl, but plunged on. "But I think you had good reasons for doing what you did. You just told us your numbers were data. Proof that there's no God. Those numbers mean something profound to you, don't they?"

Silas' dark smile was not easy to behold. "Don't all madmen think they mean something by their ravings?" He glanced out across the midnight graveyard, searching for something in the mist. "I was standing right over there when it happened." He pointed at a location near where they'd sat for lunch. "When I looked up from her body on the grass, lying there twisted and swollen, I was changed. I'd flipped to the other side."

"The other side?" asked Talia.

"I realized there's no good guy in charge of the universe. It's just about numbers and percentages. For months afterward, I focused on my work. On the chances that rule loss and tragedy."

"That's what your numbers are all about—the statistics of suffering?" Talia said, amazed.

"The words, yes, and the numbers," Silas explained matter-of-factly. "It's all there. People need hard evidence to see the real truth. Not just individual cases."

"Tell me what you mean," Talia urged.

"The Faithful Remnant waiting in vain, Josiah's failed resurrection attempt –

those are each subjective cases that demonstrate the clear absence of God. My mother leaving me stranded at the age of two without a friend in the world—also subjective. Those were good sample cases, but not enough for my thesis. Not enough to be conclusive evidence."

"Evidence for what?" asked Thomas, lost. "I thought you were – "

"Aren't you listening?" Silas snapped. Thomas kept his mouth shut. "Evidence against the Big Lie," the older man continued. "In addition to the stories, I needed objective data. Factual confirmation that God doesn't care. The numbers are all evidence. Some global, some personal." He grabbed his pick again and started stabbing at the exposed hardpack. "Try me."

"Try you?" said Thomas, startled.

"Try me," Silas repeated. "Of course, all statistics are from seven years ago. Specifics might have changed slightly over time."

"Umm…okay." Thomas racked his brain, trying to remember a few of the crazy numbers Silas had repeated over and over on his pages. "Here's one: 74. That was one of your favorites, wasn't it? It was all over your thesis."

Silas took a long pull from a bottle in his coat and grimaced. "One of my favorites," he echoed. Again, that horrible smile. "74. That's how many hours my father's dead body lay rotting on the altar before they found me underneath."

"I don't like this game, Paul," said Talia, shaking her head. "It's not healthy."

"What, too personal for you?" Silas challenged. "Okay. How about 210,000?" His pick broke clay and rock, and their shovels drew it out.

"I remember that one," Thomas said. Talia shot him a warning look, but Thomas needed to wade through this man's mind. There had to be some logic to Silas' madness, and he wanted to find it. "What is it—national or global?"

"Now we've got a player!" Silas said. "Someone who doesn't flinch." He turned to Thomas. "National. 210,000: the amount of hate crimes committed in the U.S., 1970-1980."

"How about...42%?" Thomas was recalling other numbers now, and a sick interest welled within him.

"Easy," responded Silas. "42%: Chance of a woman to have a miscarriage when giving birth, worldwide. Not quite every other birth, but somewhat close."

"480,000." Thomas' mind wove through the bizarre litany of numbers he had seen.

"Amount of people killed across the globe in natural catastrophes in 1985, estimated. Actual figures may be much higher."

"32."

"You should know that one by now, Thomas," Silas said. "That's the amount of years Josiah lived in the sanitarium after suffering a complete mental breakdown."

"8."

"The average number of significant international military conflicts happening on the planet each year. Data collection began in 1940."

"Hmm..." thought Thomas. "I can't remember any more of your numbers, Paul. They didn't stick in my mind, since they didn't have any meaning to me when I read your thesis."

"Didn't have any meaning?" blurted Silas. "Let me help you. 263: the amount of species going extinct each year. 4,138: the amount of Americans who've predicted God's return since 1860. 28: the average life span for a male peasant in Zaire, according to data from the last decade. .06%: likelihood of becoming orphaned in America by both parents before the age of ten. $466.00: the average annual income of a villager in − "

"332."

"What?" the older paused digging in mid-stroke.

"332," Thomas repeated.

Silas cogitated. "Thomas, I don't believe I have a 332."

"You don't, Paul. This one's mine."

"Oh?"

"Oh yeah. It's my own number that proves God's not doing a whole lot of rescuing."

Silas arched his eyebrows in interest, his pick hanging in mid-air.

"I walked with some refugees this summer when I visited Guatemala. It's the number of Christian *campesinos* that were massacred by paramilitary squads in their village in the early 1980's," Thomas said. "The women were raped, then shot. Kids' brains smashed on the cobblestones. The men, though, they got to be burned alive in the village church, and I'm pretty sure every one of them was crying for their savior's help when they died."

"That's a powerful data point," Silas commented without emotion. "I'll consider including it."

"You guys are sick," Talia said from the other side of the pit. "Now c'mon, let's dig." They continued to work, their palms wet with sweat and mud. Their hole was chest deep now, and it was becoming very difficult to lift the earth out of the pit. Only two could work effectively in the cramped coffin-size space, so Talia hopped out. She began lifting buckets of excavated dirt up and away from the site as soon as the pair below filled them up.

"So, as I was saying," Silas continued to Thomas as they dug side by side, "the numbers are only half the evidence that there's no God." It was as if he'd been interrupted in the middle of a sales presentation and was now getting back to it. "The rest of my proof is the shattered life of Josiah Adam Whidman."

Thomas only grunted.

"Your relative was sure of a God who spoke to him in secret messages," Silas went on. "Josiah counted syllables and noticed patterns and found hidden timelines locked within the Scriptures. He became convinced, and convinced hundreds of others, that he knew the secret plans of the divine. He was sure he knew the date of his Lord's Coming and – "

Thomas' shovel suddenly hit something large and smooth with a hollow thud. In the flickering light of their lantern, Silas crouched down and began scraping, revealing the rectangular surface of an unadorned, simple black pine box. Kneeling in the darkness, the gaunt man grinned up at Thomas and Talia, the whites of his eyes huge in his grimy face. "Contact."

78 EXHUMATION

"No freaking way! It's really happening!!!" Talia shouted, looking into the hole from above. "Be right back—don't open it without us!" She scooted off into the night to fetch Bert, who was waiting in his car at the entrance gate, ready for this moment.

With unconcealed anticipation, Thomas and Silas worked efficiently around the perimeter of the coffin with hand tools. By the time Talia returned with the octogenarian wheeling his walker and oxygen tank, the two men in the pit had exposed the entire top rim of the coffin. Talia set down Bert's old over-the-shoulder Super 8 video camera and light system and got busy.

"10:38 P.M.," Bert huffed, eyes shining in the spotlight Talia had just set up. "A moment for the ages." He fiddled with his audiovisual gear and a minute later, the video camera started to roll under Talia's fingers, capturing test footage. Bert clipped a microphone to his own lapel and to Silas, and after a quick sound check, all was ready. Talia filmed the old historian making some quick introductory comments about Gilman, then Bert Wood took over the camera work and turned the stage over to Paul Silas. Some predetermined arrangement, Thomas gathered, impressed. *These two old coots have been planning for this for a while.* They'd even dusted off some high-end video equipment.

"Life is full of strange ironies," Silas began, a solitary figure stark in the harsh spotlights, spilling a long shadow across the Gilman graveyard behind him. "Here I am, a deranged man searching for clues in the grave of a deranged man. Here I am, standing on the spot I swore I would never come to again. Here I am, an atheist, giving the sermon of my life."

446

He hoisted his pick over his shoulder and motioned to the camera to follow while he crouched at the side of the open pit and looked in. The film crew of Bert and Talia followed. "Want to know the biggest irony?" he continued to the camera. "I'm a crazy man trying to raise someone from the dead—and that someone is a man who was driven crazy by trying to raise a man from the dead." Silas gave one of his laughs, harsh and unpleasant. "Tonight, December 19, 1992, we stand at the excavated grave of Josiah Adam Whidman, who was buried thirty-five years ago. The week before he died, he left a message stating that God had revealed something to him in the last days of his life. He said he was taking a priceless secret to his grave." The camera zoomed in on Silas' grizzled face. "A few of us are foolish enough to believe he meant this literally. Tonight, we are here to unearth his secret."

Paul Silas now moved around the open pit to address the camera from behind the headstone. Bert followed with his lens. "The Reverend Josiah Adam Whidman was a true believer in a saving God. He dared to risk his entire life upon the active power of the Almighty, unlike so many other armchair Christians who never truly test their trust in the divine. Jesus said, 'if you have faith the size of a mustard seed, you can move mountains.' Josiah Whidman had that faith, and he bet his life on it."

As Silas spoke, Bert angled the camera to view Thomas down in the excavated pit. He was working with hand tools, his damp back visible, creating more space around the coffin to allow for handholds.

"Josiah was an embarrassment to polite Christianity. He dared to knock on heaven's door and expect an answer." Paul Silas' voice narrated as Bert filmed a panoramic sweep of the area, taking in hundreds of white gravestones standing out in the darkness. "Most of Christianity is happy to never knock. Then they can still hold on to the untested hope that somebody will answer."

Bert Wood brought the camera in for a close up of his collaborator's face. "Josiah Whidman not only knocked, he knocked twice. First," Silas said to the camera, holding up a finger, "he created a community that expected God to end the world in 1923." Silas now held up another finger. "Second, a few years later, he called upon God to resurrect a member of his flock in front of several hundred people. Both times Josiah knocked, he found nobody home. After his God let him down the second time, Josiah's faith finally collapsed, and he suffered a nervous breakdown." Silas stopped his speech, and the man's smile reverted to a mockery of joy. "Funny how that happens, isn't it? You fall apart when the Lord you've loved to turns out to be a sick joke?"

Silas stepped from behind the headstone and approached the camera. "What happened to Josiah Whidman when his God didn't answer?" the hollow man in the overcoat asked. "Broken, he lived thirty-two more years in a mental asylum, deserted by the God he once worshipped." Silas crouched, level with the grave marker. "During those long years in the asylum, Josiah Whidman etched his grief into rock. He insisted he be allowed to engrave his own headstone. For more than a decade, he worked his fingers bloody with hand tools and granite. Guess what he wrote as his epitaph?" The camera followed Paul Silas' gaze as he looked at the headstone next to him. Silas' harsh voice read the hand-carved inscription: "'*My God, My God, why have you forsaken me?*' Fitting, is it not? Jesus' last words were Josiah's, too."

Silas rose once more to a standing position. "Did Josiah Whidman spend the rest of his life as a man betrayed by the foulest of lies? It would seem so. The gravestone speaks for itself. It appears he died a broken man.

"But something new emerged at Josiah's time of death." Silas reached into his trench coat and brought a now-familiar packing envelope in view. "A message written by Josiah just days before he died, expressing a wild hope to those who might still listen." Paul Silas removed the yellowed handwritten letter. "In this last note written just days before his death, Pastor Whidman claimed he'd found a treasure beyond compare, a precious secret that was buried with him. It's been hidden from the world. Until now."

Silas concluded his speech. Bert brought the camera's view down into the pit. The lens zoomed in on Thomas' hands as he started to open the rusted clasp of the coffin lid, now bright under the spotlight.

Silas suddenly hopped down into the pit and put a leathery hand on top of Thomas' own. "I want to open it with you," the older man said huskily. All scripted words had stopped. "I *need* to open it with you." Under the harsh spotlight filling the excavated grave, Silas shielded his eyes and looked up into the glare. "Cut the fucking camera," he rasped. As Bert stopped filming, Silas hunched against the earthen wall. "I thought I wouldn't care," Silas breathed. His body trembled inside his black coat. "I thought I wouldn't care."

The man's emotions caught Thomas off guard. *I thought I wouldn't care either,* Thomas realized. *After Guatemala, God was dead to me.* But then Leaven came along. In the last thirty days something profound had shifted. New hope had entered his darkened life. A month ago he'd known nothing of this ancestor, this betrayed, yearning, misguided, impossible man whose secrets lied buried with him. A month ago he'd known nothing of the secret life of Paloma, of Magda, of Silas, of his own family history in Gilman. A month ago he couldn't have imagined a God who felt his own children die. A month ago there was no mystery growing in Talia's belly nor any awareness of a two-thousand year old society silently following the revolutionary path of Jesus. Over the last month all of these unknown things had become real. They had changed him. And he cared. God, he cared.

At a signal from Silas the camera again came to life. "We are about to open the casket of Reverend Josiah Adam Whidman," intoned Silas, dry-eyed once more. "Will we find nothing special? Or will we unearth a secret treasure more precious than gold? Let's find out." With deft fingers, Silas undid two brass latches and together he and Thomas opened the coffin lid.

Artifact #8: Levi ben Avram at
Shady Brook Sanitarium, 1957

Levi ben Avram was bored out of his mind once again.

Just like every nice day for the last two months, this afternoon they had him propped out in the corner of the asylum's carefully manicured courtyard to get his daily dose of sun.

Like some forgotten potted geranium.

Thirty-six other elderly male residents of Shady Brook had been shuffled out of their dim quarters and exposed to the sunshine in similar fashion. Some social hour it was: A few of his companions babbled or repetitiously hit themselves, but the majority sat silent with terrible, vacant eyes.

Levi ben Avram was so tired of it all.

He was only a patient here because of the seizures, he kept telling them; well, that, and the hallucinations. He didn't belong here among the dead. He was tired of looking at all these dry old bodies, these ancient husks so frail in their wheelchairs and bedboards. He was especially tired of waking up each day to find himself yet again in this place of eternal waiting, his own Sheol. *Get on with it!* He wanted to scream. He had spat out his medication this morning, and his dander was up. *Die already! Or live!*

Now he knew what the prophet Yechezchial must have felt like in the valley of the bones so long ago. *These bones are dried up; our hope is lost,* the prophet had written, and Levi couldn't agree more. He cackled to himself. Adonai surely had a wicked sense of humor, making a decrepit old linguistics scholar of the *Nevi'im*— the Jewish Prophets – feel just like one. Just like Yechezchial, he was trapped in his own valley of death and despair. It was driving him mad.

"Son of man, can these dry bones live?" Adonai had asked the prophet millennia ago. As a specialist in ancient middle eastern languages, Levi ben Avram had translated these words countless times—from the original Hebrew to Aramaic to Koine Greek to English and back again. He chose the Aramaic today. He looked around the plaza once again: dry men waiting in a vale of death. He was so sick of

waiting to die.

"Son of man, can these dry bones live?" he shouted in exasperation. The ancient prophetic words rolled out across the plaza. The foreign tongue of Aramaic shattered the silence of the manicured courtyard, startling the denizens. A few day nurses lifted their heads, bearing looks of professional concern, and then went back to their business. Outbursts such as this were not uncommon at Shady Brook.

"What was that?" A barely audible croak came from twenty yards away. "What did you say?"

Shading his weak eyes in the morning sun, Levi saw that it was that goy preacher, the silent one. Levi laughed out loud at the unexpected sign of life: The one who never talked *just said something.* The old gentile was an ancient tortoise in a wheelchair, craning his leathered neck from under his blanket to see better.

Now Levi remembered a few more details about the man. *Whidman,* it said on his wheelchair, *Josiah Adam Whidman.* This one, the attendants had told him, hadn't said a word for decades. No one knew exactly how long he'd been here. Some said over thirty years. Rumor was that he'd completely cracked way back in the early 1920's, when his Savior didn't come to end the world like he'd predicted. Ever since, the preacher paid no attention to the outside world.

Well he's paying attention now, thought Levi.

"What did you say?" the ancient tortoise croaked again, a little louder. Spittle flecked his drooping lips.

"Nothing you would understand, Gentile," Levi ben Avram responded dismissively, tugging at the black curls of his beard. "It was Aramaic. Dead language for the dead." He motioned with his hand, indicating the assembled cadavers in the courtyard. "Go back to sleep, Christian. Go back to Sheol with the rest of them."

"Say it again!" Josiah Whidman's brittle voice rasped. *"Do it!"*

Perhaps it was something about the preacher's tone—both pleading and demanding—that caused the old rabbi to comply. *"Son of man, can these bones live?"* Levi ben Avram shouted once more, this time even louder, and the Aramaic syllables rebounded across the docile courtyard. The old rabbi was suddenly standing at the front of his old synagogue, reading from the Tenakh for the flock of Beth Israel once again.

At this second outburst, several hovering attendants looked up from their positions, talking to each other with their eyes. Two orderlies dressed in pale blue scrubs headed toward the incident, wheeling medicine carts.

"What does it mean?" the crazy preacher croaked at Levi, his eyes burning with interest. "Were you calling on Jesus?"

"Calling on Jesus?" the rabbi scoffed. "Not everything's about your messiah, Christian." Despite his harsh words, Levi was strangely moved. *Such an outburst! Not a single word for decades, and now this!*

The orderlies had arrived with their medicine carts. The attendants at Shady Brook were accustomed to Levi's outbursts, and they had their medical protocols—Levi ranted all the time, mostly in English, but sometimes in Hebrew or Aramaic. Yet today the orderlies remained at a discreet distance, talking in hushed tones.

Could they be delaying because of the new life suddenly erupting from the silent one? This was novel indeed. They wanted to see more. So did Levi. This unexpected spark of life in this place of death deserved a response. Levi ben Avram decided to give it.

"The words are six hundred years older than your Christ," he explained to the craning tortoise confined to the wheelchair. "I was reciting from the prophet Yechezchial—you call him Ezekiel in your Old Testament. HaShem Adonai, the Lord God, is speaking to the Prophet. Ezekiel is standing in a valley of skeletons, and HaShem Adonai commands him to speak to the dry bones."

"But I heard you shout about Jesus!" Josiah insisted. "The Son of Man! What words did you start with?"

Who was this odd Gentile? Levi thought. No speech for decades, and now the man was pestering about one of the more mysterious phrases in the Aramaic language. The very phrase that the strange monk Theologos had commissioned him to write a paper about, over five years ago. *This could get interesting.*

"Bar enasha are the first words in the text,*"* the rabbi replied cautiously. "You know the phrase?"

"Of course," Josiah Whidman retorted. "It translates as – "

"In Aramaic, it's an idiom rich in meaning that gets lost in translation. But most scholars take it to mean "human" or "son of humanity.""

"No, it doesn't!" The shriveled man in the wheelchair caught Levi off-guard with his sudden ferocity. *"Bar enasha* doesn't mean just any human; it means the one and only Son of Man. Capital S, capital M. It's the title Jesus gave to himself."

"You don't know a lot about the Aramaic language, do you, goy?" the rabbi laughed derisively. "Next time, think a little before you open your mouth for the first time in thirty years."

Levi expected an orderly to come attack him with meds any minute. Agitated, combative conversations were against Levi's medical advisement, determined to be a trigger for his seizures, but they were one of the few pleasures left in the world for the aged rabbi. Even in this paltry exchange Levi was feeling a bit of the fierce joy of the old days, when he used to argue over Torah. He wasn't about to ignore this gift.

"Not this again!" he moaned. "I tell Christian after Christian, but they never listen!"

"Tell them what?" The old withered preacher demanded, twitching and clearly agitated. Slobber ran down his chin from the slack side of his jaw. Still neither attendant did anything to defuse the situation. Rather, to Levi ben Avram's glee, one of the orderlies wheeled Josiah Whidman closer.

"You think I'm talking about the Son of Man?" The old rabbi threw his hands up in the air and looked heavenward in exasperation, as if he was talking to the Creator himself. "Capital S, capital M? Ancient Aramaic doesn't even *have* capitalization, so get the idea of a special title for your Jesus out of your fool head. *Bar enasha* is a general term, a rich term, and can mean lots of things." Levi ben Avram paused, wondering how much he should say. "Man. The son of a man. Human. Humanity."

"*Humanity?*" The invalid reverend cried, now close enough to stare Levi in the face. "So now you're saying it can be *plural?*"

"Are you deaf, Christian?" The Jewish scholar smiled ferociously. "Have you never studied what you preach?" Defiant joy shot through him. Levi felt the blackness begin to creep around the edges of his vision, but held it at bay by sheer willpower. His soul was finally alive again. He wouldn't let his body betray him now. "Of course it can be plural. If you knew anything about Aramaic—the native language of your precious Jesus – you'd know this phrase can mean one individual or many. It all depends on context."

"How can this be?" The old preacher was quiet now. "Tell me. You have to tell me."

"Do you not even know the basics of your *own* language?" Levi ben Avram pulled his dark beard in victory, eyes flashing. *"Man* in general cannot live by bread alone, but a loaf of bread can be made by a singular *man,* yes? Plural, generic; singular, specific. Same word, man. But in different contexts, vastly different meanings."

Josiah Adam Whidman's eyes went wide. Then, abruptly, he attempted to rise, jerking at his restraints and twitching his stick-like legs. "This is – " he spluttered. "This is – "

"Mr. Whidman, calm yourself," soothed a nearby attendant, suddenly at the man's side with his cart of prescriptions. "Let me – "

"Don't you dare medicate me!" screamed Josiah Whidman, his eyes ablaze, one side of his mouth limp and drooling. "I might be damned, but I'm finally awake! This changes everything!" He wheeled himself even closer, batting the hands of well-meaning attendants. "Do something useful for once, and bring some paper and pens to this Jew and me! He and I have some talking to do."

Levi ben Avram laughed deeply before the familiar darkness finally took over. His eyes rolled back in his head and his muscles began to go rigid, spasmodically pulsing.

God is good, he thought just before he fell into the blackness. *HaShem Adonai has heard my cry.* Life had come to these dry bones after all. But not in a way he'd ever expected.

79 FROM BEYOND THE GRAVE

Inside the coffin, resting on the chest of Josiah Adam Whidman's skeleton, was a magazine-sized vellum envelope wrapped inside a sealed plastic bag.

"You're the next of kin," Silas said dryly. "The honor's all yours."

Thomas gently lifted the thin parcel. Talia, above, came to the lip of the grave to peer down. Under the harsh movie lights they could see through the opaque vellum to view what it contained: a small handwritten note paperclipped on top of several mimeographed typed pages.

Thomas slowly unwound the string from the circular clasp of the envelope and gingerly removed the contents, which were in surprisingly good condition after being inside a coffin for over thirty years.

Thomas first turned to the note. The handwriting was frailer than what he'd seen yesterday, but was unmistakably that of Josiah Adam Whidman. A letter sent from across death's divide.

"Read it out loud," Talia urged. Thomas complied and read:

> If you are reading this note, you have either come across it by accident, or you have sought and discovered the treasure I myself found and then hid in a field. Somehow, through God's mysterious ways, you have grabbed hold of the life yet living in these dry bones.
>
> Could it be you, Bert Wood? Did you get my final

message? Or is this someone else entirely, a spiritual cousin seeking truth from beyond the grave?

Oh, it matters not. Read on. Whoever you are, read on.

Be prepared to have your whole life changed.

-J. A. W.

Artifact #9: Josiah Adam Whidman at
Shady Brook Sanitarium, New York, 1957

Josiah couldn't tell if this cranky rabbi was an angel sent from a humorous God, or the worst of demons come straight from the Deceiver. And he didn't know which would be more frightening.

"Are you telling me that in the original Aramaic, Jesus might have been saying, 'when *the new humanity* comes, it will be like lightning east to west?' Not, 'when the *Son of Man* comes?'" The Reverend Josiah Adam Whidman pointed at a line in his King James with his skeletal index finger, laid open to Chapter 24 in the Gospel of Matthew.

"Am I stuttering?" Levi ben Avram retorted. "Do you have cotton in your ears? Yes, schleb, that's exactly what I'm saying." While the old Christian preacher's rheumy eyes scoured the text for hidden clues, the old rabbi's professorial voice rattled on. "Trust me, I know what I'm talking about, Christian. Not just anyone is interviewed by *Time-Life Books* as an expert on ancient middle-eastern languages, are they?"

Josiah Whidman stopped reading. "*Time-Life* used you as an expert resource?"

"Them, and others as well. After my article came out in '49, I briefly became known as the world's foremost authority on ancient Aramaic texts." He sniffed. "Everybody wanted my opinion on the original words of Daniel, Ezekiel, and your precious Jesus. Why, I was even commissioned to write a paper about that very line of your Scripture."

"This one, in Matthew 24?" Josiah asked, pointing down. The rabbi nodded. "Who would commission a Jewish rabbi to write a paper on a Christian text?"

"Someone who realized that Christians don't know everything about their own tradition." Levi held his bearded chin high. "Co-wrote it with a young Greek monk from Mount Athos. Theologos was his name.""

"You're telling me a monk paid you to write a paper with him about the words of Jesus?"

"No. The organization he represented did." He sniffed. "They found my Aramaic translations fascinating."

"What organization?" the old preacher demanded. "What were they trying to prove?"

"I never knew," the rabbi confessed. "They paid me handsomely for my efforts, but part of the agreement was that the organization would remain unnamed, and the final product would become their exclusive property."

"So your paper never saw the light of day?" Josiah asked, disappointed.

"Oh, it was published. But for in-house readers only, a very limited printing. The monk gave me my own copy prior to publication. Had a bit of final editing to do still, but I saw the proofs. It was to be part of a collection of commentaries."

"I very much want to see it," the former preacher licked his lips. "Do you think – "

"I'm sure I have it around here somewhere." The old rabbi took a minute to rifle through his papers.

Josiah looked up from their wooden table in the sanitarium's private study room. The pair of blue-clad orderlies were peering in through the doorway again. The staff couldn't get enough of this odd turn of events; they might shake their heads in puzzlement, but these days they never interrupted. They didn't dare, Josiah thought. The patient who hadn't talked for thirty years was finally talking. The old corpse was alive. For a solid week now, the old preacher had cornered the acerbic rabbi for three hours each day, and a kind of routine had developed. The Jew and the Christian would pore over verses from the Gospels each day, discussing the different contexts in which Jesus used the Aramaic term *bar enasha*. The New Testament recorded eighty-two individual instances in which Jesus used the term, and the duo wasn't even halfway through them.

Levi ben Avram finished combing through his files and stacks of dated research material, and looked helplessly across the table at Josiah in his wheelchair. "Sorry, Christian, I'm afraid I can't find the paper right now," he said. "Ah well, another time." The dark-haired rabbi pulled on his curly beard thoughtfully as he readjusted his sitting position. "Still seems odd, after all these years," he muttered.

"What does?"

"A young monk with money, backed by an unknown organization that paid me to help him write a paper about *bar enasha*," Levi explained. "A paper they didn't want distributed in the larger world. Very sneaky-sneaky. Guess they were worried it would make too many conventional Christians uncomfortable."

"Let's get back to this passage in Matthew," Josiah Whidman encouraged. "Jesus is addressing imperial authorities when he says, "the coming of *bar enasha* will be like lightning striking in the east and flashing far into the west.' You were saying Jesus might not have been referring to himself, or any one person, but a group."

"Yes, of course a group." The wizened scholar's voice was edged with impatience. "This is the part that makes some Christians uncomfortable. Look at the context. In this case, your Rabbi Jesus doesn't seem to be talking about himself, or just a generic group of humanity. He seems to be confronting Roman authority and describing a different kind of authority, a new kind of humanity. In our paper, we suggested that – "

"Who? You and this Greek monk?"

"Who else, goy?" railed Levi. "Yes, the Greek monk. Theologos. He was an expert in ancient Greek, and I in Aramaic. We argued splendidly." Levi paused a moment, remembering the man. "He wore the black robe of the Greek Orthodox, but he always seemed...bigger."

The old preacher looked up from his Bible. "How so?"

"He'd suggest ideas that were far from orthodox." The rabbi chortled. "About Jesus and his followers."

"Such as?"

"Well, for example, he claimed that Jesus and his relatives were all part of a desert tradition that went all the way back to Isaiah," the rabbi said. "He asserted Jesus and his brother James and John the Baptist were part of a radical sect who insisted that Adonai must be met in the wilderness."

"What?" Josiah cried. "The monk claimed that Jesus wasn't the Messiah? That he was just a part of this group?"

"That's just it. Theologos was clearly a follower of Jesus. He prayed several times a day, and he openly called Jesus his Lord. But he also claimed that Jesus was part of this resistance sect. He said they stood against Temple worship and instead called for direct experience of the divine in the desert. The goy convinced me, eventually. He even used the Torah and the Prophets. Isaiah, especially. 'There is a voice calling: in the desert, prepare a way for the Lord,' that kind of thing." Levi smiled, recollecting. "Those were heady times. It was like he was using me as a sounding board to articulate an utterly different kind of Christianity."

"Why you?"

The rabbi shrugged. "It was as if his organization had certain theories they held to be true, and they were daring a Jewish expert in ancient Aramaic to prove them wrong."

"I don't understand."

"No surprise there," Levi ben Avram said. "Theologos would always start our sessions by proposing something preposterous, and then slowly provide documentation to make it seem plausible. In fact, it was one of his more outrageous proposals that led to our assertion in the paper that you find so shocking, Christian."

"Which?"

"Which? You don't follow well, do you, goy?" Patience was not Levi ben Avram's strong suit, but Josiah would abide. "The monk asserted that Jesus used *bar enasha* in Matthew 24 in a new way, not just referring to a generic group of people who would be arriving or emerging, but a special group. As I reviewed his supporting documents, I became convinced that in all probability Jesus was referring to *his* people, a converted group who embodied his vision of the Kingdom of God."

"What are you saying?"

"Let me spell it out for you, Christian: We think Jesus used a term to define his kind of people. In Matthew 24, he's referring to the coming of *a new kind of humanity* who'd been transformed by his Way."

"How can you be certain?" the old preacher demanded. "I must know!"

"You Christians love your certainty, don't you?" the rabbi taunted. "Fool! The depths of the Divine cannot be contained in words, no matter how much you Gentiles claim your Bible is the only voice of God." By this time, Josiah knew full well that insults were the price one had to pay when learning from Levi Ben Avram. The rabbi's medication tempered his explosive temper, but only a little. But for Josiah, the fruits of the discussions were worth the cost.

Whether he was angel or demon, Josiah had to admit the rabbi was right. He *had* been a fool, for so long. He had been so certain: first, at Gilman he'd been so certain that God was coming to end the world, and then for the last thirty years, so certain that there was no God.

Now, because of this Jew, everything was in turmoil again.

Ever since this rabbi arrived, Josiah Whidman had allowed himself a wild hope. He swallowed his pride and bit his tongue until the rabbi began once more. "No one can know for certain what exactly Jesus meant here by looking just at your Book of Matthew, Christian. In our paper, we made assertions based on Theologos' other source document."

"You mentioned that before," the old preacher said, puzzled. "What document?"

"The monk had a source he called the Sayings. Fascinating. It was non-canonical, a text that your Church Fathers never included in your New Testament."

"Where did it come from?" Josiah's eyes were demanding.

"My first question too," the rabbi confided. "Theologos wouldn't disclose it's provenance. It was primitive, a sparse collection of sayings attributed to your Master and his brother James."

"Did you think it was authentic?"

"Probably. Couldn't be sure. The young monk refused to divulge its story, despite my best efforts. He wasn't interested in proving its authenticity to me. He kept reminding me my job with this text was to translate, not validate." The old Jew took a sip of water with a laugh, and shrugged. "Without provenance, I had no idea where it was found or what era of history it came from. Might have been from an eremetic splinter group, such as the Ebionites or the Essenes. But the document itself spoke to its own authenticity." The scholar's eyes shone. "It was entirely in Aramaic."

"Jesus' original language?"

Levi ben Avram nodded. "All of it. Think of that. Your precious Gospels only preserve five or six words in his original Aramaic, Christian. And everything else in your New Testament came to you through the Greek."

"What does that mean?"

The old rabbi smiled. "Is the document an authentic collection of Jesus sayings, written first-hand in his native tongue by someone close to him, maybe even his brother James? Could be. Could the document be the missing earliest source upon which your Christian gospels are based? Could be. Or is the document a subtle fraud, written later by a clever scribe who had a masterful command of a dead language once spoken by Jesus?" Levi held up his gnarled hands. "Could be this also. The origin of this source may be only known by Theologos and his organization. And they're not telling."

"You must get this source for me!" Josiah cried, curiosity burning.

"Who, me? An institutionalized seizure patient with profound behavior disorders?" The rabbi laughed. "They locked me away for good reasons, Gentile. Besides, Theologos kept it under wraps. Think about how he treated even me: six years ago he hired me for a month, had me translate the work, pumped me with all types of questions, paid me for my time and then took all my notes and disappeared. All I have left is my copy of the paper we wrote together."

Josiah Whidman moaned and cradled his head in his hands. "I need to know if it's real!"

"Maybe," Levi conceded, "but maybe not."

"But – "

"What is *real*, anyway? Whether you read the monk's secret source or just read your own sacred scripture with an open mind, you come to the same conclusion."

"What's that?"

"Are you really a former leader of your religion? I keep confusing you with a lump of coal." Levi let out a long-suffering sigh. "Isn't it obvious? Your Jesus was trying to bring about a contagious kind of new humanity, starting with himself. This theme is all through your Gospels. He was ushering in what he called God's kingdom, populated by *bar enasha.*"

"So *bar enasha* might also be translated as 'kingdom people?'"

"Kingdom people? That's good, Christian. Theologos would have liked that. Definitely possible." The old rabbi leaned back and rubbed his eyes behind his reading glasses. When he looked back up, the aged preacher was still holding his head. "What's wrong, Josiah?"

"I'm a living joke, that's what's wrong. Thirty years ago, I was so certain about this verse," Josiah Whidman muttered. "So sure it was His time."

"You mean your end-of-the-world prophecy?" Levi chortled.

The old preacher nodded. "I used this very passage to convince people that the Lord was coming in 1923," he said. "Matthew 24:27. When it turned out I was wrong, I gave up on God. But if Jesus might have meant 'the coming of *the kingdom people* will be like lightning striking in the east and flashing far into the west,' then...." His voice trailed off and the old preacher looked directly at the rabbi with pleading eyes. "Levi, look through your files again. Keep looking. I need this paper you wrote with Theologos. I need it to save my life."

80 THIS IS WHY WE CAME

After reading the handwritten note under the bright movie lights in the open grave, Thomas turned his attention to the mimeographed sheets: Josiah's buried treasure.

The enclosed pages were copied from a typewritten manuscript, perhaps dating from forty or fifty years ago; all Thomas could see at the top of each page was that they were from "Section Eight" of an unnamed larger work. It was hand-typed; some of the blue mimeographed ink had become water stained, but the document appeared legible. *Was this a chapter from a first draft of a book?* It seemed so, but it was impossible to tell.

"Go ahead, read it out loud," Silas directed. "You have a captive audience." He clambered up from the bottom to sit on the lip of the excavated hole next to Thomas, the glare of the filming lights turning the night into day. "This is the command performance, and we've got front row seats."

Talia nodded her agreement. "This is why we came."

"I'll bring some fresh lemonade from the car," said Bert with glee. "This is going to be some jim-dandy footage. Don't read it until I come back."

"Looks like a portion of a religious book, from like fifty years ago," mused Thomas as he skimmed the top page. "No title, though."

Paul Silas peered over the young man's shoulder. "More like a manifesto."

"No author or publisher, either," remarked Thomas. "Just starts with the heading, 'Section Eight.'"

Bert returned. "Get on with it, man," Talia said. Thomas began and the camera rolled:

> "In Christendom's two-thousand year campaign to sabotage the Way, perhaps no action has been more effective than the early mistranslation of Jesus' phrase *bar enasha*. With this one linguistic corruption, Christendom was able to change the Master's message from *actively being* God's kingdom to *passively worshipping* God's Son.
>
> Jesus came on the scene embodying and announcing a new reality. His startling message to an oppressed public was that the kingdom of God is here, now. He dared to proclaim that anybody could be divinely changed and be part of this new kingdom. He used the Aramaic term *bar enasha* to describe the God-filled citizens of this new kingdom. This phrase had both singular and plural connotations in Aramaic, just as English speakers use the word *man* to mean *a single man* as well as *all of humankind*. Our tradition tells us that Jesus often used *bar enasha* to refer to himself as "the new human." Yet in other contexts, he used *bar enasha* to refer to a group of God-filled disciples as "the new humanity" or perhaps "divinely revolutionized humanity." He envisioned a time when this new kingdom of God-filled humanity would spread contagiously through society like leaven in the loaf, like lightning flashing east to west.
>
> The Master's vision of an emerging, divinely revolutionized humanity embodying the Way was strangled when Christendom brought the term *bar enasha* into Greek. Was this mangling a deliberate deceit by evil powermongers? Probably not. Rather, as Paul's version of Christianity spread into the larger Roman empire, it seems likely that an early scribe took this nuanced Aramaic idiom and, in translating it without grasping its meaning, made it mean something very different from Jesus' original intention. The phrase *bar enasha,* when translated literally into Koine Greek, became *ho huios tou anthropou*--"the son of the man," a phrase that was as meaningless for ancient Christians as it is in modern English.

Did Paul and the Gospel writers understand Jesus' real meaning of *bar enasha?* Again, probably not. All these figures wrote in a much different language, and in a much different time – decades after Jesus lived. Their incomprehension of Jesus' meaning seems evident in the fact that *no one else other than Jesus uses the phrase in the entire New Testament, even though Jesus himself is recorded using it 82 times.*

Our tradition makes it clear: the Aramaic term *bar enasha* was absolutely core to Jesus' teaching, but by the time it was written down in Greek approximately fifty years later by scribes in the early church movement, something absolutely crucial had been lost. The very nature of Jesus' message was already being fundamentally changed.

After the initial mistranslation, mistakes compounded over time as scripture was transcribed and re-transcribed. In later generations someone capitalized the phrase, changing it from "the son of the man" to the title "Son of Man," which somehow came to be conflated with the unique "Son of God," which then ultimately came to be understood as the one and only Messiah who must be worshipped and waited upon.

This corruption of Jesus' message, along with the emasculation of the Lord's Prayer we examined in Section Five, has allowed Christendom to turn the transformative Way of Jesus into a powerful cult idolizing a perpetually not-yet-returning God – a cult that promotes creeds over deeds, conformation over transformation, and– "

Thomas suddenly stopped. "Section Five?" It had taken him a few seconds to process what he'd just read. He looked at Talia. "We've got to call Paloma."

"What? Now?" Talia exploded. "You've got to be kidding! You always want to – "

"No, Tal, this is different. My ancestor somehow knew of Leaven."

"What?" said Talia, incredulous.

"This is a chapter from their book," he said, searching her eyes. "*Josiah buried part of their book in his grave.*"

"Okay," she said, surrendering. "I've gone with you this far. Let's call him right now."

"No."

"No? But you just – "

"Changed my mind." A smile played on Thomas' lips. "I've got a better idea."

81 MORE VALUABLE THAN GOLD

In the darkness of Talia's apartment, Thomas turned off the home projector. "Intermission."

Talia switched on the lights in the living room. "Popcorn, anyone?" she asked cheerily, heading through a swinging door into her apartment's kitchen. "My special Parmesan recipe."

"What? Foul!" cried Magda from her seat on the couch. "You finally opened the casket! You can't stop the film now!"

"I believe he just did," Stephen Paloma said from the other end of the sofa. "And yes, I'd love some," he shouted after the swinging door. "Extra butter."

"But I want to know what's in the coffin!"

"Guess we'll just have to wait. Their house, their rules." Paloma turned from the screen to face Thomas, who was busy manning the projector behind the couch. "You wouldn't tell me on the phone what you discovered, and now you stop the film and leave us hanging. Need to take a bathroom break, perhaps?"

"Need to switch reels," Thomas said, his fingers busy threading celluloid from a new reel into the projector's loops.

Paloma arched an eyebrow. "First one still seems to have a good amount of footage left," he noted. "Why not finish it?"

"Pretty boring stuff," explained Thomas. "This one has a better ending. I think you guys'll get a kick out of it."

Talia backed her way through the swinging door, her arms loaded with two large bowls of popcorn. "Ready?" she said, giving Thomas a look.

"Ready," Thomas replied, turning on the projector bulb once again. "Hit the lights. Here comes *Night at the Gilman Graveyard, Part Two*."

When the new film reel came to life, the specifics of the scene had slightly changed. Josiah's unearthed plot was still the setting, but now Thomas was alone in the open grave, while Silas lounged at the lip, bottle in hand. Talia was nowhere to be seen, perhaps behind the camera. In the excavated pit Thomas stood next to the head of the coffin which was now closed, no longer the main attraction.

The Thomas on film raised the vellum envelope in his hand like a trophy. "Greetings, my bald friends!" he shouted at the camera.

On the loveseat, Paloma and Magda simultaneously jerked around to stare at the real Thomas. He reached forward and rubbed their shorn heads with undisguised glee. "We made this part just for you two."

"I don't even know you, bald friends of Thomas," Silas said on screen, without a trace of mirth, swinging his leg on the lip of the grave. "But your young friend insists that I comment on your lack of hair."

The Thomas on camera reached up from the pit to grab the bottle out of Silas' startled hand. "My film." He took a slug, laughing hysterically. "My jokes. My surprise." He looked off camera for a second, distracted. "Now where were we?" He took another chug and wiped his mouth. "Oh yeah. Tal, we'll probably have to cut this part before we show it back home."

"Or not," said Talia, laughing from her overstuffed chair.

Thomas on screen had composed himself and now assumed a professional demeanor. "So what was Josiah Adam Whidman's buried treasure?" he asked the camera as he stood rib deep in the open grave. "This." He held the vellum packet aloft even higher, its shiny exterior yellow under the camera lights. Paloma and Magda leaned forward on the couch. "A mimeographed sheaf of old typewritten pages simply labeled 'Section Eight.' No more. These papers were more valuable than gold to Josiah. In the last year before he died, they gave him his life back."

He took a last swig from the bottle and handed it back to Silas before starting to unwind the string from the top of the vellum envelope. "No title anywhere, no date, no publisher." Thomas shrugged. "Why did my ancestor care so much about this 'Section Eight'?" He gently removed the mimeographed sheaf from its protective envelope, and the camera zoomed in tighter to focus only on Thomas and his hands. "I had a chance to read these pages about an hour ago. And they might've given me my life back, too." He held up the brittle pages. "Ready for the punch line, bald people? Section Eight is all about the true meaning of Jesus' favorite Aramaic phrase, *bar enasha*. And the last page identifies an editor named Theologos."

From his vantage point behind the couch, Thomas was watching Magda's and Paloma's eyes growing ever wider. When they whipped their heads around in disbelief, he stopped the film and pounced.

"I knew it!" Thomas' face felt pinched. To his astonishment he realized he was crying. Crying and laughing at the same time. "It's from *The Commentaries*, isn't it?" From the projector table, he picked up the same vellum envelope he'd held in the movie. "How did my crazy ancestor in Arkansas take part of Leaven's secret book to his grave?" railed Thomas. "*How?*"

Astonishment filled Paloma's face. "I want to say random chance. But we both know I'd be lying."

"Shit." Thomas pressed his hands to his eyes. "I was afraid you were going to say that."

He stood up and paced a few steps, then turned back. "And what Jesus really meant by *bar enasha*..." he began, then ran his hands through his unkempt mane. "Blows my mind. No wonder Josiah took it to his grave. He didn't just get his life back. He got his God back."

"That chapter made his dry bones live again," Paloma said softly. "Maybe yours too."

"Just when I'd put the universe in a bitter little box, I go open a coffin and everything bursts open again." Thomas' arms felt all jangly, like electricity flowed through them. "Jesus, expecting his followers to become *divinely revolutionized humanity?*" He shook his head. "How the fuck can you resist that?"

Paloma chuckled. "A friend of mine calls it 'the irresistible revolution.'"

"And me finding the *bar enasha* message six feet deep in my own ancestor's grave?" Thomas tried to sit, but his body wasn't ready to stay in one place. "Come on! God isn't supposed to intervene like that."

"We love making our little boxes, don't we?" Magda said. A pause settled upon the group, and Thomas didn't feel quite so jangly anymore. He came to the couch with his friends.

In the warm silence, Talia spoke. "Hey, I've been meaning to ask: why'd Josiah just bury Section Eight by itself? And why was it untitled?"

"That's what I was wondering too," said Paloma. He looked to Thomas, hand outstretched. "May we see what you found?"

Thomas opened the envelope and gingerly handed the sheaf of papers to his teacher. "No title headers, no page numbers," Paloma muttered to Magda, handing her the first few pages. "But this is Theologos' work, alright. It's almost identical to Section Eight of his *Commentaries.*"

"But different." Magda examined the pages and held them up to the light. "An early version." She paused, examining. "Look. Typos. These aren't even printer's proofs." She set them down gently on the coffee table. "These copies are rough. They're probably straight from some first draft composed on Theologos' typewriter."

"But how did Josiah get it?" asked Thomas.

Paloma sat back and looked at Magda. "The rabbi."

Thomas' eyes widened. "Of course," he said. "In his letter, Josiah told Bert that Christ's real teachings came to him through a foul-mouthed Jew. But how would an old rabbi in a mental institution get a hold of part of Leaven's *Commentaries?*"

"That was my question too," Paloma said. "When you called from Gilman the night before your dig and read Josiah's note to me over the phone, a few hints you dropped sent me scrambling for answers. First, after thirty-five years of hopelessness, your ancestor suddenly was using the term *bar enasha*, which only a few people in the world seem to know about. Second, the foul-mouthed Jew who provided Josiah with new hope you told me was a rabbi, a rabbi named Levi."

"Yeah, like the jeans. So this Levi was part of Leaven back in the day?"

"I didn't know what to think," confided Paloma. "So I contacted someone who would. Pater Theologos himself is seventy now, but still an active elder of Leaven and sharper than I ever was. He wrote *The Commentaries* back in the 1960s, when he was young. I called him, and asked if he'd ever known a rabbi named Levi back then."

"And?" urged Thomas.

"He remembered him well." Paloma laughed. "'Cocky old fart,' Theologos called him. Levi ben Avram was his full name, and in the early fifties he was a distinguished linguistics scholar specializing in the ancient languages of the Middle East. Leaven contracted him to help Theologos translate from the Aramaic when he was compiling *The Commentaries*. Out of academic courtesy, Theologos remembers giving the rabbi an early draft of the chapter they'd worked on together. Section Eight."

"Makes sense, really," mused Thomas. "So a few years pass, and the old rabbi becomes mentally ill, and his family institutionalizes him at Shady Brook Sanitarium in upstate New York. There, the old rabbi meets an old preacher named Josiah Whidman in need of some serious hope. The document gets passed on."

"Ironic," laughed Magda, looking at Paloma. "I bet the rabbi never had a clue he was contributing to a training manual for an underground group of subversive Jesus followers."

"I still don't see why you call *The Commentaries* a training manual," Talia commented. "It's important stuff, but isn't it just information?"

"It serves a powerful deprogramming function. People like Thomas can come to Leaven steeped in the deceptions of Christendom, and through *The Commentaries* they can uncover the truth of Jesus' Way: what he really meant by the Lord's Prayer, what he meant by the Kingdom of God, what he meant by *bar enasha*. Apprentices seeking the Way can bring their anger and fear and wounds created by a twisted concept of God, and in the real teachings of the Master they can find healing. Hope. Transformation."

"I've still got a bunch of lies banging around in my closet," admitted Thomas. "But I'm starting to find some truth in things that at first didn't make sense. Some hope, even. Like believing in a God that doesn't rescue us, but instead is still hanging on a cross. It's a wild hope, but something."

"Sorry," Talia interjected. "I didn't get it when you said it in the graveyard, and I don't get it now. Why would a loving God bind his own hands so he couldn't do anything? What would that do?"

"That's the question I was trying to answer," Thomas said. "A feeling God who wouldn't fix anything didn't really satisfy me, but it was the only way all this suffering made any sense. Then, when I found Josiah's treasure in his coffin, it all fit: God wants allies. God's bound his own hands so that humans *need* to conspire with the divine. Become *partners* in God's dream, not just worshippers."

"*Conspire* is the perfect word," Paloma said. "It means to plot together, but it also means to breathe together. Jesus was asking humans to conspire with God to make earth as it is in heaven."

"That all sounds nice, but cooperation's a two-way street," Talia protested. "If God's handcuffed himself, how's he conspiring?"

"Divine cooperation comes through the Spirit," said Paloma. "That's why the ancients emphasized that humans had to be filled by the Holy Spirit. The word for divine spirit in Hebrew is *ruah,* breath."

"*Pneuma,* in Greek," said Thomas.

"Divine breath is right here, all around us, waiting for us to let it in, be consumed by it. Gandhi called it *satyagraha,* truth-force. Jesus called it the Helper, and said with it you could move mountains." Paloma paused. "Jesus was offering a whole new way of being human, filled by the divine breath and conspiring with God's dreams."

"I guess that makes some sort of sense," noted Talia. "If God did everything for us, we'd never have to become anything."

"Even now, part of me doesn't want to believe it." Thomas ran his hands through his hair. "Can't God just be responsible for fixing everything? I keep hoping there's something easier. But there isn't. For thousands of years God's been breathing into us, dying for us to become the messiah we've been waiting for."

Magda looked at Paloma. "He gets it. Impressive. Now all he needs is the Trial."

"First steps first, my dear," commented Paloma. "The desert comes later. First he needs to commit to being an apprentice." All eyes turned to Thomas' side of the couch.

"I want to jump in, but…" Thomas looked to Talia, who was observing with keen interest, then back to Paloma. "I don't feel like I can fully commit right now. I've got a thesis to write. Cavanaugh liked the new research and interviews I showed him this afternoon from Gilman, but remember, that was just my first hurdle. Lots more to come." He looked sheepishly at Paloma and Magda. "Can I have a thirty-day trial and then decide?"

Magda burst out laughing, then stopped. "Actually, Stephen, considering what's about to happen, that's a perfect solution."

Paloma lifted his hands, surrendering. "Thirty days it is. But let me tell you now—if you don't join our secret society after the month is up, we'll have to kill you."

An awkward pause lingered. "We're non-violent, Thomas," said Magda. "That was a joke." She looked sideways. "Wasn't it, dear?"

"Not my best, obviously, but yes," Paloma remarked. He stood up and put on his jacket. "My friends, with that, we'll call it a night. Thirty-day trial it is."

Magda followed suit, grabbing her navy pea coat. "Let the semi-apprenticeship begin," she said with a smile. "After what's coming during this next month, Thomas, you'll certainly know if Leaven is for you."

"What exactly is coming?" asked Thomas. He exchanged unsure glances with Talia.

"Keep reading the book, one section at a time," said Paloma, placing *The Commentaries* on Thomas' lap. "And get some sleep tonight." The older couple moved to the door. "Meet me 8:00 AM tomorrow at *Tolstoi's Tea House.*"

"So I'm guessing this apprenticeship thing won't be much of a consensus?"

Paloma shot his new protégé a look that needed no explanation. "Eight o' clock sharp. We've got work to do. We'll start by meeting some friends, old and new." At Thomas' questioning look, Paloma flashed a mischievous grin. "In a few weeks, we've got a date with your uncle on national television. We'll want to be our best."

82 HOLY MISCHIEF

January 15, 1993. Reverend Benjamin Whidman had been waiting for this day for months. Ever since some atheist archaeologists had dug up a bone crypt outside of Jerusalem last summer, he'd been preparing for this moment. It was his time.

"A box of bones is going to take center stage here tomorrow," Ben's voice boomed across the sea of thousands who swarmed the broad brick plaza in front of the Berkeley Museum of Man, signs and banners hoisted high. "Y'all happy about that?" A massive wave of boos washed back at him, and he smiled. Like he'd planned, a score of buses had brought supporters to the event from cities all along the west coast, from San Diego to Seattle, ready to do battle in the Bay Area. Ready to choose the Bible over bones.

"The scientists who dug up this box claim it contains the bones of James, the brother of Jesus. They claim he's the older brother of Jesus, Mary's first boy! They claim the Bible's lying. *Can you believe that?"* The crowd roared its dissent, and a hundred cameras flashed in the area up front cordoned off for the press. With quiet satisfaction, Ben could see heads turning toward him hundreds of yards away, even deep into the liberal territory of Thomas' seminary across the street. *Who are all those people listening to?* They'd wonder. He chuckled.

The pricey sound system he'd arranged for the event was paying off. In fact, everything was: the massive bus effort had brought hordes of people, the huge stage and screen behind him was a wonder to behold, the billboards and advertising had drawn a huge crowd, and three national network TV vans were parked with cameras rolling. Reverend Benjamin Whidman had called in every favor he could think of to make this moment big. And the world was watching.

"I have one question for y'all," Ben boomed into the mike. He pushed his remote, and massive images of the King James Bible and the newly-excavated Ossuary of James projected up on the giant screens behind him. "Which are you gonna believe?" he thundered. "The Bible...or *a box of bones?*" The crowd roared, and Ben knew the networks were eating it up.

"Which are you gonna believe?" he repeated. With a cutting-edge laser wand, Ben Whidman pointed at the imposing image of the Bible looming behind him. "The eternal Word of Almighty God...or the arrogant word of a few atheist scientists?"

The energy in the air notched up another level as he worked the crowd into a greater level of agitation. *"Which are you gonna believe?"* he shouted yet a third time. "The latest spin from the liberal media... or the Good News of Jesus?"

A spotlight hit the image of the Bible above him, and the crowd thundered its applause. "I got someone with me who loves sharing the Good News," Reverend Whidman told the crowd. "He'll tell you what to believe. Ladies and gents, I give you the roamin' Reverend Billy Swanson!"

— — — — — —

When Benjamin Whidman started his opening remarks, Thomas had been weaving his way through the teeming crowd that filled the vast bricked expanse in front of Berkeley's Museum of Man. His could hear his uncle tossing questions into the mike and the crowd around him roaring back, but Thomas' focus wasn't on the spectacle. His task was simple and singular: he was supposed to be near the stage steps. And he was later than Leaven wanted him to be. The standing-room-only crowd choked the plaza, and he was making slow progress through the mob by ducking hand-held signs and squeezing between jostling bodies.

Finally, he came within thirty feet of the stage steps, his uncle's voice roaring in the stacked amplifiers. Now he had to negotiate staffers, people who were part of Reverend Whidman's entourage. Twice he was asked to flash his driver's license to show he was a relative, a Whidman. To prove he had a right to be this close.

Finally Thomas was in location, poised at the bottom of the steps leading to the stage. Thomas' view of the audience was blocked by the massive tower of amplifiers that bordered the stage above—as Paloma said, the amps would be a perfect shield so the crowd wouldn't see the actions about to take place – but he had a direct line of sight to see his uncle striding back and forth on the stage, microphone in hand. For the first time in hours, Thomas relaxed. He was in place. For the first time, he concentrated on his uncle's words.

"I got someone with me who loves sharing the Good News," the voice of his uncle was booming through the amplifier and out into the crowd. "He'll tell you what to believe." At those words, a familiar figure, but with coke-bottle glasses and a bad toupee, quietly brushed by Thomas to stand on the bottom step, waiting for his stage cue. Onstage, Benjamin Whidman was finishing his introduction. "Ladies and gents, I give you the roamin' Reverend Billy Swanson!"

"Time for some holy mischief," the figure next to him whispered with a wink, and before Thomas could say good luck, Paloma was up the stairs and gone.

— — — — — —

His vision blocked by the amp tower, Thomas could only hear the roar of the crowd as Billy Swanson left Thomas' view and waddled across the stage. Moments later, a victorious Benjamin Whidman appeared at the top of the stairs, positively glowing from his performance.

"Hallelujah! It's really happening, just like we planned!" Pastor Whidman enthused to his retinue below. Eyes bright, cheeks flushed, he sprung down the flight of stairs toward his waiting staffers. Thomas, lingering near the amps, was suddenly jostled by six staff members who joined him at the base of the steps, offering their pastor hugs and handshakes as he descended.

In the midst of the small cheering mob, Thomas made his move. He jockeyed for position. "Congratulations, Uncle."

Ben Whidman started, his eyes confused, trying to make meaning of his nephew standing right in front of him. "You again?" He barked an uncertain laugh and absently shook Thomas' outstretched hand. "You love surprising me, don't you?"

"I do, Ben, I wanted to – "

"Talk to me later, Thomas," his uncle said, eyes sliding by his nephew. "Can't you see I'm busy?" Flushed from his victorious performance, Ben started to step away into the group of welcoming staffers. But Thomas only gripped tighter onto the man's hand.

"I'll talk to you now." Thomas glanced to see his own people in place. "Definitely now."

"What're you – " Ben Whidman's dark eyes blazed as Thomas darted behind him and pinned his arms in a fierce bear hug. The six members of Reverend Whidman's retinue suddenly found themselves hugged and pinned in similar manners. An army of beefy men and women had materialized out of the crowd to immobilize Ben's small crew.

"No need to struggle, folks," grated the commanding voice of one of the assailants. "Stay calm and nobody gets hurt." The burly man winked at Thomas, then glared around at the group of shocked staff members. "Name's Charlie, by the way. My friends and I are going to hug you for a few minutes, so you just relax. Don't try to do anything stupid." Thomas guessed the glistening pink scar that dominated Charlie's dark face did little to put his trapped captives at ease. "Don't worry," Charlie continued. "I'm a Christian, too. The Lord found me in prison four years ago and I haven't killed anyone since."

83 GOOD NEWS

While Thomas immobilized his uncle off-stage behind the amplifiers, Billy Swanson was having a grand time strutting across the stage.

"I looooooooove sharing the good news!" His southern twang rolled out across the museum's crowded plaza and far onto the grounds of the Bay Area Theological Union across the street. Despite his bad hair and funny glasses, his energy electrified the place, and he lifted the microphone to the crowd. *"Do you love the good news of Jesus?"*

As one, the crowd of thousands yelled its approval. Flashes went off by the dozens from the press box, and the three TV vans were filming live for the national networks.

"That's what *gospel* means, you know. From the Greek. *Good news.*" The crowd quieted down. "What is the good news of Jesus, anyway?" Swanson inquired in a folksy tone, sauntering to the left side of the stage. "Was it that Jesus died on the cross and rose again?"

The crowd roared yes, but in a tone that was less than certain. *Where was this preacher going?*

"Well, that's the good news according to *Paul*," Swanson responded. "And it is good news indeed. Great news. The risen Christ is alive and present at this event even now. Breathing with us. Conspiring with us. I feel it, don't you?" Again, the crowd cheered its approval, albeit with some apprehension.

"So what *was* the good news of Jesus? What was the first thing he declared in the Temple?"

The crowd hung on the preacher's words, waiting.

"He said, 'Change your life!' Swanson boomed. "'The kingdom of God is at hand!'"

"Amen!" shouted Clarence Washington near the front of the crowd, enthusiastic behind tortoise-shell spectacles and wearing a black shirt with a tan blazer. Magda and the others who'd stationed themselves in the front cheered outrageously as well.

Billy Swanson looked out at the crowd, questioning. "What did Jesus mean when he said the kingdom was at hand? He was saying that God's new society is already among us!" More amens rang out across the vast plaza, but most of the crowd remained unsure about the direction that this preacher was headed. *"The kingdom of God is at hand,"* Swanson said again, slowly, lovingly. "The phrase shimmers and glows, doesn't it? It's pregnant with possibility. And when Jesus proclaims the kingdom, the most amazing thing about it is that he says, *"the time has come!"*

At those four words, a well-rehearsed plan started in motion out on the street. Anyone near the Museum's plaza who'd been looking away from the electric preacher would've seen a rare sight: two dozen metal shopping carts filled to the brim with food, clothes and possessions began rattling with purpose down the sidewalks of Claremont Avenue. The battered carts were being pushed by a motley crew of homeless men and women, and though they were coming from many directions, they were all converging toward Swanson's magnetic stage.

"Jesus dared to say the kingdom of God is not a distant reality," Billy Swanson continued. "It's not just in heaven, after we die. Instead, right there in the first chapter of the first gospel, Jesus says God's kingdom is *at hand,* within reach. Near. Here. Now." As he spoke, the shopping carts rolled into the plaza brick and positioned themselves either side of the stage, as unobtrusive as two gangs of homeless people pushing shopping carts could be.

"Everyone agrees the poor should be helped someday, right?" Some wild shouts of affirmation flew up from Clarence's area of the audience, but Swanson's questions made most of the crowd uneasy. "We all want oppression and greed to be stopped someday, don't we?" A few *amens* floated up from the back. "Debts should be forgiven someday. The planet should be healed someday. Someday we should beat our swords into plowshares." The preacher paused. "But right now? Bah—that's impossible!"

"Impossible!" Magda echoed in the front row.

"Sounds impossible," Swanson admitted into the microphone, "but for Jesus, that someday wasn't hundreds of years in the future. That someday is *today*. The time has come *today* to cancel debts, to forgive those who wrong us, to treat enemies as neighbors. Right now is the time to invite outcasts over for dinner." Billy Swanson gazed out over the crowd through his thick glasses, making sure his comrades in Leaven were in place. "If you call yourself a follower of Jesus, the day to share your bread is *today*."

- - - - -

Thomas, waiting in the wings, had been listening for the phrase: *the day to share your bread is today*. At that signal, a dozen shopping carts rolled up to each side of the stage on cue. Their drivers, street people by the look of them, began tossing out donations to the crowd, shirts and socks, fruit, soap, loaves of bread. Thomas recognized a few individuals from his time in Portland: the young mother Maria was right in front of him managing one of the carts, no baby this time, using both hands to distribute cans of food. Next to her, Thomas spotted an elegant black-skinned diva in a daring dance leotard that could only be Rashaun: the figure's back was turned, but sported massive headphones and platform shoes and was throwing packages of pantyhose into the crowd. And Munch—there he was. The big guy in the army fatigues was handing out boxes of breakfast cereal with one hand while eating a package of cinnamon rolls with the other.

Thomas had the freedom to look around because Reverend Ben Whidman was contained much more securely now. Instead of relying upon Thomas' bear hug, Charlie the ex-con had wrapped the preacher's upper body with duct tape and tied him to the stage. Uncle Ben's eyes went wild with rage when Thomas, apologizing, tied a bandana gag into the man's mouth for good measure.

Thomas directed his attention back to the stage. There was Paloma, as the barnstorming preacher Billy Swanson, bad teeth, bad hair, devastating, delivering the truth to ten thousand people.

"So if Jesus said the kingdom of God is at hand," the bespectacled Swanson began, "why hasn't everything become better over the last two thousand years?" The preacher's question rang through the plaza. "Why is the world still so full of suffering and injustice?"

The crowd waited, troubled.

"Why?" Swanson echoed again. He grabbed the laser wand left by Ben on the podium. "Because Christians have been believing fantasies they think are in here." With those words, he pointed with the laser at the Bible image looming over his head. Then he pointed the laser directly at the huge image of the Ossuary. "They should be believing the truth that is found here."

The crowd roared. Thomas could read the look on their faces: *Did he really just say that? Where is Reverend Whidman?* The press box came alive. The national networks perked up on top of their vans, zooming in on the speaker as he continued.

"I'll ask you again," the bold preacher resumed with authority. "If the kingdom of God is at hand, like Jesus declared, then why hasn't everything become better?" The gathered throng was stunned into silence. "Because we haven't done our job, that's why!"

The audience flew into an uproar. Hundreds of cameras flashed. Thomas grinned hugely as he watched the TV teams in action, alternating wide pans of the outraged crowd with tight closeups of the speaker. *This is what we hoped for,* Thomas thought. He checked irate Uncle Ben, bound up like a silver mummy, and then popped his head around the amplifiers to better view the crowd.

Swanson was stalking the stage like a tiger. "The kingdom hasn't come because the people who've been in charge of the Bible have been selling us the wrong message. Misguided preachers need to stop using the Bible as a weapon to keep people scared."

Paloma's words were too much this time. A front-row mob surged forth in anger toward the stage, but as the crowd advanced, a metal barricade of carts sprung up to stop forward motion. The trained shopping cart operators moved in with precision, forming a tight metal semi-circle around the stage. *Just like in practice,* Thomas thought, impressed. *Synchronized shopping carts.* Thomas had no idea how long the rickety ring might hold, but at least for now, he and his fellow saboteurs—along with his bound uncle and the rest of Ben's captive staff—were cut off from the crowd behind a protective metal barricade.

A siren was coming closer and the crowd was surging, but Billy Swanson continued undeterred. If he was nervous about the anger in the eyes of the throng, he certainly didn't show it. "The institutional church has been telling us for centuries that Jesus is coming back someday to solve all of our problems," he cried. "All we're supposed to do is wait and worship the risen Christ. Don't worry about the old lady on the street; worry about your soul and the afterlife."

Billy Swanson paused as four police cars and a black van pulled up, tires screeching, sirens blaring. "Hello, Empire," he said softly. Twelve policemen poured out of the vehicles, donned in body armor. They began jogging in formation toward the stage.

Up front, Swanson regained his focus. "The institutional Church doesn't want you to spend too much time healing the world. That's God's job, they say. God's going to swoop in sometime soon and make everything right." Paloma-as-prophet drew a breath. "If that's the case, why does Jesus himself say strange things like, 'you shall do greater things than I?' Why does Jesus say, 'When you give food to the hungry and clothe the naked, you do it to me?'" A modest smile emerged on his lips. "What do you think? Was our Messiah just kidding?"

The crowd roared with anger. At the side of the stage, the Reverend Benjamin Whidman shouted something at Thomas, but through his bandana gag, the preacher was unintelligible. Thomas just smiled. Ben's eyes rolled in his head, wild and flashing. He stared at Thomas with injured fury.

The squadron of armored police with riot shields now forged across the plaza, driving an efficient wedge through the tightly-packed crowd, aiming for the stage. A dozen of them broke through the barricade of shopping carts and streamed up the stage steps, left and right.

Swanson knew he had but seconds. The riot police were on stage now, closing fast. "God doesn't want servants and worshippers," he cried. "Jesus dared to say God wants friends. Allies. Partners, to establish a peaceful kingdom right here on earth. Isn't that amazing? Isn't that truly good news?" With that, Billy Swanson dropped the mike and crossed his hands behind his head just before a group of riot policeman tackled him to the ground.

At that moment, chaos broke forth. The shopping cart barricade collapsed, and the crowd in front became a volcanic eruption, shouting, jostling, confusion everywhere.

Thomas pushed through the milling mob toward the front edge of the stage. At eye level right in front of him, Billy Swanson was pressed face down on the stage, hands cuffed behind him. A policeman was leaning over him reading him his rights when Swanson caught sight of Thomas.

Their gazes met. Paloma, still disguised as Swanson, was jerked to his feet by two policemen. He kept his eyes on Thomas, smiling from behind his thick glasses. "Sometimes you have to be more than normal," he said just loudly enough for Thomas to hear. The policemen led their charge off stage and as he moved, Swanson stumbled over the abandoned microphone on the ground, kicking it in Thomas' direction. "More than normal!" he shouted over his shoulder as he was dragged toward the exit.

Sometimes you have to be more than normal. Thomas looked around. The policemen had cleared the stage with Swanson in tow. Another pair of cops were approaching Ben, who was still taped and gagged just off stage, flopping like a silver fish. Thomas couldn't spot the other policemen, but he guessed they were out in the crowd, maintaining order. He looked at the microphone, laying neglected on the stage floor.

"Magda! Clarence!" Thomas called into the crowd swirling around him at the front of the stage. The retired professor materialized out of the mob, looking dignified as always in his blazer and spectacles.

"Magda's following Paloma to see how the police are handling him," Clarence reported, looking frustrated. "Our plan started so well. Who knew the police would arrive so quickly?"

"I'm going to finish what he started," Thomas said. "Will you help me?"

Clarence raised an eyebrow. "What do you have in mind, young man?"

"Get Charlie and Munch and the others and hold the stairs like we rehearsed. Don't let anyone up to the stage. I only need a minute, but I need it right now."

Clarence grinned. "I'm on it."

Without a look back, Thomas turned and ran to the stage stairs. As he did so, he came within twenty feet of the two policemen attending to Uncle Ben. They'd just ungagged him, and one stood taking notes while the other used trauma shears to cut away the duct tape wrapped around Ben's body.

"Stop that man!" Ben yelled, eyes bulging but arms still wrapped like a mummy. "He's the one who assaulted me!"

The standing police officer dropped his notepad and took off in pursuit of Thomas. Just before he reached the side of the stage, however, Charlie and Munch and three other beefy men threw their bodies across the steps, blocking passage. "Get out of the way!" the cop yelled. The five bulky figures simply held on to the railing, immobile as logs.

Meanwhile, Thomas had reached center stage and grabbed the microphone.

"Hello, Berkeley," Thomas began, his voice rolling out of the amplifiers across the plaza. "Like the other preacher said, God needs allies."

The milling crowd stopped, and turned to the stage to focus on the newcomer. "Who are you?" someone shouted.

"I'm Benjamin Whidman's nephew. The almost Reverend Thomas Whidman," Thomas replied, surprising himself. "And I'm here to tell you, God isn't in the business of rescuing us by himself. Never has been, no matter how much we like the idea. Saint Augustine got it right in the fourth century when he said: 'Man without God cannot; God without man will not.'"

The crowd stood rooted, curious: *another Reverend Whidman?*

Thomas continued. "Now when Augustine used the word *man*, did he mean a single human male? Of course not. He meant mankind – all of humanity, male and female. Jesus used a similar word: *bar enasha*. We've translated it to mean 'son of man.' Jesus used it a lot, eighty-two times. No one else used it in the entire New Testament. It was one of Jesus' favorite words. But what did he mean by it?"

As he spoke, Thomas noted Clarence and a group of other Leaven supporters had occupied the steps on the far side of the stage as well. Four policemen had gathered on either side of the stage, and were communicating on radios. None were advancing on the stairs. Yet.

"What did Jesus mean by *bar enasha*?" Thomas shrugged. "You'll have to decide. Two thousand years have passed since Jesus said the words in his native Aramaic; no one knows exactly what he meant. The people who took over Christianity have been convincing us for hundreds of years it's a title Jesus gave himself, the Son of Man, which then we've taken to mean the one and only Son of God." Up on stage, Thomas paused. "I have a question for you." He looked out across the audience. "Did Jesus think of himself as the only Son of God?" The Museum's entire plaza seemed to be holding its breath.

"Of course not."

As the crowd shouted at Thomas' heretical words, he pointed with the laser wand above him at the huge image of the stone ossuary. "This box of bones tells the truth. The bones of Jesus' brother James were placed in this stone box about thirty years after Jesus died, almost two thousand years ago. After Jesus was crucified, his brother James led the people of the Way. He was an inspiration and role model for his flock until he died. On his bone crypt, how did his followers identify James?" With the laser, Thomas pointed out three lines of carved inscriptions looming overhead. "They wrote his name. They noted he was the brother of Jesus. And, on the third line, they described him as "one of the *bar enasha*."

"So could *bar enasha* be an exclusive title for Jesus? No. Could it mean the one and only Son of Man? No again." The unruly crowd raged, but Thomas would not be shouted down. The police poised at the sides of the stage were not forcing their way up to the stairs but rather were standing vigilant, busy on their radios. After their initial zeal tackling Paloma, they had adopted a much more discreet stance of observation, watching both him and the crowd for signs of unrest.

Just then, a commanding officer strode from the side of the stage over to the soundboard near the amplifiers, led by an irate Benjamin Whidman. Thomas knew his time was about to be cut short.

"I'm here today to tell you that *bar enasha* has a much bigger meaning than you've ever dreamed of," Thomas rushed on. "For Jesus, the word meant 'the new human being.' Sometimes he meant himself, but other times he meant those who followed him. People who'd changed their lives to become partners in building the dream of God. For Jesus, *bar enasha* may have meant nothing less than divinely revolutionized humanity--"

The sound system shut down. People cheered. Thomas was left speaking into a dead microphone, surrounded by a hostile throng. Thomas noticed the network cameras were still rolling, taking in the whole scene. The commanding officer headed toward him through the crowd with a bullhorn.

"So what are you going to believe?" Thomas gave one last shout from the stage. "Ben Whidman, or *bar enasha?* Will you dare believe that we're the ones God's been waiting for?"

The officer's bullhorn screeched. "Everyone please stay calm. Thomas Whidman, come peacefully into our custody immediately or we will use all necessary force to apprehend you," the policeman intoned. "You have been warned. Come down from the stage with your hands in the air. You are under arrest for assault."

84 IT SHALL BE INTERESTING

A month and a half later, Magda and Thomas waited eighty vertical feet below the Cave of the Baptist in the cool of the Wadi Musa basin, talking in the shade while the plume of dust approached across the Judean desert.

"I bet this one is him."

They'd seen a lot of dust clouds from vehicles over the last twenty-four hours, but Thomas felt good about this one. The timing was about right, based on the news they'd heard the day before yesterday: back in the Bay Area, Paloma had been released early, and was traveling half the world to join them in the Israeli desert as soon as he could.

Magda herself didn't look confident that this new cloud signified her husband. Dust plumes crossing the Suba desert were common these days, ever since the discovery of the Ossuary of James hit the international news last summer. *Archaeologically and economically significant for the nation*, the Wadi Musa file now read, and because of that designation, the site being billed as "The Cave of John the Baptist" was slated for rapid development by the Israeli Department of Antiquities. Dr. Adinah Sharon, lead archaeologist on the dig, had gotten her hand slapped by her superiors for early indiscretions, but she'd quickly been reinstated due to her decade of knowledge of the site and her willingness to forward the government's agenda.

Two months ago, Israel's Department of Tourism started a new road cut into the dry riverbed of the *wadi*, deploying earth-movers all the way from the ruined kibbutz at Suba. The onslaught of curious visitors would need a good road with good signage, rest areas and toilets, not just an unmarked riverbed leading to an unidentified cave. The site was scheduled to be open to the public in just a week, and frantic work teams were criss-crossing the desert daily.

Despite the traffic he'd seen in the last day, Thomas still felt this dust plume might be the one. It was definitely coming their way. "C'mon," Thomas urged Magda as they crouched together in the shade of the sandstone cliff. He shielded his eyes from the desert glare. "Don't you think that's them?"

Magda didn't glance up from the stick she was using to make a design in the bottom of the sandy wash. She wore a sleeveless white t-shirt with her skirt and motorcycle boots, and the narrow band of shade barely hid her from the ferocious noonday sun. "I told you, I'm not going to look. You do the hoping for the both of us."

Thomas and Magda had come out to Wadi Suba just yesterday morning from Jerusalem, as part of an eight-day trip to Israel that Leaven had arranged for Thomas. "The Shepherd wants you to consider the trip a thank-you gift," Magda explained to Thomas when she'd seen him inside Oakland County Jail a few weeks ago. When she visited, he'd been in the middle of serving a fourteen-day sentence for his aggressive entrapment of his uncle Ben during the *Bible Before Bones* event. Originally, he'd been arrested for assault, but the charges had been reduced to criminal harassment once it was clear that the duct tape caused no real bodily injury, just detainment and humiliation. Thomas had come to expect regular visits by Talia during his brief incarceration, but he was surprised when Magda came and suggested he join her on a round-trip journey to Leaven's birthplace in Israel. "The Council is gathering one last time at Wadi Musa," she'd explained. "Considering what you did for our cause, the least we can do is show you Leaven's home base before it becomes a complete zoo."

Feels weird for me to be here without Paloma, Thomas thought, watching the plume approach across the desert. *Can't even imagine what it's like for Magda.* They'd been assuming Paloma would not be coming at all, as he still had several weeks to serve of his 60-day sentence for disturbing a peaceful assembly, a violation of California Penal Code 415. This was not the first time Paloma had been convicted of civil disobedience, so his sentence was relatively steep. But then the call came: Paloma was being released early, and might be able to join them in Israel. Due to overcrowded conditions in the California prison system, the sentences of short-term non-violent offenders were being reduced, and Paloma was one of them. During Magda's quick phone call with Adinah Sharon in Jerusalem yesterday morning, Paloma was reportedly going to be released from jail that day and then head to Oakland International, hoping to get on the soonest stand-by flight to Jerusalem. Because Magda and Thomas were outside of phone service in the remote desert, they'd heard nothing since then.

And so, the waiting. The uncertainty. The hope. Thomas and Magda made a pact yesterday that—though its mouth loomed just above them – they would not enter the Cave of the Baptist until Paloma came, so Thomas' first encounter with the birthplace of Leaven would be with them both.

The dust plume was closer now, but still anonymous. Magda again refused to look up despite Thomas' urging. "Why're you being this way, Magda?" Thomas asked. "Your man's finally coming. I thought that today, out of all days, you'd be happy."

"Happy?" Her eyes flashed briefly. "You wondering why I don't look excited?"

"Well, yeah, actually," Thomas admitted. "I am."

Magda suddenly smiled, soft. "You've never been ripped apart from the one you love, have you?" It was a huge sad smile, and she looked Thomas right in the eyes. In that one look, Thomas knew that his own love for Talia—though deeper than anything he'd felt before—was a silly little ribbon compared to the iron bond shared by Magda and Paloma. "In Leaven, we know jail time can be part of the deal," Magda said, "for any of us. Holy mischief has consequences." She paused for a moment. "Your two weeks in jail were hard for you, I know. Scary. But you knew when it would end, and you got to see Talia. For me, that kind of time apart from Paloma is hard, but okay. I brace for it. It's the not knowing that kills me." She turned back to her design in the dust. "Just because they *said* they would let him out early doesn't mean a thing. I've learned not to get my hopes up until I see his beautiful bald head with my own two eyes." She squeezed Thomas' hand. "So you be the lookout."

The plume of dust was very near now, and Thomas was feeling good about it

491

once again. The sparse, twisted Judean landscape kept the shape of the vehicle a secret for a long time, but when it finally burst around the last curve of Wadi Musa, Thomas' feeling turned from good to very good. He nudged Magda, who'd been studiously scratching in the dirt. She finally looked up. "Land Rover," Thomas grinned. "Just like you said."

- - - - -

The driver slid the beaten, all-wheel-drive vehicle to a halt in a cloud of grit in the center of the Wadi Musa, just yards from where Thomas and Magda waited. The diminutive Israeli archaeologist, Dr. Adinah Sharon, set the hand brake and jumped out of the driver's door onto the sand. She waved a greeting at Thomas and Magda before going to the rear of the auto to grab her duffel. Her British colleague, Dr. Simon Collister, disembarked from the passenger side more slowly, looking queasy in his khaki shorts and field jacket after the bumpy ride. He burped into a red bandana, then saluted the pair seated in the shade.

Finally, the one they'd been waiting for emerged. Wearing wraparound sunglasses and a loose t-shirt, Stephen Paloma unfolded himself from the back seat and smiled gently at the two waiting at the cliff base. "Yes!" he exclaimed to the sky, his bald head gleaming in the sun. He took a long drink of the Judean desert air, flung his arms wide, and stretched like a jungle cat.

While Paloma stretched, Adinah came straight over to the waiting pair. She shook hands with Thomas in a formal manner before gracing her sister in Leaven with a huge smile. "Magda!"

"Adi!" Magda said with delight, returning the embrace of the small woman. "Thanks for picking him up and bringing him out. I'm sure you're terribly busy back at the University."

"Brothers and sisters take care of each other," Adinah responded warmly. "I know how much you need to see each other." Her English was precise and strongly accented. "And yes, we're busy at the lab, but we're even busier out here, getting ready for the grand opening." The Israeli archaeologist impulsively grabbed her dear friend's hand and drew her a few steps away from Thomas, but her animated whisper was loud enough for him to overhear. "Leaven is bubbling up, Magda! Thousands of first-borns started calling from all over the globe once your mischief in California hit the world news."

Collister approached, and Adinah rubbed her hands together in excitement. "It shall be interesting to see what the Spirit's going to do with all of this wonderful mess we're making, won't it Simon?"

"Yes, yes. Fascinating," the British archaeologist muttered in his distracted manner, looking up the cliff at the Cave. "The mess we're making." He shook his head. "I only hope James' final resting place is as forgiving as he was."

"Me too," Magda sighed. "I still can't imagine the terror of tourists we're about to unleash on this sacred space."

"You two worry all you want," Adinah said in hushed, excited tones. "Me, I'm rolling with it. This is Leaven's big opportunity to rise again in the world! What did Pater Theologos say? Something about, if you're going to go..."

"Go big," Magda finished the sentence with a groan. "Not you, Adinah! Now that crazy monk is polluting the people of Israel with his stupid phrasebook."

"Simon says we're booking five tours a day, starting next week!" Adinah exulted.

"Too true," the Brit said flatly. "Spiritual seekers by the thousands are signing up. And the portable toilets still haven't arrived."

"Ah! See?" Adinah threw her hands in the air. "So much still to do. I better get going." She looked over to Paloma at the car, then back at Magda. "You three might need some time to catch up, anyway. Come on, Simon." She grabbed Collister and walked away across the sand with her duffel over her shoulder.

"We're going to check in with the Shepherd," Collister called back over his shoulder to Magda. "We'll see you later at the Cave."

Paloma, his own travel bag in hand, now approached Magda and Thomas from around the car. As soon as she saw him, Magda was up and running, meeting him halfway. Thomas saw her body shake in his arms as the pair melted into each other. He suddenly felt the physical pain of missing Talia. He wondered how she and the little life inside of her belly were doing back in the Bay Area, so far away. *My child,* he marveled.

Magda and Paloma continued to embrace in silence, lingering, getting used to each other's bodies again after the weeks of separation. Bald heads close, he whispered something into her ear, his lips nearly touching her silver bands. Hand in hand, they slowly approached Thomas, who'd been waiting at a discreet distance.

"Hey, Teach." Thomas gave Paloma a handshake, which was turned by the older man into a warm hug. "Long time, no see." The trio of Americans began walking toward the base of the sandstone cliffs looming behind them. "Glad to see you out here in your natural habitat after your incarceration," Thomas said. "Alive and well, I hope?"

"Alive," Paloma grinned, looking around the vast landscape. "And now well." Thomas followed Paloma's gaze and took in the eternal desert, wind-sculpted sandstone, dusty *wadis* aching for water, and beyond, the great sea of sand. "Very well." He turned to Thomas. "Ready to see our spiritual home, jailbird?"

- - - - -

"Our prison time didn't quite go the way your uncle expected, did it?" Paloma said as they climbed the steep goat path toward the Cave, following in the footsteps of the archaeologists.

"Pressing charges was about the worst thing he could've done," Thomas agreed. "The media went wild with our arrests. I can't believe all the news shows, the magazines articles." Thomas laughed. "You didn't tell me we were going to be famous."

"You didn't tell me *you* were going to pick up the microphone and give the sermon of your life. You carried on when I couldn't. That was brave."

"I don't know what came over me. The Spirit, I guess." Thomas shook his head. "I just saw the microphone lying there, and I knew what I had to do: finish your speech. I guess the message really mattered to some people. I got over seven hundred fan letters while I was in the county lock-up."

"You too?" Paloma smiled. He looked at Magda. "And how many did I receive at home?"

"I stopped counting," she responded. "Hundreds and hundreds. Billy Swanson's post office box was stuffed full every day for a month. And they keep coming. They all want to know what church you're from, how you're doing in jail, how they can hear more from you."

"And those letters represent just the tip of the iceberg, Thomas," Paloma said. "For every one person who actually writes, there are a thousand other people who are thinking about it. Ben's kind of Christianity is being questioned all over the world. People aren't so satisfied with the *someday* message anymore. They want to conspire for the kingdom *now*."

"You know what else people are rethinking?" Thomas added. "God's expectations of humanity. The message that Jesus wanted us to be transformed into *bar enasha*--divinely revolutionized humanity—that's spreading like wildfire."

"Spreading like lightning east to west. Spreading like leaven." Paloma smiled ruefully. "That's a message a lot different than your uncle Ben imagined when he organized *Bible Before Bones*." They reached a ledge, and Paloma stopped to take in the view. "Speaking of your uncle, how's Ben?" he inquired.

"Wouldn't know," replied Thomas. "Haven't talked to him. I'm guessing he's boiling mad, underlining his Bible with a red pen and stewing up a new enemy to attack. Probably you and Leaven."

Paloma lapsed into silence a moment. "I have to say, I enjoyed hijacking the event. I enjoyed posing as Swanson and preaching the real good news while the cameras ate it up. But I didn't enjoy shaming your uncle, Thomas."

"I did." Thomas said. "You know he deserved everything he got."

"Maybe. Maybe not."

"Are you really defending my uncle?"

Paloma shrugged. "I got to know him, being Swanson. He's a good man inside. I hope there will come a time when he can forgive me."

"Unlikely in this life," Thomas muttered as they neared the plateau. "With all that happened, rallying against Leaven is probably on the top of his list. I can see next year's billboard now. 'Who you gonna believe: The Christ...or some Caves?'"

"If he does, then so be it, but deep down your uncle has a sincere heart. He might change yet."

Thomas was unconvinced. "He'll come up with something to attack. Maybe next month he'll say these caves can't be the home of a desert school that taught Jesus anything, because the Son of God doesn't do apprenticeships. Maybe he'll – "

Suddenly, they arrived.

The dark maw of the Cave of the Baptist beckoned to Thomas, drawing him like a black hole.

85 THE CAVE

Thomas entered without words. They stood in silence for a few minutes, taking in the expansive cavern. Then Magda and Paloma led him deeper into the darkness.

Thomas followed them toward beckoning torchlight at the back of the low, wide cave. Water was dripping somewhere. Soft floor lighting had been placed in rows down the center of the cavern floor, providing an illuminated walkway. Magda and Paloma stepped to the side, and Thomas went first. In single file, their feet followed a well-worn path, an ancient trough in the sandstone that had been ground into the rock by countless pilgrims before them. Initiates dying to change their lives.

After perhaps a hundred feet of walking, the floor ahead of Thomas turned to milky blackness. He stopped in his tracks, at a loss, until he realized he was looking out across the glassy surface of still water. Torchlight danced upon it, a pool of the darkest obsidian. The young man knelt and dipped his hand into the ancient water, breaking the surface and letting the drips from his fingers echo through the silent cavern.

Magda knelt beside him. "The Drowning Pool."

"I'm guessing people don't come here to just get a little sprinkle, huh?"

"Look down," Magda said. At his feet, the path led up to the lip of the pond and then *into* it. *Were those steps?* As his eyes adjusted, Thomas made out a series of shallow stone steps descending into the water. They continued straight toward the center of the pool before being lost in the inky blackness.

"Guess how many steps there are?" Magda asked, her eyes sparkling in the torchlight. Paloma stood behind her.

Thomas tried to count, but he quickly lost them to the murky depths. "Can't tell. Twelve?"

"Twenty eight."

"Is that important?"

"Those who enter do not come out the same," Paloma said. "The number needed to be sacred. Holy."

"Twelve seems holy enough. What's so special about twenty eight?"

"The days in a woman's cycle," Magda replied. "Days of the moon. Death, and rebirth."

Thomas looked high above the pool and shivered. In the flickering torchlight, he saw the ancient images Magda had told him about, twin carvings etched into the rock itself: on one cave wall, the outline of a tall wild-haired man wearing the belted robe of some animal, holding a staff and proclaiming something; on the other, the same man's severed head floated on a platter, blood dripping from a jagged neck. Images of the Baptizer himself. He shook his head, amazed. "Still can't believe you guys can trace yourselves straight back to John the Baptist."

"That's not it."

Thomas turned, puzzled. "You told me this cave was his place."

"It is," Magda said curtly. "John baptized thousands here, and people continued the tradition long after. But that's not it. We go back a lot farther than that." She stood up and offered Thomas a hand. "Let's go find Collister."

- - - - -

"Jolly good! You get to be my first tour." The archaeologist was waiting with

Paloma when Thomas and Magda returned to the front of the cave. The rotund Brit brushed his bushy red hair back from his pale forehead and gave a big toothy grin at Thomas. "Welcome, welcome, my boy! We met briefly back at the Land Rover, but I'll reintroduce myself. Dr. Simon Collister, Leaven's chief archaeologist. Dr. Sharon and I work closely together."

"You're part of Leaven?" Thomas' eyes couldn't help but widen as he examined the hefty man. "I mean, you underwent the whole..." from the lip of the cave, he gestured out toward the wasteland below.

"The whole desert Trial?" Simon laughed and patted his midsection. "Yes I did. Some of us are just big boned, I guess."

"Great to meet someone in the group with hair," Thomas said frankly, staring at Magda and Paloma beside him. "I was beginning to think that everyone in Leaven took a vow of baldness."

"I resemble that remark," came a deep and familiar baritone from farther back in the cave, warm with humor. A dignified older black man wearing spectacles emerged from a side tunnel of the main cavern and approached the group.

"Clarence Washington, my partner in crime," Thomas said. "I hoped I'd see you here."

"Glad to have you on the team, Thomas," Clarence said, grabbing the young man's shoulders with both hands. "Nice work last month. I watched you from the steps, and just hoped I wouldn't get kicked by a police boot as you kept on preaching where Paloma left off. What you did was inspired."

Clarence then turned to his old friends, and enfolded Magda and Paloma in huge bear hugs. "Amazing job yourself, Billy Swanson," Clarence said softly. "Nice to have you back in the land of the free." The retired professor broke his embrace and looked at the group. "Well, the gang's all here and the Shepherd's waiting with the rest of the Council." He looked to Simon and Thomas. "You two continue the tour without us."

Magda winked back at Thomas as she and Paloma left with Clarence. "Duty calls. We'll come back for you soon."

"Leaven's spiritual ancestors began in these very caves, my boy," Collister began, warming to his tour. "They felt called out to the desert, and they came. We give ourselves the name of Leaven today; back then, they were simply known as Called Out Ones."

"Or the Ebionites," Thomas added. "The Roman and Jewish establishment mocked them as 'the poor ones,' because they shared their possessions in common."

Collister looked at Thomas in a new light. "Know your early Christian history, do you?"

"Just enough to be confused about the beginnings of Leaven," Thomas responded. "Up until now, I thought the whole desert Trial movement started with John the Baptist and Jesus. But just a minute ago when I saw the Drowning Pool, Magda told me your roots go much farther back. What's the real story?"

Collister cocked a bushy red eyebrow. "Long or short version?"

"Both."

"Alright, you asked for it," Collister said. "Archaeologists don't always get to run free off the leash." He rubbed his hands together with relish. "Here's the short version of what we know: The first person who came out to these caves was the prophet Isaiah, almost three thousand years ago."

"Isaiah? How do you know for sure?"

"Nothing's for sure, Thomas. First lesson of archaeology."

"Okay, but..."

"When the Gospels introduce John the Baptist, do you remember the quote they use from the Book of Isaiah?"

"Yeah. Something like..."

"As it is written, there's a voice calling in the desert," cited Collister in his booming British, his voice echoing in the cave mouth. *"'Prepare the way for the Lord, make straight paths for him.'"* He turned to Thomas. "The Gospel writers make it sound like Isaiah was predicting – six hundred years in the future – that a man such as John would be out in the desert, preparing for Jesus, yes?"

"Well, yeah," Thomas said. "They make it sound like John was foreordained to get everything ready for when Jesus showed up."

"The Gospel writers made their own punctuation," Simon muttered. "Changed everything."

"What are you talking about?"

"Ancient Hebrew doesn't even have bloody punctuation!" the red-haired Brit said in exasperation. "But Greek scribes turned Isaiah's desert into a metaphor."

"Still not tracking you."

Collister tried yet again. "Maybe the scribes were right. Maybe Isaiah was dreaming about the future and saying, 'there's going to be a voice calling in the desert six hundred years from now.' But more likely he was out here, in the desert, talking to his people about their own reality. Look at the original text of Isaiah. It says: 'There's a voice calling; in the desert, prepare the Way for the Lord. Make straight paths for him.' You see the difference a little punctuation makes?" Collister threw out his beefy hands. "Isaiah wasn't predicting Jesus and John, six hundred years in the future, and using the desert as a metaphor. He was urging his people to get out of Empire *right now*, to come out to the desert to get their heads on straight."

"You guys in Leaven sure have some interesting angles," commented Thomas. "The prophet Isaiah, hanging out in the desert, calling people out for a desert Trial? Cool theory. What evidence do you have to back it up?" Thomas inquired. "Don't tell me you found Isaiah's bones, too."

"Cheeky boy," grumbled the Brit with a smile. "I'm a scientist, remember? I'll be the first to admit, it's just a theory. But we do have some interesting fragments." With a gesture, the archaeologist motioned Thomas farther back into the cave toward a stone bench.

There, in the dim torchlight, Thomas could see countless potsherds littering the bench's surface. "We dredged the pool years ago," Collister said. "Found thousands of these fragments dating back to the Bronze Age. Proto-Isaiah."

Thomas looked close. Countless shards of thin, delicate pottery lay on the bench in front of him. Most were stained with a dark brown pigment. "Bronze Age. What's that in human years?"

"Seventh century BC, my boy. Isaiah's time. The earliest fragments were of fired clay, nicely worked, glazed with lamb's blood."

"Lamb's blood?"

The archaeologist's eyes gleamed. "Ritual vessels. Purposely shattered. Lots of them. The amount and type of these artifacts strongly suggest that in the time of Isaiah, large groups of people were coming here from surrounding cities to use this pool for water purification rituals."

Thomas took in a breath. "You mean baptism."

Collister nodded. "The stratigraphy supports the notion that there were successive Judaic schools of Isaiah, generations of desert prophets living out here and conducting rituals of transformation in these caves. Hundreds of years before John the Baptist was born."

The British archaeologist moved back toward the cave opening. Thomas followed. "The Gospels say Jesus traveled out near the Jordan to be baptized by John, who was already out in the desert proclaiming the message of life-change. *Already out*, John was. Probably here, probably trained in the legacy of Isaiah. After his baptism, Jesus was immediately led by the Spirit out into the wilderness." They approached the entrance to the cave and looked down at Wadi Suba. The vast Judean desert opened out before them, an endless landscape of tans and reds marked by tiny patches of green. "This wilderness." Goose bumps rose on Thomas' arms as the archaeologist spoke. "Somewhere not far from here, Jesus stood his Trial in the wilderness. And upon his return, the world would never be the same."

86 GRASSHOPPER

Thomas sat on that ledge long after Collister departed, looking out across the desert expanse. *Jesus was out here.* Time moved, and the tans and reds of the sandstone landscape turned to purples and browns. Shadows began stretching impossible distances across the panorama before him.

He could see Jeeps in the distance now, a crew laying gravel on a road newly cut through the desert landscape. *Tourists,* thought Thomas. Hard to imagine this desolate corner of wilderness, now an undiscovered patch of sand and rock, would soon be crawling with tourists looking for the cave that had housed the bones of Jesus' brother. Most would be coming as gawkers, but some would be like Thomas, a modern seeker searching for some true good news. Maybe the cave and the story of Leaven would lead a few hungry souls to something deeper. Maybe.

His reverie was broken by the sound of people approaching.

"Thomas Whidman." It was the voice of the old woman they'd called the Shepherd. The white-haired crone was leading Paloma and Magda down from above on a narrow cliffside trail. The three dumped out on Thomas' ledge.

"I understand you did us a great favor in front of a televised audience," she acknowledged. "For this, we give you great thanks. The Spirit was in you that day."

Thomas nodded mutely, not quite knowing what to say. Lowering his eyes, he spotted a tattoo of entwining vines and wheat on the woman's left ankle.

The Shepherd remained motionless directly in front of him, her gnarled hand holding an equally gnarled staff. "Stephen tells me you are seeking the Way, and are considering initiation into the Society of Leaven."

To Thomas' eyes, the Shepherd looked like a very piece of the sandstone cliff behind her. She was wrinkled like an old apricot. A camel-colored leather jacket covered her upper body, while a dusty muslin dressed came down to her broad splayed feet and sturdy sandals. White whiskers played about her lips, and her teeth were stained.

"Stephen tells me you might be interested in walking the Way," she said again, curious. "Have you read *The Commentaries* yet, young man?"

"Not all of it, Shepherd." Thomas had to look directly into the sun at the cave edge to look her in the face. "I didn't bring it with me to prison, and I haven't had a lot of undisturbed time to read it since."

"Make some time," she said matter-of-factly. "You'll need to meet him soon."

"Who?"

"The author himself," she replied. "Pater Theologos."

"He's here?"

"No, his health prevented him from making this Council." The Shepherd turned to Paloma behind her on the ledge. "I do pray he's healthy enough to stand as Preparer for Thomas. You're too close."

"Prepare me for what?" Thomas blurted, knowing he hadn't been addressed.

The Shepherd's level gaze shriveled any other words that might have wanted to come out of Thomas' mouth. She returned her questioning glare back to Paloma. "Have you really not told him?"

"We've both been in jail, remember, Sofia?" Paloma responded. "Thomas and I haven't had a lot of chances to chat."

"In the interim, Thomas has been in a sort of trial membership," Magda explained. "So I haven't fully oriented him to our process."

"Yeah, I've just been sort of checking it out," Thomas replied. "Leaven, that is."

"Sort of checking it out." The Shepherd folded her weathered arms. "Interesting."

Paloma shrugged. "When the time came to bring Thomas into our plans for *Bible Before Bones,* he wasn't certain he wanted to join Leaven. So we decided on a thirty-day trial."

"Unconventional times require unconventional methods." The Shepherd stroked her chin. "Please, by all means, carry on."

Paloma brought Thomas to a secluded alcove near the cave entrance. The Zen teacher glanced at his watch for the date, then at his student. "Well, Thomas, your thirty days were up four days ago. You were invaluable during our action in Berkeley , so whatever you decide, I hope you know Leaven is indebted to you. But now it's time for you to choose. You've joined us in some holy mischief; I've let you in on our secret books; and now you've even come to the Cave of the Baptist." Paloma held out his hands. "You know us, for better or worse. Time to decide, this time for real: do you wish to become part of Leaven?"

Thomas gave a tentative grin, suddenly unsure. "I've seen you, yes. But you've also seen me, at my best and at my worst."

"I have," Paloma laughed. *"Keep the change, and keep all your little secrets too?"*

"Exactly," Thomas grinned. "You know my baggage. I still have a lot of anger, a lot of fear. So before I answer, let me ask you: do you really want me?"

Paloma knelt down, just inches away from where Thomas was sitting. The teacher looked into his student's upturned face. "Without reservation, Thomas Whidman." The younger man searched Paloma's gaze and found no guile. He looked at Magda, who nodded her agreement.

Thomas looked at his friends and then out into the desert distance, and took a deep breath. "Well if that's the case, I want to be part of you. Without reservation."

The Shepherd had been standing a bit apart from the trio, but now came over. "It is to be done, then," she said. She came and stood next to Paloma. "So, Stephen. You think he's ready for the Trial?"

"As ready as any of us were, Sofia."

"Point well taken," she noted. "We'll need to find a real wilderness." The Shepherd pursed her lips. "If we're going to ask Theologos to be a Preparer again, it's fitting to use the Holy Mountain."

"My thought too, Shepherd," Paloma said.

"You approve?" the weathered old woman asked.

Paloma nodded with a fierce grin. "Athos is Theologos' backyard, so even if he's ill he should be able to do what is needed. It will take a little extra work with the monastic authorities to get Thomas a visa for the proper amount of time, but it will be worth it." Paloma turned to Thomas. "Did you know it's where I stood my Trial as well?"

"Mount Athos?"

Paloma nodded. "I've led Trials in lots of places now. It's still my favorite place to die."

"I'm not sure what you're talking about," Thomas confessed.

"You'll know soon enough." Paloma's smile was warm, but not entirely. "Time for your initiation, grasshopper."

ACKNOWLEDGEMENTS

I am deeply indebted to the many good souls who have touched this book. Indeed, throughout this project I've been aided by a communion of saints.

First, I salute those who helped shape the content and the words that eventually came to form this novel. To my wife Margaret Bartlett, I thank you for the journey. To Lauren Bjorkman and our Taos writer's group, endless thanks for your unflagging support and keen eyes in the early stages. To my core group of manuscript reviewers--John Gastil, Karen Ayala, Scott Battenfield, Ken Gingerich, Andy Bartlett, Jon Kaufman, and several others—I give much gratitude. And to Mike and Kathryn at Morrell Editing Services: know your feedback has made the novel what it is today.

Second, I want to acknowledge the following mentors: John Fife, Jim Corbett and the Sanctuary movement in Tucson, who first taught me authentic discipleship and the power of going *cimarron* through their own lives; Walter Wink, James W. Douglass and Maurice Casey, for helping me envision the deeper possibilities of *bar enasha*; Jim Wallis, for his life example as well as his thoughts regarding authentic conversion; Alan Kreider, for providing invaluable insights into the Empire-defying practices of the earliest followers of the Way; Marcus Borg, for shedding light on participatory eschatology; Shane Claiborne and Brian McLaren, whose writings help me articulate a Jesus Way that is both new and ancient; James Tabor, whose archaeological work at The Cave of the Baptist fired my imagination; Jeffrey Butz, Hershel Shanks and Ben Witherington III, whose research into James the Just and his ossuary gave me a rich history to mine; and Ched Myers, for his keen sociopolitical analysis of the Bible as well as wilderness trials.

Three individuals remain to be named, whose influence runs even deeper. Richard Rohr's wisdom, support, ideas and inspiration permeate the entire novel, but most specifically infuse Chapter 32. Direct excerpts from Stuart Murray's *The Naked Anabaptist* comprise much of *The Theologos Commentaries #2* and *#4*, his words providing a devastating critique of Christendom. Lastly, I acknowledge the passion and pathos of John Adam Battenfield, my tremendous, impossible ancestor who took up lodging in my soul and inspired all this mess. May the Lord have mercy on us all.   —T.W.

On Earth, as it is in Leaven?

**Is there really a Cave of the Baptist?
Did the Ebionites exist, and was James the Just their leader?
Did the initiation of early followers of the Way
truly take up to three years?**

**What parts of *The Secrets of Leaven* really happened?
Find out at leavenrising.com**

Take advantage of a free web exclusive! Download an appendix detailing the factual origins of the many fascinating ideas that run through *The Secrets of Leaven*. Subscribe to Todd Wynward's blog, watch exclusive Q & A videos with the author, hear about special events and gatherings, and receive unpublished excerpts of the upcoming sequel, *Leaven Rising*.

We're not just promoting a book. We're fostering a movement. Visit the website to learn more about TiLT, an intentional co-housing community emerging in Taos, NM. Or take the plunge, and sign up to join the author and other readers on a wilderness backpacking trek or week-long river trip in the American Southwest.

Join the rising.

leavenrising.com